P9-AZV-733

LOVELY,
DARK,
DEEP

LOVELY, DARK, DEEP

stories

JOYCE CAROL OATES

ecco

An Imprint of HarperCollinsPublishers

LOVELY, DARK, DEEP. Copyright © 2014 by The Ontario Review. All rights reserved. Printed in the United States of America. No part of this book may be used or reproduced in any manner whatsoever without written permission except in the case of brief quotations embodied in critical articles and reviews. For information address HarperCollins Publishers, 195 Broadway, New York, NY 10007.

HarperCollins books may be purchased for educational, business, or sales promotional use. For information, please e-mail the Special Markets Department at SPsales@harpercollins.com.

FIRST EDITION

Designed by Suet Yee Chong
Orchid photograph by Suet Yee Chong

Library of Congress Cataloging-in-Publication Data has been applied for.

ISBN 978-0-06-235694-9

14 15 16 17 18   OV/RRD   10 9 8 7 6 5 4 3 2 1

FOR
MARIANA COOK
&
HANS KRAUS

CONTENTS

ACKNOWLEDGMENTS

The stories in this volume have appeared, often in slightly different forms, in the following venues:

"Sex with Camel" in *The American Reader*
"Mastiff" in *The New Yorker*
"Distance" in *Ploughshares*
"A Book of Martyrs" in *Virginia Quarterly Review*
"'Stephanos Is Dead'" in *Yale Review*
"The Hunter" in *Boulevard*
"The Disappearing" in *American Short Fiction*
"Things Passed on the Way to Oblivion" in *Salmagundi*
"Forked River Roadside Shrine, South Jersey" in *Vice*
"The Jesters" in *Virginia Quarterly Review*
"Betrayal" in *Conjunctions*
"Lovely, Dark, Deep" in *Harper's*
"Patricide" in EccoSolo (ebook)
"Mastiff" is reprinted in *The Best American Short Stories 2014*

To all these editors and publications, heartfelt thanks and gratitude are due.

I

SEX WITH CAMEL

L OTS OF THINGS ARE OVERRATED. LIKE SUICIDE."
The boy laughed at his own cleverness. The grandmother,
who was driving in midmorning traffic, seemed distracted.

More emphatically the boy said, "There's, like, two competing *suicide hotlines* for 'teens' in just Boondock County, USA."

"Boondock County—where's that?"

"Are you kidding, Grams? *Here.*"

"Oh, here. I see—here."

The grandmother smiled but didn't laugh. Not that the boy had made a witty remark, but it wasn't like her not to laugh at the boy's remarks, however unwitty.

"At school we get e-mail announcements all the time. *If you're lonely and troubled and need someone to talk to. Crisis Counselors are waiting for your call which will be held in the strictest confidence.* There's a new one—*Do you feel safe in your home?*" The boy laughed.

"Well, do you?"

"Are you kidding, Grams? Statistics say—ninety percent of fatal accidents are in the *home.*"

They laughed together. This was good.

He liked entertaining—well, anyone. He'd been a clever bright

boy almost since he'd learned to talk. Though in cuteness, he'd probably peaked at about age eleven.

Next birthday, he'd be seventeen.

The grandmother who was elegantly dressed as always when she
left the house—smart white-silk turban, white cashmere sweater-coat,
sharp-creased pale blue linen trousers, good shoes—was driving to the
new hospital. The boy had wanted to drive of course but the grandmother had insisted, for she was nearing an age—(she was not yet
there, but she believed she was nearing *there*)—where such basic skills
as driving a vehicle might begin to atrophy, if she didn't practice them
daily.

Superannuated. The grandmother didn't want to be that, she'd
said. The boy had been impressed with the word which he'd appropriated as one of his own.

As a young boy, he'd collected words. *Zygote, parallax, exsanguination* were examples. Now, *superannuated.*

This morning's drive was something of an adventure—the new
hospital was, according to the Google map which the boy had printed
out, 6.7 miles farther from their house than the old hospital.

They'd worn out the old hospital. It was time for the new hospital
which had just opened the previous week, on the far side of a rushing
six-lane state highway.

"Suicide is, like, some kind of dumb *hobby*. Ninety percent of suicides are mistakes—the person hadn't actually intended to kill himself."

"And why are we talking about this?" The grandmother, who'd
been an administrator in a small liberal arts college in a former lifetime, spoke with an air of bemused disbelief. The grandmother cast
a sidelong glance at the boy that would have been, if the boy had
acknowledged it, withering.

The boy shrugged. He'd only meant to be entertaining, nothing he
said had the slightest significance or depth.

"Who brought it up?" the boy asked. "Not me."

"Well, not *me*."

In fact as the grandmother drove the boy had been skimming e-mails and text messages on his smartphone. It was one of the slew of mostly unwanted e-mails from his school that provided a link to the crisis hotline, he'd deleted without a second thought.

"Tell me something funny. I mean, *funny*."

"There's this kid accompanying his grams for something to do on this perfect autumn day when he could be hiking in Peace River Canyon with his friends or alone with his Nike D200."

"Very funny."

"'Dyslexic guy walks into a bra.'"

"A what?"

"A *bra*."

The grandmother laughed. "That is funny."

"'You're so ugly, in the sandbox the cat tried to bury you.'"

"No. That's not funny."

"C'mon, Grams—there's, like, a million 'You're so ugly' jokes. That's one of the least nasty."

"I don't like jokes that turn upon people being ugly, or stupid, or"—the grandmother's voice shifted just perceptibly, so the boy knew she meant to be funny—"Polish."

The boy wanted to point out to the grandmother that jokes are based upon insults mostly. Where's she been all her life? The jokes he hears from his friends and tells are pretty crude, taken from the Internet or cable TV.

"'There's this guy riding through the desert on a camel. He'd been alone for days so he felt the need for sex. No women anywhere in sight so the guy turns to his camel who has become wary of him, like the camel had had some kind of experience like this before. So the guy tries to position himself to have sex with the camel but the camel runs away.

The guy runs to catch up with the camel and the camel lets him on, but just to ride. But soon the guy feels a need for sex again so he tries the same thing again—but the camel runs away. Finally after crossing the desert the guy comes to a road, and on the road is a broken-down car with two gorgeous blond women in it. The guy asks the women if they need help and they tell him if he fixes their car, they'll do anything he wants. The guy works on the car and gets the motor going and the women thank him saying, 'Now what can we do for you?' and the guy says, 'Could you hold my camel?'"

The grandmother seemed to be contemplating this. But the grandmother did laugh, finally.

"OK, that's funny. Only just not very."

"There's dirtier jokes that are funnier, Grams. But I'd guess you don't want to hear them."

There was an edge to the boy's voice. The grandmother declined to reply.

The grandmother continued to drive, now engulfed in a swirl of traffic at a rotary. The boy knew to remain silent as the grandmother navigated the exit—not the first, not the second, but the third exit.

The boy felt really old sometimes. But that was his secret.

When the grandmother had exited the roundabout properly and was driving at a normal speed again the grandmother said, "At least five people have asked me, over the phone, who is coming with me to the hospital and who will be driving me home. What they don't want is someone stepping out of their unit after waking from a 'procedure,' fainting and falling down. Worse, falling down some stairs."

"What they don't want," the boy said, "is a lawsuit."

The grandmother chewed at her lower lip, thoughtfully.

"I guess you must be right. I never thought of it that way. I'd thought they gave a damn about me."

"They can give a damn about you, Grams, and still not want to be sued."

"CAN YOU READ the directions to me? Please."

"I *did*. I *have been*. Jesus!"

The grandmother was driving slowly along a newly paved road in the direction of a high-rise building that looked to be made of dull-green shimmering glass, in several flaring wings. Beyond this building were smaller and flatter buildings. All were surrounded by parking lots. The boy was trying to match up the Google map with the actual landscape and was having difficulty.

The "new hospital" was a congeries of sleek buildings constructed at the edge of town in a lunar-landscape of parking lots and mostly bulldozed soil. Yet, there were areas planted in fragile new grass, and sprinklers rising and falling in the sunshine.

Though everything was new, the parking lots closest to the hospital were near-filled. And these lots were vast and daunting. Even the boy was feeling daunted.

There was a drop-off place for patients and visitors near the front entrance of the high-rise green-shimmering building and the boy and the grandmother were trying to determine how they could spare the grandmother walking what looked like a mile from the parking lot. Finally the boy said, "Just get out, Grandma. I'll park the damn car. There's not gonna be New Jersey traffic cops on private property, asking to see my license."

It was a measure of the grandmother's mounting desperation that she agreed to this. The boy slid into the driver's seat when she got out of the car, and drove into Lot B.

By the time the grandmother had made her way into the fiercely air-conditioned foyer of the sparkling new building, and was glancing about looking for assistance, the boy had parked the Acura and had run back to join her.

The boy was a damned good runner. At times like these especially.

In school sports, the boy was too lazy, or dreamy, or distracted. Couldn't take seriously what the other guys took seriously. All that crap was like living your life with your face pressed up close against a mirror, you couldn't see your own face let alone anything surrounding it. Kid stuff didn't engage him, now he wasn't a kid.

Everything was shining-new in the new hospital. Glancing up you expected to see welcome balloons bouncing against the ceiling several floors above.

"Hel-lo! Can I be of assistance?"

A smiling young woman in clothes color-coordinated with the soft pinks, greens, blues of the foyer appeared at their elbow. The grandmother said yes thank you. As if she hadn't memorized the words, the grandmother frowned at a form she was holding saying carefully, "It's the Ambulatory Surgery Unit we're looking for."

The appointment was for 9:30 A.M. It was 9:22 A.M. now.

The smiling young woman informed them that they were in the wrong building—the hospital. The Ambulatory Surgery Unit was in the Medical Arts Pavilion at the far side of the hospital. "You should have parked in the east lot and entered by that entrance."

"How'd we know that? 'East lot.'" The boy was feeling belligerent.

"If you've come for an appointment, you should have been given directions and a map to the Medical Arts Pavilion."

"'Pavilion'? What's that—like, a carnival or something? A band plays on a 'pavilion'?"

The smiling young woman looked perplexed. "'Pavilion'—it's just what it's called. Where Medical Arts *is*."

Quickly the grandmother intervened. "The Medical Arts Pavilion is in—this direction? Through here?"

The smiling young woman said yes. She was pointing into the interior of the hospital—you could see a bank of elevators, a long wide gleaming corridor, an atrium with potted trees, an "outdoor" café. Workmen were noisily installing something involving electrical wires beyond a sign that smartly read PARDON OUR PROGRESS!

The boy, whose blood had begun beating hard since he'd run in a fast sprint from Lot B, said to the smiling woman, "How'd anybody know that? They told us to come to the *hospital*."

Strictly speaking, this was probably not true. When the grandmother had spoken of her appointment at "the new hospital" she'd spoken in a general and therefore careless way, which the boy had taken literally, and now was reluctant to surrender, the way a loyal dog will not surrender something his master has tossed for him to fetch, to the wrong person.

"If you've come for a medical procedure, you should have been given information, a sheet of paper with a map, " the young woman said evenly. She was still smiling but her smile had become strained. "But there's no problem, I'm here to guide you."

The boy was fuming. Hard to say why. Maybe seeing the grandmother through the young woman's practiced eyes, a woman in her late sixties too elegantly dressed for the circumstances, determined to play the role of *composed, calm.*

"Just tell us which direction, we can find our own way," the boy said, but the grandmother said, "Thanks! That would be really kind of you."

Together they walked into the interior of the high-rise building, the smiling young woman in the lead.

The boy was smoldering and grinding his back molars.

The boy nudged the grandmother who was clutching her over-priced oversized handbag in a way that annoyed him.

"The grandma routine gets old, fast."

"The bratty grandkid, faster."

The boy laughed, harshly. The boy observed in a voice heavy with sarcasm that they must've taken a wrong exit to bring them here—"I think we're in the Marriott."

The corridor led into another building, the "Pavilion"—which did resemble an upscale hotel. In the center of the foyer was a burbling fountain into which, already, though the Pavilion had been inaugurated just a few days before, wishers had tossed copper pennies. Overhead were mobiles in the shapes of birds with outspread wings, Disney-renditions of austere Calder sculptures.

Both the shiny pennies and the floating birds annoyed the boy. A medical clinic isn't a *fun place*.

The smiling young woman prepared to leave them now. "Take the first elevator to the right. On the second floor, turn right. You can't miss it—'Ambulatory Surgery.'"

Now, the strange thing. The unexpected. Too often, in the boy's recent life, there was this—this *extra thing*.

For the young woman was smiling at them, but in a new way. As if she hadn't taken in both of them, the grandmother *and* the boy, until now. The boy felt a shiver of dread.

"You know? I think I remember you. From the old hospital? The two of you? And someone else?" The young woman glanced around as if a missing person might appear. As if one of the strangers passing by in the corridor might turn and smile and identify herself.

Hi. Bet you wondered where I was.

Unfamiliar places could be more dangerous than familiar places, unexpectedly. The boy had been discovering that an unfamiliar place was more easily "haunted" than a familiar place simply because there was less there to distract the memory.

"I don't think so. I think you must be confusing us with someone else." With a cool smile the grandmother turned decisively away, as the boy glared at the shining floor in silence.

On the second floor they turned right. Here was, not a medical unit, but a *suite*. Very lavishly furnished and decorated, seen through floor-to-ceiling glass panels.

The grandmother murmured ambiguously, "There are worse places than the Marriott."

The boy halted outside the doors to Ambulatory Surgery. It was as if his legs were refusing to function, like comic-robot legs.

The boy was beginning to experience *that feeling*—it didn't have any name, and he couldn't have described it. And after it lifted, he could not really remember it.

The grandmother said, "You can wait out here, Billy Bob. You can explore the grounds. You can hang out in the café. What do kids *do?*"

Billy Bob was a playful name. A joke-name.

Nothing very bad could ever happen to *Billy Bob*, seemed to be the promise.

The boy indicated his new smartphone, that fit in the palm of his hand. "Grams, never have to ask what kids *do.*"

THE BOY DIDN'T ACCOMPANY the grandmother into the suite designated Ambulatory Surgery but the boy remained outside looking in. Through floor-to-ceiling glass panels you could see people in the waiting room who might have been people anywhere, in an airport perhaps, except some of these people were in wheelchairs and some were bald—(bald at a wrong age, and in the wrong sex)—and the boy knew from experience that if he stepped inside the room a certain *alteration of the air* would unnerve him—he'd begin to feel that strange sad clutching sensation, that was also a sensation like that of sand slipping away beneath your feet, he'd do anything to avoid.

The grandmother was giving her name to the receptionist. The grandmother would be asked *Do you have a living will?*

The boy was sweating in the air-conditioned air.

The grandmother turned, to point out the boy to the receptionist—there was her *designated driver*, it was he who would take her home.

The boy waved to the receptionist to signal *That's right. I'll be here. No worry!*

The boy was tall: five feet ten. *Tallness* gave him confidence at times like these.

For ten minutes or so the boy stood outside the glass panels and made faces at the grandmother who was leafing distractedly through a magazine (the grandmother had brought herself: she knew not to rely on waiting-room reading) and who glanced over at him smiling, or half-smiling—for she was distracted, the boy saw, though pretending not to see or not to register seeing.

Being a grandkid, you can so easily regress. All the ages you ever were are all recalled by the grandparent, in a shimmery love-haze like those blurred faces on TV in which identities have been disguised.

The boy was behaving strangely outside in the corridor as others came and went. Outpatients, and their companions. The boy did not want to go away, neither did the boy want to remain.

You want something to happen, finally. You want something to be decided and the results revealed.

You did not want anything to happen. You did not want any results.

The boy knew of *results*. The boy knew that some results are *irrevocable*.

The grandmother's name must have been called, for the grandmother stood suddenly, looking frightened, which the boy wished he had not seen, but he'd seen, so he would try to forget seeing, which is not so difficult as you'd think. A smiling youngish nurse in pastel smock and pants came to escort the grandmother into the interior of the medical unit walking with her as if steadying her, and they disappeared. And the boy was dry-mouthed, observing. And the boy backed away, and turned away.

Approximately ninety minutes, the grandmother would be in Ambulatory Surgery. All this time, unfolding before the boy like an elaborate card trick.

THE BOY WAS CRAZY for his smartphone which could occupy him for many minutes. On the boy's smartphone were countless *apps*—a small galaxy of *apps*. But the boy had more than the smartphone in his sweating hand, he had also his geometry text weighing down a pocket of his khaki cargo pants. He'd become the sort of wiseass kid who tells adults he likes geometry for its *orderliness and sanity.*

The boy was wandering on the second floor of the Pavilion. Discovered a stairway, and ascended. Too restless to stay in one place plying the smartphone.

He thought *I should have the car keys now. In case something happens, Grandma has to stay in the hospital overnight.*

It began that way, usually. Tests, overnight.

Through floor-to-ceiling glass panels on the third floor the boy observed a waiting room furnished exactly as the waiting room in Ambulatory Surgery. Here too were rows of chairs, and a few wheelchairs. Except here, the patients were all young girls.

Slender girls with long straight hair to their shoulders, falling down their backs. Girls with size-zero figures. Beautiful angel-girls, with faces that clutched at him. Hot-looking except they were, on second glance, too skinny—scary-skinny. Though they wore loose-fitting clothes you could tell they were scary-skinny for there were girls like that at his school, not many but a few, and of these some of the most beautiful girls, you learned not to stare at, but you stared. He'd turn away now but a face on the other side of the glass panel so clutched at him, such a face, he was paralyzed. Counting nine girls in the waiting room. And with them—he'd hardly noticed—older women who had to be their mothers. *A waiting room exclusively female.*

The boy stored up the information to relay to the grandmother on the drive home—"Guess what it was?—Eating Disorders Unit."

The grandmother would say, "*Eating Disorders!* I could envy them, that kind of condition."

The boy would say, reprovingly, "Actually, they die. A lot."

He knew, he'd read statistics on the subject. And a girl in his class had died—(of a heart attack?)—who'd weighed only seventy-seven pounds at the age of fifteen.

The boy would entertain the grandmother, but maybe not with Eating Disorders.

The boy exited the Pavilion and was struck by hot gusts of wind rushing across the vast parking lots.

The boy hiked around the hospital to check out Lot B, a half-mile away. Just to see that he knew where he'd parked the car. (He did.) The landscape was part primeval, gouged-out earth, mounds of red earth. Hot rushing winds that took away his breath. *Hi. Bet you wondered where I was.*

Back inside the Medical Arts Pavilion the boy liked feeling invisible among a continuous stream of strangers. At sixteen you're an invisible age. He sprawled on a vinyl sofa by the burbling fountain. Couldn't prevent himself from counting the shiny copper pennies in the fountain, that he could see: thirty-two.

If he counted again, possibly he'd get another number. He thought in wonderment *Why? Why do people do such fucking stupid useless things?* It was envy he felt, not scorn.

The boy checked his smartphone for the fifteenth time that morning. Mostly, he deleted messages. His thumbs had become practiced assassins. His life had become a series of rapid deletions—you deleted *them* before they deleted *you.*

Boring! The boy was restless suddenly, jumped up and took an elevator to the fourth floor—Pulmonary, Acute Asthma—took stairs down to the third floor where he leaned over the railing gazing down at the burbling fountain. From this height, you couldn't see the shiny copper pennies and you would not speculate on what asshole-useless wishes they were.

One of the girls from Eating Disorders was walking slowly in his direction. Except that the girl's eyes were open and unnaturally wide, she might have been sleepwalking.

She might have been nineteen though she looked fifteen. Crinkly red-brown hair fell halfway down her back. Unlike most of the Eating Disorders girls she wore tight-fitting clothes—black Capri pants, a sweater so tiny her tiny breasts were showcased like Dixie cups. Her wrists were so small, the boy stared seeing how he could loop his crude guy-fingers around them twice. He was staring at the girl so intensely, the girl took notice and laughed at him.

"Am I somebody you think you know? Or—are you somebody I'm supposed to know?"

The girl was just so gorgeous. The boy hoped his mouth wasn't drooping open like a dog's.

Anorexic girls had breaths like acid. It was part of all that the girls didn't know about themselves. The boy knew that, when the girls looked in mirrors, they saw something totally different from what normal people saw, but he couldn't imagine what they saw.

"Sorry. Am I scaring you?"

The question, from the girl, should have made no sense, but made sense. The girl laughed. Her laughter sounded like small flames darting.

Clumsily the boy said, "I'm looking for the elevators."

"Not looking very hard, are you? Elevators are over there."

The boy was telling one of the guys boastfully *This girl I met, she's really cool. She's a little older than I am. Smart . . .*

"Are you in 'Eating Disorders'? There's almost no guys, I never run into guys."

The boy laughed. He didn't know whether to be flattered or insulted.

"Do I look like 'Eating Disorders'?"

"Well, don't be so smug, Fred," the girl said, "you could be, one day."

"I don't think so. I like to eat too much."

"We all like to eat *too much*. That's the definition of 'Eating Disorders,' stupid."

She was the most gorgeous girl he'd ever seen in actual life but being called *Fred* or *stupid* wasn't a turn-on for him.

He'd turned away. He had somewhere to get to. The girl caught the look of surprise and hurt in his face and relented.

"Excuse me? Hey."

The boy turned back, but hesitantly. Body language suggesting he didn't trust her but maybe, he'd be surprised.

"I'm on fucking meds, see? That's why I say fucking stupid things I don't mean, Fred."

The boy said OK. That was cool.

"Yes, but you don't mean it. You're looking like you want to escape. My point is, I didn't mean it. I *don't mean it.*"

The boy said OK. But he had to leave now.

The girl said, in a rising voice, "*It isn't OK, asshole!* I'm talking to you."

"Miranda!"—a woman was approaching the girl, agitated. A mother-looking woman from whom the girl flinched with a look of such juvenile loathing, the boy was shocked.

"What the fuck do *you* want? Where the fuck did *you* come from?"

The woman tried to placate the girl but her mistake was to touch the girl's flailing arm.

"Fuck fuck fuck you. I said—*fuck you.*"

The boy escaped to the elevators. He heard angry sobbing, and angry whispering, and a sound of struggle, but he did not glance back.

THIS GIRL I met yesterday, she really came on to me. Must've been, like, twenty years old. So hot . . .

"Fuck you, Fred. This is going nowhere."

The boy's aloud voice was cracked, hostile. The boy was feeling loosed as an electron spinning into space—no gravity, no "orbit."

HE'D SKIPPED BREAKFAST that morning, now he was ravenously hungry.

In the first-floor café he ate. Stuffed his face. Washed all of it down with a giant chemical-Coke. You'd think you couldn't buy such toxins in a hospital café but you'd be mistaken.

He loosened the belt of his jeans. He was a skinny kid, and skinny kids bloat fast.

Why *was* there so much bias against suicide? People should do what they fucking want.

The boy checked his smartphone on the average of once every three minutes. He wasn't *addicted*, it was just something he did. Other things felt boring, or old. You'd done them already. You'd heard them already. His geometry text he'd lugged to the hospital with the intention of catching up on the assignment but the environment was too distracting for concentrated work. The grandmother had said it was not a good idea for him to miss school for her but then the grandmother had relented saying he should get his assignments from his teachers and try to get some work accomplished waiting for her and the boy had said irritably that that was exactly what he'd planned to do, for Christ's sake.

At each table in the café there were these trapped people—you had to be trapped if you were here, nobody would be here who'd chosen to be here even in the shining new hospital with bobbing welcome balloons. Even if the café was kind of attractive, not a bad place—the menu not-bad, for a place like this. Each person in the café was a visitor to the hospital or the medical center and each had a probably sad, possibly awful story to tell. (The medical center had a notable Oncology department, for one thing.) The boy who'd been stuffing his face didn't want to hear a single one of these stories. The boy was sick of his own sad story.

Yet he was listening to two women talking together at a nearby table: one was in civilian clothing and the other was in a blue hospital nightie with a robe over it, hospital-issue socks. There was a needle in the back of the woman's hand dripping intravenous fluids into her from a pole she hauled around with her, with a jaunty smile. The women looked like sisters—not-young, but not-bad looking—laughing more than would seem normal.

At the old hospital, patients would sneak outside with their IV poles and smoke. It was against hospital rules as it was against common sense but the boy had abetted one of these patients more than once.

One of these times she'd said, "Good news and less-than-good news."

"Will I be able to tell which is which?"

The patient laughed. Laughter turned into a coughing fit. The plastic IV container quivered. "You're right. There's not much difference."

Later she said: "The good news is, they're stopping chemo. The bad news is, they're stopping chemo."

That had been the old hospital. The boy thought, The hell with the old damn hospital.

THE BOY TOOK the elevator to the second floor, turned right. He was feeling a little panicked now.

It was precisely ninety minutes. He'd had to resist coming early for it was a fact of this life, medical things are never completed *early.*

This time, the boy pushed open the doors and stepped inside. The boy checked in with the receptionist, gave the grandmother's name and his own name. The receptionist called back to the medical unit. The boy was told please take a seat for the grandmother wasn't out of recovery yet but the boy pretended not to hear for the boy did not want to be trapped in a seat, the boy wanted free use of his legs. The boy was too tall and too old to be drifting around the waiting area annoying patients in chairs, some of them in wheelchairs, drifting about the waiting room taking up magazines like *Smithsonian, Scientific American, Your Health* leafing through them then shoving them back in the magazine racks.

After about twenty minutes, the grandmother appeared in a wheelchair pushed by a nurse.

The boy stared at the grandmother and something began to fade in his head and he began to feel really weird but quickly recovered, pretty much recovered by the time the grandmother was wheeled to him with her hand uplifted—to him.

"Billy Bob: you're looking kind of *sick*."

The grandmother spoke in a jovial way. The grandmother had applied fresh lipstick to her bloodless lips, to suggest she was in a very good mood, looking and feeling damned good after the ultra-"invasive" procedure.

It was just—it was just the sight of the grandmother in a wheelchair was—a kind of a, a shock . . .

"Yes, my young friend. You're looking kind of *ghastly*."

The nurse who'd been pushing the grandmother in the wheelchair laughed at the grandmother's humor. As the nurse helped the grandmother up and out of the chair the grandmother thanked the nurse saying in a voice of notable clarity that she felt "one hundred percent recovered" and did not require any more assistance.

It was medical protocol to wheel patients out of recovery, whether they felt weak or not. It didn't *mean anything*, as the boy knew.

The boy was shaky. The boy was trying to think of a jokey response. The grandmother was laughing at him.

"Fooled you, eh? I saw your face."

"Problem was, I saw *your face*."

(This was pretty lame. The boy searched his brain for witty one-liners. All he could think of was *you're so ugly* jokes. Like shoving your hand in a pocket desperate for a tissue—nothing there. Have to blow your nose in your hand.)

The grandmother was feeling good, she said. Oh maybe a little light-headed but *good*. There was no pain—none! Or, if there was, it was like in another room—not immediate. Taking the boy's hand, so the boy felt her icy fingers, and another time worried he might faint, but didn't.

Oh Jesus: the grandmother's fingers were *so thin*.

The boy escorted the grandmother from Ambulatory Surgery, down to the foyer. The boy would leave the grandmother at the entrance and the boy would run, run—run to Lot B—to get the car to pick her up.

"THE FUNNY THING about anesthesia—you've been *out*, but you don't remember. When you wake up you aren't really sure you are not dead, but you guess you aren't fully alive either."

The boy sniggered as if this was meant to be a particularly witty insight by the grandmother.

The grandmother was settling into the passenger's seat. Now, the grandmother conceded, maybe she was feeling a little—tired. Maybe she'd close her eyes on the way home. Maybe at home, she'd have a nap.

The boy was thrilled by the new-model Acura in Bellanova White Pearl, that held the road so beautifully. A quiet engine, like a heart that doesn't rattle.

He'd helped the grandmother select this vehicle. They'd traded in an older, inferior vehicle.

The boy felt good, driving. The boy felt very good.

"What did the doctor say? Was there an X-ray? Blood work?"

The boy hadn't planned to ask these questions. Yet the boy heard himself ask these questions.

The grandmother was silent for a moment. The boy chose to ignore this moment.

Then, deftly the grandmother pitched her thin soprano voice in imitation of a singsong male voice, presumably Chinese.

"'Results not in yet, Mrs. Cosby. Will call tomorrow morning.'"

The boy laughed. The boy felt great relief, laughing.

MASTIFF

Earlier on the trail, they'd seen it. The massive dog. Tugging at its master's leash so that the young man's calves bulged with muscle as he held the dog back. Grunting what sounded like *Damn Rob-roy! Damn dog* in a tone of exasperated affection.

Signs on the trail forbade dogs without leashes. At least, the massive dog was on a leash.

The woman stared at the dog not twelve feet away wheezing and panting. Its head was larger than her own, with a pronounced black muzzle, bulging glassy eyes. Its jaws were powerful, and slack; its lips shone, and the large long tongue rosy-pink as a sexual organ dripped slobber. The dog was pale-brindle-furred, with a deep chest, muscled shoulders and legs, a short taut tail. It might have weighed two hundred pounds. Its panting was damply audible, unsettling. The straggly-bearded young man who gripped the leather leash with both hands, in beige hoodie, multipocketed khaki shorts, hiking boots, squinted at the woman, and at the man behind her, with an expression that might have been apologetic, or defensive; or maybe, the woman thought, the young man was laughing at them, ordinary hikers without a massive monster-dog tugging and straining at their arms.

The woman thought *That isn't a dog. It's a human being on his hands and knees. That face!*

Such surreal thoughts bombarded the woman's brain waking and sleeping. So long as no one else could know the woman paid little heed.

Fortunately, the massive dog and its master were taking another hiking trail into Wild Cat Canyon. Eagerly the dog lunged forward sniffing at the ground, the young man following with muttered curses. The woman felt relief, the ugly dog hadn't attacked her! She and her male companion continued on the main trail which was approximately two and a half miles uphill to Wild Cat Canyon Peak.

The man, sensing the woman's unease at the sight of the dog, made some joke which the woman didn't quite hear and did not acknowledge. They were walking single file, the woman in the lead. She waited for the man to touch her shoulder as another man might have done to comfort but she knew that he would not, and he did not. The man said, in a tone of slight reproof, that the dog was an English mastiff— "Beautiful dog."

The woman felt the man's remark as a rebuke of a kind. Much of what the man said to the woman she understood was in rebuke of her narrow judgment, her timorous ways. Sometimes, the woman amused the man, for these reasons. At other times, the woman annoyed the man and she saw in his gentlemanly face an expression of startled disapproval, veiled contempt. She thought *He sees through me. My subterfuge, my ignorance. My desperation.*

The woman said, over her shoulder, with a wild little laugh, "Yes! Beautiful."

The hike that day to Wild Cat Canyon Peak would be a hike uphill, into the sun. Splotched light and shadow on the trail, momentary spells of sun-blindness. The woman was thrilled to be outdoors, and hiking with the man. *This* man, to whom she'd been introduced with great promise seven weeks, four days before at a dinner party in a mutual friend's home in the north Berkeley hills.

The hike had been the man's suggestion. Or, rather, in his oblique way, which might have been (the woman thought) a strategy of shyness, like her own, he'd simply told her that he was going hiking that weekend, and would she like to join him?

In this way, the man had not risked being rejected. The woman had been made to know that if she came with him she was accompanying *him*.

The woman and the man had gone on walks together, by this time. But a hike of such ambition, to Wild Cat Canyon Peak, seemed to the woman something very different.

She'd said, with her wild little laugh, "Yes! I'd love that."

IT WAS LATE AFTERNOON. Several hours the man and the woman had been hiking. And now single file down the mountain from Wild Cat Canyon Peak they were making their careful way. The woman was descending first, then the man. For the man was the more experienced hiker and wanted to watch over the woman whom he didn't trust not to hurt herself. She'd surprised him by insisting upon wearing lightweight women's running shoes on the trail and not, as he was wearing, hiking boots.

She hadn't thought to bring water, either. The man carried a twelve-ounce plastic bottle of water for them both.

The man had been amused by the woman. Just possibly, the man had been a little annoyed by the woman.

Yet, he was drawn to the woman. He hoped to like her more than he did—he hoped to adore her. For he'd been so very lonely for too long and had come to bitterly resent the solitude of his life.

At the outset of the hike it had been an unnaturally balmy day in late March. At midday, the temperature might have been as high as sixty-eight degrees Fahrenheit. Now as the sun sank in the western sky like a broken bloody egg darkness and cold began to lift from the earth. The man had suggested to the woman that she bring along a light canvas jacket in her backpack, he knew how quickly the mountain trail could turn cold in the late afternoon, but the woman had worn just a pullover sweater, jeans, and a sun-visor hat more appropriate for summer. (The woman's eyes were sensitive to sunlight even with sunglasses. She hated how easily they watered, tears running down her cheeks like an admission of female weakness.) She'd confounded the man by not bringing any backpack at all with the excuse that she hated feeling "burdened."

Now in the gathering chill the woman was shivering. If she hadn't clenched her jaws tight, her teeth would have chattered.

The trail had looped upward through pine woods to a spectacular view at Wild Cat Canyon Peak where a stone monument had been erected to the early twentieth-century environmentalist landowner who'd left many thousands of acres of land to the State of California for the park. Then, the trail looped down, in tortuous switchbacks, to the trailhead an hour's hike away, and the parking lot which would be "gated," as signs warned, at 6:00 P.M. It was already 4:40 P.M.

At the peak, the man had taken photographs with his new camera while the woman gazed out into the distance, at the spectacular view. At the horizon was a rim of luminous blue—the Pacific Ocean miles away. In the near distance were small lakes, streams. The hills were strangely sculpted, like those bald hills in the paintings of Thomas Hart Benton.

The man had given the woman water to drink. Though she'd said she wasn't thirsty, he'd insisted. There's a danger of dehydration when you've been exerting yourself, he said. Sternly he spoke, like a parent you could not reasonably oppose.

The man spoke with the confidence of one who is rarely challenged. At times the woman quite liked this air of authority, at other times she resented it. The man seemed always to be regarding the woman with a bemused air like a scientist confronted with a curious specimen. She didn't want to think—(yet she thought, compulsively)—that he must be comparing her with other women he'd known, and was finding her lacking.

At the peak, absorbed in his photography, the man seemed to have forgotten the woman. How childlike, how self-contained and maddening! The woman had never been so at repose in her *self*.

For nearly an hour the man would linger at the peak, taking photographs. During this time other hikers came and went. It was no effort for the woman to speak with these hikers briefly while the man seemed oblivious of them. It wasn't his way, he'd told the woman, to strike up conversations with "random" persons. Why not? she'd asked, and he'd said, with a look that suggested that her question was virtually incomprehensible to him, *Why not? Because I'll never see them again.*

With her provocative little laugh the woman said *But that's the best reason for talking to strangers—you will never see them again.*

At least the straggly-bearded young man with the massive dog—the English mastiff—hadn't climbed to the top of Wild Cat Canyon Peak.

But other hikers with dogs made their way there. A succession of dogs, in fact, of all sizes and breeds, fortunately most of them well-behaved and disinclined to bark; several trailing their masters, older dogs, looking chastised, winded. The damp subdued eyes of these older dogs seemed to seek the woman's own eyes.

"Nice dog! What's his name?"

Or, she'd ask, with widened eyes, "What breed is he?"

The woman understood that her male companion had taken note of her fear of the mastiff, at the start of the hike. How she'd tensed at the sight of the ugly wheezing beast that had to be the largest dog of its kind she'd ever seen, nearly as large as a Saint Bernard, but totally lacking the benign shaggy aura of the Saint Bernard. How she'd stared at the slobbering jaws and glassy blind-seeming eyes—as if in recognition of something not to be named.

And so at Wild Cat Canyon Peak the woman made it a point to engage dog owners in conversations, in her bright airy friendly way. She'd asked about their dogs, she'd even petted the gentler ones.

As a child of nine or ten she'd been attacked by a fierce-barking German shepherd. She'd done nothing to provoke the attack and could remember only screaming and trying to run as the dog barked furiously at her and snapped at her bare legs. Only the intervention of adults had saved her, she'd thought.

The woman hadn't told the man much about her life. Not yet. And possibly never. Her principle was *Never reveal your weakness.*

Especially to strangers, this was essential. *Never reveal your weakness.*

In a technical manner of speaking the woman and the man were "lovers" but they were not intimate. You might say—(the woman might have said)—that they were strangers, essentially.

The woman liked to say to her friends, to amuse them, that she wanted not *to marry* but to *be married.* She wanted a relationship that seemed already mature, if not old and settled, at the start. Newness and rawness did not appeal to her.

"Excuse me? When do you think we might leave?"—hesitantly the woman spoke to the man, not liking to interrupt his concentration.

In their relationship, the woman had not yet displayed any impatience. The woman had not raised her voice, not once.

At last, the man put away his camera, which was a heavy, complicated instrument, into his backpack. And the water bottle, which contained just two or three inches of water—"We might need this, later." The man's movements were measured and deliberate as if he were alone and the woman felt a sudden stab of dislike for him, that he took such care with trivial matters, and yet did not love her.

There were no restrooms on the damned trail—of course. These were serious hiking trails, for serious hikers. Longingly the woman recalled the restroom facilities at the trailhead, a considerable distance downhill. How long would it take, to hike back down? Another hour? For male hikers, stopping to urinate in the woods was no great matter; for female hikers, an effort and an embarrassment. Not since she'd been a young girl trapped on a hateful long hike in summer camp in the Adirondacks, had she been forced to relieve herself in the woods. The memory was hazy and blurred with shame, and humiliation at the very pettiness of the discomfort. If she'd told this to the man he would have laughed at her.

Driving to the park that day, the man and the woman had felt very happy together. It sometimes happened to them, unpredictably—a sudden flaring-up of happiness, even joy, in each other's company. The man had been unusually talkative. The woman laughed at his remarks, surprised that he could be so witty. She'd been flattered that, a few days before, he'd visited her art gallery, and had purchased a small soapstone sculpture.

The woman had slid over in the passenger's seat, to sit closer to the man, as a young girl might do, impulsively. How natural this felt, a rehearsal of intimacy!

They'd spent time together in the woman's house, upstairs in her bed—but they hadn't yet spent an entire night together. The man felt self-conscious in the woman's house, the woman felt as if the man were a houseguest, to be treated graciously and not intimately. She hadn't been able to sleep yet beside the man for the physical fact of him was so distracting, he took up too much space in her bed. Naked and horizontal, the man seemed much larger than he did clothed and vertical. He breathed loudly, wetly, through his opened mouth, and though he woke affably when she nudged him, the woman had not wanted to wake him often. She'd resigned herself to lying awake, listening to him breathe. Yet, her physical discomfort was acute—*I can't sleep, I will never sleep if this man is in my bed.*

The woman had not ever been comfortable with a man in close quarters, unless she'd been drinking. But the man scarcely drank. And the woman no longer lost herself in drink, that life was behind her.

On the car radio a piano piece by the Czech composer Janáček—the title was translated "In the Mists." The woman recognized the composition within a few notes. She'd played the piano cycle years ago as a girl. Her eyes filled with tears as she remembered.

Through the somber, distinctive piano notes in a minor—"misty"—key the man continued talking, as if he didn't hear the music. Avidly the woman listened to the piano notes and not to the man's words but the man's voice was suffused with the melancholy beauty of the music and she felt how she loved him, or might love him.

He will be the one. It's time.

The woman was forty-one years old. The man was several years older, she believed. The two had been introduced by a mutual friend, closer emotionally to the man than to the woman, who'd said to the man *You will like Mariella. You will like her face* and to the woman *Simon is an extraordinary person but that might not be evident immediately. Give him time.*

The man had been the director of a distinguished research laboratory in Berkeley, California, for many years. His work was predominant in his life. Scientific truth was sacrosanct, unassailable, as it was impersonal and transcendent. His work was what he'd leave behind of himself. He was idealistic, a zealot for science education and the preservation of the environment. He was famously generous with younger scientists. He was a legendary mentor to his graduate students and post-docs. He'd never married. He wasn't sure he'd ever been *in love*. He had no children, though he'd always wanted children. He was dissatisfied with his life, outside the lab. He felt cheated and foolish, that others might pity him. Especially those younger colleagues whom he'd helped in their careers.

He'd been disturbed earlier that year, visiting one of his protégés at the Salk Institute who was married, had several children, and a scientist-wife; the young family lived in a split-level cedar house on three acres of wooded land. In this household the man had felt sharply the emptiness in his own life, in the underfurnished rented house near the university in which he'd lived for more than twenty years, imagining a kind of pride since, from this house, he could so easily bicycle or walk to the lab.

He'd gone away from the young family's house shaken and shattered. And not long afterward, he'd been introduced to the woman of whom it was said *You will like Mariella's face.*

The woman was also lonely and dissatisfied, but it was others with whom she was primarily dissatisfied, not herself. She'd had intense relationships with men since college but invariably she'd been involved with several men at the same time, seeing them simultaneously so that she was prevented from feeling much emotion for any of them. At the same time, she was deeply hurt if a man wasn't involved exclusively with *her.* She'd seen her mother obsequious in her marriage. Her tall handsome father hadn't valued the wife who'd humbled herself for him; he'd left her, when the woman had been a child, and he'd rarely visited his children. All her life she'd yearned for the absent man even as she'd resented him. Her fantasy was her father returning, and she and her mother spurning him with gales of wild laughter.

She'd thought *It's insane to be vulnerable, as women are. Nothing is worth such hurt.*

Yet, she was an attractive woman. Within a small circle of friends she was highly popular, admired. She dressed stylishly. She had many social activities. She'd invested wisely in an art gallery. Despite this, much of her mental life was preoccupied with how she appeared in others' eyes. She could barely force herself to contemplate her image in a mirror: far from beautiful, not even pretty, her face too small, heart-shaped, her chin too narrow, her eyes too large and deep-set. She hated it, she was *petite.* She'd have liked to be five feet ten inches tall, to walk with an air of female swagger, sexual confidence. At five feet three inches, she had no choice but to be the recipient, the very receptacle, of a man's desire.

It disturbed her that she was so detached from her family, her relatives and girlhood friends. In the midst of a buoyant social occasion something inside the woman seemed to switch off. She could feel the deadness seeping into her, the chill indifference. Her women friends close as sisters hugging her, kissing her at the end of an evening, a friend's husband slipping his arm around her waist to kiss her, just a little too hard, with too much vehemence—"Good night, Mariella!" And the coldness in her responded *I don't give a damn if I ever see any of you again.*

She laughed at herself, such emptiness. A hole in the heart.

She could have wept. She would soon be forty-two years old.

Yet it happened, in the new man's company, the woman felt a rare hopefulness. If she couldn't love the man it might be enough for the man to love *her*; enough for them to have a child together, at least.

(What would the man have thought, if he'd known how the woman plotted? Or were these harmless fantasies, not likely to be realized?)

(In the woman's weakest moments, she lamented that she had no children; she would soon be too old for children. Yet, young children bored her, even her young nieces and nephews, who she conceded were beautiful.)

Now, making her way down the trail, eager to be out of the park that had seemed so beautiful hours ago, the woman was feeling disconsolate. The long rest at the peak had enervated her. The man's indifference had enervated her. As the sun shifted in the sky so she felt strength leaking from her.

Brooding and silent the man was walking behind the woman, sometimes so close he nearly trod upon her heels. She wanted to turn to scream at him—"Don't do that! I'm going as quickly as I can."

So absorbed was the woman in the voice inside her head she only half-realized she'd been hearing a familiar sound from somewhere close by—a wet chuffing noise, as of labored breathing. The trail continued to drop, turning back upon itself; another, lower trail ran parallel with it now, and would join with it within a few yards, and on this trail two figures were hurrying, one of them, in the lead, a large beast running on all fours.

The woman heard panting ahead. A sensation of fear washed over her.

She had no choice but to blunder forward. Appalled, she saw the massive dog ahead, unavoidable. The damp shining eyes were fixed upon her, not blind-seeming now, but sharply focused. With a kind of canine indignation quickly shifting to fury the dog barked at the stricken woman, straining at his leash as the straggly-bearded young man shouted for the dog to *sit*.

The woman knew better than to succumb to panic, certainly the woman knew better than to provoke the massive dog. It is always a mistake to expose one's weakness. Her terror of what those teeth and sharp claws could do to her.

She couldn't help herself—she screamed, and shrank away. It was the worst possible reaction to the dog that, maddened by the woman's terror, leapt at her, loudly barking and growling, wrenching the leash out of his master's hands.

In an instant the mastiff was on the woman, snarling and biting, nearly knocking her onto the ground. Even in her terror the woman was thinking *My face. I must protect my face.*

Behind her, the man quickly intervened. He seemed to her fearless, astonishing—pulling her back, behind him, shouting at the dog's master to call the damned dog off.

Futilely the young man was shouting—"Rob-roy! Rob-*roy!*" The dog paid not the slightest heed to his master, viciously attacking the man, on its hind legs and pummeling him as if to knock him down, that it might tear at his throat with its bared, yellowish fangs.

The frantic struggle could not have lasted more than a few seconds. Fiercely the man tried to shove the dog away, striking it with his bare fists, kicking at it. The straggly-bearded young man yanked at the dog's collar, cursing. With great effort he managed to pull the furious dog away from the man who was bleeding badly from lacerations on his hands and arms and face.

The man had been knocked to one knee. The dog might have torn out his throat but the young man yanked back hard, as if to break the dog's neck.

The terrified woman was cringing behind the man. Always she would remember how unhesitatingly the man had leapt forward to protect her, taking no heed for his own safety.

In the confusion of the struggle, the woman felt something warm on her face. Not blood but the dog's loathsome slobber.

The dog's master managed to extricate the dog from the couple. Still it was barking hysterically, lunging and leaping with bared fangs.

The woman cried, "Help him! Get help for him! He'll bleed to death."

The young man apologized profusely. He was holding the struggling dog down with both arms. Claiming the dog had never done anything like this before—not ever . . . "Jesus! I'll get help." There was a rangers' station a half-mile down the trail, the young man said. He'd run, he'd get help from the rangers.

Alone with the injured man, the woman cradled him in her arms as he moaned and writhed with pain. He appeared to be dazed, stupefied. Was he in shock? His skin felt cold to the woman's touch. She could barely comprehend what had happened, and so swiftly.

The crazed dog had bitten and scratched her hands, too. There were cuts and abrasions in her flesh, bleeding. But her fear was for the man. She fumbled for her cell phone, tried to call 911 but the call failed to go through. She wondered—should she try to make a tourniquet to stanch the flow of blood from the man's forearm? Years ago as a high school girl she'd taken a course in first aid but—could she remember, now? For a tourniquet you had to use a stick? Her eyes darted about, searching for—what? So slowly she was thinking, with the effort of one trying to walk through sludge in a dream. Like a foolish trapped bird her heart beat erratically in her chest.

The man was insisting he was all right, he could walk to the rangers' station—"Hey, I'm not going to die."

Grotesquely, he tried to laugh. He had no idea how torn and bloody his face was.

The woman helped the man to his feet. How heavy he was, and how uncoordinated! His face was a mask of blood, it was terrifying to see flaps of loose skin in his cheeks and forehead. One of the man's earlobes had been torn.

At least, the man's eyes had been spared.

The woman gripped the man around the waist, clumsily. With effort he was able to walk leaning heavily on her. The woman was trying to comfort him—she had no idea what she was saying except that there would be help for him soon, he would be all right . . . She saw that the front and sleeves of her sweater were soaked in dark blood.

By this time the sun had sunk below the tree line. It was now dusk and the air was cold and wet as if after a rain. The woman's teeth were chattering. The woman and the man made their stumbling way along the trail. They'd begun to hear calls, cries—two rangers were running up the shadowy trail with flashlights, shouting. The man was limping, wincing with pain. His clothes had been torn as if with a giant scissors. Though he must have weighed sixty pounds more than she did, the woman was managing to hold him erect, trembling with the effort. As she was about to collapse the man was lifted from the woman's grip.

They were taken to the rangers' station and treated with first aid. Sterilizing liquid, bandages. For the man's lacerated forearm, a tourniquet deftly applied by the elder of the rangers. It was observed that the man was lucky—"The artery wasn't severed." A dog attack was a serious injury, there was the possibility of rabies. It was imperative to locate the dog.

The straggly-bearded young man had fled the park with the mastiff. Incredibly, he had not reported the attack. But others had seen him, and had reported him. A hiker returning to his car in the parking lot had taken down the plate number of the young man's Jeep.

Beneath the bandages, the man's face was ashen. His breath came quickly and shallowly. He was urged to lie down on a cot. Despite his protests, an ambulance was called. Dog bites are highly dangerous, the ranger said. A vicious dog-biting has to be reported. The dog's owner would be prosecuted. And leaving the scene of the attack—the son of a bitch would be charged for that, too.

The man's facial injuries required stitches, that was clear. First aid wouldn't be enough. The woman had seen with horror what the dog's teeth and nails had done to her friend. Already the gauze bandages on his face were darkening with blood.

Within minutes the ambulance arrived in the now near-deserted park. The tearful woman wanted to ride with the injured man in the ambulance but the man insisted that she take his station wagon, and meet him at the hospital; he didn't want his vehicle locked in the park overnight.

Even with his injuries, half-dazed by the attack and speaking with difficulty, the man appeared to be thinking calmly, rationally.

The woman took his key from the man's shaky fingers, and his wallet and backpack, and followed in his station wagon. Followed the ambulance along curving mountain roads. She could not breathe, the loneliness was palpable and suffocating as cotton batting.

Inside the man's station wagon, and the man not at the steering wheel! This seemed unnatural to her, baffling.

She thought *He will be all right. We will be all right, then.*

She could leave him, then. She would call a taxi, and be driven to her home approximately twelve miles away.

Yet it was shocking to her, she could not quite fathom it, the dog's young master had fled the park without reporting the attack. The straggly-bearded young man who'd seemed so concerned about them had cared so little about their welfare, he'd fled knowing that, if his dog wasn't located by authorities, both bite-victims would have to endure rabies shots.

She'd been told by the park rangers that the dog's owner would be apprehended within a few hours. The attack had already been reported to local police. A warrant would be issued for the dog owner's arrest. She'd been assured that authorities would find the man and examine the dog for rabies but in her distressed state she'd scarcely been able to listen, or to care.

At the brightly lighted medical clinic, the woman hurried inside. She understood that she was wild-eyed, splotched with blood, looking distraught and disoriented. She saw—the man was being carried into the ER on a stretcher. To her horror she saw that the man seemed to be only partly-conscious. He didn't seem aware of his surroundings. She asked one of the medical workers what was wrong and was told that her companion had had a kind of "seizure" in the ambulance, he'd lost consciousness, his blood pressure had risen alarmingly and his heartbeat had accelerated, in fibrillation.

Fibrillation! The woman knew only vaguely what this meant.

"Oh God save him," the woman begged. "Don't let him die!"

She was prevented from following the man into the ER. She found herself standing at a counter, being asked questions. Her face was streaked coarsely with tears like a billboard ravaged by weather and rain. She fumbled with the man's wallet, searching for his medical insurance card. His university ID. How slowly she moved, her bandaged hands were clumsy as if she wore mittens. One of the EMTs who'd brought the man into the ER was telling her that she should be treated as well, her lacerated hands and wrists should be examined in the ER, the rangers' first aid wasn't enough. But the woman refused to listen. She had more important matters with which to deal. She flushed with indignation when the woman at the counter asked what relation she was to the injured man and sharply she said:

"I am his fiancée."

HOW LONG SHE REMAINED in the ER waiting room the woman would have no clear idea afterward. Time had become disjointed, confusing. Her eyelids were so heavy, she couldn't keep them open. Yet she was sure she hadn't slept for even a few seconds.

Several times she inquired after the man and was told that he was undergoing emergency treatment for cardiac arrhythmia and she could not see him just yet. This news seemed terrible to her, unacceptable. He'd only been bitten by the damned dog! He had not seemed so badly injured initially, he'd insisted upon walking . . . The woman was light-headed, breathing quickly. Her bandaged hands and wrists throbbed with pain. She heard her thin plaintive voice begging—"Don't let him die!"

With her affrighted eyes she saw how others regarded her. A woman slightly crazed with worry, mounting fear. A woman with a voice raised in panic. A woman of the sort you pity even as you inch away from her.

The woman's clothes were damp with blood. Her blood, and his.

She saw that her coarse-knit sweater, that had been one of her very best, most beautiful and most expensive Scottish sweaters, had been torn and mangled by the massive dog past repair.

On the trail coming down from Wild Cat Canyon Peak she'd been so cold her fingers had stiffened but now her fingers burned and stung beneath the bandages. In a bright fluorescent-lit restroom outside the ER unit her face in the mirror above the sink was blurred like those faces on TV that dissolve into pixels to disguise the guilt of identity. She was thinking of the way in which the massive dog had thrown itself at her and the way, astonishingly, in which the man had protected her from the dog. Her brain felt as if it were throbbing, flailing to comprehend. Did the man love her, then? Or—was she meant to love him? What a coward she'd been, the craven way in which she'd ducked behind the man to save herself, desperately she'd grabbed at him, as she'd have grabbed at anyone, cringing, crouching, whimpering like a terrified child. The man had thrust himself forward to be attacked in her place. A man who was virtually a stranger to her had risked his life for *her*.

Now the woman found herself in possession of the man's wallet. She had his backpack containing his camera equipment. In her state of nervous dread she looked through the wallet which was a leather wallet of good quality but badly worn. Credit cards, university ID, library card. Driver's license. A miniature photo of a tensely smiling middle-aged man with a furrowed forehead and thinning shoulder-length hair whom she would have claimed she'd never seen before. And she discovered that he'd been born in 1956—he was fifty-seven years old! A decade older than she'd have guessed, and sixteen years older than she was.

Another card indicated that the man had a cardiac condition—*mitral valve prolapse*. A much-folded prescription dated several years before for a medication to be administered intravenously. Nearest of kin to be notified in case of emergency, a woman with the man's last name, possibly a sister, who lived in San Diego.

The woman hurried to the ER, to speak with a nurse. She pressed the prescription onto the woman who promised her, yes she'd report this discovery to the cardiac specialist who was overseeing the man's treatment.

They would only humor her, the woman supposed. The hysterical fiancée! They'd performed their own tests upon the stricken man.

"Ma'am?"—the waiting room was nearly empty when an attendant came to inform her that her companion was hospitalized for the night, for further tests in the morning and observation in the cardiac unit.

The cardiologist on call had managed to control the man's fibrillation and his heartbeat was near-normal but his blood pressure and white blood cell count were high. The woman tried to feel a rush of relief. Tried to think *Now I can go home, the danger is past.*

Instead she went upstairs to the third-floor cardiac unit. For several minutes she stood outside the doorway of room 3112 undecided whether to enter. Inside, in a twilit room, the man lay in a bed, unnaturally still, as nurses fussed about him. His heartbeat was monitored by a machine. His breathing was monitored. The woman saw that the first-aid bandages hurriedly applied to his face had been removed, his numerous wounds had been stitched together and bandaged again, in a yet more elaborate and more lurid mask of crisscrossing strips of white. The man's arms and hands had been bandaged as well.

The horror was, the ugly dog had wanted to tear out the man's throat. Tear off his face. And how easily that might have happened.

A kindly beautiful face the woman thought it.

She'd entered the hospital room, her knees were weak with exhaustion. Almost she felt that she might faint. A sick, sinking sensation rose in her bowels, into her chest, a dread beyond nausea. Yet she felt gratitude for the man's courage, and for his kindness. Shame for herself, that she'd valued the man so negligently.

In the room, the woman pulled over a chair and sat beside the man's bed. Slowly the woman moved like a person in a dream not her own.

The man had been undressed, his torn and bloodied clothes removed from him. In a hospital gown he lay unnaturally still, eyes shut. His breathing was quick and shallow but rhythmic. The bed had been cranked at a thirty-three-degree angle to allow for easier breathing.

His eyelids fluttered, startled. Was he seeing her? Did he recognize her?

The tear-ravaged face. The bandaged hands and wrists. The woman thought *He has forgotten my name.*

From what the woman could make out of his stitched-together face beneath the bandages, the man was trying to speak. Or—trying to smile?

He was asking her—what? She tried to understand but his words were slurred.

The woman reached over, to take the man's hand. His fingers too were bandaged, and felt cold, stiff. She squeezed his fingers, and the man squeezed back.

She heard herself explain that she would be staying for a while. Until visiting hours ended. She had his wallet and his camera and the key to his station wagon and other things of his, for safekeeping.

She said she would return in the morning, when he was to be discharged. She would drive him home, then. If he wanted. If he needed her. She would return, and bring his things with her, and drive him home. Did he understand?

In the cranked-up bed, the man drifted into sleep. They'd given him a sedative, the woman supposed. Powerful medication to calm his racing heart.

His mouth eased open, he breathed heavily, wetly. This was the night-breathing the woman recalled, and felt comforted to hear. The woman practiced pronouncing his name: "Simon." This seemed to her a beautiful name. A name new to her, in her life, for she'd before never known anyone named Simon.

Now they were safe, tears spilled from the woman's eyes, and ran in rivulets down her ravaged face. She was crying as she had not cried in memory. She was too old for such emotion, there was something ridiculous and demeaning about it. Yet, she was remembering how at the top of the steep trail the man had insisted that she drink from his plastic water bottle. She hadn't wanted to drink the lukewarm water, yet had drunk it as the man watched, acquiescing, yet with resistance, resentment. In their relationship the man would be the stronger, the woman would resent the man's superior strength, yet she would be protected by it. She might defy it, but she would not oppose it. She was thinking of the two or three occasions when she'd kissed the man in a pretense of an emotion she hadn't yet felt.

Like the man, the woman was exhausted. She continued to hold the man's hand on the outside of the covers, less tightly now. She lay her head against the headrest of the chair beside the bed. Her heavy eyelids closed. Vividly she saw the man at the peak of Wild Cat Canyon trail, holding his heavy camera aloft, peering through the viewing lens. A chill wind stirred his thinning silvery-coppery hair—she hadn't noticed that before. She must hurry to him, she must stand close beside him. She must slide her arm around his waist, to steady him. This was her task, her duty. He was stronger than she, but a man's strength can drain from him. A man's courage can be torn from him, and bleed away. She was terrified of something, was she? The pale-blue rim of the Pacific Ocean, far away at the horizon. The bald-sculpted hills and exquisite little lakes that seemed unreal as papier-mâché you could poke your fingers through. And to her horror she realized she'd been hearing a heavy panting breath, a chuffing-wet breath, somewhere behind them, and below them on the trail, in the gathering dusk, waiting.

DISTANCE

M A'AM? YOU CAN'T OPEN THE WINDOWS, SORRY."
      Coolly she turned to the boy. Prissy Mexican kid
wearing white-boy wire-rim glasses who'd brought up her single lightweight suitcase she'd have preferred to have brought herself, to save a
tip. But at the hotel check-in downstairs the suave brisk young woman
behind the counter had finessed Kathryn, handing the card-key to the
bellboy, with no chance for Kathryn to intervene.

"'Can't open the windows'—why not?"

Evasively the boy mumbled what sounded like *sealed.*

"The windows are 'sealed'? But why?"

Kathryn's voice betrayed surprise, dismay. A room in which other
occupants had slept recently—their odors left behind, faintly disguised by disinfectant, room "freshener"—was not the ideal setting
for what she anticipated.

Asking again "Why?"—but the bellboy ignored her. Adjusting a
wall thermostat, a rush of air-conditioning from overhead. In his pose
of concentration there was a mild rebuke, Kathryn thought. A warning

*Don't be ridiculous. Don't ask questions if you don't know the answers.
Sealed windows in high-rise hotels in Vegas, you can figure.*

ON THE THIRD DAY she called L____.

She would have said *I am testing distance.*

Two thousand two hundred thirty-seven miles and three hours separating them.

Except she'd left his telephone number behind. Or she'd lost his telephone number. She'd been hurried packing for her trip and careless as frequently she was careless in small matters despite her wish to be otherwise—seeing now with a stab of dismay clothes, toiletries, papers scattered across the unused hotel bed where she'd unzipped her suitcase and shaken it in search of the slip of paper she was sure she'd brought with her—she'd meant to bring with her—bearing such crucial phone numbers as his.

What did it mean, she hadn't memorized his telephone number.

What did it mean, she didn't know the man's middle name—not even his middle initial! She wasn't sure of the precise name of the road he lived on though she'd been brought to his house—by him—several times and in her mind's eye she could make that journey along that suburban-rural road again at a distance of two thousand two hundred thirty-seven miles and three hours. Thinking *I can't be sure, I don't know. None of it has entered that deeply into me.*

It was her decision then, to call *directory assistance* for his number.

In fact it was *nation-wide directory assistance. City and state please?*

Calling information for his number wasn't identical with calling him of course. Maybe she wouldn't call him. There was that option, purely hers.

Still it seemed urgent to her—she could not have said why—to have his telephone number written hastily in ballpoint on a notepad on the bedside table of this hotel at the edge of the desert two thousand two hundred thirty-seven miles and three hours distant from him. Whether she made use of this number or not. *It's in my power. My choice.*

At the other end of the line a (female) recorded voice in a neutral tone neither warmly engaging nor coolly disapproving provided her with a number which was presumably his number—how quickly it was summoned, before she'd been fully prepared—and this number when punched into the phone receiver with the brash optimism of a child playing at a game warned to be slightly dangerous, maybe more than just slightly forbidden and for this reason irresistible triggered a brief spat of ringing presumably two thousand two hundred and thirty-seven miles away and a *click!* and a (male) recorded voice *This is the L___ residence. No one can come to the phone at the present time so please leave a detailed message and you will be called back*—which confused her—stymied her—for her lover lived alone—didn't he?—or had someone else lived with him until recently, and he hadn't gotten around to changing the recording?—the voice wasn't precisely her lover's voice but resembled it to a degree to lure her into leaving a message even as a part of her mind remained skeptical *This can't be him, such formality isn't like him.* Yet once embarked upon the brief message she could not break it off—feeling like a fool—so stupid!—embarrassing!—leaving a message in a breathy faltering voice like air leaking from a balloon.

She thought *Enough! He will never know.*

In fact it was a relief to think—to assume—that whoever received the message would simply erase it, as a wrong number. For surely—she was certain—that formal oldish voice hadn't been her lover's voice. Whatever voice was her lover's voice—she could not recall, just now—in any case her lover would never hear the message she'd left exposing herself so unambiguously—now she was thinking with a thrill of euphoria why call him at all? Where was the need to call him? Where was the need to attach herself to *him?*—she was more than two thousand miles away, the man could not touch her and render her weak, unnerved, frantic with sexual desire nor could she have touched this man had she wanted to touch him. His body that seemed to her of the weight and density of clayey earth, smelling of damp, of leaves, of the sweetest sort of rot, the taste of her own body in his mouth and his mouth in hers as they lay together like swimmers who have drowned together clutching each other thrown at last upon a desolate littered shore, and high overhead the figures of long-winged shrieking birds . . . What need had she of *him*! She disliked him. She hated him. He had hurt her, her body was bruised. He'd laughed hurting her. She had scoured his shoulders and back with scratches, he'd laughed seeing blood on the sheets. She hated him, such intimacy. It was an insult to her, such intimacy. All that—the life of *feeling*—she would have liked to squeeze from her veins drop by drop.

It was so: her soul was of no more substance than the shadows of long-winged birds—a western species of hawk? gull?—eagle?—across the drawn blind of her hotel room window. With a cruel smile she thought *I will never call him. Never speak with him again.*

In this way she would end it between them, this morning. This was within her power.

As in the east he was three hours into the morning and for her it wasn't yet dawn.

There was such pleasure in heedlessness, as in cruelty! Eagerly she opened the blind. Pushed aside the drapes that were made of a heavy synthetic fabric. It was exhilarating to her to see that the sun was only just rising at the mountainous horizon. That in every direction she could see beyond the sprawl of the city there was an open lunar land-scape, unnameable. She thought *He has no idea where I am, he will never know.*

As he would never know how she'd been awake much of the night as she'd been awake much of the two previous nights. How she resented him, that she'd been awake on his account. Despite the air-conditioning she'd sweated through her nightclothes and the nape of her neck was damp and sticky and the places he'd touched her were bruised and sore and her mouth still swollen and the fleshy lips between her legs swollen and singular and perverse with their own little heartbeat. *He will never know. No more!*

Yet—so strangely!—even as she was thinking she would not call him, she would tear into shreds the slip of paper with his number on it, that she wouldn't be tempted to call him at a later time, she'd lifted the receiver of the bedside phone and got an outside line and another time consulted *directory assistance* and another time a (female) recorded voice came on and this time she made a point of providing both her lover's name and the name of the street on which he lived in that city two thousand two hundred and thirty-seven miles away and three hours into the future so that there could be no chance of a second mistake—previously she'd given just her lover's name—and now she was provided with a number that seemed familiar to her—at least, the first three digits seemed familiar—and this number she called without giving herself time to think *No! no why are you doing this, you should not risk it* and after several rings a man answered at the other end of the line amid a crackling of static and the man's voice which she could not hear clearly sounded abrupt, unfriendly as if the ringing telephone had interrupted him at a time inconvenient to him and she was saying in an unexpectedly anxious voice *Matt? It's me—it's*—her voice breaking as she uttered her name, what pathos in so uttering her own name, her name uttered as a kind of plea, a kind of begging even as the man at the other end of the line said impatiently *What? Who? Can't hear you* for the line continued to bristle with static like jeering laughter as she repeated her name, how plaintive and piteous her voice for she could not grasp the situation—was this man her lover? Had she caught her lover in a mood unlike any she'd ever known in him?—for in truth she barely knew him, their intimacy had been preceded by the briefest of acquaintances—or had he sensed her ambivalence about calling him, at last on the morning of the third day of her absence, and was now taking revenge as rudely he said *You've got the wrong number, sorry* and hung up.

She was barefoot, shivering. In sweaty nightclothes and the most secret parts of her body throbbing with hurt, with insult and mute outrage she found herself standing at the hotel window. With the most frantic bare hands you could not pry open such windows nor could you smash them for they were double- or triple-plated, unsmashable. *Ma'am you can't die, so easily. Throw yourself from a window?—no.*

She saw that it was 6:20 A.M. in Nevada—so early. In the east it was 9:20 A.M. and a reasonable time to have called him, she'd thought. Except he'd discovered something about her, in her absence. He'd discovered the elemental fact that he could live without her as she'd discovered that she could live without him. He was older than she by a number of years, he was more experienced and wiser and why then should he need *her?* With his mouth he'd made love to her in a way that had unnerved and frightened her with its blunt intimacy and now he was repelled by that intimacy and by her and wanted nothing more to do with her *You've got the wrong number, sorry* in a voice thick with disgust leaving her sickened, staggering. How swift and how deadly God's grace came as a spike in the heart. Telling herself with a measure of calmness *This is my punishment. I knew better, I had been warned.* Yet like one stepping forward to the gallows, to allow the noose to be lowered over her head, perversely she saw herself take up the phone receiver again, there she was calling the number again, and after a half-ring the impatient man answered again as if knowing it must be her whom he despised and quickly in a pleading voice she said *Matt this is Kathryn! Don't you know me—Kathryn?* and the reply was annoyed, grudging *Look miss I'm not the man you want. I'm not "Matt." My last name is L____ but I'm not "Matt." I don't know who the hell you want but I'm not him—OK?*

The line went dead. The unknown L____ had vanished from her life as if he had never been.

This was a relief! Should have been a relief. But she was shaken, uncertain. Swaying on her feet as if she'd been struck on the head with a mallet—in such circumstances, the elemental fact is that one is still alive, still standing.

I will end this folly now. I can do this.

She seemed to be staring out a window—where?—a tall wide plate-glass window she knew to be sealed, for her own protection: many and varied were the suicides of this famed city in the desert-basin but plunging from a high-rise window was no longer an option. The sun was now a fierce red-neon bulb beyond the mountains that were serrated like knife-blades and flat-seeming like cardboard cutouts and the city that had been glamorous and glittering by night was now flat, dull, and indistinct with the haze of air pollution, its mysteries exposed like cracks and stains in soiled wallpaper. She thought *I have been warned. God has given me a second chance, to spare myself.*

She had not believed in God in a lifetime. Nor in any minimal secular god. She was contemptuous of such beliefs, but also envious. With no one to forbid suicide, you were more or less on your own.

Her room was on the twelfth floor in a hotel of approximately twenty floors. Not one of the newer hotels, nor one of the older glamorous hotels, rising totem-like amid the sprawl of the city—a safe neutral place she'd believed it, sufficiently distant from her point of origin and from her lover whose face she'd begun to forget. His voice, she had forgotten: confused with the voices of strangers.

She'd decided not to call him, she'd been granted a second chance to spare herself, to avoid humiliation, and yet—with the blank open eyes of a sleepwalker she observed herself in the reflecting glass returning again to the phone—taking up again the lightweight plastic receiver with the heedlessness of one who, having been snake-bit, stung with venom, takes up again the glittery slumberous length of snake, coolly dry to the touch, both terrible and splendid, with a crazy smile. *Why not? Toss the dice.* Again she dialed 411. Again the appeal to *directory assistance.* But this time she requested *operator.* And with care she spoke to the operator—a woman with a just discernible southern accent. Kathryn spelled out her lover's name—so far as she knew it—and she spelled out the name of the suburban-rural road on which he lived; she explained to the operator that she'd been given two wrong numbers in the past ten minutes and this was a crucial matter, an emergency nearly, she could not afford to dial a wrong number again . . . In all this she remain polite, poised. You would not have guessed how close she was to screaming, cursing. Her reward was a third number both like and unlike its predecessor.

Must have dialed this number for suddenly—so very suddenly!—the phone was ringing—two thousand two hundred and thirty-seven miles to the east—ringing and ringing and abruptly then the line went dead.

What was this!—her lover's phone line had gone dead. Utter deadness, blankness she was listening to, out of the lightweight plastic mechanism. With a sob she broke the connection.

In a bureau mirror was a woman's face flushed and smudged as if partially erased. Her mouth resembled a pike's mouth, thin-lipped, frozen into a grimace, hideous. Madness pinged in the woman's blood like tiny carbonated bubbles. She thought *I am shorn of all pride. I am desperate, broken. I am an addict. I can stop this.* Yet she continued: she did not stop: her icy fingers punched out the very number the operator had given her another time, and another time the phone rang, and rang. She saw her lover staring at the phone as it rang—his face came to her now, his eyes narrowed and turned from her—but he had no intention of answering the phone, he had no intention of speaking to her. He wanted nothing further to do with *her*. But this time the ringing ended with a *click!* and a recorded voice came on—*This is Matt. Sorry I can't come to the phone please leave a message thanks*—and at once she recognized his voice, of course this was her lover's voice, how could she have mistaken another's voice for *his*! She was physically weak now, exhausted. She felt the impulse to quickly hang up the phone, that the man's feeling for her would be untested. She foresaw never calling him again. Now that she had done it, and now she'd heard his voice and knew him, and felt a jolt of recognition deep in her body, that she knew him, and wanted him, and knew the bond between them, that distance could not dissolve, she had the power to end it, that nothing further would be risked between them. Her pride would remain intact, in time she would forget him . . . Yet she left a message for him, in a voice not so faltering as previously; as if leaving a message for her lover was the most natural thing in the world; in a rush of feeling she said she missed him, she was sorry to have left so quickly without saying good-bye, she gave him the hotel number—*If you want to call.* She added *I love you.* Quickly then she hung up the phone.

She laughed wildly, both hands over her mouth. Like a child who has muttered an obscenity that can't be called back.

Only just 6:43 A.M. and she was spent, exhausted. It was something of a shock—a mild shock—seeing how quickly the sun had risen now, above the mountains. For once sunrise began, it could not be slowed, or impeded. Of course the sun was not "rising"—the earth was "turning on its axis" toward the sun—Kathryn knew this, for what it was worth to know such things; in her brain was an arsenal of such knowledge, loosely attached to facts, her education which had not come to her inexpensively mostly a snarl like yarn or shoelaces in a duffel bag. In any case, this "sunrise" was a spectacular sight. She was a reluctant pilgrim, she was one who *saw.* How the sky in the east was brilliant blinding flame-red riddled with clouds vaporous and fleeting as thoughts—how the sky was crisscrossed with mysterious funnel-like bands of cloud that widened and thinned in the wake of what might have been fighter-planes though the planes weren't visible from where Kathryn stood.

Love you! I never said that.

Smiling to think that he might believe her. The thin-lipped pike's mouth in a cruel smile. *Let him believe what he wants!*

With clumsy fingers she was fumbling to remove the sweaty nightgown, that fell in a puddle at her feet. She kicked it free of her ankles, repelled. It was disgusting to her, to smell so frankly of her body—a rank animal smell—a sexual smell—she must scrub herself clean. *For the wages of sin is death. Everlasting death is the wages of sin* she wished to believe, she might clutch at such a belief as one clutches at a wall, for support as the floor tilts, shifts, collapses. *Wages of sin, I am in love with sin. My body sick with sin.* She would step into the shower and turn the water on hot, hot as she could bear it, scalding-hot to cleanse herself, better yet in a scalding-steaming tub she might scald the interior of her body, up inside her belly where the man had been. Shut the bathroom door and the shower-stall door and the sound of the shower would be deafening, she would hear no phone ringing, she would not be tempted to answer any phone. *No more! I am finished.* Yet—so strangely—as if to spite her the phone on the bedside table began to ring. She had not heard this phone ring before—a high-pitched bat's-cry ring that seemed to her utterly astonishing—unanticipated. Yet calmly and matter-of-factly as if nothing was wrong—of course, what could be wrong?—it was only a ringing phone—a ringing phone in her hotel room on the twelfth floor of the high-rise hotel surrounded by desert—she went to answer the phone seeing her hand above the receiver trembling in anticipation. How ridiculous she was, to be so frightened! So in dread of what was to come calmly thinking *I don't want this. I don't need this.* Her numbed fingers lifted the receiver as a sleepwalker might have done, heedless, yet attentive; her voice that was faintly quavering yet at a distance of so many miles might have sounded warm, assured murmured *Hello!* and there came at once a man's answering voice, close in her ear in the sudden catastrophic collapse of all distance as if he were in this very room with her saying *Kathryn? For Christ's sake is that you?* and simply she said *Yes. It is.*

A BOOK OF MARTYRS

Y*ES. I WANT THIS.*
　　　He asked if she was sure. She said again *Yes.*

The vow was unspoken between them: once started on their drive into a more northerly part of the state, once embarked upon this journey, they could not turn back.

It was a drive of approximately three and a half hours on the interstate highway if there were no delays: road construction, accidents, state police checkpoints.

In fact there was a police checkpoint just outside Madison. Triple rows of cars moved slowly, reluctantly like ice congealing, to form a single lane. Her heart beat hard in dread. *They will turn us back. They know.*

Stiffly-politely the Wisconsin state police officers asked the driver of the vehicle to show them his license and the vehicle registration. In the passenger's seat she sat very still. She expected the police officers to ask for her ID but they did not.

She dared to ask who they were looking for? She did not fail to call them *officers.*

Not able to bring herself to say with schoolgirl propriety *Whom are you looking for?*

That is—*For whom are you looking?*

It is protocol, police officers don't answer such questions from civilians. Police officers are the ones to ask questions. She felt a crude blush rise into her face, she'd made a fool of herself.

She was behaving as guilty people do. With a hope of disarming authority, a wish to appear *innocent*.

In any case she was of marginal interest to the police officers: Caucasian female, hair dark blond, early twenties, weight approximately 110. So they would size her up, impersonally.

Maybe eyeing her for possible drug use?—deciding *no*.

That she was attractive, very likely a college student, or a graduate student—this was of no interest to them for clearly they were looking for someone else.

And the man beside her, at the wheel of the car: at first glance maybe her father, second glance maybe her husband. Yet, the driver and his passenger didn't seem married. They wouldn't have seemed, to practiced police-officer scrutiny, to belong in any discernible way *together*.

The driver was a rawboned Midwestern type, you would think. Tall, slope-shouldered, sawdust-colored hair worn long, receding from a high forehead. White shirt, khakis. Genial, cooperative. Maybe a little edgy. Eyes lifting to the police officers' suspicious eyes, to signal to them *Hey—I'm a good citizen. Average guy. Nothing to hide.*

Conover was of an age somewhere beyond the older of the police officers which would make him in his early forties, very likely. Though his manner was youthful, even playful. And the furrowed lines in his face were not age-lines. The man had an easy authority to which, in other circumstances, the officers might have deferred. Possibly, he'd been in the U.S. armed services. (In fact, Conover had not "served" his country. Conover loathed the very institution of *armed services*.) The faculty parking sticker on Conover's rear window, issued by the University of Wisconsin-Madison, would have alerted the police officers to his possible, probable identity: one of those hip university professors determined not to resemble a professor.

"I hope it isn't anything serious, that has happened. Whoever it is you're looking for." Conover paused, smiling. His words were innocently inane, like the murmured afterthought—"Officers."

They took away the driver's license, and the auto registration, to run data through a computer in their vehicle. In the car, Conover and his companion whispered together like abashed children.

"Naïve question, asking if it's something 'serious.' It must be, or they wouldn't be stopping cars."

"You meant *seriously* serious—like a terrorist attack."

"No terrorist attacks in the American heartland. Not worth the effort."

Drewe laughed. Conover was the one who made her laugh, in the most stressful situations.

The police officers returned, at a deliberate pace neither slow nor hurried—in the car the couple tried not to betray the unease they felt, watching the uniformed men approach them from the rear. Drewe thought absurdly *If they draw their guns!*

Almost it would seem to her afterward, she'd seen this.

Behind Conover's steel-colored Toyota a line of vehicles was forming, traffic brought to a halt. No one made an attempt to turn around at the barricade and flee.

Without explanation the police officers handed back Conover's driver's license and vehicle registration and asked to examine the glove compartment, the rear of the car, the trunk. Now a little stiffly Conover said, "Of course. Officers."

She knew: her lover was a longtime member of the ACLU. By temperament, training, and principle he was an adversary of what he'd call the police state. He distrusted and disliked police officers. Yet, without being asked a second time, Conover stooped to push the little lever on the floor that unlocked the trunk.

"Maybe they're looking for drugs."

"Maybe somebody has kidnapped somebody."

"And put them in the trunk?"

"Maybe the victim is dead. The trunk is the logical place."

"They're looking so *grim*."

"Because they suspect, with us, that we're 'innocent'—of whatever it is that has happened, that has caused them to look *grim*."

Conover spoke lightly. Much of his speech was dialogue, meant to evoke amusement in listeners.

She had become his most ardent listener. And so, she knew herself privileged to hear, from time to time, usually unpredictably, what the man truly thought, beyond what the man believed might be cleverly presented.

But Conover wasn't so relaxed as he was pretending, she knew. He had not scheduled enough time for them to make the drive to Eau Claire without feeling rushed; he'd been coolly pragmatic, planning the drive. Neither had wanted to make the appointment in Madison, or anywhere near Madison.

Now, a police checkpoint was slowing them down. She would not mention this to Conover, of course.

A wifely impulse, such reproach. And the intimacy of reproach.

But she was not Conover's wife and had not the luxury of such intimacy.

She saw, Conover was rubbing his jaws. He'd shaved that morning hastily, there was a swath of silvery stubble on the underside of his jaw. And six minutes late picking her up at her residence so she'd been awaiting him anxiously and eagerly and had run out to him, oblivious of who might, in fact, be observing.

"You don't have anything incriminating in the trunk, I hope?"

Conover tried to think. His mind had gone blank.

"Just the spare tire. I think."

"No mysterious clothes, shoes? Bloodstains? Nothing to be mistaken for a—weapon?"

"Jesus! I hope not."

At the rear, the state police officers were taking their time examining the trunk. Drewe had the idea that they were picking up bits of desiccated leaves, to smell them—as if the leaf-fragments were evidence of a *controlled substance*. She felt an impulse to laugh, this was so ridiculous.

"Maybe they will arrest us. They will stop us."

"Don't be silly, Drewe. Just don't talk that way."

"'Conspiracy to commit murder.' That's a crime."

"You're not being funny."

"I'm *not*. In fact."

They sat silent. Conover was staring through the windshield, unseeing. He'd scratched at his jaw, and started a little, just-perceptible bleeding. She was perspiring inside her loose clothing.

Now you've gone too far. Good!

Her demon-self chided her, teased and tormented her through much of her waking day. And in the night, the demon concocted her dreams in a swirl of fever-anxiety and nausea.

Drewe's demon-self was nothing new. He—it—had sprung into a powerful and malevolent independent life by the time she'd been eleven years old when it was beginning to be said of her half in admiration and half in disapproval *That girl is too smart for her own damned good.*

Her parents were religious Protestants. Not extreme, but definitely believers. Her father was a superintendent of public works in Glens Falls, New York. Her mother had been a kindergarten teacher for twenty years. They were not unintelligent people yet their reiterated criticism of their only daughter who'd gone to college and then to a distinguished Midwestern university on full-tuition scholarships was something on the order of *Pride goeth before a fall.*

She was feeling nausea, now. The chilling-sweating-clawing grasp of nausea.

In recent weeks these purely physical spasms came upon her, in rebuke of her public poise and self-control.

Conover had been drawn to her, he'd said. Her cool demeanor, the elegance of her public manner. That she was a sexually attractive young woman as well, in the most conventional of ways, was not a disadvantage.

But now she was gagging. She took a deep breath, and held it. To give in, to vomit at the side of the highway, the Wisconsin police officers looking on in surprise and disgust—she could not bear such a humiliation.

Conover nudged her. Was she all right?

Mutely she nodded *Yes*.

It had been suggested that Drewe eat a light meal two or three hours before the procedure. But this wasn't practical for they were on the road early. And an early breakfast would have truly turned her stomach. And she'd had virtually nothing to eat the previous night, so maybe it was only hunger. Voracious and insatiable hunger, that felt like nausea. And a dull headache, and the sweating-inside-the-clothes which were deliberately plain, ordinary clothes—none of her eye-catching consignment-shop costumes—a pale blue long-sleeved shirt which was said to be mosquito-proof, that Conover had bought her for one of their hiking trips; dark blue corduroy pants with deep pockets. On her feet, sandals. For there would be no hiking today.

On the third finger of her left hand was a silver star-shaped ring, which Conover had brought back for her from an academic conference in Delhi. He had not (probably) meant for Drewe to wear the ring on the third finger of her left hand, she supposed. But Conover was too gentlemanly to object.

It was helpful, yet a kind of petulant rebuke, the way the police officers shut the Toyota trunk, with a thud. Disappointed that they'd found nothing—no evidence of criminal activity.

"OK, mister."

The younger of the two police officers waved Conover on. Both were stony-faced. Conover waved at them in return as he moved his vehicle forward, a kind of salute, playful, not at all mocking, in its way sincere—"Thank you, officers. I hope you find whatever—whoever—you're looking for."

There would seem to have been nothing funny in this remark yet they laughed together, in the vast relief of co-conspirators who have not been caught.

IT WAS SEVEN WEEKS, two days now.

She'd counted, assiduously. Like a fanatic nun saying her rosary she'd counted, counted again, and again counted the *days since your last period.*

There was something so vulgar about this! She resented her situation, the banality of her *biological destiny.*

She had not told Conover. Not immediately.

To keep such a secret from your lover is to feel a thrill of unspeakable power. For always there is the possibility *He doesn't have to know. He can be spared.*

Or—*His life can be altered, irrevocably. This is in my power.*

She wasn't a careless person. But she was sometimes reckless, defiant.

What is the worst you can do to yourself or another. This, you will one day do.

Her demon-self predicted. And so it would be.

The very fact of *conception, pregnancy* was astonishing to Drewe. For all her reputed brilliance she hadn't quite understood that such biological facts pertained to the unique individual who was Drewe.

When she told Conover, his expression could only have been described as *melting.*

He did not say *My God how has this happened, we were so careful.*

He did not say *This can't be an accident, Drewe. You are not the sort of woman to have accidents.*

He said *Oh honey. How long have you known?*

Meaning, *How long have you been alone, knowing?*

She'd made two appointments with a gynecologist in Madison. She'd had an array of tests, blood work, Pap smear, mammogram. She'd been very quiet during the initial examination. The gynecologist had said several times *Excuse me? Are you all right?* She'd alarmed the young Asian woman by staggering light-headed when she slipped down from the examination table in her paper gown but quickly she'd laughed and assured the doctor that she was fine.

Just a little surprised. And I guess—scared.

But laughing. Wiping at her eyes, and laughing.

The procedure at the Eau Claire clinic was scheduled for 11:30 A.M. Arrival no later than 11:00 A.M.

It would be a *surgical procedure* and not a *medical procedure*, now the pregnancy was seven weeks. The *medical procedure* had appealed to Drewe initially, for it involved merely pill-taking, but her gynecologist had dissuaded her. *Too much can go wrong. You don't know how long you will be bleeding, and where you might be. The more protracted the discharge, the more opportunity for an acute psychological reaction.* Drewe had felt sick, a sudden indraft of terror, at these matter-of-fact words.

She was not a minor. She was twenty-six.

Except now feeling much younger. Helpless.

Your decision, Conover had said. Of course.

No. Not my decision alone. *Our* decision.

It's your body. It's your life. You will decide.

Gently, yet with a chilling sort of equanimity, Conover spoke these words. And so she knew: Conover was the one to decide.

She did not "want" children—this was a statement she'd often made, to herself and others. As she did not "want" to be married.

So she'd made the arrangements. She'd chosen WomanSpace in Eau Claire, out of several possibilities. Driving three and a half hours to Eau Claire, Wisconsin, would be a strain on them both, a kind of punishment for Conover as well as her, yet worse the strain of returning after the procedure.

She could not imagine. The return home.

What intimacy between them, then! It was the terrible intimacy she most craved, with the man. Not with any man had she had a true, vital intimacy, that had entered her deeply, into the most profound and secret depths of her soul. In fact she had not known many men, in her young life. Conover, who'd impregnated her, against their calculated plans and their wishes, would be that man.

And so, it was arranged. They had only to execute their plans.

Probable arrival back in Madison in the early evening.

Stay with me tonight, OK?

If you want me.

Don't be ridiculous! I always want you.

She wanted to believe this. She smiled, so badly wanting to believe.

Though the great land-grant university at Madison was very large—(45,600 enrolled students, a campus of over 900 acres)—yet the Madison community was somehow small. You saw the same people often. You recognized faces, knew names, even of people whom you didn't personally know.

Both Conover and Drewe would have been mortified to have been seen together and recognized at the Planned Parenthood clinic in Madison, that was so prominent in the university community.

To the Eau Claire WomanSpace clinic she was bringing a hard-cover volume of Milton: *Paradise Lost*. There was desperation in clinging to this hefty volume, which she'd first read as an undergraduate of nineteen. She'd been ravished by the austere sublime poetry of Milton, that was a reprimand to the doggerel of her demon-self.

Of man's first disobedience , and the fruit / Of that forbidden tree, whose mortal taste / Brought death into the world, and all our woe . . .

Milton's Lucifer beguiled her. Also, Milton's Eve.

Such beauty in the poet's grave sonorous blank verse yet behind it was an implacable and unyielding façade of something inhuman. *Justifying the ways of God to man.*

Conover asked what the book was?—and Drewe told him.

Conover said he'd read only just a little of Milton, as an undergraduate. "Read me something now, darling. Convince me that poetry matters."

Drewe thumbed through the familiar, much-annotated pages. In her most level voice she read to Conover the passage in which Lucifer, the fallen archangel, says *Better to reign in hell than serve in heaven*. (To which Conover grunted in approval.) She read the longer, surpassingly beautiful passage in which Eve sees her own reflection for the first time in a pond, in Eden:

> I thither went
> With unexperienced thought, and laid me down
> On the green bank, to look into the clear
> Smooth lake, that to me seemed another sky.
> As I bent down to look, just opposite
> A shape within the watery gleam appeared
> Bending to look on me: I started back,
> It started back, but pleased I soon returned,
> Pleased it returned as soon with answering looks
> Of sympathy and love; there I had fixed
> Mine eyes till now, and pined with vain desire.

When she'd finished, Conover remained silent for a while, then said, as if there might be an answer to his question, "This myth of 'paradise'—it's always *lost*. Ever wonder why?"

They were approaching Eau Claire: thirty-six miles to go.

But it was 10:20 A.M., they would not be late.

"OH GOD. **Look.**"

As they approached the WomanSpace Clinic on Hector Street they saw them: the demonstrators.

Pro-Life picketers. Milling together on the sidewalk in front of the clinic, and in the street. Some were carrying picket signs. Drewe's contact at the clinic had cautioned her *There might be demonstrators on the morning you're scheduled. Try to ignore them. Walk quickly. Don't engage them. They are forbidden by law to touch or impede you in any way.*

Stunned and dismayed Drewe stepped out of the car. Quickly Conover came around to her, as the demonstrators sighted her, and hurried in her direction as if recognizing her.

Like piranha, they seemed to Drewe. Horrible, in their rush at her.

There might have been thirty of them—there might have been more. Drewe had a confused impression of surprisingly young faces, young men as well as women, even teenagers. At once she felt sick with guilt, these shining faces were massed against *her.*

Unlike her friends and acquaintances in Madison, these strangers in Eau Claire knew her secret.

Immediately they knew, and they did not sympathize. They would not forgive.

"God-damn! This is unfortunate."

Conover took hold of Drewe's arm, urging her forward.

The demonstrators' voices lifted, pleading. Yet sharp. Excited, aroused. *They were happy to see her.*

As she was surprised to see teenagers, so Drewe was surprised to see so many men. Easily, there were as many men as women among the Pro-Life demonstrators. And they were of all ages—young, middle-aged, elderly. Though she'd been instructed not to look at them yet Drewe could not stop herself; she could not stop herself from making eye contact with some of them; they were on all sides of her, blocking her way as they'd been forbidden to do, forcing Conover to shove against them, cursing them; there came a Catholic priest of about Conover's age, with something of Conover's furrowed forehead and earnest genial coercive manner, dressed in black, with a tight white collar; like a raven the man seemed to Drewe, a predatory pecking bird intent upon *her*.

Hello! God loves you!

Listen to us! Look at us! Give us five minutes of your time—before it's too late!

Your baby wants to live—like you.

Your baby prays to YOU—LET ME LIVE! You have that choice.

Look here! Look at us! Your baby is pleading . . .

There came a WomanSpace escort, a lanky young man in dark lavender sweatshirt and jeans, to take hold of Drewe's other arm. Just come with me please, just come forward, don't hang back, you will be fine. Just to the front door, they can't follow us inside.

Yet the demonstrators clustered boldly about them, defiant, terrifying in their fanatic certainty.

Look here, girl! You had better know, it's murder you will be committing.

And God knows, God will punish. You'd better believe.

The woman blocking Drewe's way was heavyset, in her forties perhaps. Bulgy-eyed, with a strong-boned fattish face, shiny synthetic russet-red hair that must have been a wig, a floral maternity smock covering her drooping-watermelon breasts. There was something gleeful and demented about this woman, that set her apart from the other demonstrators. She was holding a rosary aloft, practically in Drewe's face, praying loudly *Hail Mary Mother of God pray for us sinners now and at the hour of our death Amen. Hail Mary Mother of God pray for us sinners now and at the hour of our death Amen. Hail Mary . . .* In her other hand the woman held a picket sign—a ghastly magnified photograph of what appeared to be a mangled baby, or embryo, lying amid trash. Drewe had been warned not to look at these picket-sign photographs—(which were said to be digitally modified, and not "real")—yet this ghastly photograph she saw clearly. *Hail Mary! Hail*

Mary! Hail Mary save this baby from the abortion-murderers! Strike the sinner down dead.

You could see that the heavyset woman in the maternity smock was thrilled to be in combat, she'd been awaiting this moment to spring at Drewe. She was jeering, and disgusted, but thrilled, fixing Drewe with a look of derisive intimacy.

She knows me. She knows my heart.

They were almost at the front door of the clinic, which was being held open by another WomanSpace assistant. Yet the heavyset woman followed beside Drewe, taunting her. Drewe wrenched her arm out of Conover's grip to push at the woman—"Leave me alone! You're religious fanatics. You have no right! You're *sick.*"

The woman, surprised at Drewe's reaction, took a moment to recover—then shoved Drewe back. She was strong, a small dense mountain of a woman, with a flushed and triumphant face.

Murderer! Baby-murderer! Jesus will harrow you down to hell.

Oh!—the woman had hurt her. A shut fist, against Drewe's upper chest.

Conover and the lanky escort hurried Drewe away, up the steps and into the clinic, where the demonstrators were forbidden to follow. With what relief, Drewe saw that the door was shut against them.

She wasn't crying. She would not give the heavyset woman that satisfaction, to know that she'd hurt her.

Not crying but tears trickled down her hot cheeks.

Not crying but she could not stop trembling.

Pro-Life. Their certitude terrified her.

THE *SURGICAL ABORTIONS* were running late.

There'd been complications that morning at WomanSpace. Many more demonstrators than usual, a bus-load of particularly combative League of Life Catholics from Milwaukee. The Eau Claire PD had been called earlier that morning, summons had been issued.

But no arrests?

Conover complained to the staff: why wasn't there another way into the clinic?

He was told that, no matter which entrance was used, the demonstrators would flock around it. Other strategies had been tried, and had not worked out satisfactorily.

"The civil rights of your clients are being violated. That's an aggressive mob out there, and could be dangerous."

It was not a secret, abortion-providers were at risk for their lives. Abortion doctors had been killed by snipers, Planned Parenthood offices had been firebombed.

Incensed, Conover sat beside Drewe, in a vinyl chair nearly too small for him. By degrees, he quieted. He'd brought work with him for the long wait, and would take solace in his work.

Drewe sat in a haze of such startled thought, she could not coherently assess what had happened.

A woman, a stranger, had assaulted *her*? Yet more astonishing—Drewe had assaulted the woman?

And all this had happened so swiftly. A terrible intimacy, in such close quarters.

"They seemed to know me. They recognized me."

"Don't be ridiculous. They don't know *you*."

"They know my type—my category. They know why I am here."

"I should hope so. They aren't total idiots."

They aren't total idiots at all. They are true believers.

Drewe had to fill out more forms though her gynecologist had faxed a half-dozen documents to the clinic. The receptionist, a harried-looking woman with a strained smile, took her name, checked her ID, asked her another time about allergies, asthma, any recent surgery, silicone implants—next of kin.

Next of kin: what were they expecting?

Conover said she could leave it blank probably.

In a hurt voice she said shouldn't she give them his name?

"Sure. I'll be right here, in any case."

It didn't seem like a convincing answer. Yet Drewe could not put down her mother's name, her father's name . . . No one in her family must know.

In the event that Drewe died, it would be mortifying to her—(yet, how could she *know?*)—that her family knew of her secret.

Not that Drewe was ashamed of herself—(though in fact, yes Drewe was ashamed)—but rather, Drewe resented others knowing of her most personal, private life.

Even knowledge of Conover, who wasn't divorced quite yet— separated from his wife, who lived in another part of the country—had to be kept from Drewe's family, who would have judged her harshly, and pityingly.

A married man. Of course he says he's "separated."

Too smart for her own good. Headstrong, never listened to anyone else. Pride goeth before a fall . . .

She returned to her chair, to sit and wait. Brightly she wanted to ask Conover if she'd really hit that awful woman, who'd thrust a rosary into her face?

Drewe was an entertaining storyteller. But to whom could she tell this story?

The waiting room was ordinary, nondescript as a dentist's waiting room, except for the pamphlets, brochures, and magazines on display, all on feminist themes, abortion procedures, federal and state laws; yet, perversely, for WomanSpace was a Planned Parenthood clinic as well as an abortion provider, there was a wall rack entirely filled with pregnancy/birth/infant information. Drewe wondered at the incongruity, and the irony.

Slatted blinds had been pulled shut over the windows at the front of the waiting room. Yet you could hear raised voices outside, that seemed never to subside.

Drewe could have wept with vexation: she'd left *Paradise Lost* in Conover's car, after all. And there was no way of retrieving it.

Drewe said, to Conover, "Waiting rooms! Think of *No Exit*. Even a waiting room to Hell would be boring, wouldn't it?"

Conover, who was reading his Kindle, responded minimally.

Drewe told Conover, in a discreetly lowered voice, for she did not want to annoy or distract or further upset others in the room, who were very likely waiting for consultations or procedures like her own, of how, when she'd first been taken to a dentist, by her mother, at the age of four, she'd become panicked in the waiting room, and in the dentist's chair she'd become hysterical. Her mother and the dentist— (male, middle-aged)—had tried to calm her with N_2O—"laughing gas"—but this too had frightened her. In disgust the dentist had told Drewe's mother *Don't tell a child "this won't hurt" when it will hurt.*

She was speaking in her quick bright nervous way that did not seem to involve her frightened eyes, or her frozen mouth.

Conover said, touching Drewe's arm: "Not now, honey. Just be calm now. Maybe later."

Had she been talking too excitedly? Had she been laughing, unconvincingly?

At first she had no idea what Conover meant: *Later?*

Of course she knew: it was not really surgery, only just a *procedure*. Vacuum suction through an instrument called a cannula, and she would be sedated, though conscious, thus not running the risk of an anesthetic.

She'd read all about it of course. It was her way to know as much as she could of whatever subject might be approached intellectually, coolly. She'd memorized much of what she'd read.

As if in one of the pamphlets she'd read, a vision of the heavyset woman—the jeering face, accusing eyes.

Baby-murderer. You.

Sick. You are sick. You!

Drewe glanced about the waiting room. Was she being watched?—was she somehow special, singled-out, more guilty than the others? But why?

There were two or three women in the waiting room of Drewe's approximate age. But she seemed to know they were not university students. And a girl of perhaps seventeen, soft-bodied, in a paralysis of fear; her mother close beside her, gripping her limp hand.

The scoldings, the disgust, had ended. Now, there was a mother's sympathy, and anxiety.

Drewe would not have told her mother about this *surgical procedure*. Not ever.

Drewe would not tell her mother about becoming, by accident, *pregnant*.

When they'd entered the waiting room, there had been no man. Conover had been the sole man. Since then, another man had entered, with a thin ashen-faced heavily made-up woman; both of them grim, not speaking to the other.

Drewe wondered if men, in such situations, glanced at one another, to establish some sort of—bond? Or whether, and this was more likely, they assiduously avoided eye contact.

Conover appeared oblivious to the other man in the waiting room. Yet, Drewe guessed that Conover was well aware of his presence.

Drewe guessed too that Conover had been disconcerted by the Pro-Life demonstrators. Conover was accustomed to *demonstrating* and not being *demonstrated against*.

His sympathies were naturally with protest. This was his background, his instinct.

Conover had been involved in the Occupy Wall Street events in Madison. He'd organized a teach-in at the university. His politics were "leftist"—"activist"; he had a history of participating in marches and protests, particularly when he'd been younger. (On a protest march on State Street, on the eve of the American invasion of Iraq in 2003, Conover had been injured by a riot policeman's club, dislocating his right knee. Since then, he walked with a limp, and sometimes winced with pain when he believed no one was watching.) His father had been a high-profile labor attorney arguing federal cases.

It was against Conover's political principles to "cross" any picket line—but this was a different situation, surely.

Conover was a distinguished man in those circles—academic, intellectual—in which he was a distinguished man: outside those circles, few would have known his name. He was an Americanist-historian whose books on pre–Civil War America, particularly a history of Abolitionism, had won him tenure, visiting professor-ships, prizes. Yet he was a man whom confinement made restless, anxious. He sweated easily. In the waiting room he crossed his legs, uncrossed his legs. He shifted in the vinyl chair, that was almost too small for him. In bed, his legs frequently cramped: with a little cry of annoyed pain he scrambled from bed to stand on the afflicted leg, to ease the muscle free of the cramp. Sometimes his toes cramped too, like claws.

Don't be scared he'd said several times. *I will be with you.*

He was reading an article on his Kindle, submitted to a histori-cal journal for which he was an advisory editor. Drewe, who had no reading material of her own, tried to read with him, but could not concentrate.

At last the receptionist called Drewe's name—but it was not her name, as Conover told her, startled; tugging at her wrist, to pull her back. Still, Drewe rose from the vinyl chair, seeming to think that her name had been called. "Drewe, that isn't your name," Conover said, and Drewe stammered, "Oh, but I thought—maybe—there had been a misunderstanding." She had no idea what she was trying to say.

Someone else will murder her baby. It's a strange dream, but it isn't my dream.

Was it true, the baby *wanted to live?*

But she wasn't carrying a *baby.* Only just a cluster of congealed cells.

She might explain to Conover. Try to explain.

And calmly he would say *You've changed your mind, then. This is for the good, I think.*

Is it? For the good? Oh—I love you.

We can love the baby. We can make a life for the baby, in the interstices of our lives.

She was saying *Yes!—I mean no . . . I don't know.*

Conover hadn't heard. Conover continued reading, taking notes as he squinted at the shiny Kindle screen.

Another woman had come forward, to be escorted into the rear of the clinic.

Drewe had wanted to make an appointment in Eau Claire under a fictitious name. Conover had thought it wouldn't be feasible, or even legal; as it happened, Drewe's gynecologist wouldn't have cooperated. And there was the matter of the faxed tests and documents. And health-care insurance.

Someone in the waiting room was crying softly. Drewe did not want to glance around for fear that in this bizarre waking dream she would discover that the afflicted person was herself.

In fact, it was the young girl with her mother. Very young, pale and wan, and scared. Probably not seventeen, nor even sixteen. It was difficult to imagine such a child having sex—maybe "having sex" wasn't the appropriate term, having had sex inflicted upon her was more likely.

Maybe she'd been raped. That was an ugly possibility.

With a pang of envy Drewe saw how the mother continued to hold her daughter's hand. The two whispered and wept together. And how, when the daughter's name was called, both the daughter and the mother rose to their feet.

Drewe's eyes locked with the daughter's: warm-brown, liquidy, terrified.

Drewe looked quickly away.

"Drewe?"

Conover was watching her. His face was strained, the tiny shaving nick on the underside of his jaw was bleeding again, thinly.

"You're sure, are you? About this?"

He is trying to be generous, Drewe thought. It was an effort in him, he was trying very hard. Like a man who has coins in his closed fist he wants to offer—to fling onto a table—to demonstrate his generosity, even the flamboyance of his generosity, which will be to his disadvantage; but his hand is shaky, the coins fall from his fingers onto the floor.

She reassured him, her lover. The woman was the one to reassure the man, he had made a proper decision.

She heard herself say, another time: "Yes."

STRIKE THE SINNER down dead.

Baby wants to live. Baby prays—LET ME LIVE!

By the time her name was called, sometime after 12:30 P.M., Drewe was exhausted. She had not slept more than two or three hours the previous night and her head felt now as if she'd been awake for a day and a night in succession.

Something was happening in front of the clinic: some sort of disturbance. The demonstrators had interfered with one of the clinic's patients, there'd been a scuffle with one of the WomanSpace escorts, the Eau Claire PD had been called another time.

There were shouts, a siren. Drewe was trembling with indignation. The fanatics had no *right*.

She'd used the women's lavatory at least three times. And each time she'd scarcely been able to urinate, a tiny slow hot trickle into the toilet bowl, she'd been desperate to check: was it blood?

It was not blood. It was hardly urine.

The abortion-clock was clicking now, defiantly in her face. She saw how all of her life had been leading to this time.

The life-time of the cell-cluster inside her would be no more than seven weeks, three days. Conception, suction-death. From the perspective of millennia, there was virtually no difference between her own (brief) life of twenty-six years and the (briefer) life of the baby-to-be.

Sick. You are sick. You!

But her name had been called, at last. Numbly she had no choice but to rise to her feet, and be led by a nurse into the interior of Woman-Space.

Conover had leaned over to squeeze her hand, a final time. But Drewe's fingers were limp, unresponsive.

The woman was speaking to her. Explaining to her. Calling her "Drewe"—she felt uncomfortable at this familiarity. Conover had been left behind—that was a relief.

A man might participate in his lover's natural-childbirth delivery but a man would not participate in any woman's *surgical abortion*.

He would not be a witness! He would never know.

Drewe was naked and shivering inside the flimsy paper gown, that opened in the front. Her lips were icy-cold. Her skin felt chafed as if she'd been rubbing it with something abrasive like sandpaper.

She'd been allowed to keep on her sandals.

A middle-aged woman doctor with skinned-back hair and a hard-chiseled face had entered the room. Her manner was forthright, with an air of forced and just slightly overbearing calm. She spoke in a voice too loud for the room as if there was some doubt that the trembling patient would hear her, and would comprehend what she was saying.

Dr. _____—Drewe heard the name clearly yet in the next instant had forgotten.

Dr. _____ was asking how she felt?

How do you think I feel? Ecstatic?

Mutely and meekly Drewe nodded. As one deprived of language, making a feeble gesture to suggest *Good! Really good.*

Dr. _____ was telling her it was required by law that she have a sonogram before the procedure.

A new law, recently passed by the Wisconsin state legislature.

A sonogram, so that Drewe could look at the cluster of cells—the "fetus" in her womb, at seven weeks. And she must answer a fixed sequence of questions.

Do you understand. Are you fully cognizant of.

Have you been coerced in any way.

You are certain—you have not been coerced.

Drewe was astonished. She'd been through all this—these questions—not a sonogram: she had not had a sonogram—but all this *talk*. She wanted to press her hands against her ears and run out of the room.

Dr. _____ was explaining that there are different sorts of coercion. Drewe would have to declare whether anyone had exerted pressure on her in any way contrary to her own and best interests.

Drewe stammered—she'd already answered those questions many times.

Yes. But this was a new law. They were required to ask her more than once.

She shut her eyes. No no no no *no.*

No one had coerced *her.*

"Are you feeling all right, Drewe? Did you have anything to eat this morning?"

Eat! She'd forgotten entirely about eating.

The thought of food was repulsive to her. She could not imagine ever eating again.

"Let us know if you feel nauseated. Immediately, let us know."

The nurse was administering a sonogram. An X-ray of the pregnant womb. This was a requirement of the "new" law.

Drewe was lying on an examination table, on her side staring at an illuminated dark screen, an X-ray showing a tiny ectoplasmic shape, ever shifting, fading. She recalled fraudulent photographs of "ectoplasm"—spirits, ghosts—at the turn of the previous century. But the sonogram wasn't fraudulent. In the screen she could see her own pulse, the fierce beat of her blood.

Baby wants to live. Just like you.

The baby's father did not want the baby. He had not said so, but she knew. Of course, she knew.

Conover loved her—but did not love her *enough*.

He certainly did not love her enough to want to have a baby with her. To start a family with her. She'd known this, but had not wished to acknowledge it.

The man had his own children of course. His children who were already born. Grown to adulthood, or nearly. Safely in the world, and their very existence no longer precarious, dependent upon any whim of their father, or mother.

A daughter, a son, seemingly on cordial terms with Conover, but not very intimate terms. And the separated-wife had been deeply wounded by Conover, and could never forgive him. The divorce, if there was a divorce, would be bitter and debilitating. Drewe had come belatedly in Conover's life.

The doctor with the skinned-back hair was regarding Drewe with surprise. Were Drewe's eyes welling with tears? Where was Drewe's old resolve, that had caused her family to say of her *It's like she isn't even one of us, sometimes. Like she doesn't even know us.*

The doctor was asking Drewe if she was having second thoughts? She didn't need to make a final decision of such importance today.

Yes. She was saying, insisting.

Yes. That was why she'd come—wasn't it!

She was not going to go away without . . .

Her voice trailed off, uncertainly.

The patient was given sedatives. Some time was required before the sedatives began to take effect.

The voice would be diminished, as the sedatives took hold. She saw a tiny pinprick of light, the baby-to-be, fading, about to be extinguished.

They helped her lie on her back, on the table. Her feet in the stirrups.

So open, exposed! The most secret part of her body, opened to the chilly air.

She was feeling panic in spite of the pills. But much of this she would forget, afterward. As her uterus was sucked empty, so her brain was emptied of memory. A machine thrummed close by, loudly.

She saw now: the sequence of actions that had begun in the early morning of that day, and was now irreversible. Running from her residence hall to the curb, to climb into the steel-colored Toyota into the passenger's seat beside her lover; kissing her lover on the lips as an act of subtle aggression, and buckling herself in the seat belt, her hard, curved little belly that had not yet begun to show, as her small hard breasts had not yet begun to alter, or not much. (The nipples were more sensitive, and seemed darker-hued. But she could not bring herself to examine her body, that filled her with dread.) Almost gaily—brazenly—she'd begun that sequence of actions, that had led to this: naked, on her back, knees spread. And the tiny pinprick of light all but extinguished.

She would be awake through the entire procedure, it was explained to her. Not fully awake, but in the way of someone seeing a movie without sound, at a little distance.

When the mask was fitted to her lower face she felt an impulse to push it away, panicked. She'd forgotten the purpose of the mask—the self-monitored laughing gas for the control of pain.

There was a natural lock on the mechanism, Drewe was told. So that she could not inhale too much of the gas at one time. So that she wouldn't lose consciousness.

The procedure would take no more than minutes.

So fast! Yet so very slow, Drewe felt herself drifting off to sea, her eyes heavy-lidded, the sickly-smelling gas in her nostrils and mouth so that, as she breathed, she felt an instinct to gag.

The cervix was being dilated. She did not think *My cervix!*

A straw-like instrument was being inserted into her body. Up tight between her thighs. The machine began to hum, louder. A sucking noise, and a sucking sensation. Quick-darting cramps wracked her lower abdomen. These were claws like the claws of sea-creatures, locking into her. She began to count *One two three four* . . . but lost her concentration, for the suction-noise was so loud, close beside her head, and the cramps so quick, biting and sharp, and the laughing-gas was filling her brain like helium into a balloon, she was in danger of floating above the table to which (she realized now) she was strapped, as her knees were strapped, wide-parted.

The cramping came now in long, almost languorous ripples. Almost, a kind of sensuous cruelty, as if a lover were hurting her, with crude fingers, fingernails, deep inside her body.

She'd begun to cry. Or, she was laughing.

Please no. I don't want this. It was a mistake.

Let me up, this was a mistake.

God help me . . .

SHE FUMBLED WITH the paper-thing, that clung to her sweaty thighs.

Into a wicker basket it went crumpled. Then, her clothes—into which she bound herself with badly shaking fingers. Telling herself in an ecstasy of relief *It's over!*

She was herself again. *Only* herself.

Though the cramping continued. And she was bleeding, into a sparkling-white cotton-gauze sanitary napkin.

For a while she lay dazed, comatose. The N_2O was still in her bloodstream: she tried to think what might be funny, so that she could laugh.

She had no idea how much time had passed. The procedure itself had been less than eight minutes, she'd been told. On her left wrist was a watch but it was too much effort for her to look at it, to see what time it was.

The silver-star ring on the third finger of her left hand felt loose. Or, her fingers were sweaty . . . There was the danger that the ring would slip off.

Then, she was being rudely awakened. She was being led out of the recovery room. She was leaning on the nurse's arm. Sweat oozed in tiny beads at her hairline. She was being told that she should make an appointment to see her gynecologist in Madison in two weeks. And she was not to "resume relations" for at least two weeks. Did she need contraception?

She laughed. Contraception!

She'd always used contraception. She'd been terrified of any intimate encounter that was not contra-conception. Yet, the contraception she and Conover had been using had failed.

Conover was waiting for her. Conover looking tired, and the lines in his face deeper.

Conover took her hand. Conover stooped to kiss her sweaty forehead. Conover said in a lowered voice in her ear what sounded like *My good girl! I love you.*

This was so un-Conover. Drewe pushed a little away from him, laughing.

"'Good girl.' Sounds like a dog."

Bad luck, or maybe good luck: there was a commotion in front of the clinic as another woman arrived outside to enter, forced to run the gauntlet.

And then, when they left the clinic, to hurry out to Conover's car, it was a surprise that the demonstrators paid little heed to them—in their focus upon the frightened-looking new arrival, a dark-skinned woman in her mid-thirties, in the company of an older woman. The lanky-limbed WomanSpace escort had come to the assistance of the woman, aggressively.

Drewe looked for the heavyset woman in the maternity smock, with the perky-shiny synthetic wig—the woman who'd dared to strike Drewe with her fist—but she couldn't see her.

Look straight ahead, Conover was saying. We're almost there.

His arm around her waist. She was stumbling, feeling weak and light-headed—the cramping in her belly was like quick-darting electric currents. She'd understood that Conover had been shocked to see her, when she'd reappeared in the doorway of the waiting room, on the nurse's arm, not seeming to see him seated almost in front of her. She'd been smiling and blinking in the dazed way of one who has been traumatized without knowing it.

Get in! Take care . . .

Conover helped her into the passenger's seat. Behind them, swarming after the new arrival, the demonstrators were loud, excited. Conover had locked Drewe's door for her. She was staring out the window—looking for someone—she wasn't sure who . . .

Conover was shaken, but Conover quickly recovered. Near the entrance to I-94 south he stopped at a deli where he bought sandwiches and bottled water for Drewe and for himself, and a six-pack of cold beer, for the long drive home.

Try to eat, he told her. Then maybe try to sleep.

Drewe couldn't eat much of her sandwich. Conover ate his, and the remainder of hers. Conover drank most of the Evian water, thirstily. And, in furtive illegal swallows, at least two of the beers.

Though he'd urged her to sleep, yet Conover couldn't resist talking to her as he drove. He was too edgy to drive in silence, or even to listen to a CD. He laughed, and talked, and told her stories he'd told her already, but not at such length, and with such detail.

These were stories out of history. These were not personal stories. Judging by the way in which he told them, he'd told them to other audiences, at other times. Abraham Lincoln caricatured in pro-Confederacy newspapers as a Negro, or a black ape—"The hatred of Obama is nothing new in U.S. politics." Draft riots in New York City—notable Wall Street "Panics"—the defeat of the Bank of the United States by wily "Old Hickory"—Andrew Jackson. Conover did not specialize in personal stories.

Drewe didn't know her lover's children's names. Possibly he'd mentioned these names, but not frequently. Drewe knew the former wife's name but little of the woman. And Drewe had not asked, out of tact as well as shyness. Or maybe it had been disdain, for the lover's family whom she had hoped to supplant.

They arrived back in Madison by nighttime.

Drewe said, I think I want to be alone. Just drop me off, thank you.

Her lips were parched. Her eyes ached as if she'd been staring into a hot sun.

Conover said, Don't be ridiculous, Drewe! You're staying with me.

I don't think so. I think I'd better be alone.

I thought we'd planned this. Tonight.

I don't think so.

Drewe, look—I'm here.

He took her hand. Both her hands. She was feeling very weak, there was little strength in her hands. Something like her identity had leaked away, like liquid down a drain.

She did not say *You are here but not-here. Better that you are not-here in a way that I can see.*

He relented, and drove her to her residence hall. Seeing that she was adamant, and just very possibly on the brink of hysteria.

In his car parked at the curb in front of her residence hall Conover talked to her earnestly. Lights on all six floors of the building were on. It was an aged stone building of some distinction. A women's graduate residence in which Drewe had lived, in a single room, spare as a nun's cell, for two and a half years.

Conover lived in a large but somewhat shabby Victorian house, a mile away in a neighborhood called Faculty Heights. Drewe had visited this house often, and often stayed overnight, but had never lived there, and understood now that she would never live there.

The relief in his face! She'd seen.

The dread in his face. That she would weaken, she would plead with him to love her as she loved him.

Or worse yet, as women do, plead with him that she could love enough for two.

She was bleeding into the sanitary napkin. That was enough of pleading, for now.

He said, I'm not going to leave you. Come on.

She said, No. Thank you.

She said, I need to be alone. For now.

She opened the car door. She saw her hand on the door, and the door opening, and she saw herself leaving the steel-colored Toyota and walking away. It was the edge of a precipice: the fall was steep, and might be fatal. Yet, she saw herself walking away.

Conover hurried after her, to the door of the residence hall. Drewe said, sharply, It's all right. Please—I need to be alone.

You don't need to be alone, that's—that isn't true. I'm not going to leave you alone.

She turned away. She left him. In secret bleeding into the already-soaked napkin she walked away, not to the stairs but to the elevator for she was too weak and too demoralized for the stairs and would wait for the sluggishly-moving elevator instead. At the opened door—through which several young women passed, into the foyer, glancing curiously at Drewe and at Conover—he called after her, he would not be leaving but waiting for her in his car.

From her room on the fourth floor, she saw his car at the curb, and his figure inside, dimly. When vehicles passed in the street their headlights lit upon him, a stoic and stubborn figure in the parked vehicle. He'd turned on the ignition to listen to the radio, probably. He would finish the six-pack of beer.

Cautiously like one composed of a brittle breakable substance—very thin glass, or plastic—she lay down on her bed. Her skin was burning, she was very tired. The cramping was not so bad, dulled by Vicodin. Her life would be a painkiller life: she would be aware of pain but would not feel it, exactly, as her own.

She was bleeding, thinly. She'd changed the sanitary napkin and replaced it with a fresh sparkling-white cotton-gauzy napkin for the WomanSpace nurse had thoughtfully provided her with a half-dozen napkins in a plastic bag.

There was no serious danger of bleeding to death yet the word *exsanguination* sounded in her head like a struck gong.

Forty minutes later, when she struggled to her feet, the Toyota was still at the curb.

He'd been trying to call her on her cell phone, she discovered. She'd turned the phone off at Eau Claire and had not turned it on again.

She slept again, fitfully. Sometime after midnight parched-mouthed and her eyes aching as if she had not slept at all she staggered to her feet and to the window. And the car was gone.

"STEPHANOS IS DEAD"

H AVE YOU HEARD?—STEPHANOS IS DEAD."
       "Oh no! When—?"
"Just this morning, I think."
"But—how?"
"A heart attack, or an aneurysm—something sudden."
"My God! Stephanos. . . ."

Mickey was standing beneath an overhang just outside the quaintly titled Smila's Sense of Organic Foods, waiting out the worst of a sudden thunderstorm. Despite the loud thrumming of rain on the overhang and on the pavement it was impossible not to hear this emotional exchange between a Nordic-looking professor of math at the university and a middle-aged woman who was someone's wife. (Mickey knew: this was insufferably snobbish. In fact, in certain quarters, Mickey herself, despite her Ph.D. and post-doc status, was no more than "someone's wife.") And she knew Angelo Stephanos, or had known him, slightly. Mickey met the glances of the math professor and his companion with an expression of surprise and sympathy, for it seemed only tactful; she wasn't prepared for the looks of extreme sorrow, even horror, in their faces, nor for the way in which they seemed not to see her, as if she were invisible.

"But—where did it happen?"

"In his house, I think. Just—within minutes."

"He can't be very old—not fifty . . ."

"He'd been sick, someone was saying, after he'd returned from India . . ."

"That wasn't Stephanos, that was Bandeman, he came back with malaria, I think you're confusing them . . ."

"Stephanos was such a world traveler! He went to all sorts of dangerous places, like Kashgar, and Tibet, and then, to die at home—"

"Poor Beata! She's so devoted to him . . ."

"My God! Are you sure? It's impossible to believe that—Stephanos is *gone.*"

Now another woman joined the two, astounded and aggrieved—"Stephanos? Angelo? *Died?* What are you saying?"

Mickey recognized Abigail Burdine, wife of one of Mickey's husband's older colleagues in the political science department: a woman Mickey considered cold-blooded and aloof except at this moment she was looking stunned as if someone had struck her in the face.

Abigail Burdine was a woman whom Mickey knew, but not well; who hadn't been particularly friendly to Mickey in the early, difficult years at the university when Mickey's husband hadn't yet been granted tenure and exuded, in the eyes of tenured faculty and their smug spouses, something of the precariousness of a rock climber on a near-vertical slope: you felt sympathy for such vulnerability, but did not want to become involved with it.

Eventually, when Mickey's husband was promoted, and women like Mrs. Burdine were marginally friendlier to her, Mickey hadn't been able to respond with any sort of convincing warmth. She'd perfected a method of *not-seeing* which was a kind of reverse social radar.

Now crowding beneath the overhang, grocery bags gripped in both arms, the Burdine woman repeated in breathless disbelief: "Stephanos is *dead*? You mean—Angelo Stephanos? Are you serious? *How*?"

"Heart attack, or maybe an aneurysm . . ."

"My God—*when*?"

A surprise to Mickey, and something of a rebuke, that the woman who'd snubbed her for years was capable of such emotion.

"The news is just going out. It's on the university Web site. You can check your cell phone . . ."

"My God! Oh."

By this time a half-dozen individuals were standing beneath the overhang as rain pelted the pavement. A sleety sort of rain striking the pavement like machine-gun fire.

It was a relief to Mickey, shoppers emerged from Smila's who had no awareness of or interest in news of Stephanos's death. They stood quite quietly by themselves staring out at the rain and biding their time until they could rush out to their vehicles.

Mickey saw with a smile how one straggly-haired young man, wearing a shiny yellow poncho, placed his purchases in his bicycle basket, covered with something waterproof, and pedaled out bravely into the storm.

Smila's Sense of Organic Foods was a small food and herbal supplement store at the edge of the university's older, central campus. Mickey had seen Angelo Stephanos shopping here, she was sure— she'd exchanged greetings with the man, numerous times—but could not have claimed to know him. He was a short springy gleaming-bald youngish man with a bluntly ugly yet attractive face, olive-dark, with sculpted-looking features like a European film actor of decades ago: burnished skin, dark goatee, flashing smile. Even as a younger faculty member he'd been something of a campus celebrity—often on the local arts TV channel—his photograph in local newspapers. Stephanos gave public lectures on such topics as "The Semiotics of Religious

Experience" and "Deconstructing Derrida"; his Introduction to Comparative Religions course had to be capped at three hundred students, not counting a score of community auditors who adored him.

Now as talk of Stephanos's death swirled about her Mickey felt a keen sense of loss; and embarrassment to know so little of the man, thus to care so much less than the others cared.

It was a curiosity, a part of the Stephanos mythos, that the man was usually called by just his surname—"Stephanos"; to students he was "Professor Stephanos." Mickey, if she'd called him anything, had probably called him "Angelo."

She tried to recall if she'd ever exchanged more than a few words with him. At a university gathering, a reception—not recently. And the short bald olive-skinned smiling man with the sculpted-looking face had made a gesture meant to be kindly, courtly—he'd seized both her hands to congratulate her on something, or to compliment her; and Mickey had reacted with surprise, and Stephanos had laughed: "Excuse me! I did not mean to *alarm*." (Which wasn't like Mickey in any case. She was hardly a fastidious or formal sort of person.) She seemed to recall that her husband Cameron had played tennis with Stephanos and mutual friends, years ago in the university courts off Broadmead Avenue where they'd lived for almost ten years. She had an impression of the wiry thick-chested man in tennis whites, with his short muscled legs, bounding about the court and making his opponents swing their rackets desperately, lunge, miss, send balls into the net.

Another time Abigail Burdine was demanding *when* this had happened, and *how*; as if there might yet be some mistake, or loophole, to rebut this news that so upset her.

Mickey was thinking, with a shudder—(for the air was wet and cold and she hadn't dressed warmly enough that morning rushing off to the medical center)—how strange, the phenomenon of human attachment and grief; we can care genuinely only for those whom we know; even when the deceased is obviously a much-loved, superior and good man.

You'd never heard anything but praise for Stephanos. Mickey thought so. Maybe a few demurrals—the man was so *vain*. (But what male professor, Mickey thought, was not *vain* in his heart of hearts? And what woman would not wish to be *vain*, if circumstances rendered such a wish not foolish?) His political allegiances—*Amnesty International, Doctors Without Borders*—his support of the Obama/Biden presidential campaign; his legendary generosity with students, and with younger colleagues; his robust good nature, good humor—(he'd had a reputation perhaps as a European male who appreciated good-looking young women, and attracted them irresistibly)—Mickey felt the loss of all this, that she hadn't really known; dismay that she and Stephanos had not been social friends, that their social circles had not overlapped.

Why was that? Hadn't Cameron liked Angelo Stephanos, or, for whatever reason, hadn't Angelo Stephanos liked *him*? Or hadn't Stephanos liked *her*? In the University Heights community everyone knew everyone else; everyone's public-school children were tangled together like distant cousins; yet, lines of social connections were not always evident to the observer. Impossible not to think, as Mickey was now thinking, that she and her husband had been, in an essential sense, *excluded*.

What an arduous day! And now, this God-damned rain.

Mickey had driven to the food store after work to buy a few things she knew her husband wouldn't have purchased, though his office was closer to Smila's than her own; food-shopping had once been a mutual enterprise but had become, with the passage of time, a marital chore like others which she and Cameron pushed back and forth between them, never having clearly defined who was responsible for what, and how often. It was hard not to exude the air of a martyr, if one did just slightly more than the other, as it seemed Mickey frequently did. For Cameron's position at the university was *more important* than hers—his career *far more important* than hers.

"Would anyone like a ride? I could drive someone home . . ."

The downpour was lessening. Mickey dared to interrupt the talk of Stephanos's passing with her offer that was spontaneous, impulsive. She would have to know that most of her companions huddling beneath the overhang would have cars of their own but, as it turned out, both the Nordic-looking math professor and the woman with whom he'd been originally talking had walked to Smila's, to make just a few purchases.

"Would you? That would be so kind . . ."

"Thanks so much!"

Mickey made a rush for her Toyota which was parked a short distance away, amid mud puddles; almost gaily she tossed groceries into the trunk, and hastily drove back to the store, as if fearing the math professor and his woman companion might have decided that they didn't need her.

It was good—this reckless physical exercise. For Mickey was not feeling so very robust. And so, Mickey felt the need to publicly disprove any possibility that she might not be feeling so very robust.

The woman sat beside her, breathless and distraught, her wetted grocery bags in her arms; the long-limbed professor climbed in the back of the car, urged by Mickey to "just push things aside"—the rear of her Toyota had an air of affable clutter, and it didn't matter if much of it was pushed onto the floor.

Mickey felt a childish thrill of excitement, driving these strangers in her car. It was not unlike the thrill you'd feel giving a lift home to popular students in high school—really popular students, or older students, in a clique superior to your own. She had appropriated their intensity, their grief—was that it? For she felt so sadly distant herself, from the late Stephanos.

But the woman beside her—(the name was Madelyn McCall)—was turned to speak to the man in the backseat—(his name was Andy Funkhauser, as Mickey should have known)—and their continued talk of the deceased Stephanos was distracting to her as she drove in the rain. To her annoyance, they'd forgotten to tell her where to turn until it was too late—"Please, I know you're upset about your friend, but let's be practical." Her voice was sharper than she'd intended. She stared at Funkhauser's blunt sand-colored face in the rearview mirror. On his head was an idiotic METS cap, soaked with rain.

Now there was silence in the car. Mickey apologized—"Hey, sorry. Just, I'm a little anxious about driving in this rain."

"Oh, we appreciate it! Is it—Mickey? You're so kind."

"Yes! Thanks so much."

"You were close friends of Angelo Stephanos, I guess?"—Mickey spoke hesitantly.

"Yes. I think so. I mean—I'd like to think so."

"Yes. My wife and I—we've known him and Beata since we moved here from Iowa, eleven years ago. He made us feel so welcome."

"I wish I'd known Stephanos better. He was obviously a remarkable individual."

Mickey spoke uncertainly, not knowing if this was the right thing to say. Rain lashed against her windshield in a delirium. She was tasting something ugly and metallic in her mouth and the sensation made her want to spit.

It seemed to her that her words, foolishly inadequate as a paper grocery bag in a downpour, were met by her companions with a stiff sort of embarrassment.

At a red brick house on Mercer Street Mickey pulled into a driveway, to let Madelyn McCall out; at a Colonial a block away, she pulled into a driveway, to let Andy Funkhauser out. Both McCall and Funkhauser thanked her profusely for the ride but Mickey thought

Will they remember me? Fuck, no.

SHE'D BEEN TO CHEMO that morning: 7:00 A.M. to 10:00 A.M.

She was one of the "lucky ones"—she understood. The gastroenterologist who'd discovered her colon cancer had told her *You won't think so right now but when you think back to this day, you will realize that it was the luckiest day of your life.*

Mickey wanted to think so. There were *good thoughts* and *not-so-good thoughts* in this matter of fighting cancer.

It was her secret, or so she hoped. No one but Cameron knew.

No one at the Institute knew. (Where Mickey was, after six years, still an adjunct instructor with no medical benefits. The enormous cancer costs—surgery, oncology, chemotherapy—were borne entirely by Cameron's university insurance.) She'd so arranged her schedule this term, her chemotherapy days didn't intrude upon her work-days; she had not yet missed a class, or even a staff meeting; she liked to think that her colleagues and students would be astonished to know she was undergoing chemotherapy, and why.

Of course, some mornings even when she hadn't had chemo recently she could barely force herself out of bed. She could barely drag through the day. All of her effort, and she had to think it was an effort in a good cause, lay in her imposture in public: behaving exactly as she'd always behaved, or a little more so.

Going to the medical center was trickier. If Mickey encountered people who knew her in the grim infusion room she'd concocted a plausible-sounding story about a deficiency in her gamma globulin count. No one but a practiced clinician could detect the difference between a gamma globulin infusion and the aggressive chemotherapy that involved fluorouracil and oxaliplatin.

These were chemicals enlisted to kill cancer cells. A strategy not unlike, Mickey had to think, spraying napalm in the jungle in the hope of killing the hidden enemy amid the fecund vegetation.

Keeping the colon cancer secret was essential to her. Even from her relatives and closest friends. It was a *Mickey* thing—not wanting sympathy, pity. Not wanting attention. The wrong kind of attention.

Cameron was willing to keep her secret. He, too, did not want to be the object of sympathy or pity or even marked concern among his colleagues and friends.

It wasn't so bad—she'd lost weight. At last, size seven as she hadn't been since the age of fifteen. Her favorite foods made her gag, like old friends she hadn't seen in years turning up looking all wrong. She hadn't (yet) lost much of her thick dark-blond hair. She hadn't (yet) had the most extreme side effects of the treatment—fainting, seizures, extreme vomiting and diarrhea, death.

Sometime in the first night following an infusion her cheeks became flushed as the cheeks of a girl skater in a Norman Rockwell painting and by morning, her right eye was bloody.

She'd learned to think *This is lucky! Only one eye.*

Cameron hadn't noticed the bloody right eye. Cameron might have noticed the weight loss but said nothing. But then, Cameron hadn't looked at Mickey very often, in recent months. Nor did Cameron touch her very often, in recent months. An impulse came over her at times to wave her hand in front of his eyes to attract his attention—*Hi! This is me, Mickey!*—but, then what? Did she really want Cameron's attention, up close?

Cameron had reacted to her brassy-chemical breath. She'd only realized belatedly.

Leaning up to kiss him, just a friendly good-bye kiss as Cameron was about to rush off, and seeing how, just perceptibly, in a way that suggested stoic restraint on his part, Cameron stiffened.

For of course her breath must smell. The interior of her mouth tasted like battery acid that no amount of mouth-rinsing with alcohol-free mouthwash could dispel.

Sorry hon. I won't, any more.

After dropping off the aggrieved friends of Stephanos, Mickey hadn't been in the house for more than a few minutes when the phone rang. An agitated-sounding friend was calling from Berkeley—"I just got an e-mail that Angelo Stephanos is dead? Can that be right?"

"Yes—I think so. I haven't seen anything official, but . . ."

"My God! Stephanos! He was just here at Cal, he gave the keynote address at a LAPA conference, really a brilliant, warm man—he was impressed by a paper I gave, and he was going to invite me to your campus—and now . . ."

Mickey said, sympathetically, "People are very upset here, of course. I mean, people who know him. Knew him. Evidently he was a very charismatic person . . ."

"I wouldn't call it 'charismatic'—that sounds phony and shallow. Stephanos just radiated *life*. I'd been feeling kind of depressed about some things, and he really listened to me and said the most thoughtful, subtle things. I scarcely knew him but he said that when I came there to give a talk, he hoped I'd stay with him and his family."

This friend had stayed with Mickey and Cameron in the past, visiting their campus. The gratitude with which he spoke of Stephanos's invitation was slightly hurtful.

"He died at home? In his bathroom, in the shower? They're saying an aneurysm? My God."

"Or a heart attack . . ."

"Just like that! Terrifying."

"Well. It might have been merciful, so abrupt. He wouldn't have known what was happening."

Hesitantly Mickey offered her friend this banal consolation. But her friend seemed scarcely to be listening.

"Is Cam there?"

"No."

"He knew Stephanos, right?"

"Did he? Not well."

"I'll call later. We can commiserate."

"E-mail is best, with Cameron. You know how he is about phone messages."

Their friend—who was Cameron's friend from graduate school days at the University of Minnesota, not so much Mickey's friend—didn't hang up immediately but reviewed, in a voice of genuine loss, how exceptionally gracious—and helpful—Angelo Stephanos had been to him, when he'd sent him a rough first draft of his new book on the "politics" of transgendered texts; the book had just been published by Cal-Berkeley Press and one of the few but laudatory reviews cited points that Stephanos had supplied, which he'd intended to write Stephanos about, to thank him. But—he'd procrastinated. And now it was too late.

Of all that he'd missed by dying, Mickey thought, a thank-you e-mail from an ambitious younger colleague would probably not have been paramount to Stephanos.

But she had to console Cameron's friend, who was genuinely upset. She was feeling how bizarre the situation, in this matter of the evidently catastrophic death of Angelo Stephanos: she understood it was a personal loss, possibly a flaw of character, to be unable to share in the commiseration others felt so naturally.

"Angelo Stephanos certainly was beloved," Mickey said dryly. "When most of us die, we'll be lucky to be *missed*."

But this was mean-spirited, adolescent. This did not come out as Mickey meant it, as a statement of fact. Fortunately the friend in Berkeley hadn't heard.

"Stephanos was such an ageless person, somehow. He was so *alive*. Jesus! This is a shock. . . . I should call—is it Beatrice? Beata? She must be devastated . . ."

Beata Stephanos? Mickey tried to recall if she'd ever met this woman.

"Tell Cam I called, will you? And if there's a memorial service for Stephanos—of course, there will be—I'll try to get there."

"Yes. Of course. You can stay with us. Please."

Please. Was Mickey begging him, this man who was her husband's friend, whom she scarcely knew?

Of course, she'd spoken spontaneously. She was a generous person only because she was heedless and reckless; this was not a virtue, but you could see how it might be mistaken for a virtue.

Mickey hung up the phone and wandered into the kitchen like a dazed person—seeing, there, the wetted grocery bags on the counter. She had to put away the groceries—(of course, Cameron wasn't here to help her)—and she had to think about—whatever it was, she had to think about—something urgent and essential in her own life that was a million pixels swirling in a thunder-cloud about to burst.

HER PROBLEM, Mickey thought, began with *Mickey.*

It was a high school name. It had been the perfect, gratifying, coveted high school name. *Mickey* quite suited her long legs on the basketball court, her streaked blond ponytail swinging with its own antic life, her quick unfettered high-pitched and spontaneous laughter; *Mickey* was funny and sexy and good-looking (if not beautiful) with a smooth freckled face, creamy skin and wide-set sea-green eyes and a sly sweet smile—so you could forgive her for also being a good student, one of the half-dozen excellent students in her class, and one of the few who'd gone on to a university career, and then to graduate school. (B.A. in biology, Ph.D. combining in ecology/evolutionary biology.)

It was a *Mickey* thing to make jokes about the artificial-vein implant in her upper-right chest, that allowed blood to be taken, fluids to be dripped into it, without the excruciating usual routine of a nurse poking for a vein; and it was a *Mickey* thing to make jokes about the plastic chemo-bottle she sometimes had to carry, in secret, in a jazzy black fanny-pack around her waist, that fed more chemicals into the artificial vein to be carried, via her bloodstream, throughout her body.

And it was a *Mickey* thing to joke about the "Sexuality" section of the *Medical Center Patient Chemotherapy Handbook*:

Women Undergoing Chemotherapy May Experience
the Following:

> Lack of sexual desire
> Vaginal dryness
> Discomfort during intercourse
> Inability to experience orgasm
> Hot flashes
> Interruption of menstrual cycle

Note: DO NOT CEASE BIRTH CONTROL.
BIRTH CONTROL IS STILL NECESSARY.

Mickey had to laugh. It *was* funny—*Discomfort during intercourse!*—this was tantamount to suggesting, to a quadriplegic, that he/she might experience some muscular discomfort while sprinting.

As for *birth control*—maybe that wasn't so funny. Just sad.

These clumsy jokes, Mickey did not make in the presence of others. Certainly not Cameron.

These were *inward, brooding* Mickey-jokes.

Now at almost thirty-seven she'd outgrown *Mickey*; but it was too late to try to convince others that she merited being called *Michelle*.

Worse, she'd grown into *Mickey*. She'd been shaped—misshapen—by *Mickey*. Like one of those stunted little Japanese bonsai trees except her stuntedness was mostly inward.

Mickey failed to evoke *gravitas*. Not a name likely to be attached to one who merits respect, attention, a fellowship from the National Academy of Science, or, in time, the tears of a grief-stricken community.

Cameron had fallen in love with *Mickey*—he'd never met *Michelle*.

Now, not so much in love with *Mickey*—he'd have even less interest in *Michelle*.

As *Mickey* she'd been the one to absorb bad news like a deep-sea sponge bred for such a purpose. She'd been the one, in the marriage, to understand, forgive, and forget. (Amazing how volitional amnesia could be. Misdeeds of Cameron's had been whited-out as in a nova explosion.)

Waiting for Cameron to come home she called a few friends. The combination of that morning's chemo and the catastrophic death of Angelo Stephanos had left her shaken—she had *no feelings*, she was *totally numb*.

Of several friends only one woman, of Mickey's approximate age, spoke of Stephanos as if she'd suffered a personal loss. It was news to Mickey that Jacky Spires had been such an intimate of Stephanos but there was Jacky mourning the man in the most extravagant way, on the verge of crying—"What a tragedy! He was so *young*." Mickey asked Jacky to explain to her why Stephanos had been so remarkable; wanting to feel something of what the grieving woman felt. If only the acid-taste in her mouth didn't make all else seem irrelevant.

After chemo, Mickey was supposed to avoid alcohol—of course. And cold drinks, in fact anything cold. *Cold* seemed to attack tissue like something alive, leaping.

Still, a quarter-glass of white wine wouldn't hurt. She didn't think so. She had to open the refrigerator and remove the bottle with a woolen glove on her right hand, kept on top of the refrigerator for that practical purpose. And she sipped the cold tart liquid very, very slowly for fear that her mouth and throat muscles would spasm.

On the other end of the line Jacky was saying, like a migraine sufferer speaking through pain, "Stephanos was just, I don't know—a wonderful person, Mickey. So generous, and so funny. Beata is rather prim, she seems almost like his mother at times. He's so funny, making jokes the poor woman couldn't begin to comprehend—of course, she's thoroughly *Greek;* he's only just half-. Well, Stephanos gave off an air of something like *love.* It's difficult to explain . . . But you must have met him, too . . ."

As she listened to this lovesick elegy, emotions of adolescent yearning and loss welled up in Mickey. (Or was it a faint surge of nausea? She'd remembered to take her anti-nausea medication.) She recalled her first love—not a lover: a friend—in college. A poet who'd gone on to publish, with some success. And, not long afterward, her first lover—not a friend. (She'd lost track of him after his second marriage.) Seeing Cameron for the first time at the University of Minnesota where she'd been a new, young graduate student and Cameron had been completing his Ph.D., Mickey had felt a sense of intensity, urgency—she'd been twenty-five years old and had believed herself *old.* She'd been drawn to biology as natural history; but biology was now becoming computational, mathematical. In her environmental lab it had seemed that men were clearly preferred; sexism prevailed; that she was *Mickey Lewenstein* was a disadvantage, like a withered leg; that she tried to compensate for the withered leg by being brightly articulate, energetic and hardworking, seemed to annoy others in the lab including the principal investigator whose assessment of her stalwart effort had been probably reduced to a pithy utterance *Works too hard for too little.* Or *Smart but not smart enough.*

If she'd been a star in the U-Minn department she might not have married Cameron, or anyone; she might now have a professorial position, with tenure, at a good university; yet by now, to be reasonable, she might also be burnt out. Molecular biology was the cutting-edge science of the new century, like neuroscience. And the colon cancer would have caught up with her, being, she guessed, genetically-predetermined to strike her approximately when it had.

Strange, she rarely thought of it. Of this mysterious voracious *it* residing in her very guts.

That she wasn't afraid of the cancer, much—this was more surprising to her. She trusted her (excellent, Asian-American, woman) oncologist and believed that the chemo would prevent the spread of the cancer elsewhere; the tiny tumor had been surgically removed, very deftly done, and had left a small precise puckered-looking incision almost immediately above her belly button, like a tattoo.

If he'd loved her, Cameron would have kissed that sweet little puckered tattoo. Since he hadn't, so he didn't.

She tried to see it that clearly. Such clarity was a *Mickey*-thing.

SO RISKY, to love another person!

Like flaying your own, outermost skin. Exposed to the crude air and every kind of infection.

Some months ago she'd seen him. She was sure. Walking with a stranger.

By chance she'd seen. Returning from a late-afternoon run at the university arboretum and crossing the engineering quad which was contiguous with the consortium of buildings that housed the Grant Clark Institute of International Affairs where Cameron had an office and so seeing, though at first not knowing what it was she was seeing, her husband in the close company of—was it a young woman? A *girl*?

So long had Mickey been one of these herself, that legion of voracious *girls*, she'd failed to realize that *girl* isn't a noun but an adjective, applied to a condition. A phase of being and not a *being*.

No longer would you call Mickey a *girl* unless (for instance) you'd seen her at a little distance, walking/jogging in the hilly arboretum, in denim shorts, pullover, university jacket, leg warmers and well-worn running shoes; sometimes, still, her streaked-blond hair pulled back in a ponytail to whip behind her.

Closer, you'd see that Mickey had become, inescapably, a *woman*.

Since the chemo, there were new, faint lines in her forehead and the skin was both flushed and alarmingly papery. In the interior of her mouth, in the days following treatment, small canker sores that burnt like tiny peppers.

Sometimes after chemo she had a delayed physical reaction—shivering, shuddering, quaking and so cold, her teeth began to chatter. It was her temperature, as they said *spiking*—the intense cold actually a symptom of imminent fever.

So long as her temperature didn't inch beyond 100.1 degrees F., she was not in immediate danger.

Such quaking episodes were—oh, she wanted to think this!—like the aura preceding an epileptic fit. The mystic-transcendental aura of Dostoyevsky, for instance. An elite sort of pathology and not just—pathology.

At such times she was compelled to think that her mistake wasn't *Mickey*. Not just the name. She was thinking that her true mistake, if it had been a mistake, had been to blindly persevere in a field in which so very few women excelled that each had to be unique. And she hadn't been *unique*.

In certain fields of scientific research, as in politics, finance, and law, the female and the intellectual ran along parallel lines that did not converge, as the male and the intellectual did. You could be thoroughly an intellectual while not surrendering maleness; you could not be so totally intellectual and not surrender some degree of femaleness. It seemed to be a law of nature, or of culture so deeply ingrained in the species that it felt like nature. This was true of Mickey's academic women friends as it was true of her. Married, unmarried—it made no difference.

Her friend Jacky Spires had become a highly prolific, productive researcher in the volatile field of social psychology. Jacky attended conferences, she published papers, articles, books. It helped that she was unmarried—it helped that she had few distractions. She'd become a star in her department yet never felt confident, always harried, pursued—"At least there's the compensation of a new book next year. I try to think of it that way. If there was only next year, and no new book, or new work . . ." Jacky made a gesture of eloquent dismay.

Mickey had lost the momentum of research, conference papers, publication. She'd lost the impetus to start a family. But she was still *alive*.

Except: she'd seen Cameron walking with one of them.

Might've been a first-year graduate student. So young!

On a side street near the political science building. A couple walking together, talking intensely, Cameron's arm brushing against the girl's arm, and the girl glancing up at him, one of those smiles-inviting-a-kiss. And Mickey who'd been about to cross the street in their direction froze, and turned away, and fled like a kicked dog.

A sensation like a hook in the heart. And she'd thought *This is not new. This is not lethal. The marriage will survive.*

"Cameron? I saw."

"'Saw'?"

"I know about her."

"'Her'? Who?"

Patiently Mickey said, as if Cameron were a precocious young child, and this was a game they were playing, "I don't know her name— how would I know her name? But I know about her."

Cameron frowned. Cameron glanced down at his feet, frowning.

"Not sure what you mean, Mick."

"Don't 'Mick' me! I saw you with her, and it was evident—you are a couple."

"When was this? Today?"

Mickey's face was burning. This was so ridiculous—her husband interrogating *her*.

"Yes. Today. This afternoon. About four o'clock. On McCormack Street near—what's it?—Elm."

"Really? *Today?*"

"Yes! Today. It was an accident, I just happened to see you—and her. At first I didn't realize that it was you, and then—I saw."

Cameron shook his head, baffled. He was a tall solid-built man of forty-one whose alternative life, he liked to say, would have been skiing—Ski Patrol Olympics, snow-mountain rescue, working for the National Park Service in, for instance, Yellowstone. His wrists and ankles were twice the size of Mickey's wrists and ankles and she never saw him without feeling an involuntary sensation not unlike melting, or decomposition. *Ohhhh. Yes.*

She knew, he'd been unfaithful to her. Probably.

In twelve years of marriage, inescapably.

It was a *male thing.* For some, a *female thing* as well, but not for Mickey.

And now, she wanted to think she'd been mistaken. Certainly, she was mistaken. The look of hurt, surprise, indignation in her husband's face—she had to be mistaken.

"I can see you're upset, Mickey. It's the stress of these weeks"— (Cameron wouldn't say *chemo,* as he would not ever say *cancer*)—"and you're not sleeping, I can tell. But at four o'clock today I was at a poli-sci faculty meeting, that lasted until almost five-thirty. Would you like witnesses' statements, notarized?" Cameron's sarcasm was masked as humor so it wouldn't sting quite as much.

"All right, then."

"'All right, then'—what?"

Mickey laughed. Another little peppery canker sore had emerged, in the soft moist flesh of her cheek. But Cameron knew nothing of these sores, no reason for Cameron to know.

"Just—'all right.' I didn't see what I saw. I believe you."

LATER SHE'D WONDERED: the young person, the stranger, slender-bodied, so eagerly accommodating to the elder who was Mickey's husband—could it have been, not a *girl* but a *boy?*

IF HER EYES had seen *boy* her brain would've registered *girl*.

SHE TRAVELED to the city by train to select a wig. In secret.

It was advised to select a wig before actual hair loss.

In the literature it was said *Hair loss can be more traumatic for cancer patients than the threat of cancer itself.*

She should have her hair buzz-cut, she was told. Oh but not just yet, she protested.

"Next time you come to see us."

In the unsparing mirror a shadow-eyed woman regarded her with a brave smile. Same brave smile she'd seen since the myriad public-lavatory mirrors of adolescence. *Well! Here we are.*

She was shown a beautiful human-hair wig, priced at three thousand six hundred dollars. This was classy/glossy wavy hair just slightly lighter in color than her own and about the length of her own, now slightly ragged hair.

She was shown a synthetic wig of approximately the same color, curlier, just perceptibly more festive. Eight hundred ninety dollars.

She was shown a synthetic wig, not so showy, but attractive, adequate. Six hundred fifty dollars.

"But I want a wig like my own hair. I don't want a wig that looks better than my own hair. I'm not trying to look *glamorous.* Can't you approximate that?"

Pink-smocked Mimi whose own hair was glamorous, blow-dried and gaily-streaked-blond, said, with a little frown, "Yes. We could. But it would mean taking one of these great wigs and thinning it so much, there would be almost nothing left to hide the netting."

Thinning it so much. Almost nothing left. For the first time Mickey had some sense of her condition.

❀

IMPULSIVELY SHE DECIDED: SHE WOULD PAY A CALL TO THE widow.

She would *offer condolences.*

This morning a new spurt of energy. The old buoyancy, she'd almost forgotten.

In University Heights it was known, Stephanos's widow was having a kind of open house 5:00 P.M. to 7:00 P.M. and all were invited. A memorial service would be scheduled for later in the term.

In the late afternoon then she dressed in glamorous black: a taffeta dress with a stylish little jacket which she hadn't worn in (at least) a decade; high-heeled black shoes and black net stockings. So unlike Mickey's usual attire even when "dressy" she hoped people wouldn't think she was in costume.

Amazing how the black taffeta dress fit her. She'd lost at least fifteen pounds.

Sexy-chic. Mickey hadn't looked so glamorous since her high school senior prom.

Combing her hair cautiously with a wide-toothed comb as she'd been instructed. Still, hairs began to be "released." After the first two chemotherapy treatments her hair had not seemed affected but now, after the third, she saw a subtle yet unmistakable difference and her scalp was feeling singed.

In a near-panic noticing strands of hair backlit by sunlight from a window, drifting, falling. A sort of halo framing her face.

Wanting to protest *I'm still a young woman. My life is before me.*

Stephanos took her hand, and brushed his lips against the knuckles.

Of course your life is before you. But you must reach out and take it.

She drove to Stephanos's house on Arden Avenue which was less than a half-mile from her own house. She was feeling such sorrow for the widow whom she scarcely knew.

For Stephanos, she felt only a kind of numbness. A vague sense of loss but also resentment at this loss. For the man hadn't been her friend—not hers and Cameron's.

But for the widow she felt something like pain. A pain that left her breathless. A shared—(but how could it be shared? Beata Stephanos knew nothing of *her*)—terror at the abrupt loss of the husband which must feel like an amputation. She thought *I hope she will let me be her friend. I hope I can help her.*

This was naïve, probably. Ridiculous. The Stephanos family had relatives, countless close friends. A phalanx of people who'd loved Stephanos and would protect the widow.

So many vehicles were parked in front of Stephanos's house, and on side streets near the house, Mickey had to walk a considerable distance in the sexy high-heeled shoes and in her arms bearing a lavish bouquet of flowers—calla lilies, roses, gardenias, mums. Impulsively she'd stopped at a florist in town and bought up the store saying a friend had just died and the high school girl behind the counter said *Ohhh. Is this the professor? Lots of people been in here all day.*

Stephanos had lived in a stately, just slightly shabby old English Tudor built in the early years of the twentieth century, like numerous others at this end of the older campus. At one time the residential neighborhood was considered the most prestigious in the area: the university president lived close by. Now, younger faculty preferred to live in the hilly, expansive suburbs.

Mickey drifted inside the house, in the company of several others who were carrying flowers, or casseroles, or baskets of fruit. Their greetings were murmured as if embarrassed.

So many people! Half of University Heights had to be crowded into the downstairs rooms of the Stephanos house. Mickey had to restrain herself from looking quickly about—as if Stephanos might appear. Almost, in a part of her brain, she expected to see him.

Mickey! So kind of you to come. My sweet girl.

She'd become chilled on the walk from the car. Shivering, mildly quaking. The sexy black taffeta dress fitting her hips seductively and the stylish little jacket, button-less, fell open to show the tops of her creamy-pale breasts. (The puckers at the sides of the breasts, a result of Mickey's weight loss, and a curious brittle discoloration of the nipples, were hidden from view.)

She felt clumsy, bearing her armful of flowers like some sort of Greek peasant girl. She did see familiar faces, she exchanged smiles. The atmosphere was somber, heightened. Music was playing— sounding like Greek Orthodox chorale music. Everyone was excessively courteous. Except there were small children, darting about. On a long dining room table vases of flowers, floral displays, fruit-baskets, casserole dishes. Bottles of dark red wine. Stuffed olives, stuffed vine leaves, crusty white bread. A smell of something baking in the kitchen—quiche?

There were tear-streaked faces, there were muffled sobs. Mickey guessed that some of the mourners were relatives. A frightened-looking dull-eyed boy of about fifteen, a disabled child in a wheelchair who resembled Stephanos about the eyes. Mickey handed her armful of flowers to a high-school-aged girl who took them from her muttering *Thanks, ma'am!*

Mickey knew few people here. In her sexy black taffeta dress and high-heeled shoes she drew eyes. No one knows what to make of death. Never did and never will. Mickey wondered if she should feel ashamed for having intruded upon private grief but someone was greeting her, making her welcome—"Hello! I think you are—Elena?"

"Mickey. I mean—Michelle."

"Thank you for coming, Michelle. Beata is in the kitchen."

It was a vast cluttered kitchen. A harried-looking little woman was scolding a sulky adolescent girl. Somehow, Mickey had picked up a glass of the dark red wine. The first sip was delicious, like a tap to the pleasure center of the brain with a felt-tipped mallet.

"Oh! Sorry."

She'd collided with one of the Stephanos relatives. She was trying to approach Mrs. Stephanos, to offer condolences; she would speak quickly and quietly and retreat, for she needed to return home, and fall upon her bed. Too much was crowding into her head, she had to lie very still to process it. *A girl, or was it a boy. That close-companionable familiarity.*

Except: she'd imagined it. The man hadn't been Cameron but someone who'd resembled Cameron who'd been at a faculty meeting at that very minute.

She'd been reckless, heedless. After chemo, she should have set an entire day aside for rest. Her imposture of *healthy-Mickey* was becoming a strain. Cameron tried to take no notice as one would take no notice of a forced theatrical performance.

There was no denying it, a sickly-yellow chemical malaise filled her being. Not wine but water, not cold water but tepid water, was prescribed so that her tender throat muscles wouldn't spasm.

"Marta? Are you—"

"Michelle. We live over on Reardon Lane."

"What a sad, sad occasion this is! I can't believe it."

"I—I can't believe it, either. Stephanos was so . . ."

Could not bring herself to say *alive*.

Maybe she wouldn't survive after all. Her almost cheery equanimity in the face of surgery, recovery, chemotherapy was a paltry performance, and Cameron had caught on. His once-lustful love had turned to pity. Pity has no (sexual) potency. He was looking for a new, younger, healthy sex-companion. You could not blame the man: it was nature.

On the dining room walls and on a wall beside the staircase were family photos. Many were of the deceased man, smiling with his wife, children. Several were of the deceased man smiling in academic garb— honorary doctorate hoods gaily colored as Hallowe'en costumes. In the living room, the Greek chorale music had ceased; someone was playing the piano, a lovely slow etude of Chopin executed with music-school precision.

There came Beata Stephanos into the dining room as if in search of someone. In such a gathering, in your very home, you would naturally seek out your husband. Beata was a short plump woman with black eyes fierce as a falcon's eyes. She wore black—layers of black. Her mouth was a thick smear of red in a doughy-pale face that had been an attractive face once, not long ago. The widow was in her mid-forties. Yet seemed, in her grief, ageless. Mickey was reminded of those excruciating drawings and woodcuts of the German artist Käthe Kollwitz.

Mickey saw that Beata Stephanos was blinking and staring at *her*.

Advancing upon her with a look of fury. Not grief but hatred distorted the woman's bulldog-face.

"You! Dare to come here! So he liked you—eh? His weakness. Pretty girls. 'The blondes'—he called you. That's why you're here—is it?"

Mickey was too shaken to comprehend. It was difficult to hear even raised voices in the crowded dining room. Pretty girls? That's why she was here?

"You and the others—'blondes.' You didn't think you were the only one, did you?"

Mrs. Stephanos was furious, sneering. She appeared to be drunk. A dark-eyed adolescent girl with a look of utter mortification tried to restrain Mrs. Stephanos but she cast off the girl's arm with a muttered curse.

Then, abruptly, Beata Stephanos turned away, as if Mickey's expression of dismay had deterred her. Or so Mickey wished to believe. The widow pushed her way into an adjacent room, a small book-lined study off the dining room. Not knowing what she was doing but feeling that she must do something, if only murmur into the widow's ear *Excuse me, I hope you will accept my condolences for your loss* Mickey followed after her. She wanted to explain, and to apologize; since childhood, she was in terror of being misunderstood, and wrongly/ harshly judged. She wanted Stephanos's widow to look at her more closely to see that (1) Really, she was no one whom Stephanos or Mrs. Stephanos had known; (2) She wasn't young/sexy. But Beata was shoving something at her.

"Yes. Good. You are here. Good! Take it. I don't want it. No more! You left it in our bedroom—you, or someone like you. He would say— 'It is nothing, it is just'"— Beata made an airy contemptuous gesture, or tried to, snapping her fingers—"but now, you will—please—leave— me—alone." She was thrusting at Mickey what appeared to be a silk shawl—Japanese?—very beautiful, aquamarine, visibly soiled.

"A gift from *him*. I don't doubt. So take it with you—*go*."

Mickey opened her mouth to protest, to explain—but there were no words. And the widow had turned away, in disgust. Shouting at someone in the kitchen, who shouted back, in Greek.

Mickey departed. Mickey staggered from the house, clutching the silk shawl that was aquamarine silk embroidered with cream-colored threads, tiny gardenia-blossoms. The shawl, though soiled, was yet beautiful. She had never seen anything so beautiful close up, let alone held it in her hand. She could see that the shawl had been selected by an individual of impeccable taste.

Quickly she walked to her car, parked some distance away. Both her feet were aching in the absurd high-heeled shoes of another, innocent era. Her breath came short, with a little stab of pain in the region of the heart. *Stephanos!* A light rain had begun, again. The air was wet and cold. She drew the shawl about her shoulders. She began to shiver, to quake. She drew the shawl tighter.

II

THE HUNTER

IN PRIVATE, A NERVOUS COLLAPSE IS AN ILLNESS. IN PUB-
lic, it can be a career.

On the evening of my arrival, there was a dinner in my honor
at the small Midwestern college on the Mississippi River where, as
my father was dying, in a longitude/latitude approximately one thousand miles to the east and north, I'd agreed to be Caldwalder Poet-
in-Residence for two weeks. The dinner was held at the President's
House which was a small Georgian mansion atop a hill overlooking
the leafy college campus in one direction and, in the other, in the
near distance, the Mississippi River and the "border state" (Missouri)
beyond. The President's House was a national historic landmark,
I was informed. The president's wife took me on a brief tour of the
older part of the house, which dated to the early nineteenth century;
these were called the "historic rooms." The president's wife told me
that the President's House had played a significant role in the Underground Railway, as Illinois had been bordered by several slave states.
I felt something sharp in the region of my chest hearing such casual
words—*slave states*. I considered the phenomenon of a house *playing a
role*. I said, it must be a very interesting experience to live in a national
landmark and the president's wife assured me yes, it was. I'd hoped

to be shown the entrance at least to the *Underground Railway* but the president's wife led me back to the party where my presence was eagerly awaited as an actor crucial to a scene is eagerly awaited by her fellow actors. And during the course of the lengthy dinner I became restless, though I'd been seated in a place of honor to the right of the president and to the left of the wealthy donor elderly Mrs. Caldwalder, and excused myself to slip from the table; a uniformed server escorted me to an old-fashioned bathroom in another part of the house, all brass fixtures and gleaming mirrors, and afterward, instead of returning to my place of honor at the table, I made my way back to the "historic" part of the house that smelled of its stone foundation and of the dark earth beneath. Here it was cooler and damper. The hardwood floor was atilt and ceilings were lower. I switched on a light in the back hall, which the president's wife had switched off when we'd ended our tour. At a little distance I heard the murmurs and quiet laughter of the dinner guests; there were perhaps twenty guests, all strangers to me. I found myself at the threshold of a long tunnel-like room which the president's wife had not shown me. Furnishings in this room were covered in sheets that glimmered in shadow like hunched-over ghosts. I groped in the dark to switch on an overhead light—an antiquated crystal-chip chandelier with transparent flame-shaped bulbs. There was a cavernous fireplace of stone, mortar, and brick. There was a massive mahogany table covered in glass figurines, porcelain and carved-wooden clocks of all sizes, ornamental paperweights, elaborate candlestick holders and other household items as in a museum display. A smell of dust assailed my nostrils. Everywhere were cobwebs—broken remnants of webs, and freshly-spun, perfectly executed webs. The Oriental carpet beneath my feet was faded and frayed yet still beautiful. On my heels I squatted to peer into the cavernous fireplace, that had the look of a shadowy entrance; I wondered if the *Underground Railway* opened out of it. With the soft palms of my hands I pushed at the bricks, rapped my knuckles—but nothing gave. There were no logs in the fireplace, and a light dusting of ashes.

Set in the wall close by was a pantry with a tall, narrow door, and into this pantry I peered also, but my way was blocked by shelves. I could not find any suggestion of a tunnel here.

Through a square-cut window in this wall I could see, so dimly it might have been an illusion, one of those hypnagogic images that flash at us with sickening vigor as we sink into sleep, the shimmering Mississippi River at sunset; the mythic river that confounds the eye, it is so wide, and bears the illusion of being shallow.

The thought came to me, as if it were waiting for me here—(for thoughts await us unexpectedly, in places that are new to us)—*Well, I am here! Now I must discover why.* The realization was both liberating and frightening.

Where was the historic *Underground Railway* in this house? I was eager to see this remnant of our shameful American past. (Though not mine, precisely: my parents' parents had emigrated from Europe in the early twentieth century.) I'd ceased hearing the murmur of voices and laughter in the other part of the house—possibly, I'd forgotten the lavish dinner party *in my honor.* With the curiosity of a heedless child I lifted one of the dust-sheets to discover a cushioned couch with intricately carved cherrywood arms and legs, and an impression in the plush fabric that suggested the outline of a body. I quickly lowered the sheet. From a jumble of cushions and pillows I lifted a strikingly designed needlepoint pillow to my face, and inhaled deeply a scent of dust and a faded, flowery perfume. I examined the mahogany table. Here was a treasure trove of useless, antique items! Each of the clock faces "told" a different time. This did not suggest chaos as you would think, but a kind of graveyard calm that is past time. One of the smaller clocks was ticking—or so I thought. A cream-colored (German? eighteenth-century?) porcelain clock with exquisite floral ornamentation, about the size of a grapefruit. In my clutching hand it felt warm, and had the "feel" of a clock that has been ticking until just a moment before, though the slender ivory hands were pointing to "three" and to "five"—twenty-five minutes after three o'clock.

The bizarre thought came to me—*This will be the time of my father's death, or of my own. That is why I have been brought here.*

Something moved in a corner of my eye. Strands of cobwebs wafted overhead as if stirred by my breath. I thought—*The fireplace! Of course, it is the entrance to the underworld.*

At the oversized fireplace I squatted on my heels, in my dark-wool jersey dress, and in my high-heeled shoes, that were not ideal for such exertions; I thumped methodically at the interior of the fireplace, which was badly smoke-scorched brick. By this time there were ashes on my clothing. Cobwebs brushed against my face, caught in my eyelashes. My heartbeat quickened in anticipation for I believed that the secret passageway that was the *Underground Railway* had to open out of this fireplace and if I could open it, I would crawl inside . . .

"Excuse me? Are you looking for something?"

Awkwardly I turned to look up. It was the president of the college to whom I had been introduced less than an hour ago. He was a man of vigorous middle-age, very straight-backed, and he was staring frankly at me as if not knowing how he should react—with embarrassment? amusement? concern? The president's eyes were particularly striking, so dark as to appear black, and his eyelids were blinking rapidly as if to keep pace with the rapidity of his thoughts.

Had I forgotten that I was a guest of honor in his "historic" house and among these strangers?

I was not accustomed to being a *guest of honor*. Maybe that was it. Or maybe—I'd dismissed the distinction for such distinctions are like paper hats to be worn, or removed, with equal aplomb.

Sang-froid too. I've always liked the sound—*sang-froid*.

"Miss N___? I hope there is nothing wrong . . ." The president pronounced my surname carefully for it was a name that had acquired an unexpectedly somber and quasi-exalted tone in its association with *contemporary American poetry by women* not unlike the sound of a crystal glass delicately struck by a fork. If there was disapproval and incredulity in the man's deep-baritone voice, it was well disguised.

Quickly I straightened, and brushed ashes from my clothing. I assured the president that nothing was wrong. But I did not smile for the first instinct in such an awkward circumstance is to smile, apologetically or in chagrin.

Between us was a strained silence. More words were expected from V___ N___ as the honored guest at this small, distinguished liberal arts college on the Mississippi River, and as a poet of some (minor, recent) distinction, but no words were forthcoming. In his gentlemanly way the president had extended a hand to mine, to lift me to my feet, but his touch was cautious and fleeting.

"We can take you on a more extensive tour of the President's House tomorrow, if you like. D'you have an interest in border-state history? Slavery?"

"Yes. But no—I don't really need a private tour."

"It would be no trouble, Miss N____."

I should have known the president's name of course—but had forgotten it. Almost, I could not have said where I was, except for the president's remark about border-states.

Graciously the president managed to re-introduce himself, sensing that I'd forgotten his name: "Rob Flint."

Something about the name stirred hairs at the nape of my neck—*Rob Flint!*

You could see that Rob Flint was deciding to interpret his poet-guest's behavior as "eccentric"—perhaps, "charmingly eccentric." As an administrator he was also a skilled raconteur; he knew how to entertain, to make people laugh, as he knew how to manipulate and coerce when required; he would tell this story afterward, in a tone to inspire wonder in his listeners, and possibly laughter. Rob Flint was one not easily thrown off balance, quick to laugh and even, in his way, to forgive—so long as an offense was mild.

He'd been president of Garrison College for just three years. In those years, he told me, not boastfully so much as matter-of-factly, he'd led a campaign to increase the college's endowment by twenty-two million dollars; there'd been further pledges by prominent donors in the tri-state area. And then, as if impulsively, Rob Flint added, "But I've been lonely, too. This isn't my home."

He wanted me to know this. As I was a stranger in this place, and alone, Rob Flint too was something of a stranger, and did not feel at home.

"Will you come back to our dinner, Miss N___" — (pronouncing my name as if it were a privilege)—"you'll be missed." As Rob Flint led me out of the historic part of the house, and back to the dining room, he told me in his casual expansive way that he'd graduated from the University of West Virginia with a degree in engineering but soon after he'd gone to graduate school at Vanderbilt, and had a Ph.D. in economics. He had an additional degree in economics and history from Oxford—he'd been a Fulbright fellow. He'd received other fellowships, numerous grants. He'd taught at UVW, Drexel (Philadelphia), Bevell State (Nashville); he'd been a dean—a "very young dean, only twenty-nine"—a provost, and now a president. He'd been brought to Garrison College from Bevell State to succeed a president whose tenure had prevailed for seventeen years—the Garrison trustees had thought it was time for a "radical change." Rob Flint was boasting to his poet-guest in an almost boyish manner—as if making a reluctant statement of fact.

Oddly then he said, as he led me back to the party, "I'm a deer hunter who hasn't touched a rifle in years—almost twenty years." Adding, "You're a poet, you see into the heart. You understand." Gently, yes and firmly, Rob Flint touched the small of my back.

I understood: a hunter is a hunter for life.

I understood: you never give up that good feeling of knowing that you can pick up a rifle, aim it, pull the trigger and some living, breathing creature oblivious to you will die suddenly—stricken, bleeding, utterly surprised and utterly dead. *That* good feeling.

"Please. Be seated."

Rob Flint pulled out my chair at the elegant, candlelit dining room table. Eyes moved onto us, and expectant smiles. I had to suppose that in my absence there had been some mild concern about me, which my re-appearance assuaged. It was a beautiful setting—I wondered who might have been here in my place, if I were not the Caldwalder Poet-in-Residence; and, if not, where I would be at this moment.

The dinner continued, with a stiff sort of festivity. More ice water poured tinkling into goblets, more wineglasses refilled. There were briskly efficient dark-skinned servants in attendance, whose thoughts you would not want to decode. There was a sparkly crystal chandelier not unlike the chandelier in the historic part of the house, and this too was cleverly lighted by transparent flame-shaped bulbs. On the dark-silken walls were portraits of the president's predecessors at the small liberal arts college on the Mississippi River—faces indistinct but uniformly male, and gravely putty-colored. The president's wife, Elvira Flint, smiled at me with thin lips, eager and distressed. Yet the woman's eyes were not friendly, for she had seen Rob Flint escort me into the dining room, and she'd perceived something in the hunter's face no one else might have perceived.

It was expected of me that I would behave strangely—in the tradition of Emily Dickinson, I was a *half-crack'd Poetess*. Already I'd fulfilled the expectations of the company, and was humbled by my own performance. (In my hair was a thread of cobweb—graciously Mrs. Caldwalder detached it for me, without a word.) Conversation turned to poetry as it often did in my presence, in such circumstances, with forced gusto, for Poetry is the secret vice of those who never read it but harbor faint nostalgic memories of having read it long ago, or having had it read to them as children.

It was not surprising that a wealthy widow like Mrs. Caldwalder might endow a million dollars to a small college like Garrison, in the service of Poetry. Other arts might make their own halting ways, but Poetry must be given an enormous artificial boost.

And so to entertain and to impress and because I so yearned for an interruption of our desultory dinner table conversation I recited, with something of an improvised Irish lilt, Yeats's "The Wild Swans at Coole"—shutting my eyes to remember the beautifully honed stanzas more clearly, and to suggest a suppression of tears.

At the end of the evening, elderly Mrs. Caldwalder clasped my hand in both her hands, frail-boned as sparrows. Mrs. Caldwalder could not have been more than four feet eleven inches tall and wore bravely high-heeled shoes to bring up her height an inch at least. Tearfully she told me that that very poem of Yeats had been a poem her husband, deceased since 1981, had recited to her soon after they'd met in Lycoming, West Virginia, in 1946. We clasped hands for a brief tremulous moment.

IT WAS AN ERA WHEN MOST NEWS CAME BY PHONE.

Good news, bad news.

News to make you fibrillate with joy, news to crush you to the floor where you quasi-wake minutes later dazed and deboned and your underwear wetted.

By phone also meant *land phone*. Or, a more comforting term, *home phone.*

Cell phone can be defined as a mode of instant (if not universally reliable) communication between unicellular life-forms. I was in fact in possession of a *cell phone* at this time, in an early year of the twenty-first century, for I liked to think of myself as drifting somewhat ahead of the curve, but it was my *home phone* I picked up to receive what I would later classify as the first, innocent-seeming installment of a series of very bad news.

No. I am not that sick. You're busy, you have your own life, your responsibilities. Don't be ridiculous!

He'd been bemused at the prospect of my coming to visit him when (he knew) I had *responsibilities.* But it was a phase of his life when bemusement shifted abruptly to irritation, anger, even fury—*I said, don't be ridiculous!*

Then again, more reasonably—*There's plenty of time. I'm fine—for now. "Stabilized." You can't interrupt your professional life—your obligations. You can't let people down. A woman is no less responsible than a man.*

He'd paused, to let me absorb these words. He'd been the parent who had encouraged my determination to be a poet—at any rate, to live the precarious and uncharted life of a poet.

When you're through with the—what's it—"residency"—drop by here. I'll be here.

He'd laughed, obscurely. His voice was just loud enough to be comforting.

Several times I'd spoken with my brother, whose news was terse and guarded. Possibly he, too, had been having difficulty communicating with our father. He'd given me the hospice number to call but cautioned me not to upset our father by calling—at least, not frequently. "Hospice? But that means—" Weakly my voice trailed off.

My brother was evasive and impatient. We had never been close—he was older than I was by seven crucial years, and had never taken me seriously; now that I had accumulated, by slow degrees, something like a *reputation,* he seemed resentful of me, and had made it clear that he'd never read more than a few poems of mine, and had found them incomprehensible.

When I called my father he hadn't wanted to discuss his illness—
"That's personal, honey." He'd laughed irritably as if to acknowledge
that, in this phase of his life, nothing could be *personal* again and he
knew it. He seemed mildly insulted that I was concerned for his well-
being, as if I were an intrusive stranger and not his only daughter. To
my questions he answered with a vague sort of careless good humor
like one swatting away flies.

I could not speak with my mother—I'd never been able to speak
with my mother about serious matters. She had reacted with childish
terror at my father's illness, withdrawing ever more deeply into her
lifelong self-absorption in which all things related to *her*.

But I did speak with one of the hospice nurses who assured me
that yes, my father seemed to be "stabilized" for the time being—such
remissions sometimes occurred even in hospice. She told me that my
father was "one of our favorites" and that the hospice had a backyard
barbecue and picnic area for families who came to visit patients.

A backyard barbecue and picnic area! I had no idea what to say.

The nurse asked me when I might come to visit my father and I
told her two weeks. "That's when Dad wants me."

There was a beat. The nurse seemed to be pondering a reply.

"Well—yes. Two weeks is—good. But if you could come a little
earlier, that might be—a better idea."

Two weeks, I told her. My father insisted.

"You know how my father is by now—stubborn as hell."

It was a buoyant thing to say—*stubborn as hell*. You would not say
stubborn as hell about a mortally ill man.

The nurse, who sounded middle-aged and tired, not so upbeat as
she'd seemed at the start of the conversation, said, "Yes, I know—a
little—how your father is."

I waited for the nurse to say something more, but that was all she
said.

❀

DURING MY TWO-WEEK RESIDENCY AT GARRISON COLLEGE, ROB Flint and I met a number of times in private, and in secret. These were not easily arranged meetings. For an academic administrator is a very busy man, with a schedule deftly constructed as a cat's cradle; an administrator is likely to be closely watched by subordinates, most of whom are female. He is also likely to be observed by individuals eager to take up his time in the hope of influencing him on their behalf. Yet, Rob Flint took time to pick me up in his car, at the Bickerdyck Inn in which I was staying, in the late afternoon, when my responsibilities at the college were usually over for the day. (The Bickerdyck was an "historic" inn of faded luxury to which I'd insisted upon moving after two days in the antique-crowded Alumni House in which the college had installed me. It was explained to me that the Caldwalder Residency included room and board on campus, but not elsewhere, yet I insisted upon being moved to the hotel downtown, and I did not offer to pay for the hotel; I assumed that I would be billed, but I would not volunteer.) As Rob Flint drove us along the river and into the hilly countryside in his burgundy-colored Mercedes he talked to me in an impassioned voice—of himself, of course; Rob Flint had no other subject that so enthralled him—and I listened enthralled as well, or seemed to listen; thinking *So this is where I am, now! And with this stranger.*

I thought *If not here, where?* A sensation of cold swept over me, at the prospect of being elsewhere.

For where I should be, I'd been forbidden.

From where I badly needed to be, my father had banished me.

And so there was nowhere, except here. With this strangely elated, urgently eloquent stranger who dared to squeeze my hand as if we were already intimate—as if there wasn't the slightest possibility that his masculine aggressiveness might be repulsed.

"So happy that you're here! Such *serendity*."

This word, Rob Flint mispronounced in a way that made me smile, with tenderness.

There was no man in my life at this time—there had been no man in my life for some time. Enforced celibacy brings with it a kind of sardonic stoicism—as an individual with a limp might limp more emphatically, to forestall pity in observers.

In Rob Flint's lightest touch there was a sexual charge. In Rob Flint's brooding gaze, a predatory air.

I'd wondered, at the formal dinner, if anyone else was aware of Rob Flint staring at me so openly, even as he led the conversation, lightly and entertainingly. In the back of the house, when he'd gripped my hand to help me rise from the fireplace, I'd felt the imprint of his strong fingers, and had tried not to wince; for Rob Flint was a man who could not help himself, shaking hands, gripping hands, inflicting a sort of innocent hurt upon others. I thought that only the object of the man's sexual interest would be aware of it—for Rob Flint was discreet, by instinct. Yet the wife couldn't escape feeling the diminution of such a husband's desire, like a white-hot and blinding light suddenly switched off. I didn't take pleasure in the humiliation of the wife, or anyway not much pleasure. I did think—*She knows what he is, but in secret. She is too proud to acknowledge what she knows.*

On a bluff overlooking the river, Rob Flint parked the stately Mercedes. Out of the glove compartment he took a silver flask—(*Could this really be happening?* a scandalized voice wondered, close in my ear as a gnat)—and offered me a drink, a small sip—"Please, just a taste at least."

It had to be very good, very expensive Kentucky whiskey, I knew. Nothing but the best for Rob Flint who would not have wanted to drink alone.

Rob Flint reiterated much of what he'd told me on our first evening, now adding details, and at length. He laughed at my "witty" commentary on the Mississippi River—how strange it seemed to a visitor that people actually lived on the banks of the Mississippi, lived close beside it, the great mythic river; over this river they drove routinely and with no particular attentiveness on bridges of no distinction; they spoke of the river as, merely, *the river*—as if unaware of its mythic status.

"Nothing is 'mythic,' close up. Nothing is 'mythic' where you live."

Rob Flint spoke wistfully. On our return to town driving with his left hand, knuckles big-boned and covered in coppery hairs, while with his right hand, his stronger hand, he held my hand, and exerted a bruising pressure, unaware.

To this remark, I made no reply. In Rob Flint's company I was mostly silent, a vessel into which the man spoke as one might speak—freely, with no risk of being judged—when he was alone.

"Though I'd guess that, if we could come back from the dead, to see where we'd lived—we would see that it had been 'mythic' then. Too late!"

But Rob Flint laughed, to show that, for him, nothing would ever come *too late*.

LATER, ROB FLINT said that he'd "loved" me—from the first moment he'd seen my photograph, on the dust jacket of one of my books. This had been nine or ten years ago, at least. And so when he'd learned that the Caldwalder residency was being discussed he'd suggested my name, and the committee had invited me—"Unanimously."

Rob Flint smiled, to suggest that *unanimously* might not have been the complete story. But it would do, for this was Rob Flint's story.

"Thank you! I'm very grateful."

Though rapidly my mind worked: the committee had not wanted *me*, but had deferred to the president's suggestion. Very likely, the president had coerced the faculty members into inviting me as an exercise of presidential will.

They would have preferred someone older, more distinguished. A male poet, burdened with the most prestigious awards, who'd have sneered at their invitation; or, if he'd accepted, would have fulfilled his obligations minimally, and gazed over the heads of the young poets he was obliged to teach.

I was embarrassed, to be told this. But I was grateful for having been told in such a way that my embarrassment wouldn't be noticed.

"And I'm grateful, too, Violet. That we've met at last. That this— between us—has begun."

THE BICKERDYCK INN had once been an opulent place. Here I felt comfortably entombed.

Carved mahogany paneling shone in the dim light and on the walls of the downstairs, public rooms were faded murals of heroic military scenes of the Civil War. There may have been scenes of slaughter involving horses—I did not allow myself to look too closely.

There were three elaborately brass-grated elevators of which only one was operating but I seemed never to guess which elevator this might be.

In my suite on the eleventh floor were faded velvet drapes on all the windows that, operated with a power switch, sprang to life and opened with startling vigor. Outside were sky, clouds, a gleaming river below and in the waning sun the river glowed red like something molten. Freighters made their way like great amphibians of a long-ago time.

The windows were not very clean but they were floor-to-ceiling along an entire wall, plate-glass and impossible to open. I took a strange sort of solace in the fact that the cloud-formations above the river, like brain-masses of varying degrees of texture and color, beautifully eerie, hypnotic, were not part of the early-evening sky my father might be gazing at from a hospice window one thousand miles to the east.

Several times, I placed a call to the hospice. Each time, I fumbled my message saying there was *no urgent need* to return my call.

By 9:30 P.M. the downtown of the old riverfront city had darkened. Traffic had dwindled to isolated vehicles and there were few pedestrians. Except for the Bickerdyck Inn and several neon-lighted taverns on adjacent streets, the area was desolate. Within a quarter-mile of the dour granite county courthouse were blocks of once-stately granite office-buildings now FOR SALE OR LEASE. Many storefronts were empty. An Art Deco movie theater on Main Street had been converted to a discount furniture store and its exclamatory bargains posted on the marquee. How lonely, a dying city! Yet there was something thrilling about such emptiness, that spoke to the emptiness in my soul. I thought—*If my father is dying, it is life itself that is the betrayal. I hate life!* This was an exhilarating thought for it seemed to me an irrefutable truth and all truth makes us free—pushes us, however horribly, to Truth. From the windows of my suite in the historic inn I watched individual figures on the sidewalks eleven floors below, I observed vehicles slowing to red lights at deserted intersections. Though there was no other visible traffic, yet each vehicle remained at each red light until it turned green. One night, near midnight, I observed a gathering of men on the street outside one of the taverns and wondered what bond defined them—vehement male voices lifting faintly. I had the idea that the men were planning a desperate and irrevocable act but soon afterward they broke off their excited exchange, walked away and disappeared from one another and from me.

If you are a fatalist, you understand that someone has to be observing these men at this time, and from this perch on the eleventh floor of the Bickerdyck Inn. It is futile to inquire *Why?—Why me?*

One night at about 11:00 P.M., after Rob Flint had left me, I rinsed the hotel glasses in which we'd drunk whiskey—(which Rob Flint had brought to the room)—and washed my face that had become heated and blotched. I rinsed my mouth, that had acquired a sourish taste,

and pressed a washcloth soaked in cold water against my slightly swollen lips. Too restless even to attempt sleep I descended in the slow-
paced hotel elevator, crossed the deserted lobby where my heels rang
against the marble floor, made my way along darkened and deserted
Main Street in the direction of the river. There were few vehicles here,
and no one visible on foot except me; in doorways, homeless men hud-
dled, as if comatose, but would not glance up at me, or speak to me.
The taverns were minimally lighted, like caves; from the street, you
could scarcely tell if a tavern was open. And beyond the dim-lighted
area was the great dark river.

   This has begun. This—between us . . . Rob Flint's words replayed in
my head, like a stuck record.

   Whether the words were ominous, or thrilling, I did not know.

   That morning as usual I'd risen early to walk along the river. At
10:00 A.M. I was to be driven to the college where for most of the day
I would deftly impersonate the *Caldwalder Poet-in-Residence.* (One of
the English faculty picked me up, not Rob Flint. Each morning there
was a different individual in a different vehicle, and each seemed eager
to speak with me.) Private time was precious to me and so quickly
each morning I made my way along Main Street—to South Main
Street—to the river's abrupt edge—a desolate stretch of parkland
adjacent to a railroad yard. And there, at the end of the railroad yard,
was an asphalt road badly cracked, with a look of being superannuated,
replaced by an elevated interstate highway on which traffic whirred
and thrummed overhead; on this road, I began tentatively to run. The
river-air was chilly as the sun rose by slow degrees in the eastern sky.
I had no idea what the longitude was here, what the latitude was here,
or why I was here. I smiled to think how the most elemental truths
struck me as profound and unsettling—that, if one were *alive,* one
must be *somewhere* and not rather *nowhere.*

   It did not seem possible to me that, one day soon, my father
would be *nowhere.* That's to say—I could search for my father every-

where, through all of the world, and yet I would not have been able to find him.

For this dying, too, had *begun*. And once *begun* it would run its course.

Yet, knowing this beforehand, I was powerless to see my father. I could not risk his wrath. I could not risk the loss of his love. I could not disobey my father, for I was not strong enough.

And also, the most pitiless truth was, in my deepest self *I did not want to see my father.*

I did not want to see the wounded, diminished, frightened man. I did not want to see his eyes, that would clutch at mine in denial of what was gathering in a corner of his room, what darkness and density of darkness. I did not want to be inveigled into a childlike pretense between us that my father was "all right"—his condition "stabilized." I did not want to approach my dying father.

As no one would wish to approach Rob Flint in some future, terrible time—the once-handsome, once-vigorous, once-so-commanding and so masculine a man weakened and frail, emaciated and fading; the voice once so charismatic in self-enthrallment, faint and failing.

But that was a future time, you could say a time of reckoning. At that time, there was no likelihood that I would be in Rob Flint's life, nor even a name, a face, an intimate gesture, in Rob Flint's faltering memory.

Unless—(this was madness, I knew!—the madness of a certain sort of poetry, not currently in style)—I would be Rob Flint's wife, and widow.

There'd come a confused fragrance of blossoming fruit trees and honeysuckle, muddy river-water, a faint stench of chemicals. Some miles downriver were factories not visible from where I walked. Here in the derelict riverfront park were plaques, monuments to Civil War officers, steamboat captains, pioneers. A monument to Senator Stephen A. Douglas, who'd campaigned against Abraham Lincoln for the presidency, and lost. It is natural for men to erect statues of their kind, to commemorate what is meaningful in life, yet little of the outer, public life bears any actual meaning to individuals, who dwell inwardly, intimately with a very few others. At such times it came over me like a sweep of muddy water—the career-life was of virtually no significance, without the inner, intimate life. What madness, to have wished to live through poetry, like a swimmer who clutches at a frail limb, to keep from drowning! Yet, I'd given up much, in this effort. I would give up more.

Unless indeed, I would become Rob Flint's (second?) wife.

Rob Flint was in his late fifties, perhaps. His wife was surely his age, but looked older. *Replacing the superannuated wife. There is a small thrill to this, in proportion to the achievement. But it is a thrill.*

I could envision: a provincial life with this man, not here perhaps, for the scandal of divorce and hasty remarriage would make Garrison College impossible, but at another small college of no particular academic or historic distinction, in another fading American town. Disappearing into such a life, as one might disappear into faded wallpaper. Of course—I would *continue to write poetry*. In the interstices of life.

At that hour of the morning there'd been virtually no one in the river-park. Storm debris lay scattered on the ground—at the college, I'd been told that tornados routinely whipped through this part of the state. There were rotted trees, gutted tree trunks. Overhead on the interstate were diesel trucks and buses emitting black exhaust and on the inside of the overpass, graffiti-defaced walls. Since high school I'd been a runner and during times of distress there was no happiness for me other than running for in running you are alone in the most elemental and uncomplicated of ways.

At such times I felt like a long-legged girl. Not a woman in the thirty-ninth year of her life, with no idea what her fortieth year might bring. I yearned to run and to feel a mad strength course through my legs, until my sides clenched with pain, and my breath came short. *Run, run! There is no escape otherwise.*

But each morning, after a carefully calculated thirty minutes, I had to turn back. As if a leash were fastened about my neck, jerking me to a halt. Turn, and return along the same embankment path. For the car from the college would be coming for me promptly at 10:00 A.M. For I was a responsible person, as my father understood. I would surrender a final visit with my dying father out of a wish not to violate the expectations of strangers. *A woman is as responsible as a man—a woman must forgo the personal life, in the way that men have always done.*

At night, however, though I was as restless as I'd been in the early morning, and with more of a sense of desperation, I dared not walk far from the Bickerdyck Inn. The river seemed ominous by moonlight, threatening. The crude beauty of the river by day was transformed into something very different by night—the "water" appeared living and sinuous, like a vast swarm of snakes. To cross one of the bridges—to feel the spell of the dark, rushing water beneath—I did not dare.

And there were homeless men, in the area. I'd seen their melancholy camp sites beneath overpasses, by day.

At the first of the taverns, the River House, I entered a smoky interior like a cellar. There came a blast of music, a smell of beer, cigarette smoke. In my excitement my vision dimmed: I could see figures but no clear faces. With a mild stab of alarm I saw—thought I saw—Rob Flint at the bar, gazing at me with a look of startled interest.

And other men, lone men. Turning to look at me, too.

I thought—*They are hoping to recognize me. But I am no one they know.*

Boldly, unless it was recklessly, I went to the bar. Space was made for me, like a parting of waters.

I settled myself upon a wobbly stool. I ordered a drink—gin, ice.

At the hotel, Rob Flint had urged whiskey upon me. I had the idea that Rob Flint did not travel far without a flask or a bottle of good Kentucky whiskey at his fingertips like one of those emphysema-sufferers whom you see, in public places, wheeling oxygen tanks with them. But I'd only taken a sip or two out of the hotel glass, to placate him.

Now, sobriety seemed an awkward choice. Like virginity, outgrown.

I heard myself order the drink in a quiet voice. No one but the bartender—staring just short of rude—could hear me.

"Yes, ma'am."

This was the first time in my life I would order such a drink in such a place, as it would be the last. My voice was soft and melodic with a faint Irish lilt. Clearly my voice betrayed its outsider origins. The bartender's eyes fastened on me like burrs and in a brisk bemused voice he said a second time as he set the drink down before me, "Yes, ma'am." A slight emphasis on *ma'am*, as in the punch line of a joke.

There may have been other women in the River House at this time. In booths at the rear. Yet I had the impression of having made some sort of blunder. As a single woman I often stepped into places, into circumstances, in which, one could surmise, a "woman" had not been expected, yet was not forbidden—a sort of social error, yet not a fatal error. So I felt in the River House, drinking my solitary drink. I was awkwardly out of place but had not committed any outrage for which I would need to be punished by being raped, mutilated or strangled. Of course I understood that no one from Garrison College would have patronized the River House, and so no one would recognize the *Caldwalder Poet-in-Residence*.

Probably it had been inferred, I was "someone from the college." I'd gathered from remarks made to me in the hotel that the college on its several hills north of the city was both admired and resented for few local students were admitted to Garrison College.

The man at the bar who'd seemed to resemble Rob Flint was not

Rob Flint of course. He was younger, less carefully dressed. His eyes on me were frankly curious rather than admiring as Rob Flint's eyes were admiring. I ignored him in a way that didn't feel rude (to me at least). I sipped at the gin-and-water, that did not feel comforting but faintly mocking. My tongue had begun to feel numb. The fingers of my right hand were numb. I thought—*Am I having a stroke? Is that what it is—to "have" a stroke?* I thought it was curious usage, a way of blocking the thought that one doesn't *have a stroke* but *suffers a stroke* as one would suffer a sharp blade piercing one's flesh. I wondered if my father would "have" a stroke—the elderly ailing are sometimes so struck—and disappear from us. It was an abstract wonder that carried with it a particular daughterly terror and yet it did not interfere with my essential happiness seated on the wobbly stool at the River House. My poet's brain was heightened though (I would not have wished to confess) I had not even attempted poetry in weeks. In weeks, I had not been capable of thinking coherently. I seemed not to be thinking language-thoughts at all. Such relief, that no one knew me here in the River House! V__ M__ was anonymous, and to most eyes she was invisible.

Rock music was playing loudly from some unknown source—rock music of a long-ago era. It was belligerently loud, with a pounding and elemental beat, a primitive music for primitive adolescents. We'd all been so young then. Some of us had not grown beyond that age. Like the eyeball of a fetal twin absorbed in the mother's womb before birth, preserved in the fatty tissue beneath the heart, or in the bowels, or in the brain. All our former selves remain inside us, embryonic. I wondered what would remain of my father, in me—what faint, fading DNA coursing through my body.

When I left the River House after twenty minutes, no one seemed to take note—unless to think *That desperate woman! Has to be from the college.*

Next morning, Rob Flint called me at the hotel.

"I'm concerned about you, Violet. I think you might be putting yourself at risk."

NEAR THE INTERSTATE OVERPASS, beside the wide choppy river. In a derelict no-man's-land of stunted trees, wild honeysuckle and grasses and thistles, scattered debris. And amid that debris, just beneath the overpass, a homeless man who might have been any age between forty-five and sixty-five, metallic-colored matted hair to his shoulders, broken teeth in a glistening canine smile. He'd set a small smoldering fire at the center of his camp, that smelled of garbage. His possessions were rolled into bundles and crammed into a rusted grocery cart. His clothing was filthy, yet colorful—tight-fitting dark-red jacket, brightly green tie, pajama-like sweatpants with yellow and gray stripes, on his knobby feet knitted patterned socks. His battered quasi-leather boots were placed side by side, left-foot/right-foot, before him on the blanket on which he sat. Also on the blanket were books, numerous books, hardcover and paperback, which looked water-stained and warped . . . I could see just one title—
When Worlds Collide. *A few yards away from the man who stared and squinted at me I stood staring in return, hesitant to speak. The man murmured something that sounded like* Hello! G'morning! *His words were slurred and buoyant. His accent was Southern. His swollen eyelids blinked slowly. His tongue swiped at his lips, that appeared swollen and cracked, blackened at the corners as if he'd been eating something black as tar. In a faint friendly voice I said* Hel-lo! *I was panting and sweaty from having run too fast, and too far. Again the homeless man greeted me and added what sounded like,* Have you come for me? Who are you?—*but these words too were very slurred. On hands and knees he began to crawl toward me—I wondered if he were crippled. He appeared to be moaning, grunting. In amazement I stared at him and could not move away. Foolishly paralyzed in my light-woolen black slacks and gossamer-knit jacket that were hardly appropriate for running, black crepe-soled "walking shoes" inadequate for serious running, the arches of my feet aching.*

Barely I managed to say to the homeless man Excuse me—I'm sorry to interrupt you, I—I am no one you know . . . *With a grunt the man heaved himself to his feet before me, to his full height; almost, I wanted to help him, but dared not come so near. He swayed on his feet, one of his legs appeared shorter than the other. In an uplifted apocalyptic voice he spoke rapidly to me—smiling gat-toothed—grimacing—bloodshot-eyed and a cast in one blind-looking eye—arguing something to me, a rush of words I could not decipher except to understand that there was considerable emotion to it—a grievance?—indignation? Or was he claiming that he did know me, after all? In my strange paralysis I could not seem to move. My legs felt leaden, as if I'd been running for hours and not merely minutes. Before I could step back in alarm, the homeless man grabbed my arm at the elbow, and gave me a shake as he accused me of— what?—something unspeakable, I knew. His expression was contorted as in a terrible orgasm. The bloodshot eyes shone with fury. For now it seemed that the man with the badly matted shoulder-length metallic hair recognized me—had been waiting for me—was berating me for having taken so long to get to him . . . In both hands he seized my shoulders and brought his boiling-hot face to my face, his scummy mouth to my mouth, a fetid breath, stooping he pressed his mouth hard against mine, and caught my upper lip between his teeth, and bit, and bit—such pain!—I screamed and struck at him in terror he would bite through my lip, like an animal . . .*

Then, he released me. With crude elated laughter he released me—I had been powerless to free myself—always I would remember this: I had been powerless to free myself. My lip was bleeding profusely but I felt no pain. In terror and in humiliation I turned—tried to run—not as a practiced runner runs but as a panicked woman runs—a woman no longer young, and the muscles of her legs no longer springy, elastic. In terror and in humiliation and in utter surprise I was running from my assailant in this unknown place that smelled of smoldering garbage, my hand against my bleeding mouth, my badly bleeding mouth. Whimpering with pain

and shock, running clumsily from the graffiti-defaced overpass and into
the suddenly hot sun, and the mud-colored river close beside me whose
exotic name I had forgotten.

"MISS N ___? What has happened to your mouth?"

Calmly I explained: a fall, on concrete steps. Nothing serious.

They stared at me, aghast. *He* stared at me.

"Have you seen a doctor? Maybe you should have stitches . . ."

It was nothing serious! I didn't need stitches. I was sure.

I smiled, to show that the (disfiguring) upper-lip wound didn't
hurt.

Or, if it hurt, didn't *seriously hurt.*

"Maybe—a tetanus shot?"

But I didn't care to discuss the wound. It was an entirely superfi-
cial, temporary wound. Thank you!

This was painful to me, or rather to my pride: of the fondly eccentric memories they would have of V___ N___, *Caldwalder Poet-in-*
Residence, this stupid little mouth-wound would be foremost.

AND DID V ___ N ___ discharge her duties as *Caldwalder Poet-in-*
Residence, indeed yes she did.

And did V___ N___ inspire in others an avidity for poetry and
a patience in the craftsmanship of poetry sadly missing in herself,
indeed yes she did.

Leaning over earnest young poets' manuscripts with them and
encouraging them to read their work aloud—"The test of poetry isn't
in the eye but in the ear. Trust the ear."

And, "Whatever your 'true subject' is, it can bide its time. What
you're doing now is apprentice work. Don't judge yourself harshly. Be
patient. Time is on your side—ten, twelve years. Twenty years. Poetry
is timeless, you'll always be young when you return to poetry. Write
every day—the way you dream every night."

And, "Poetry is what frightens. It is rare, and worth waiting for. But in the meantime, a lesser poetry can be your companion. You should not ever scorn companionship."

The young poets seemed grateful for such advice. They seemed grateful to be taken seriously. It is preferable to be scorned than to be humored but most valuable to be taken seriously, which is something V___ N___ could provide.

Strange that it was not so very difficult for me to discharge my responsibilities as the *Caldwalder Poet-in-Residence*. Far easier than to discharge my responsibilities as a daughter.

Several times, it was arranged that V___ N___ join a gathering of poets and writers—"creative writing students"—at luncheons catered by the College. At the head of the table V___ N___ was seated, appropriately for V___ N___ was the adult among gifted young people with shrewd eyes and questions to ask. The luncheon atmosphere was gravely festive, with intermittent nervous laughter and among this laughter, my own.

Not a wild or a shrill laughter, I think. A sound as of a startled creature that finds itself released and in the same instant is re-captured, as a cage door slams shut.

My wounded upper lip had begun to throb. Cleverly I pressed an ice-water glass against it, to numb the pain. The more I addressed the students (who listened to me with a flattering sort of attentiveness), the less actual pain I felt; when I quoted lines of poetry, or recited entire poems, the pain diminished. *This world is not conclusion. / A Species stands beyond— / Invisible, as Music— / But positive, as Sound—*

Such happiness in my voice at such times—such *certainty*.

In my life, *uncertainty*. But in poetry, *certainty*.

There seemed to be a kind of hunger in the young writers for someone with whom they could speak openly. I gave them reading lists, patiently I read their work and wrote detailed commentary. *This is what I am doing, because this is where I am.* I felt elated, though very tired. At the end of a typical day at the college my throat was dry from the effort of protracted and enthusiastic speech and my hand ached from writing comments on manuscripts. My head buzzed with words like drunken, elated bees.

There were hours that moved slowly, like wagon wheels mired in mud. Yet the days of the two-week residency moved with stunning swiftness. I thought—*I am safe so long as I am here.* The future was a blur, like a mirror that has faded with time.

A call came from the president's office: "Well! They love you, it seems. Our 'Caldwalder Poet-in-Residence.'"

And: "They say they've never met anyone like V___ N___ —a person who is 'known' taking time with them. They say you are so *kind*."

Rob Flint spoke with great satisfaction. I told him I hoped that some of this might be true, at least.

Sharply then Rob Flint said, "If I say this is so, it's so. I don't exaggerate. And I don't humor—anyone."

The man's tone was a rebuke. Stung, I broke the connection.

Mostly I felt relief that my secret, sick self had not been found out. I felt a childish and perverse pride that the poet's public self appeared so *radiant*.

That night, Rob Flint came to see me another time. He had suggested that we not see each other for a while—a day, two days—he had family obligations and was very busy with office work—yet at 11:08 P.M. he appeared breathless and eager at the door to my suite in the Bickerdyck Inn. And he brought with him, in a discreet paper bag, a bottle of Kentucky whiskey. His handsome face was ruddy with emotion.

"Are you taking notes? Are you writing about us? If you write about me," Rob Flint said lavishly, "—you'll disguise me, of course? I've seen your poetry, dear Violet, and I know it's discreet."

"It's impersonal, therefore seems discreet."

"It's very powerful, and it seems personal, because of that power. But it is discreet. You have an uncommonly pure soul, my dear."

Rob Flint talked like that, yes. A successful administrator is one for whom the airy inflations and enhancements of speech come readily. And so, I would find myself responding in a similar way telling him that there was something unexpected in my life here—in this place—"and the Mississippi River"—"and having met *you*." My voice trailed off, in the way of a sleepwalker who has walked out of sleep and into a dazzling daylight. I had approached but had not dared to utter the name *Rob*. But my eyes shone with tears of conviction and the little wound in my upper lip throbbed like a livid vein.

Rob Flint kissed me, in a precise way to avoid the little wound. I staggered a little with the pressure of the man's kiss, that felt like a strong shove with the palm of a hand; and a quick prodding tongue, that would not have tolerated resistance. I thought—*He is repelled by the disfigurement. He doesn't know this yet.*

Like my new friends at the college Rob Flint had expressed some concern about the wound, which had acquired a black zipper of a scab, and was still slightly swollen. I assured him that the wound was healing, and that it did not hurt. Rob Flint asked if I'd seen a doctor to make sure there was no infection and vaguely I said yes I had, I'd seen a doctor, and there was no infection.

"You're a stubborn person, Violet, aren't you! I suppose that's what makes you a poet and not, like the rest of us, a person of *prose*."

This remark was startling, and made me laugh. But I sensed some resentment in the words, and understood that, in a clash of wills, the president must always win.

Rob Flint was an abrupt and crushing lover. There was something exuberantly impersonal in his lovemaking—his desire was like an avalanche, unstoppable. Even his curiously formal speech was a prelude to lovemaking that rushed like a flood, breathtaking, near-suffocating; such lovemaking did not require more than minimal cooperation on the part of the woman, who needed only not resist. And Rob Flint was the quintessential *hunter*—teeth damp and gleaming in pursuit, skin exuding a fever-heat. The pleasure in his exertions was explosive, to him; you could feel the shock of sexual release coursing through his body like a bolt of electricity. But he would say nothing, he would emit no sound. His face twisted in an effort of stoic silence.

And then he would say, later—"And you, Violet? Are you happy, Violet?"

This question was posed with some anxiety. And so of course I said *Yes!*

I did not ask Rob Flint personal questions. I understood that Rob Flint would tell me all that he wanted me to know—beyond this, any curiosity on V___ N___'s part would be intrusive. I knew that Rob Flint preferred to drive his own car but that the college owned a black Lincoln Town Car manned by a driver in which he was taken frequently to the airport and to civil occasions; on presidential missions to meet with trustees, alumni, donors, politicians, bankers. I knew that Rob Flint had a family—children now fully adult and moved away; the age of his adult children would be a source of (minor, chronic) anxiety to Rob Flint, whose conception of himself was exclusively masculine.

I knew that his wife was deeply unhappy, as she had to be a very lonely woman. To have been, even temporarily, the object of so ardent and fixed a sexual gaze would be to know immediately when that gaze shifts elsewhere. Yet I understood that his wife loved Rob Flint unstintingly. Such blindness, such desperation—the very essence of a certain kind of wifely love.

Rob Flint returned to the subject of having "discovered" me—the early book of poems, the dust jacket photo. "You were wearing your hair in a single, long braid. You were gazing into the camera, without a smile. This had to be fifteen years ago at least—I was in a Barnes & Noble store in Philadelphia. I'd thought—I am going to meet this woman—this 'poet.' And I will meet her on my own terms, when I am ready to meet her."

How proud Rob Flint was of himself! For here was the hunter's elation at the outcome of the hunt.

I'd never worn my hair in a "single, long braid." Rob Flint had not said he'd bought my book in the Barnes & Noble.

I wondered if the conflict between the president and the Caldwalder committee had been more heated than I'd been led to believe. I felt the floor shift beneath me, that V___ N___ hadn't been wanted at all. Rob Flint gloating to a subordinate how he'd succeeded in *thrusting V__ N__ down the committee's throats.*

Rob Flint laughed now, as if recalling exactly this.

Later, as we lay together unclothed in the ridiculously large "king-sized bed" beneath a fringed four-posted canopy and an ivory satin coverlet Rob Flint said that he hoped I would not write "too overtly" about him, or the College—for already he'd come close to "creating scandal" at Garrison, having had policy disagreements with his board of trustees. "Trustees think, since they've hired you, that you are *in their hire.* But they are mistaken."

I said, "You're a man of integrity. They hired you for that."

Rob Flint said, "Yes. You are right—'a man of integrity.' But when 'integrity' conflicts with personal interest, it's 'integrity' that is expected to compromise."

As if to seal this remark, Rob Flint kissed me. My arms around his heavy shoulders tightened, and I thought—*These are the things people say to each other, in this bed.*

Later, Rob Flint said, now in a rueful voice, "My marriage—it isn't what people think."

I did not ask—*What do people think?*

"It isn't what it seems. Even in the eyes of our family—our children."

I wondered if I was being prompted to ask—*But what does your marriage seem?*

I could not recall Elvira Flint—a kind of smiling ectoplasm hovered in her place. I felt rather than saw the woman's covert, wistful expression when Rob Flint ushered me into the dining room in triumph, hand light against the small of my back.

Like a hunter, Rob Flint had rituals. As a lover, he fell into a pattern of memorized behavior. A way of lovemaking, and a way of postlovemaking. I would become in his arms the absent wife. He said now, "I can't believe you'll be leaving so soon, Violet. We will see each other again, won't we? I want to see you again."

Tentatively I said, "I would like to see you again."

We were making statements, vows. You might have thought that we were speaking before witnesses.

As I was rarely hungry until I began to eat, and then became ravenously hungry, so I'd had little feeling about Rob Flint until I uttered these words. Then, I felt a sharp pang, as of loss. And the little wound in my upper lip throbbed with renewed pain.

Only now, I understood. I'd come to the old riverfront town on the Mississippi to fall in love with a man named Rob Flint who was the president of the local college, and a lifetime hunter. As my father was dying back in the East, so I was coming into my own life, as a woman, in the Midwest. This was the story: the (poet's) (secret) biography.

At the door Rob Flint kissed me in a way to avoid the wound in my upper lip. Remembering then the bottle of whiskey, and returning to the living room to take it with him. And in his ruddy face that look of relief, elation, guilt, satisfaction of a man who has been released from one woman but is not yet within the gravitational pull of the other woman.

"Violet, good night! I will see you tomorrow."

THAT NIGHT, though it was very late I called my brother and left a message on his answering service.

I called the hospice, and left a similar message.

By 10:00 A.M. the next morning no one had called me back. I

left for the college feeling like a condemned prisoner who has been reprieved for another day at least.

THERE WAS A FAREWELL LUNCHEON for the *Caldwalder Poet-in-Residence*. Most of the guests were students, and a few of the guests were professors and instructors. It seemed that the students had "learned" from me. It was touching how, one by one, they lifted their glasses of cola, iced tea, sparkling water and ice water to honor V___ N___. The name (which had, for some reason, embarrassed me as a schoolgirl, though it was a quite ordinary quasi-"ethnic" name) pronounced with such ceremony! A straw-haired girl with whom I'd seemingly become close, whose prose-poetry I had praised, became emotional and could not speak . . . And a (gay?) boy, the most gifted of the Garrison undergraduates, who'd been a favorite of mine, wiped at his eyes . . . I was touched; I was astonished; I was grateful; I was humble; I was disbelieving . . . As they took pictures of me with their cell phones, some of them posing beside me, I did not protest

But—your admiration is misplaced! I am not writing poetry now—I am not a poet any longer. I am a hypocrite and a liar and I am not a good person but despicable and you should despise me for I have hidden away here on the farther bank of the Mississippi River while in the East my father is dying. As I'd been too cowardly to call the hospice that morning before leaving for the college, so I was too cowardly now to utter these words.

I might have wept, but I did not weep. My (wounded, throbbing) mouth trembled. Witnesses would say that V___ N___ whose reputation was that of an "aloof" and "carefully calibrated" poet was revealed as a vulnerable and sentimental woman, with a mysteriously swollen mouth and anxious eyes. In a faltering voice I was trying to say how much I'd learned from my students at Garrison College, that instruction is not "one-way"; how, at this particular, difficult time in my life,

I was touched by their warmth, their openness . . . (But why had I said *Difficult time*? I had not meant to say *Difficult time*.) As the halting words issued from me I recognized them as true, or true in some way—for the moment, in this place.

With some ceremony, a gift was presented to me by the straw-haired girl. An unwieldy object, in elaborate gift-wrapping.

Was I expected to open this? As everyone watched?

The gift was an accordion file with a Chinese design of flowers and butterflies. A file in which to keep letters, or poems. It was quite a beautiful file and had surely been expensive. I felt my face heat, with a kind of shame. I thanked the students, stammering. I wiped tears from my eyes. "I—I will never f-forget . . . This has been a . . ."

Unobtrusively at the rear of the room Rob Flint entered. He wore a beautifully tailored dark suit, a tasteful red necktie. He was glowing with presidential pride, like the owner of a prize steer at a county fair. "May I say a few words?" Rob Flint called out with the assurance of one whose request to speak had never been denied. The president of Garrison College had not been invited to this luncheon, it seemed. Or he'd been invited, but had had a more important engagement elsewhere. At once everyone turned to Rob Flint with smiles of happy expectation. For Rob Flint was a popular president, you could see.

To the room of avid listeners Rob Flint spoke of my "devotion" to poetry and to the "young poets of Garrison College"—another time speaking of having "discovered" my poetry years ago. And Rob Flint expressed a hope that I would "return again, soon." A faintness rose in me, a roaring in my ears.

Was he offering V___ N___ a position at the college? I didn't think so but—the president had that power, if he wished to use it, or misuse it.

In a shaky voice I expressed the wish that this would occur, too. Yes, I hoped to return to Garrison College . . . My faltering words were lost within a sudden eruption of applause.

Later that afternoon, at the inn, as I packed my two suitcases, I tried to recall how this awkward scene had ended. I'd been deeply moved and might have made a fool of myself—if anyone had noticed. (My sharp-eyed brother, no lover of poetry and hardly an admirer of his younger sister, would have noticed.) A small crowd of students and faculty members asked me to sign copies of my books and in this affable confusion Rob Flint disappeared as quickly and unobtrusively as he'd appeared. But already the memory was fading, like the carpets of the historic old inn. I had brought just two medium-sized suitcases to the college. I always traveled lightly, even negligently, like one who has been forced to pack for another person for whom one cares little. Most of the time I wore black on public, professional occasions for black is always appropriate. Cashmere-black, silken-black, black brocade. Black I could vary with colorful scarves, or necklaces, that were gifts from people it might be presumed I'd loved, and had once loved me—or so it would seem from this evidence. There had not been many.

Since I had so little identity of my own, it was a practical strategy to dress in the gifts of others. I was a youngish-American-woman poet variant of H. G. Wells's Invisible Man, who could make himself visible only by wrapping strips of gauze and bandages around his body, that he might clothe himself against the cold.

For even if you are invisible, you will feel the cold.

The phone rang, as I had been dreading it would ring. I could not bring myself to answer it, trembling badly.

But then, the phone rang again, and blindly I lifted the receiver—shut my eyes like one stepping off a ledge. And the voice was not my brother's voice, or my father's faint, accusing voice, but the voice of Rob Flint who was saying that he was downstairs in the lobby—he'd had to see me "one more time" before I left for the airport.

A taxi was coming, to take me to the airport. No more Garrison College escorts.

"But should you come here, now? To my room?"

I felt a pang of concern for Rob Flint. It was day, and not night: the chief administrator of Garrison College was behaving recklessly. I had the idea that he'd strode into the hotel by the front entrance, and not by the side entrance. He would be recognized in the lobby. He was a flamboyant local personality, he was *known*.

Yet, Rob Flint came to my room, and shut the door behind him, and took my hands in his. I was terrified of what he would say— *Look, Violet, I love you. I'm making my claim. You can go away from me but only if you promise to come back.* The words were so vivid to me, almost I could not hear what Rob Flint was saying: how much he would miss me, what an opportunity this had been for all of the college community.

I was moved. I was feeling shaky. Leave-takings are always difficult even when one hasn't exactly been in the place in which one has been perceived to be.

"Violet, we will all miss you!"

"I—I will miss all of you . . ."

We paused. We were breathless. Rob Flint was just slightly taller than I was, and at least forty pounds heavier. His silvery-brown hair lifted in airy tufts around his ears, which were larger than seemed normal. His face, overall, was a large face. Creases in his skin, particularly around his eyes, were kindly. His teeth were the teeth of perfection, providing him with confident smiles upon which a personality might be shaped. He was smiling, yet his smile had become tinged with concern.

I was so frightened, I could almost not hear Rob Flint's words. I dreaded him saying that I could not leave. In a flash of a fantasy I saw the man blocking the door and refusing to let me out.

Rob Flint said, frowning, "Forgive me, Violet. I have something I must ask you."

"Yes?"

Don't ask if I might love you. Don't tell me you love me.

Rob Flint hesitated. You could see this straight-backed man lifting his rifle to his shoulder, sighting carefully along the barrel. His finger on the trigger. It requires a certain strength to pull a trigger, when something upright and living is sighted in your scope.

"The first evening, the dinner at the President's House, you remember . . ."

"Yes. Of course."

"Did you, in the back room, where Elvira had taken you a few minutes before, happen to see—I mean, did you happen to take, by mistake, a little clock? A German ceramic clock, an antique, about this size . . ." Rob Flint made a circle of his hands, of the approximate size of a grapefruit. "It was fairly heavy, a white ceramic base, with some sort of floral design painted on it. My wife discovered that it was missing only just today . . ."

There was a stunned pause. Though I was listening closely, I could not comprehend what Rob Flint was asking me.

Quickly adding, "Violet, I have to ask."

"Are you asking me—did I take an antique clock from your house?"

"From the President's House. Not mine."

"Did I—steal something from the President's House? You are asking me?"

"Well—by mistake, you might have taken it. You seemed tired and distracted that night . . ."

"If I stole it. You are asking me."

"No. But if, by mistake, you happened to . . ."

"'Walk off with it.' A ceramic German clock, the size of a grapefruit, and heavy. Your antique clock."

"Not ours. I've explained—it belongs to the President's House. It belongs to the college."

I'd turned from Rob Flint and was making my way, not entirely steadily, to one of the windows. Though the inn was old, the windows were new: long, horizontal, plate-glass. Sunlight flooded through the glass, but it was sunlight filtered by a layer of grime on the outside of the glass. Dust motes in the air like manic atoms. I was stunned as if Rob Flint, who had been my lover, had struck me a blow to the solar plexus. A powerful blow from a practiced boxer can stop an opponent's heart, it is said. It's a cruel blow but it can be thrown easily if you have the strength and the skill and the will to do such lethal hurt, and if your opponent has no skills of self-defense.

Carefully I licked my lips, that were cracked and aching.

"Rob, you're asking me, a woman you'd claimed to love . . ." (But had Rob Flint actually used the word *love?*) " . . . a woman who feels very strongly about you . . ." (But was this so?) " . . . if I've stolen from you and your wife and your college, what is it, a German clock . . . ?"

"An antique clock, early eighteenth century. I don't know what it's worth, but—Elvira says it's an expensive antique, and it belongs in the President's House at Garrison College."

Rob Flint was looking both defiant and apologetic. He was stroking his chin in a gesture I had not seen before. In his presidential clothes he looked strangely distressed, like a mannequin with a cracked face. Belatedly he came to me, as if to comfort me. "Violet, I knew you hadn't seen the damned clock. But I had to ask. Because it's gone from the house, evidently, and there was no one . . ." Rob Flint paused, considering what he was saying. "My wife says there was no one else who could have—I mean, she thinks . . ."

"No one else ever enters that part of your house? No cleaning woman, handyman? Not your wife herself?"

I spoke quietly. I would not defend myself. I was feeling suddenly very tired. I yearned for the vertigo of thirty thousand feet above the earth. The possibility of lightning striking the plane's wings, detaching its tail from its body. I had seen such photographs, records of disaster. Passengers and crew consumed in a flaming holocaust. I yearned for the freedom in that moment—glancing up from a hopelessly stalled scribble of poetry in my notebook to see flames leaping from the plane's jet engines.

Rob Flint only repeated, more aggressively now, that he'd had to ask.

"You might ask your wife, you know. 'Mrs. Flint.'"

"My wife would not do such a thing, Miss N____. There is no question of that."

My suitcases were on the bed, packed, but not yet closed. Like helpless creatures on their backs, spread-eagled. I went to the bed and lifted the suitcases, to dump out their contents on the bed. Mostly clothes. Underwear. Soft things. Several books, a notebook. As at airport security, these personal items were exposed, somehow damning, of so little consequence. My "toiletries" were in my shoulder bag, to be shown separately in my demonstration to security guards that I was not a terrorist.

Rob Flint stood above the bed. I nudged him to look, with a wifely sort of intimacy. He touched nothing, but he did look: I saw the canny eyes moving swiftly. Both suitcases had zippered compartments, I took Rob Flint's hand and pressed it against the compartments, so that he could feel, as he could see, that there could not possibly be anything of the size and density of a clock secreted there. Rob Flint recognized the absurdity of the search, and drew away. "Wait. Here." I handed him my shoulder bag to examine, but he did no more than weigh it in his hands; in virtually the same instant, he handed it back to me.

"Of course. I'm sorry."

"*I'm* sorry."

"I didn't really think, Violet . . ."

"Your wife thought so."

I spoke with sudden bitterness. I felt my mouth twist into a wounded smile.

Rob Flint frowned. His face was flushed, he was not so attractive now. His flushed scalp showed through his hair. "I don't care to discuss my wife, Violet. I'm not comfortable discussing my wife with a stranger."

Rob Flint had been glancing toward the bathroom. The door was shut. Was there something hidden in the bathroom? My awkward visitor seemed reluctant to ask and so I pulled at his arm, with similar wifely impatience, to lead him to the bathroom. I opened the door to this large, white-tiled, quite attractive if windowless room, that he could see that there was nothing in this room, that had been cleared of my belongings.

Except, in the wastebasket, there was an odd, unwieldy object: not an antique clock but an accordion file with a Chinese design on its front.

I'd forgotten this. I'd forgotten that I'd thrown away the expensive gift from the students. Now my face heated again, with embarrassment and regret.

Rob Flint peered into the wastebasket as if he'd found what he'd been looking for. He lifted the accordion file, to look beneath it.

"Why did you throw away your gift, Violet?"

"I—I didn't realize I'd thrown it away . . . It must have fallen into the wastebasket." My voice faltered, shamefully. I was not a skilled liar and in that instant Rob Flint's insult to me was countered by the very clumsiness of my attempt to lie to him. He all but laughed at me. Plaintively I said, "There wasn't room for the accordion file in my suitcase. It's so large . . . Would you like it back? You could return it to the students, they could get their money back."

Rob Flint seemed not to hear this spiteful remark. He left the bathroom, still smiling; he paused to glance again at the bed, where my clothes were mutely spread. I understood that the man who'd been my lover was seeing again, as I was forced to see, our unclothed bodies on that bed, vulnerable, entwined. Oh, we had loved each other!—desperately, unmistakably. And now the memory had become improbable. Impossible to believe.

Unsteadily—yet with determination—I walked with Rob Flint to the door of the suite. At the door as he paused to speak to me I shoved at him as a child might shove another child, suddenly and without premeditation. My voice was sneering, nasal: "Go away. Go home. Tell her you couldn't find it, I'd hidden it so well."

Quickly I shut the door behind Rob Flint.

AT THE AIRPORT, I called the hospice another time. A woman answered—not the nurse with whom I'd spoken the other day. She identified herself as "Holly" and she seemed surprised to hear from me when I identified myself. And when I asked to speak to my father she said, in an agitated voice, "Oh but—hadn't you been informed? Your father passed away yesterday—yesterday afternoon . . ."

My flight was boarding. A woman's amplified voice drowned out the nurse's words. I heard myself reply, and heard her speak, but could not decipher the words. Numbly I made my way onto the plane, carrying a single suitcase and my heavy shoulder bag. The other suitcase had been checked in baggage. I was trying to speak, and the nurse's voice had grown faint. In my confusion, I seemed to think that it was my father who was speaking—my father's faint, fading voice I was trying to hear.

The flight attendant was concerned for me, after the plane had taken off, that I was crying and seemed disoriented. The passenger beside me was an older Asian man, who appeared embarrassed, and I did not want to upset him. I was crying strangely, as if choking, trying to cough up dry sand in my throat. In my hoarse voice I managed to stammer—"There has been a death in the family." It was an impersonal announcement, intended to forestall concern, for I did not know what else to say. "There has been a death in the family."

Soon then I heard the flight attendant repeat in a lowered voice to others in my vicinity—*There has been a death in the family. There has been a death in the family.*

THE DISAPPEARING

THINGS HAVE A WAY OF DISAPPEARING. BUT—WHERE DO they *go?*"

She was speaking to someone. Speaking on the phone. Her reputation was for saying such things—astute in their way, but light, amusing. Her voice was always buoyant, she meant only to make you laugh, or smile. She did not ever mean to make you alarmed, or embarrassed.

Later that morning, as if to bear out her casual remark, in the dim light of the garage she saw that something was missing.

Amid the dense accumulation of *things*, an emptiness.

There is comfort in such accumulations. Layers of lives, of years. Gardening tools, wheelbarrow, aerosol cans, old bicycles, recycling bins, battered trash cans, cardboard boxes stacked in a corner. Cracked clay pots, exiled kitchenware and furniture. Antique television, dog-food bowls. You could do an inventory of a household by all that has been worn out or excluded, exiled from it. You could do an inventory of a life.

But yes, against the rear wall, something sizable was missing. She could almost see its ghostly outline against the wall.

Theft? But who would steal from their garage?

Nothing in the garage was worth stealing, this was a principle of storing things in the Vanns' garage.

Then she saw: her husband's bicycle was missing.

There was her English racing bicycle, and there was another bicycle she'd once ridden, leaning against the wall, tires long flat. There was a part-dismantled bicycle that had belonged to their son. But the space where her husband's hefty black mountain bike had been was empty and she wondered how long it had been missing, how many times she'd glanced in that direction and failed to *see*.

She went to Ryan breathless, excited. "Your bicycle! Your bicycle is missing."

She hadn't wanted to say *stolen*. She hadn't wanted to sound that sort of alarm.

But Ryan surprised her by telling her calmly that the bicycle wasn't missing, he'd given it away.

"Given it away? But why? It's a beautiful bicycle, you've always loved it . . ."

This was not literally true. The mountain bicycle wasn't beautiful any longer. Nor was it true that, in recent years at least, Ryan had loved it.

For many years in their marriage, they'd bicycled frequently. They'd bicycled from their home to the Delaware River, and back, in hilly terrain; they'd taken their bicycles on their car and bicycled along the Hudson River. They'd bicycled in Nova Scotia, Cornwall, Scotland, Italy, the South of France, sometimes with another couple who were also avid cyclists. But the past several years they'd bicycled less, and less. The past summer, they hadn't bicycled together at all—Julia hadn't wanted to acknowledge this. Ryan was too busy, or not in the mood for bicycling; or, Ryan was both too busy and not in the mood. And Ryan had "health issues"—arthritis, hypertension. Julia had gone out by herself on neighboring country roads, but there was little pleasure in it, bicycling alone. Little pleasure in doing anything alone, that had once been done with another.

Where in the past she'd had to pedal hard to keep up with her husband who was likely to pedal heedlessly ahead, forgetting her, now she had no one with whom to keep pace; she should have felt a kind of liberation and relief, but she did not; she found herself squinting ahead, straining to see him in the distance . . . *Oh where was her husband! So far out of sight.* And now she was made to feel the loss of Ryan's bicycle, the acute disappointment, something like betrayal in her husband's casual explanation. *Gave it away.*

He'd given it to his nephew Kevin, he said.

"Kevin? But—why?"

"Because I haven't been using it."

She knew—as the husband of the household Ryan didn't care to be interrogated. Nor did he care to be interrupted while reading the *New York Times*—it was something of a marital taboo, to interrupt him.

The husband didn't like it that the wife should be staring at him with an expression of hurt, as if the matter of his bicycle had anything to do with *her.*

"Kevin's bike was stolen so I told him, come over here and you can have mine."

"Couldn't Kevin's parents buy him a new bike?"

"Of course, Dave and Carrie could buy him new *bikes.* That isn't the point."

"But what is the point? I don't understand."

"The point is, the bicycle is gone."

"But—Kevin could return it, when he gets a new bike of his own—couldn't he?"

"Julia, I said the damned bike is *gone.*"

The wife felt the rebuke. For some rebukes are *husbandly.*

There was something here having to do with the fact that Kevin was her husband's nephew, not hers; Julia wasn't close with Ryan's brother's family. Always she'd felt, since she'd married Ryan more than forty years before, that, if something happened to Ryan, if he passed away before her, she would never see his family again, nor would they make any effort to see her.

It was remarkable to Julia—(it did not hurt or offend her, but only amused her)—how Ryan's family managed to take photographs or videos of themselves that excluded her. At holiday gatherings there was Ryan, and there was—not Julia beside him, arm linked around his waist—but a sister, a cousin, another relative. *We've only been married more than half our lives*, Julia would say, lightly. *Can't expect your family to accept me so quickly.*

Ryan turned pointedly back to his newspaper. For him, the subject was closed. For Julia, all that day she would bear the minor wound of a marital rebuff; she would hear a faint echo, a disturbing echo, the bleak and irrevocable word *gone*.

"I'M NOT HURT. It isn't that serious—just a bicycle. I am not *betrayed*."

Speaking to herself as a way of instructing herself.

In marriage, the most intense conversations are often with oneself.

Julia's bicycle remained in the garage, near the space where the mountain bike had been, alone and abandoned. It was a classy-looking English bike, thin tires and numerous gears. From time to time that summer she would take out the bicycle and ride along country roads near the house, out of stubbornness, and loneliness; not troubling to wear a safety helmet, as Ryan would have insisted, reasoning that she wasn't going far, and she wasn't bicycling in dangerous circumstances. She wouldn't tell Ryan where she'd gone unless he asked—and he never asked.

How she'd loved bicycling! It was one of the happy activities of her life. She was a youthful woman for her age, her legs hard with muscle, her reflexes quick and stamina undiminished. It hurt her to think that bicycling might not be appropriate for her any longer.

Eventually, without Ryan bicycling with her, she would give it up.

She knew this would happen, but could not acknowledge it just yet.

Like other things, in their close, intimate life. Things they would give up, or had given up; things they'd abandoned of which they would not speak nor perhaps even think, as days, weeks, months and years washed over them, warm water lapping over their mouths.

The husband, the wife.

Disappearing, and gone.

HE WAS BECOMING MYSTERIOUS to her. He was making her uneasy. Forty-four years they'd been married. In those years—obviously— she'd had every opportunity to know Ryan Vann thoroughly— intimately; yet, she'd begun to understand that the husband whom she knew, or believed she knew, was not altogether the man with whom she lived. Often now seeing Ryan at a little distance, in a parking lot or on the street, she could not always recognize him.

He was "older"—of course. But that was not the mystery.

When his hair had begun to thin in his early fifties, out of vanity the husband had gone to a barber and had his head shaved—totally, abruptly. At once then he'd seemed smaller, less distinctive. For so many men—(Julia now noticed)—were totally bald, out of vanity per- haps; in vague emulation of those iconic black athletes and rap stars who shaved their heads for reasons of sexual glamour. The husband's head was of a normal size but seemed diminished, as his ears were more pronounced. His face now seemed wider, flatter, stretched from ear to ear like a clown's face, but perhaps Ryan didn't notice, as he had no awareness—(Julia was certain)—of the curious labyrinthine lines, creases, and dents in his scalp. She thought—*The hair was a disguise. The scalp can't be disguised.*

For thirty-two years Ryan had been a well-paid research consul- tant for a New Jersey pharmaceutical company that specialized in medications for blood-related diseases like leukemia and lymphoma. His training had been in chemistry and molecular biology. He was now part-retired. He had a private, professional life apart from his wife—an office several miles away, and a "laboratory" which she'd never seen. Julia wasn't sure of Ryan's work-hours, for he seemed to set his own work-hours that varied from week to week. She wasn't sure who his associates were any longer; when she asked after one of them Ryan was likely to say, "He's no longer with us." Or, more cryptically, "Him? He's gone."

Gone. But where?

Still, she wanted to think that she knew her husband intimately—as he knew her. For there was nothing secret in her life—(she didn't think so). Their life together—(it was a single, singular life, not lives)—had been worn smooth as the stone steps of their front walk, upon which countless feet had trod over the decades.

Yet she found herself recalling—with an involuntary flinching as if a shadow had passed swiftly over her head—an incident from their early life.

This was not a good memory. This was not a shared memory. In the years following the incident, neither the husband nor the wife had spoken to the other about it.

They'd been married just three years and they were living in another part of the country, in a large Midwestern city on the southernmost shore of one of the Great Lakes, when they'd returned one afternoon to their (first, newly purchased) house, a two-bedroom Colonial in a residential neighborhood, and discovered that the side door, which was the only door they routinely used, was unlocked—what a sinking sensation, to push open that door!

The door had been locked, when they'd left earlier that afternoon.

And so it was bizarre how, at first, as they stepped into the house, they hadn't seemed to understand that something had to be wrong.

Walking into the kitchen, and beyond, staring—was something out of place? Missing?

The very air felt altered, as in the aftermath of agitation. There was a smell—smells . . . Then, they saw: books had been pulled down from shelves, scattered on the floor as if they'd been kicked. Chairs dragged out of place. A mirror on the floor, badly cracked.

The rage of the thief or thieves, discovering that the household contained so little of value.

"Someone has been here . . . My God."

Very like a fairy tale, it seemed. Someone had intruded into their house and into their life. And yet—who?

Julia felt faint, disbelieving. Ryan's breathing was harsh, quickened. When Julia clutched at Ryan's arm, half-consciously he pushed her away, in his effort of concentration.

Yet neither thought to quickly leave the premises, and to call 911 immediately.

They hurried upstairs, Ryan in the lead. The acrid smell was stronger here, an odor of both sweat and urine. In their bedroom, that was so private and so intimate a place, the intrusion was shocking: closet doors flung open, bureau drawers yanked open and their contents dumped on the floor. Clothes and shoes scattered rudely on the floor. Even then, they were thinking slowly, with effort. As if they were wearing iron shoes, and could not move easily. They couldn't seem to grasp—*This has happened. It is real. Something has broken into our lives. We have been violated.*

The bathroom—in the toilet, a hot-looking, yellow urine, that had not been flushed away. Julia would recall a moment's relief, naïve gratitude, that the perpetrator hadn't defiled the floor, or the walls. Quickly holding her breath she leaned over to flush the toilet.

"Son of a bitch. God-damn bastard cocksucker *son of a bitch*"— Ryan slammed the bathroom door shut.

Julia had never heard her husband speak in such a way, his voice furious but high-pitched, near-hysterical. She had never seen him so angry, and so helpless.

Ryan had had his wallet with him of course, and Julia, her handbag. These crucial items hadn't been taken by the thieves. They hadn't a cache of bills hidden anywhere in the house, fortunately—Julia was sure of this—and so no money had been taken. The frantic way in which the rooms had been searched seemed to mean that the thieves were looking for hidden cash.

"Call 911! Hurry."

"I *am.*"

Ryan made the call downstairs on the kitchen phone. Numbly the wife heard the husband reporting a break-in, a burglary. Please send police officers! The wife heard the husband stammer providing the address, as if he weren't certain of it.

They'd been living in this house for less than two years. Just inside the limits of a large Midwestern city.

The city was "racially troubled." Their neighborhood was "newly integrated."

Waiting for the police to arrive. A very long wait, it seemed.

"It's lucky we don't need an ambulance. Lucky the house isn't on fire."

"That's a different kind of emergency. They'd send an ambulance or a fire truck if—"

"Yes. You'd like to think so."

It was a political issue in the city. Emergency calls from inner-city neighborhoods weren't answered with the alacrity with which emergency calls from other, residential parts of the city were answered. The Vanns wanted to think that they lived in a "good" residential neighborhood and that the color of their skin—"white"—could be deduced by their address.

Waiting for the police they were too nervous to remain still. Was this a *crime scene,* which they shouldn't disturb? Julia had to restrain herself from gathering up fallen books and reshelving them. Ryan foolishly lifted the fallen mirror whose cracked glass now broke, and fell onto his shoes. Julia cried, "Ryan, don't! You'll cut yourself."

Blindly they made their way through the house another time like sleepwalkers. The alien smells were more evident now—sweat-smells, man-smells, smells of strangers. A prevailing odor of urine suggested that maybe after all the thief or thieves hadn't confined themselves to the upstairs toilet.

So disgusting! Julia's nostrils contracted, she was feeling faint and nauseated.

"He—they—were black. You can tell."

"You can? But—"

In his furious state, the husband wasn't to be reasoned with. And the wife was having difficulty thinking coherently as she was having difficulty walking as if she were very tired, or had been struck a blow to the head.

The way Ryan had uttered the word *black*. Julia knew, he would never remember after the fury-flame had passed.

Here was a surprise: the violation of the household was more obvious than it had seemed initially, when they'd just stepped inside the door. For in each room something was out of place, or had been altered. Furniture, small rugs. A lamp overturned. On a wall, a framed print, Rodin's *Gates of Hell*, was crooked, as if someone had brushed his shoulder carelessly against it.

Ryan was discovering that more items had been taken from his study than he'd thought. His face was flushed and indignant, with a look of fear beneath. Was his briefcase gone?—his old, frayed-leather briefcase he'd had for years? On his hands and knees Ryan searched for the briefcase beneath his desk, beneath a sofa . . . He'd examined desk-drawers, whose contents had been heaped out onto the carpet, several times. He was becoming irrational, muttering and cursing loudly.

Julia asked if anything important had been in the briefcase? Print-outs, lab-data? Panting and cursing, Ryan ignored her.

His electric typewriter was missing, that had been set on a table, beneath a black plastic cover. Out of a closet, a portable radio had been taken.

Ryan was looking sick, confused. Julia could not bear to see her young husband so helpless.

She forced herself to return upstairs to the bedroom, dreading to discover—yes, much of her jewelry was missing. Squatting on her heels she pawed desperately through clothing on the floor—where were the pale pink pearls that had belonged to her grandmother?— where, the girl's wristwatch that had been a birthday present from her grandmother? And where was the jade necklace Ryan had given her, brought back from a trip to China? She couldn't find her favorite silver bracelet, and the beautiful necklace made of blue Venetian glass, also a gift from her husband . . .

Trying to tell herself—*Nothing you own is expensive.*

Trying not to think—*Everything that is gone is irreplaceable.*

Downstairs, Julia discovered more damage. More thefts! Silver candlestick holders missing from the dining room table—a wedding gift from Ryan's parents, that had been conspicuously tarnished. Out of the sideboard other silver items had been taken—a large ladle, spoons—all tarnished, of dubious value. Julia thought, with a sudden wild elation—*Good! No more God-damned silver polish.*

Ryan's new Nikon camera was missing from a closet shelf. Julia's old Polaroid was missing.

Out of the front hall closet, a pair of Ryan's boots was missing— *boots!* Julia saw to her dismay that her good, black cashmere coat was missing. Her *coat!*

Numbly they would say—*Our house was burglarized.* A curiously passive expression, this was—*Burglarized.*

Though we locked the doors and windows and were not gone long, our house was burglarized. As if the intrusion were a kind of weather, an act of God, and not the act of an individual or individuals.

After forty minutes, police officers arrived. They were two stocky swarthy-white men in their mid-thirties, uniformed, with heavy-looking holsters, prominent billy clubs and pistols on their hips. So outfitted, they seemed virtually to creak as they moved, and they did not move swiftly. They did not seem very concerned about the break-in and they betrayed no excess of sympathy for the agitated (white) couple residing at 294 Wildemere Drive, rather a kind of mock courtesy masking a scarcely concealed contempt. They asked Ryan—(pointedly, they ignored Julia)—if he'd searched the entire house including the basement, if he was sure no one was hiding in the house, and Ryan said, stammering, that he and Julia had looked through the house upstairs and down but not the basement; and so the police officers descended into the basement, cautiously, yet heavy-footedly, pistols drawn.

(The abashed couple exchanged a glance: not for a moment had they thought of the basement! Someone might well have been hiding there, and they were too distracted to have given it a thought.)

The police officers returned to the kitchen, pistols back on their hips. Nobody in the basement, and no signs that they could see of anything out of place.

"We don't really have much that anyone would want," Julia said nervously. She hoped she wasn't sounding apologetic. "Especially in the basement, where . . ." But no one was listening to Julia.

The officers asked Ryan routine questions—when they'd left the house, if they'd locked the doors and windows, when they'd returned home. If they'd had a break-in before. The officers determined that the house had been entered at the rear by the forcing of a lock—"Not very secure these cheap kind of locks, see?"—on a sliding glass patio door. The officers discovered what neither Ryan nor Julia had discovered, a smear of blood on the patio door—"Where he wiped his hand, see?" (But why would the intruder be bleeding? Ryan and Julia had no idea, nor was this ever explained. There was no broken glass in sight.) Somehow, the officers determined that there were two perpetrators—"Probably kids looking for drugs, or money for drugs." With stubs of pencils the officers took notes, or pretended to take notes. The elder of the two addressed Ryan with a barely concealed sneer, still ignoring Julia as if she didn't exist: "Mr. Vann, why'd you come inside this house? Your mistake was pushing open that door, see. If you'd known the door was locked when you left, and it was unlocked when you returned, you would know that someone had broken in, OK? You would know that that person or persons might still be inside, and that they might be dangerous. You would know that."

You would know. It was a curious bullying way to speak. Julia could not believe that the police officer was reprimanding her husband, who stood stiff and abashed, mortified. A man reprimanding another man, in the presence of his wife. And Julia too stood silent, frightened. Was this break-in somehow their *fault*?

"See, if they had a gun, and you and your wife walked in—they might've shot you. Happens all the time."

The officer spoke with a grim sort of satisfaction. The husband was forced to agree, shamefaced.

"Did you have money on the premises, Mr. Vann? Did they take money?"

Ryan shook his head *no*.

"No money? You're sure?"

Ryan shook his head *yes*. He was sure.

"Could you make an inventory of what they took?"

Ryan and Julia said *yes*. They would try.

"Do you have a gun, Mr. Vann?"

Quickly Julia interceded—*no*. No gun!

But Ryan paused, not answering. Julia looked at him, astonished.

"Do you have a gun, Mr. Vann? Did they take your gun?"

"I—yes—I have—I had—a gun. Yes, the gun is—missing."

Ryan spoke miserably, not looking at Julia. Julia stared at him openmouthed.

Both police officers were frowning. The elder of the two persisted: "Do you have a homeowner's permit for the gun, Mr. Vann?"

Yes. Ryan had a permit.

"Could you identify the handgun, Mr. Vann?"

Ryan stammered trying to recall—trying to identify—the gun. He had not examined it much, he said. He thought it was—it would be called—a "revolver." He had not ever fired it.

"'Not ever fired it'?"

No. Ryan had to confess, he had not.

"And was this 'revolver' loaded?"

No. Ryan did not think the gun was loaded.

"You had this gun in your household for protection, Mr. Vann, and it was not loaded?"

The officers exchanged a glance. Inscrutable, it seemed.

Julia thought—*They think we are such fools!*

"And this gun is now missing, Mr. Vann? You are sure."

Yes. Miserably, Mr. Vann was sure.

"Any other weapon, Mr. Vann?"

No. No other weapon.

"You're sure? No other weapon on the premises?"

Ryan asked if "weapon" included knives? Kitchen knives?

"No, Mr. Vann. Not a kitchen knife. Like, another gun, or a switchblade. An illegal-length blade."

Miserably Ryan shook his head *no*. No other gun and no *switchblade* in the household.

Ryan was obliged to show the officers his homeowner's permit for the missing gun, which turned out to have been a .22 Ruger pistol; the document had been filed amid Ryan's financial records. As if to humiliate Ryan further, as Julia stared from a doorway, they asked him to show them exactly where he'd hidden it—in the lowermost desk-drawer. (No wonder he'd been so anxious about his study, Julia thought.) Ryan explained—he'd purchased the gun in a gun store in Austin, Texas, preparing to drive north one summer by himself. This had been years ago, before he'd met Julia.

"And you never test-fired the gun?"—again, the officers regarded the husband with neutral expressions.

"I—I don't think so . . ."

"Did, or did not, Mr. Vann?"

"N-No."

The weak answer seemed to hover in the air, as if no one wished to claim it.

The officers continued to take notes with their stub-pencils that seemed too small for their large fingers. They had not appeared surprised that the homeowner at 294 Wildemere had owned a gun, still less that the gun had been stolen from him; their disdain seemed to be that the gun had been hidden in an obscure place, hadn't been loaded or ever "fired."

The Vanns were to file an inventory of stolen items with the local police precinct, and with their insurer. When Ryan asked if it was likely their things would be returned to them, the police officers murmured what sounded like *Might be.* When they left the house Julia looked after them in dismay—Wasn't anyone going to take fingerprints? Didn't the police *care?*

Alone with her husband in the violated house, Julia felt shaky, uncertain. She knew that he would try to embrace her—he was repentant, ashamed—and when he came to her, and touched her, she pushed from him with a little cry.

She could not bear for him to touch her, at that moment. The heat that lifted from his body, as of an obscure but defiant humiliation.

"A gun! You had a gun in the house, and I didn't know."

They were both breathing quickly. Julia's heart was pounding quickly and shallowly and she seemed to be having difficulty shaping her words: her tongue felt too large for her mouth, and numb.

It was hurtful to her: her husband had been intimidated by the police officers. He had seemed oblivious of their rudeness to *her*.

"Julia, the gun was for our protection."

"But why didn't you tell me?"

"I didn't want to worry you."

"Didn't want to worry me! A gun in the house . . ."

"It wasn't loaded. I rarely glimpsed it. It was just—there."

"All this time, years we've been together—we moved into this house—you brought the gun with you, and you didn't tell me." Julia's voice lifted in wonderment. She did not say—*How can I ever trust you again?*

And so in the weeks and months to come the wife would inquire of the husband, with an air of subtle reproach—"Is there a gun in the house now, Ryan?"—and Ryan would say, pained, "No. There is no gun in the house."

And again, a few months later—"Is there a gun in the house now, Ryan? You would let me know, wouldn't you, if there was a gun in the house?"—and Ryan would say, "No, Julia. There is no gun in the house."

"But you would tell me, if there was a gun?"

"Yes. I would tell you, darling."

No police officer ever called them, after that day. No one came to the house on Wildemere Drive.

Their first house, this had been. So long ago, it seemed that others had lived there—the young husband, the young wife.

After the break-in, the house felt subtly poisoned to them. The foul odor of urine did not fade for some time. By the time they moved away they'd come to dislike the house that had once seemed so wonderful to them, the place of their eager, young love.

Their stolen things were never returned to them—of course. The inventory of items the Vanns had so carefully assembled went unacknowledged by anyone at the local police precinct; eventually, they were informed that it had been "misplaced"—"lost."

Months were required for the insurance company to reimburse the Vanns, and then only partly, after numerous telephone calls.

They never spoke of the burglary. Very few of their relatives knew they'd been burglarized, and no one knew about the stolen gun.

Until finally they moved from the large Midwestern city at the southernmost point of the Great Lake, to a suburban community in central New Jersey where most inhabitants were "white" and there was very little crime. And the wife had no need to ask about a gun.

HIS TELEPHONE VOICE WHICH WAS JOVIAL, GREGARIOUS. THE voice of a happy man, you would say.

Fascinated she listened. From another room, she listened.

Who is he talking to, with such emotion? Who can make my husband so happy?

DRIVING TO TOWN she saw posters newly affixed to trees, telephone poles: MISSING DOG.

In town, MISSING DOG on fences, walls, in the grocery store and in the library. Photo of a dog with damp hopeful eyes, upright ears.

MISSING DOG –"GEMINI"—"GEM"

3 YRS OLD BEAGLE/BOXER MIX

COAT BROWN COLORS

FRIENDLY THOUGH MIGHT BARK

LAST SEEN CREEKSIDE PARK 5/13

******REWARD******

At the bottom of the posters was a local telephone number replicated on little strips of paper to be torn off. At the library, only one of these strips had been torn off. Julia tore off a strip.

The little dog in the photo looked so forlorn! Julia could not bear the thought of "Gem" wandering lost, frightened. Slowly she drove along country roads and Creekside Park feeling strangely optimistic. In a circuitous route that would bring her back home, but not immediately. Still optimistic, though beginning to tire, seeing a number of dogs but no dog not accompanied by a person, and on a leash.

I'VE BECOME A frightened person, I think.
But why? Frightened of what?
It has not happened yet. It is beginning.

SHE WAS ASKING HIM something, or she was remarking upon something, casually, not accusingly, and her voice was certainly not sharp, her voice was certainly not reproachful or harsh, though she might've expressed curiosity, and an undercurrent of irony, or mild indignation, asking where he'd been, where he'd been when he'd returned late that afternoon or possibly she'd asked him with whom he'd been speaking on the phone in his study, not once but more than once, she had not eavesdropped but she was wondering, and he wasn't listening, or he was walking away—or, he was listening, as she spoke to his back, even as she spoke and he was walking away distractedly, or rudely, and now she did raise her voice, and now she did follow after him and pull at his arm, not hard, not (as he would afterward claim) squeezing his arm in a way to cause pain, only wanting attention from him, so rarely did he give her his fullest attention, even facing her his eyelids were hooded, his gaze drifted from her, and now he was walking away from her and she pulled at his arm, and he turned suddenly, pushing at her with a curse, and his fisted arm shot out—it was involuntary he would claim, it was "reflexive"—and struck her a palpable blow on the chest; and she saw in his flushed face a look of anger, and inexpressible loathing. And she recoiled from him, giving a little cry, the blow *had hurt* but it was more the surprise of the blow that had hurt, and the look in the husband's face; and she ran from him and slammed a door crying *I hate you too. I can hate, too—I hate you.*

SHE DID HATE HIM! She hated him that he no longer loved her, as he had loved her once.

"Jesus, Julia! I'm sorry. You know I didn't mean it."

He'd meant it. She knew.

She'd seen the look in the husband's face, of unfettered loathing. She'd felt a sudden flaring of loathing for him, as a struck match may light another match, very quickly, before there is time to extinguish it.

"*I'm* sorry. I shouldn't have—whatever I did, to provoke you."

Through the years of her marriage she'd been loved by the man. She'd been prized, protected. The husband's love had been a warm light shining upon her, a continuous light, sunshine of the sort we take for granted until, one hour, a cloud eclipses it and we find ourselves shuddering in the cold, bereft.

So saying to him, in her soft plaintive guilty voice, "Yes, I forgive you, Ryan. Will you forgive me?"

IN THIS WAY, days passed. The remainder of their lives.

Each understood that the other had been deeply shocked. If marriage is a masquerade, there is the very real danger that masks may slip.

The wife had seen that the husband did not love her, and was lost, as if she'd kicked free of gravity, for without the husband to love her, how was it possible for the wife to love *him?*

She'd loved in the husband his regard for her. His respect for her, and his wish to protect her. She could not imagine her life without this fierce love for the man, that was her reason for being, as, years before, being a mother to their child had been her reason for being, unquestioned as breath.

Terrible things she told herself, as if to test herself.

It's over. The masquerade. Now, we can die.

SHE MEANT NONE of this! Of course.

She was anxious for him. She loved him, and was fearful of losing him—she wasn't sure how, or why.

In his closet, in their bedroom—Ryan's clothes on hangers seemed fewer than she recalled, no longer crammed tightly together.

On Ryan's side of the cedar closet in the hall, where his winter suits, sport jackets and trousers were hung inside plastic, moth-proof bags, Julia was certain there was more space than there'd been previously. At the bottom of these plastic bags were neatly folded sweaters of Ryan's, mostly gifts from Julia, and these too seemed to have diminished.

Was Ryan giving things away? Or—was Ryan moving things away, to another residence?

She felt stricken to the heart. She felt betrayed anew.

She couldn't trust her husband to tell her the truth. No wife can trust her husband, the very relationship *wife* makes deceit inevitable.

When she asked Ryan if he'd discarded some of his clothing he'd seemed at first not to know what she was talking about. Then he said, not meeting her eye, "That Vietnam Veterans' organization that comes by in vans—I gave them some things, a few months ago. I think that was it."

"Where was I?"

"Where were *you*? How the hell would I know, Julia?"

"Did someone ring the doorbell? Did they come to the house here? Why didn't you tell me?"

Ryan laughed, irritably. Julia knew that she was annoying him, indeed she was annoying herself, but could not seem to stop. It was the very *pettiness* of the situation that provoked her.

"I think I did tell you."

"No. You did not, I'd have remembered."

"I left their card in the kitchen. On the counter, with the mail."

"I don't think so."

She could not give it up, she knew he was deceiving her. Giving away expensive clothing, sweaters that had been presents from Julia, cashmere, hand-knit, beautiful—why would Ryan do such a thing? Why, so secretly? Perversely? It wasn't as if their closets were overflowing, and winnowing was necessary.

Another time, Julia checked Ryan's bureau drawers—socks, underwear. These, too, seemed to be diminished, somewhat.

But she couldn't be sure. She couldn't ask *him*.

Of course, the issue was trivial. It shouldn't matter. She didn't truly think that her husband of forty-four years was moving out, to another, secret residence. (Did she?)

Still, some weeks later she checked Ryan's closet again. And the cedar closet. And it seemed to her, yes—more of Ryan's things were missing. She could even identify some of them: favored neckties, shirts, sweaters, the camel's hair sport coat, his older gray pinstriped suit. *He is abandoning his old life. He is going—where?*

OFTEN NOW, she felt panic. A sensation as of great beating wings descending upon her, sucking up oxygen, leaving her cringing, faint.

Embarrassing to love another person more than the other person loves you. Like wrong-sized persons on a teeter-totter. The heavier determines the motions of the teeter-totter, the lighter is in the other's control and might be dropped to the ground, unceremoniously.

Impulsively she resumed the old antagonism: "Ryan, tell me: we don't have a gun in the house now, do we?"

"A gun—? Don't be ridiculous, Julia. Please."

"But—do we?"

Ryan was looking pained, and Ryan was sounding evasive. But Ryan said, forcing himself to look Julia full in the face: "No. We do not."

"If someone broke into our house, he wouldn't find a gun? He couldn't use it against us? Is this true?"

"Julia, this is true."

She went away shaken, seeing the expression in his face.

She had already searched the house, Ryan's part of the house, desk-drawers, high closet shelves, shelves in remote areas of the basement. She had found nothing—no gun.

Yet she knew—*He is betraying me. He is abandoning me. And there is nothing I can do.*

AND THEN SHE DISCOVERED—the husband was withdrawing money from their joint banking accounts. There were mysterious expenditures—$1,200, $4,600, $17,000. A singularly large withdrawal—$58,000.

Of course, Ryan had explanations. When Julia inquired.

He'd transferred money from one account to another, or—he'd purchased bonds that yielded a "higher rate of interest than we were getting." He could provide figures, he could be utterly convincing. Julia listened, and a pulse beating in her head warned her—*He is preparing to leave you. He is stealing from you. Don't trust him!*

It did seem that Ryan was startled by her curiosity. By even her awareness of their finances. For Julia had rarely shown the slightest interest in money, she'd entrusted to the husband virtually all of what she'd called *money matters*. It had been a measure of her femininity, in a way.

Also, Ryan told her he'd been giving donations—"in both our names"—to several charitable organizations.

Ryan rummaged through a desk-drawer to show her several thank-you letters and documents of receipt. These were for smaller funds—$800, $1,000. Julia only glanced at them, embarrassed. She felt so foolish, doubting the husband.

"Why didn't you tell me? I could have co-signed the cards."

"I'm sure that I did tell you, Julia. Around January first. You usually tell me to 'use my own judgment'—so that's what I did."

Ryan spoke evenly, with an edge of impatience. Since he'd struck her several weeks before—(by "reflexive" accident, as he'd claimed)— there was a precarious tenderness between them as if both were convalescents. The checks were to Amnesty International, Doctors Without Borders, New Jersey Hospice. Others were names new to Julia. Figures swirled in Julia's head, she made no effort to add them up, the husband was so convincing.

Saying, in a chiding voice: "These are all very good causes, Julia. We have to do something meaningful with our God-damned money."

SOMEHOW IT HAD HAPPENED, the husband and the wife had had a child together. Out of their young bodies, a son named Patrick.

The son had become an adult and lived several thousand miles away in Southern California where he, too, though in a way very different from his research-scientist father, worked in that indeterminate zone between "biology" and "commerce." The son had become an entity shared by the husband and the wife of whom they could speak at any time in their special, private way of speaking of their son, which was an (intimate, inviolable) bond between them.

For approximately twenty years *the son* had been their single most obsessive subject of conversation—how bizarre that seemed to them, now.

For Patrick was gone from them now, irrevocably. Strange and unsettling to think of *the son* as an adult man, thirty-three years old; a man who had not only his own, private and secretive life but was involved in the lives of others totally unknown to the parents, a divorced woman (Hispanic judging by the name: Diaz) and her two young children who lived in San Diego, California. In this new alliance, which was in fact an alliance of more than a few years, utterly peripheral to the lives of Patrick's parents, Patrick was ever more distant to them. He'd taken on the emotional and financial responsibility of a family Julia and Ryan called *ready-made, non-returnable* from which they knew themselves excluded.

Ready-made grandchildren did not greatly excite them. Especially Ryan.

Patrick had left them at the age of eighteen and had returned only sporadically since. The more successful a son, the less you will see him. They took pride in this fact, and a kind of grudging pleasure. They understood that Patrick would never again return as the son of their household; he would never again be their child. Those years he'd loved his mother, even adored her—all that was finished. The precious years of Julia's *mothering*.

When Patrick had first left for Stanford Julia had wept for days. There'd been something savage and unspeakable in her grief. She'd wanted to think that it was an exceptional grief and that she could not survive the loss of her *mothering* but of course she survived, as everyone had assured her she would. She'd learned to laugh at herself, eventually. She'd thought—*Each death is laughable, maybe. All that is required is perspective.*

Now, there were days when Julia had to remind herself that she'd been—she *was*—a mother. And that she and the husband had created a child out of their young, ardent bodies, as a flame had whipped through those bodies pitilessly.

Wistfully she said to the husband, "Well—ready-made grandchildren are better than no grandchildren. Don't you think?"

Ryan said, "I have no idea what you're talking about."

THE HURT WAS a bruise you longed to press, to establish that it is a bruise, and that its hurt is natural.

She was waiting for him to love her again. To discover her, as he'd discovered her forty-five years before. A lifetime!

Don't leave me. Don't go away. Where are you going?

In terror she woke in her bed, such thoughts churning in her brain. And there was the husband to console her, sharply speaking her name.

He was a master of sudden, emergency situations. At times, like one captured in a spotlight, he was kindly, patient, placating, wise. In the way of a healer he called her *Julia, Julie*. He called her *darling*.

"It's only a dream, darling."

Sleepily admonishing her, "Whatever it was, just forget it. Dreams are nothing but vapor."

HE LEFT THE HOUSE calling out to her *G'bye!* He made no effort to know if she heard him, in another part of the house.

Quickly and in stealth one day she followed him, as she'd planned.

She took care to keep her car a discreet distance behind his station wagon.

The husband in the station wagon. The wife in a smaller vehicle.

He drove at a moderate speed in just the direction she'd have predicted. At the pharmaceutical company approximately seven miles away he turned into the driveway as she'd predicted. The wife told herself—*You see? There is nothing.* The wife returned home by a circuitous route taking her through Creekside Park where she saw few dogs, and those dogs on leashes. It saddened her that the DOG MISSING posters had become frayed, rain-lashed.

She wondered if "Gem" had been found, or if his owners had simply given up the search. She'd lost the tiny slip of paper with the telephone number.

SHE THOUGHT *Is he moving out? Going to live with—who?*

It was painful to think that just possibly the husband had another family, not so far away. You heard of such things. You were mildly shocked, or you were amused, but you were not terribly surprised for such things happened, and were not considered exceptional. There was another, younger family in north Jersey perhaps. The husband had chosen another wife, a woman young enough to be their daughter, whom he'd met in his lab, a younger biologist, a lab technician, possibly someone on the clerical staff, and Ryan was departing soon to live with this young family for he would be a doting father to the young woman's children. (Julia did not want to think that Ryan had fathered young children, himself.) In weak moments Julia thought—*Take me with you! Don't leave me alone.* The young wife might be lonely for her own mother, who'd died of breast cancer, or worse yet pancreatic cancer, swept off the surface of the whirling Earth.

No, that was ridiculous. The young wife would not want *her.* She was so weak thinking of these things, she could barely stand. She poured red wine into a glass, and not a clean glass, and drank. The man—the husband—(sometimes she was forgetting his name, but she knew exactly who he was)—had been the one to introduce Julia to wine, to the ceremony of drinking wine slowly, savoring each mouthful, when she'd been a girl of nineteen. That warm astonishing sensation running through her throat, into her chest, belly, groin . . . That sensation of almost unbearable longing, she felt still, so many years later, though the object of the longing held himself teasingly from her, at a little distance.

Out of that sensation of longing, the child had been conceived.

Out of such longing, all of life—raw, grasping, blind—is conceived.

To her surprise she saw: their stock of wine was depleted, considerably. Where once there'd been too many bottles in the lower cupboard to have easily counted, now there were but a few. She thought—*Have we been celebrating? What have we been celebrating?* She could not recall the last time they'd drunk wine together, seriously together, on the rear deck of their house in summer.

Only dimly could she recall wine-sweetened kisses. Long ago their quiet laughter, caresses. Her fingers in the husband's hair, his strong spread fingers against the small of her back.

My love. You have made me so happy.

IN THE NIGHT she wakened with the realization—*Of course!*

The husband slept beside her, turned from her and facing the dark of the bedroom. No idea of what the wife had guessed.

This time she followed him in her car along the country highway at a discreet distance as before, and when he turned his station wagon into the entrance of the pharmaceutical research headquarters she continued to drive along the road, at a slow speed; within a few minutes, she saw the husband's station wagon reappear, from another driveway, leading back onto the road. Shrewdly the husband had simply driven through the grounds of the pharmaceutical company, which covered a number of acres. Now, the husband was driving at a higher speed.

Another six miles into town. He was meeting someone there, she knew.

Unexpectedly the husband turned into the vast grounds of the medical center and hospital, that had been newly built and opened within the year. Where was Ryan going? Had he an appointment there, about which he hadn't told his wife?

Julia felt a clutch of surprise, and alarm. She thought—*Or maybe he's visiting someone in the hospital. Doesn't want me to know.*

A woman, possibly. A new, young woman. Or an older love. Someone he'd never told Julia about, to spare her. Or, someone in his family who had never cared for the wife.

Someone who was ill? How seriously ill?

She parked behind the medical center. There was Ryan's station wagon not far away. She believed it was Ryan's station wagon though the late morning sun blazed and blinded her and she could not decipher the license plate. She tried, rubbing at her eyes. But she could not. And she'd arrived too late to see which entrance the husband had taken into the massive building.

It was like their old days of bicycling—Ryan ahead, and almost out of sight; Julia behind, pedaling furiously, panting and resentful. Where had he gone! He couldn't have known that she was following him—could he?

Her senses were alert, her heart was beating rapidly. She wondered if hunters felt this way. There was something raw and carnal in it, the pursuit of prey.

He would be furious if he knew.

But he would know then, how I love him.

The medical center was attached to the hospital though it was only three floors, and the hospital, seven. You walked through a large atrium-foyer, and followed corridors arranged like spokes, each clearly designated. The medical center/hospital resembled a hive that thrummed with life, and much of it not-visible to the visitor's eye. Tile floors gleamed underfoot, ceilings were high, provoking a sensation of vertigo. Julia was feeling short of breath. "Please! I need to see him, so badly. My husband." In the near distance she did see Ryan, or thought she saw Ryan—each time, the man turned out to be a stranger. And once, the man turned out to be a woman, big-boned and tall with very short-cut, taffy-colored hair flat against her head.

Much of the ground floor of the medical center was Radiology. There was a dispiriting familiarity to the very name—Radiology. Julia had had numerous mammograms in the old medical center as well as, over the years, C-scans and MRIs. Her medical history swam up at her, a glimmering-white shark beneath a sea green surface. She turned away, she shut her eyes. But this visit was not about *her*.

She took up her cell phone and called the husband's cell phone number. The little ringing went unanswered until Ryan's voice mail switched on.

Was he here? Somewhere? The medical pavilion, as it was called, contained a dizzying variety of doctors, specialists—Internal Medicine, Gynecology & Obstetrics, Respiratory, Dermatology, Asthma Clinic, Pediatrics, Oncology, Neurology, Eating Disorders.

Was that Ryan?—in the hospital café? This was an attractive café meant to mimic an outdoor café, in the atrium. Decorative stands of bamboo, of a uniform height of about twelve feet, surrounded the white plastic tables and chairs, of which approximately one-half were occupied.

Julia saw to her dismay that the husband, seen from the back, was seated at a table with a woman, a stranger—(Julia was sure the woman was a stranger)—who appeared to be a hospital patient for she was attached by an IV line to a portable trolley beside her chair. A woman of no discernible age except *not young* in a pale blue striped hospital gown, and over the gown an oversized cardigan sweater, haphazardly buttoned. And on her head, a scarf; for her head seemed to be bare, her scalp was hairless, without the scarf she'd have looked newborn as a baby chick, touching and vulnerable. And very thin. Julia was puzzled—she'd never seen this emaciated woman before, she was sure.

In a stammer of horror she thought—*Is that me? Is that who I've become? And Ryan has come to see me, to say good-bye.*

Tenderly the husband was touching the emaciated woman's arm. The husband was himself thinner than the wife recalled, with a scalp that shone as if waxen. His back was to her, she could see his sharp shoulder bones like wings poking through skin and cloth. The shirt he wore was no shirt Julia recognized. What were he and the woman speaking of, so earnestly? It was a startling sight—the woman was able to smile, she and her companion laughed together.

But what could be so funny? Was Death funny?

The wife felt excluded, cheated. She felt betrayed. The husband had never shared his death with *her.*

Soon then, the woman rose unsteadily to her feet and left the café.

A nurse, or a nurse's aide, had come for her. A handsome dark-skinned girl with a bright smile. Taking the sick woman by the arm, and tugging at the IV trolley which moved with practiced ease in their wake. The husband stood, not altogether steadily on his feet either, preparing to leave the café. He was checking his watch—Julia saw, he'd been waiting for an appointment. The sick woman in the café hadn't been the sole object of his visit after all, his meeting with her might have been accidental, innocent.

It was quite probable Ryan was visiting a relative in the hospital. If he'd had an appointment with one of the medical specialists she would have known, he would have told her. Those effusive conversations he sometimes had on the telephone, in his study with the door shut— might've been a relative. Ryan had an easy jocular bantering relationship with cousins both female and male. He loved them, Julia knew. He'd grown up with them, they were his closest and oldest friends.

Julia wasn't jealous. Julia didn't allow herself such petty emotions. If jealousy was an emotion.

And so, who was in the hospital? One of the (elder) Vanns, who had never liked Julia, for what reason she could not comprehend. Decades since she'd cried herself to sleep over such inexplicable rejection.

But now—where was the husband? His gait had been stiff, as if one of his legs gave him pain. Possibly, Ryan was seeing a back specialist. She'd begun to follow him belatedly, but he was gone—in a men's restroom possibly.

Long high-ceilinged corridors. Elevators with Plexiglas panels.

The hospital opened out of the atrium, corridors like spokes. This was Julia's first visit to the new hospital. If Ryan had come here previously, he hadn't brought Julia, and he hadn't shared his news with Julia.

This visit was his secret. The identity of the patient was his secret.

She went to the hospital information counter and asked if there was a patient in the hospital named "Vann." The receptionist told her that such information was "restricted." She said, "But I'm sure that a relative of mine is hospitalized here, and I'd like to see him. As long as I'm here."

"And what is the patient's full name?"

Julia hesitated. She had no idea what to say. It made no sense to say "Ryan"—for "Ryan Vann" wasn't a patient here—was he?

"Ma'am? What is the patient's first name?"

Her breathing came labored and thick. Somehow, the air had turned viscous. Or, she'd fallen, and was being sucked into a kind of quicksand.

"Ma'am? Ma'am? Hello, ma'am . . ."

They were leaning over her, where she'd fallen. Something like a great mouth had been sucking her down. The interior of the mouth was tepid, lukewarm, not chill as you'd expect. A briny odor as of old, stale urine which was a surprise in this sparkling-new hospital.

"Ma'am? Can you stand up? Sit up? Are you breathing all right?"

"Ma'am, just lean on me."

So embarrassing! In the hospital of all places she'd fainted; or not exactly fainted for she hadn't lost consciousness—(she was sure she hadn't lost consciousness for even a moment). And they were making a fuss over her, and didn't want her to stand up too quickly, take her handbag from them, and escape.

A blood-pressure cuff was being put on her upper arm. She hadn't given permission. Tight, tighter, tighter—Julia winced with the sharp pain.

Her blood pressure was very low, she was told. And her heartbeat—(one of the young black girls had dared to press her thumb against the underside of Julia's wrist)—was rapid.

"I—I'm fine. There's nothing the matter with *me*."

They wanted to take her into the ER. She was too weak to walk and so they would carry her on a stretcher. She insisted—No! She would not.

She was sitting on a bench. They'd allowed that. At the edge of a little gathering of observers, Julia dreaded to think that Ryan might be among them—staring in amazement at his wife! But she didn't see him. She was feeling vast relief, he hadn't seen *her*.

At last after several contentious minutes she managed to break free of the strangers. Managed to convince them she was all right. In their chiding voices they were saying, "We can't force you, ma'am. But you should check into the ER. You were unconscious, you 'fainted.' Did you wet yourself?"

"No! I certainly did not."

Furious and ashamed Julia turned away. She knew they were watching her—waiting for her to weaken, falter and again fall to her knees on the polished floor—but she did not. A safe distance from the information counter she saw a women's restroom, entered a stall and checked her clothing—yes, her underpants seemed to be "wetted" but odorless. (*Was* this colorless liquid urine? It didn't smell at all.) In one of the toilet stalls she waited patiently until no one was in the room before leaving but couldn't locate her car in the immense parking lot that dazzled and blinded with light. Where was Ryan's station wagon? Had he moved it? Had he driven home?

Eventually, Julia located her car. When she returned home she saw without surprise, Ryan's station wagon wasn't in the driveway.

WHERE YOU ARE GOING. Take me with you!

She lay close beside him. Stealthily, she embraced him from behind. She did not want to wake him. His breathing was raspy, wet-sounding. She pressed her warm face against the wiry hairs of the man's upper back. It had been years since she'd held the husband so close, so intimately. And she, the wife, so exposed and vulnerable, her arms open to him. She was risking rejection, a shrugging sleep-blunted rebuff. But Ryan was asleep and couldn't know. His was a deep gasping medicated sleep that excluded all awareness of the wife, as of the exterior world. But in this sleep he murmured as if speaking to her, and this was a surprise. Clumsily he turned in the bed, as he rarely did in his deepest sleep. He pulled at the covers, partially detaching the upper sheet, and he gave a little moan, and pressed against the wife, his soft, limp penis, that stirred against her thigh, the most subtle stirring of life, a kind of sigh, an indrawn breath, a vow.

THINGS PASSED ON
THE WAY TO OBLIVION

WHEN DOES *FATAL* BEGIN. YOU LIVE IT, BUT YOU CAN'T name it.

HER FIRST RESPONSE was *No.* But this was only the first response.

Her most forceful girl-cousin had brought her in the late-Saturday-night midsummer craziness of the East Village to Avenue B to *Fleurs du Mal (Tattoos).* She'd protested laughing nervously—the last thing she needed in her jangled life right now was a tattoo—she'd always felt a fastidious revulsion for tattoos—but Carroll had a way of insisting that made you think that, when you gave in, you were making her personally happy and so—somehow—Leanda's protest had turned into a weak *Well—all right . . .* Carroll hugged her fiercely, the kind of quick hard hug you'd get from a teammate after a score. *Fantastic! We'll pick something really beautiful for you beautiful Leanda.*

IT WAS SO: she was *beautiful Leanda.* You had to know Leanda intimately to know that beauty had never been enough.

IN THE BRIGHTLY-LIT tattoo shop amid deafening rock music she'd felt a thrill of daring as if—at last—she was doing something to define herself. Something risky and risqué no one in the family would expect of *her*.

Black butterfly! Terrific.

Your first? Great choice: it's Chinese.

Like, from a Chinese scroll? Ancient.

Well sure—it will hurt, some. The needle will sting. That's what a tattoo is—a little (temporary) pain for (permanent) beauty.

THE PLEASURE OF GIVING in, weakly. To people who mattered: family. All her young life the keenest pleasure.

GUESS HOW OLD my cousin Lee-lee is?

Foxy Joe Hall the tattoo artist at *Fleurs du Mal* had guessed—nineteen? Twenty-one? Totally surprised to learn the stiff-smiling girl was twenty-seven.

As long as she isn't underage. We don't do underage.

A reputable tattoo shop also will not oblige customers who are obviously drunk, high, or mentally ill. Professional ethics!

Leanda wasn't drunk, and Leanda wasn't high. This was a fact.

Foxy Joe Hall had executed all three of Carroll's super-action-heroine manga-tattoos. These were smart, cool, sexy tattoos nothing like the black butterfly which was too girly for Carroll Johnston. Like black-lace lingerie Carroll wouldn't be caught dead in.

How's your tats? Enjoying them?

You know I am, Joe! Absolutely.

No one saw Carroll's tattoos except very special people. No one was so trusted except very special people. The stylish three-inch manga-tats were on her belly, on the inside of her left thigh, on her right buttock. Carroll was a solid-muscled girl of almost-thirty built like a Henry Moore sculpture. You might mistake her for hefty or overweight seen from a little distance but not up-close. She was plain-faced, snub-nosed, icy-blue-eyed, *cool*. Her hair was metallic-blond. In Vineyard Haven, Edgartown, and Chilmark she'd been going door-to-door that summer requesting signatures on a petition to recall those Martha's Vineyard officials who hadn't been vigilant enough regarding sand dune conservation and it was said Carroll Johnston was so force-ful she'd accumulated more signatures than any other petitioner in memory.

These tats she'd had now for several years were kept secret inside her baggy clothing—cargo pants, T-shirts, prized old Dartmouth swim-team sweatshirt—if older family members/relatives were any-where near.

Carroll looked on while Foxy Joe worked his miracle-precision needle on Leanda's pale shoulder. The girl's skin did seem to him weirdly thin—the girl was *mixed-race*—some kind of Asian or South Pacific—but her skin was whiter than his. Delicate like silk a rough-calloused thumb could tear.

Oh oh oh!—the needle did hurt.

Like anything physical, almost. What was called *love-making*—though Leanda had learned to pretend otherwise, *love-making* always hurt.

She was a stoic, however. She'd learned, young.

A stoic, good-sport, *l'il dude*. As a child of five or six already she'd learned how to inveigle the Johnstons into liking her, that's to say find-ing a place in their hearts for her, with her shy stammering ways and shiny-black-winking eyes.

Adults you can fool, usually. Your own generation sees through you with a smirk.

Like wading in the surf at the private beach in Chilmark. She'd never tried to swim there like the others who threw themselves into the water without hesitation shouting with laughter. And the crazed family dog Paolo—Portuguese water spaniel—rushing among them colliding with Leanda if she wasn't careful. She'd weighed approximately ninety-seven pounds at her heaviest. If she waded out too far in a pretense of swimming she was in danger of being swept up by the waves, thrown down gasping for air and her skin scraped raw, bruised by pebbles.

Swimming is such a *fun-thing*, she'd had to hide the fact she hated it. Like *love-making* she tried to see was necessary, and practical, if any man was going to "love" her.

(At the beach no one had judged her harshly. She was sure. Carroll, Jody, and Quinn had been star team-swimmers at their schools, and would go on to compete at Dartmouth, Williams, Sarah Lawrence. Of her tall strapping blond boy-cousins all but one or two were jocks for whom swimming had been just one of the sports they'd been good at. They'd laughed at *l'il dude Lee-lee* but they'd liked her too. She was sure.)

How're you doin', Leanda? We're at the halfway mark now—almost.

Too distracted by the buzzing pain to respond. She'd have thought—twenty minutes? Thirty? Already forty excruciating minutes had passed. Not even halfway!

Stiff and straight in the swivel chair she sat, so short her feet didn't reach the floor. Her jaws were locked with strain. The chair was like a dentist's chair, and the buzzing needle was like a dentist's drill. In the mirror-to-the-ceiling she watched with fascinated horror the black butterfly materialize on her left shoulder. In bright lights that made her eyes water, she saw her quick-oozing blood wiped away. The butterfly was "life-sized"—in fact, a little larger than a typical monarch butterfly, that seemed to be pushing out of her very flesh.

What Daddy would say! He'd been disgusted with her frequently, but never for anything visible and incontestable as this.

The more beautiful the skin, the more it hurts. Like Einstein says there's no free lunch in the Universe, eh?

Leanda had no idea what Foxy Joe was talking about. The tattoo artist was one of those easy talkers—bull-shitters. Most guys you met were bull-shitters. Since she'd been a young girl Leanda had learned not to look startled but to smile in a kind of sly complicity.

Einstein means no energy is ever totally lost, Joe. It's just converted— energy into matter, matter into energy.

What the fuck's that, my friend?

What I said, Joe: energy into matter, matter into energy. E equals MC squared.

Carroll was one to weigh in on intellectual subjects. All of the Johnstons—except Leanda's mother and Leanda herself, of course— were like this. You'd think that someone had handed them a microphone. There were politicians in the family, in Maine and New Hampshire—U.S. congressmen. A Johnston had been chief justice of the New Hampshire Supreme Court in the 1950s and another Johnston had been an Eisenhower advisor. Leanda knew little of the family's history for little had been told her, she was *of the present generation.* She wasn't always sure if her cousin Carroll knew half of what she was talking about but Carroll spoke with such confidence, no one questioned her.

Carroll leaned close to observe Foxy Joe's quivering needle and the startling-red blood that oozed out around it. So absorbed, she hadn't answered her cell phone when it rang—the opening bars of "Paint It Black."

Ordinarily Leanda would have been stricken with embarrassment, this stranger, Foxy Joe Hall, so close to her, breathing his hot breath on her, that smelled of something like licorice; nudging his groin against her, as if he wasn't aware of what he was doing. A tattoo was a sexual—sexy—thing Leanda was doing, or having done to her—she guessed that Carroll saw it that way.

Foxy Joe was telling Leanda to sit still please. And could she try not to shiver so much.

Was Leanda shivering? Air-conditioning was blasting onto her face and her partially bared torso, her tank-top pulled down her shoulder so that Foxy Joe could ply his needle. But the tattoo artist needed AC, the bright lights and the "high degree of concentration" raised his temperature.

Foxy Joe had graying rust-colored hair in a ponytail and appeared to be, inside his clothes, covered in tattoos. Clusters like coiled snakes on both his arms and rising onto his neck, just the look of it, such density, made Leanda feel dizzy. Carroll had introduced Foxy Joe Hall to Leanda as "the crème de la crème of tattoo artists."

Foxy Joe dressed like a hipster in his early thirties but up close you could see the man was fifty at least. The skin on his forehead was unnaturally tight but the soft puckered skin around the eyes was unmistakable. Piercings in his nose, eyebrows, ears, and cheeks made him glitter like a pincushion. Carroll had boasted that Foxy Joe was so picky, he'd turned away customers because the tattoos they'd wanted were "unaesthetic"—or they themselves were "unaesthetic"—("that is, ugly")—it was like getting admitted into an exclusive club, having a tat by Foxy Joe.

At *Fleurs du Mal*, the smallest and simplest tattoos started at $199 excluding taxes.

Carroll had said, squeezing Leanda's chill little fingers *This one's on me, Lee-lee. Next one you can purchase for yourself.*

LATER IT WOULD BE NARRATED—(within the family initially, then in the media)—that Leanda had insisted upon a tattoo on the night of July 29. She'd asked Carroll to take her to the tattoo parlor on Avenue B where Carroll had gotten her tattoos. It would be narrated that Leanda had been in a "mood"—(maybe code for *high? coke-high?*)—she'd been sulky, vengeful—she'd known how a tattoo would upset her father with his ridiculous antiquated notions of feminine beauty, and she'd wanted to upset the old man, for sure.

Really? Leanda? Doesn't sound like her.

Well, she was high. I was surprised, too—I'd always thought I knew Leanda. A lot of a quiet person's personality comes out when she's high and not being observed by her elders. I don't mean that Leanda was a hypocrite or anything like that but—she wasn't aware of the rage she felt, I think, for all of us, growing up with us, and for her father and how he treated her. You never get over being adopted, and there's the—race thing. And at the wedding she'd made a fool of herself, she kept obsessing about some stupid wine spilled on her stupid dress asking me if any of it had gotten online.

Any of what?

I don't know—pictures of her. The stained dress, and this old geezer pawing her, who'd been some old lover of her mother's.

Did Uncle Jayson ever know?

About what, the old guy?

No, the tattoo.

I guess maybe. But he never saw it with his own eyes.

He didn't see the body?

Sure Uncle Jayson saw the body—in the funeral home in Chilmark. But you couldn't see the tattoo in the coffin, obviously.

He didn't come into the city to identify her . . .

Are you kidding? You know Uncle Jayson—he more or less fell apart when he got the news. They shipped the body to the funeral home.

Oh God that's sad. So soon after Brook's wedding . . .

Jody came with me to do the ID at the hospital morgue. Nobody seemed to know what the hell was going on. Who was in charge. Worst fucking hour of our lives, that's for sure.

THEY'D TAGGED HER *probable druggie, overdose.*

Seeing the dilated eyes rolled back in her head. Not-quite-healed tattoo on her back exposed by a clammy-sweaty T-shirt that had pulled off her shoulder.

In this part of Manhattan even on a "good" street—West Tenth at Fifth Avenue—it wasn't uncommon to answer such calls. In the

Magdalen Hospital ER nights in summer, many such calls. Overdose, panic.

Usually the caller wasn't alone. Maybe this one had had a friend with her, a druggie-companion. He, or she, might've left before the girl began to OD. Might've fled.

Summer nights half the population out on the streets and half of this population drunk or high or both, you were quick to identify such calls and even before blood work you were rarely mistaken.

This one's 911 calls were incoherent, bizarre. Had to be tripping.

By the time they'd arrived at 44 West Tenth, #3B, at 11:39 P.M., August 9, the girl had passed out. She'd had the presence of mind to unlock her door. Three medics had rushed up the stairs not wanting to take time waiting for the elevator and they'd found her on the floor just inside the door, pale-toffee skin, slutty black butterfly tattoo on her left shoulder, half-dressed, barefoot. She'd had a rich-girl look, even on the floor, sweaty and unconscious and a trail of vomit on her chin. Her hair was black, straight, disheveled. The apartment was sparely but stylishly furnished, nice things, oatmeal-colored sofa, black leather chairs, hardwood floors and small elegant woven rugs and framed photographs on the walls, conspicuously large black-and-white photographs of the quality you'd see in a museum. And there was an enormous state-of-the-art computer. And built-in floor-to-ceiling bookshelves. And the small bedroom attractive too though the bed was unmade, the sheets churned-looking, and the adjoining bathroom was messy—damp towels on the floor, toilet seat up and a stink of vomit and a ceiling fan turned high. (No visible sign of drugs or paraphernalia only just Tylenol, ibuprofen, bottles of vitamins, herbal medications. But if she had junkie friends they might've panicked and taken away the evidence.) Must've been she'd staggered into the other room lost her balance and fell heavily onto the floor for you could see the beginning of a bruise, considerable swelling on her right knee, in the ER the knee would take on a grotesque appearance like a bulbous growth on the girl's leg. *Mixed-race female, blood pressure sixty-four over ninety-nine, almost no pulse, clammy skin, open and dilated eyes, estimated age early twenties, estimated weight one hundred pounds, estimated height five feet two inches, failure to respond, probable overdose.* The small unresisting body that smelled of both vomit and urine they'd strapped to a stretcher bearing her skillfully down the stairs and to the ambulance at the curb with as much excited zeal as if she hadn't been an artsy-druggie who'd brought this collapse on herself but an innocent young woman stricken by some mysterious illness or malaise that had caused her dilated eyes to roll back in her head, her opened mouth to be damp with spittle, her bladder to release urine and her skin to exude clammy sweat so she'd looked like she was covered in a fine scrim of grease.

Heroin OD, want to bet?

Nope.

(OH GOD she'd said *No*—hadn't she?)

(Hadn't even wanted to see Carroll after the wedding where she'd been made to feel ashamed. And there was Carroll calling Leanda on her cell at 9:00 P.M. even as she was climbing out of a taxi on West Tenth outside Leanda's brownstone, uninvited.)

(NEVER REGAINED FULL CONSCIOUSNESS in the ER where, 12:12 A.M., she was admitted thrashing and writhing in the throes of a probable drug overdose. Oxygen mask attached. After some difficulty with her small veins blood was drawn but the vials may have been mislabeled, or misplaced. IV tube in her sallow-skinned arm she'd been tied to the gurney so she couldn't pull out the needle and injure herself. Given a powerful sedative and wheeled to a post-op room to wait for lab results. Soon then a new shift of medical workers came on duty. And most of the younger staff was new since the first of July—admitting resident, interns. By the time she was given an identity—*Leanda Johnston*, 27—after forty-eight hours, dehydrated, sinking blood pressure, cardiac arrhythmia, so powerful a sedative her organs shut down one by one, she'd lapsed into a deeper coma, and died.)

THE FIRST THING WRONG but she hadn't understood it would be *the first in a sequence of things-wrong.*

Not the tattoo—(which, examining in a hand mirror reflecting a bedroom mirror, she'd stared at for long minutes at a time rapt in a sort of hypnotized dread—unless it was elation: the black butterfly was truly beautiful and yes, it was *sexy*)—but the wedding she'd been so anticipating. Or, maybe it had been the afternoon before the wedding, the long trek through glaring sun, beach grass and nettles to the Johnstons' private beach on the Atlantic Ocean off Chilmark.

Her father, shuffling with his foot in a cast, sweating, cursing, had needed her to help him walk. He hated to use a cane, he preferred to lean on his daughter, who was also carrying his camera and tripod. Alone of the little party Leanda hadn't worn proper shoes, only just sandals, and she'd been bare-legged, though she'd been warned about ticks.

Deer ticks, not the other kind. Deer ticks are so little they're the size of a pencil point. You don't see them, that's the problem. They burrow deep and they infect you and if you're unlucky you don't feel the pain of the infection.

News of deer tick "infestation" and Lyme disease "epidemic" on Martha's Vineyard had the effect of making younger people rebellious for it was older people who obsessed about these matters. Even Leanda who was cautious by nature had quickly become tired of the subject by the early summer. The Johnstons' next-door neighbors on Menemsha Cross Road who made a fetish out of showering *twice a day washing every inch of their bodies with a rough-textured washcloth*—Leanda's aunt Elsie and uncle Davis, Carroll's parents, who were convinced they'd just gotten infected with Lyme disease each time you saw them—Leanda's mother Gabriele who'd stayed away from the island for much of the summer like a recluse in the perpetually-air-conditioned condo on

Central Park South—and Gabriele's friend Helene Yarburgh who'd claimed to have had Lyme disease resulting in semi-paralysis of her facial muscles though (it was said behind her back) it had really been a minor stroke Helene had had, she hadn't wanted to acknowledge.

(Helene Yarburgh, a wealthy quasi-glamorous widow who lived in Edgartown, was notorious on the Island for an alleged love affair she'd had with William Styron twenty years before. When Helene had first seen Leanda, as a young adolescent, she'd blithely assumed that the *mixed-race* girl had to be an au pair, otherwise what would a Filipina be doing in the Johnstons' house in Chilmark?)

Jayson Johnston, Leanda's father, now in his mid-seventies, was a paragon of carelessness in hygiene—Jayson ate food he'd dropped onto the floor, ate unwashed fruit, neglected to wash his hands even after using the bathroom. He laughed at his family's insistence that he see his small team of doctors regularly and he'd continued to smoke after a lung-cancer scare in his fifties, he didn't take precautions against deer ticks when he went out tramping in the woods and through deep grass; and yet, he too obsessed over Lyme disease— "They say it eats your brain. Microscopic parasites." When Leanda assisted her father, as she'd done intermittently for the past six years since graduating from college, she'd been astonished to observe at close hand how Jayson Johnston both revered and despised himself; how he'd seemed at times, in his heavy-drinking fugues, not to care if he lived or died.

"Am I too old for you? Too old to be your God-damned *Daddy*?"— he'd taunted her, cruelly. "Maybe you think you'd have been better off with your 'birth mother,' eh?"

Leanda had shook her head mutely. *No Daddy.*

She had no idea who her *birth mother* was. She'd known as a very young child that the woman who called herself "Mummy" wasn't her true mother as she wasn't the mother of her sisters or her brother Casey—these were the children of previous Mrs. Johnstons, now departed. She'd known, because she was told so often, that she was *special*.

"We picked you out, Leanda. No 'pig in a poke' with you!"

She tried to see: a pig in a poke? Was a poke like a paper bag?

Was *she* the little piggie, in the paper bag?

The corners of Daddy's eyes crinkled when he smiled so broadly, you understood you had to smile, too. Or Daddy would take offense.

He'd had assistants, sometimes more than one, working for him. But Leanda had liked to be Daddy's "assistant," too. Sometimes he called her "my apprentice." None of this was serious of course. Jayson Johnston's serious photography required travel—Brazil, Patagonia, Antarctica, Africa, remote provinces in China and in the Australian outback. It was only in recent years, since his health had begun to fail, that Leanda's father concentrated on subjects close at hand. Like his friend the late, distinguished photographer Paul Strand whom he'd known as a young man, he was now photographing trees, flowers, leaves, skies and moonlight just outside his door. These photographs were minimal, spare, modest in ambition, "poetic." (On the walls of Leanda's father's house in Chilmark were a number of signed prints by such classic photographers as Brassaï, Alfred Stieglitz, Cartier-Bresson, Edward Weston, Minor White, Paul Strand. Of these, Strand's *Winter Garden*, *Great Vine in Death*, and *Things Passed on the Way to Oblivion*, work of the early 1970s, were clearly models for Jayson Johnston's newest work, which Leanda knew to be very beautifully composed but, she thought, sadly diminished, small in scale.)

Retired to Chilmark, her father had been embittered and ironic at first, like a crippled giant; more recently, he was trying hard to adapt to the changed circumstances of his life. Leanda could never remember her father's age—she thought it might be seventy-five.

Or, seventy-six.

Gamely Leanda had carried Jayson's heavy Hasselblad for him on the island, the previous spring. His tripod. His backpack which contained bottles of Evian water and wheat germ bars as well as lenses. She was half his size. She was in reasonably good physical condition— but she wasn't a hiker. In school, she'd been a slow cautious swimmer in the shallow end of the chlorinated pool. At sports she'd been hopeful and sometimes inspired but easily discouraged by aggressive competition, and soon breathless, fatigued. She'd been too small to take seriously. Not the last chosen for sports teams but next-to-last. The (adopted) Chinese-American girls had snubbed her, in their cool subtle way. In the Johnston household it was crucial to be a good sport, not to complain and above all not to *weaken*. Especially at their summer place where much of the time was spent outdoors. (Secretly, Leanda hated summers. She'd hated summers on Martha's Vineyard where so much time had to be spent outdoors and where so much time was spent talking about weather, real estate, "new people," threats to the Island.) At Squibnocket Point they'd tramped into the dunes. She'd crouched shivering in freezing April wind from the ocean as her father photographed shorebirds for hours—relentlessly, tirelessly. Astonishing to observe this frequently morose aging man quickened to life by the camera in his hands that were still steady, thrilled by the sight of herons, egrets, hawks, cranes, curlews, gulls—amazing, Jayson Johnston could identify herring gulls, laughing gulls, black-backed gulls, species of terns.

She was the one to stagger in exhaustion. Though she was nearly a half-century younger than Jayson Johnston.

The legendary Jayson Johnston! This was a joke not entirely a joke.

But it was deer ticks she'd been thinking of, for some reason. What was the neurological disease they caused—Lyme disease? But why was she thinking of this?

Recalling her handsome dark-tanned cousin Mitchie Johnston who went everywhere barefoot on the Island, driving his Jeep, hiking in dune grass, in hot sand. Fearlessly running into the crazed crashing waves that foamed at Leanda's bare toes on the beach, freezing even when the sun was warm. Mitchie she'd been in love with—at a little distance—since she'd been twelve, and Mitchie had been sixteen. He'd appalled female relatives by blithely pulling ticks out of his skin with tweezers or burning them out with matches, wincing with pain but laughing.

(But these hadn't been deer ticks. The other species of tick, large enough so you could see them. Looking like tiny spiders. Very black, and very easy to detect against skin as pale and smooth as Leanda's.)

Mitchie hadn't come to Brook's wedding but he'd sent an e-mail video. Mitchie'd been traveling in Nepal, trekking with several companions and a Sherpa guide, making a documentary film.

She hadn't loved Mitchie Johnston in years. She rarely thought of him now except sometimes with Nick—shutting her eyes, as Nick touched her, caressed and kissed her, seeing then her dark-tanned cousin with surf crashing about his perfect boy-body, shielding his eyes from the sun, laughing at her.

YOU'RE PRECIOUS TO ME, Leanda. You are the only child I chose, because you are special.

Did Daddy really say these remarkable words? Or had she invented them? It almost didn't matter which, in her delirium she could make no distinction.

CARROLL HAD TEXTED just once, to ask how the tattoo was healing.

Leanda had texted back *Good! Thanks, C.*

In fact the tattoo didn't seem to be healing as she'd been promised it would. Or (possibly) she'd misunderstood how quickly it would heal. That entire tattoo-episode—like much of the wedding—was a blur and a buzz in her head she preferred not to recall.

She'd slipped away from the wedding party. She was sure no one noticed.

And the tears on her silly hot face, like the old fool's wine staining her beautiful silk shift, no one noticed.

Brook hadn't asked her youngest (half-) sister to be a bridesmaid. Diplomatically Brook had explained she'd wanted a "balance" between sisters/cousins and friends—it was certainly nothing personal.

Of course, it was personal. Brook disliked Leanda.

Though Leanda adored Brook, as she adored all her (half-) sisters, and her (half-) brother Casey, they disliked her.

Or if they didn't dislike her, they were indifferent to her which was worse.

At family occasions Leanda was given to know—just *know*—that, if she hadn't been present, if she hadn't *existed*, essentially nothing would be changed in the gathering.

Mummy had said sighing *I tried. God knows I tried. She's a sweet sad child she's just not—you know.*

These not-quite-sober words she was sure she'd overheard. More than once.

Just not—you know . . . My own daughter.

Gabriele had had at least two miscarriages, Leanda had learned. If one of these pregnancies had come to term—Leanda wouldn't have been brought into the family.

Pig in a poke! That was exactly what Gabriele had wanted.

Though she'd been involved at first in planning her stepdaughter's wedding, and the party of nearly two hundred guests to be held at the Chilmark farm, Gabriele had claimed to feel too "stricken" by the heat to travel to the actual event. (This July, 2012, had been the hottest in recorded history in New York City and New England.) Leanda knew that her father was furious though he was professing indifference.

Brook had said she was disappointed, and hurt. At the Champagne party Jody had said with a giggle *Oh come off it, Brook-ie! Why'd you or anybody else give a shit.*

This too, Leanda had pretended she hadn't heard.

Now she was safe from them. Now she'd fled the Vineyard and returned to her own place on West Tenth Street. She was at her computer trying to work the Photoshop program which was too complicated for her. Now, she did miss Nick!

When she'd first started to feel sick, running a mild fever, and mildly sick to her stomach, and a mild headache—she attributed it to the computer, her long mostly frustrating and futile hours at the computer. And then, it had been just a few days after getting the tattoo and the tattoo was still sore, like a patch of burnt skin, and so she hadn't thought *Maybe it's a tick bite, infected*—for she was in Manhattan now, on West Tenth Street.

Immediately she'd thought *The tattoo.*

How impulsively she'd behaved! Nick criticized her for rarely behaving *spontaneously* which showed how little he knew of her, whom he claimed to love. Yet she'd behaved *spontaneously* the other night, *impulsively.*

It was a reckless thing to have done. In the Johnston household such pop-culture gestures as getting a tattoo were signs, in most people, of imbecility, inferiority. Only a loser defiles her body, unless she's a rock star which is different, but only barely. The summer fifteen-year-old Maggie had streaked her platinum-blond hair red, purple, green—no one had stopped talking about it.

Getting a fever, nausea—this was an appropriate punishment for what Leanda had done. Knowing beforehand that it would be a mistake.

Why had she trusted her cousin! She had to believe that Carroll had had a mischievous reason for coercing Leanda into defiling her body—(as her father would see it)—with a sleazy tattoo on her shoulder.

What in God's name have you done, Leanda! You know I hate tattoos on women.

She was feeling panic, for Jayson would learn about the tattoo eventually. Even if she kept it hidden, as Carroll did her tattoos, in the presence of relatives. She felt a thrill of horror—what if Carroll had recorded some of the tattoo session on her cell phone, and sent it out? A multiple mailing?

That night, she hadn't wanted to go out with Carroll, or with anyone. She'd had enough of going out—of being "festive"—several days on the Vineyard helping to prepare for the lavish party—at a time when she needed to prepare her portfolio for the Camden (Maine) Arts Colony. The deadline was August 15 for a place in the fall/winter.

Her friend Nicholas had sent his application already. It was certain that Nick would get a place there since he'd been a Camden arts fellow several times in the past, and the director was enthusiastic about his work. It had been their plan to go together—Leanda had promised to tell Jayson that she couldn't be his assistant any longer.

That evening, Nick was going to call her—but she'd gone out with Carroll, and hadn't answered her cell phone when the call came. It was essentially a life that wasn't *adult*—she knew this. To be an *adult* you had a serious job, you supported yourself, you were married or living with a loyal companion; you might even have a child, or children. (It was like a gull's shriek in her head: she was *twenty-seven*.) You didn't live much of the time with your family, you didn't sacrifice your (still reasonably young) life working (for no pay) for your demanding father.

Like one of the voracious shorebirds, Jayson Johnston was— flapping its feathered wings, stabbing its beak into what was edible, mad glaring eyes, shrieking cries of insatiable hunger.

A sudden swirl of nausea. This had to be—what?

She hadn't gotten around to listening to her voice mail since she knew that Nick would have called, and she felt guilty about not seeing him. She'd invited him to the wedding and then—unconscionably, in a text message—she'd dis-invited him.

It had to be the tattoo. A dirty needle!

Maybe—she was infected with AIDS?

(But not from a tattooist's needle, was that possible?)

(Of course it was possible. Very likely, Foxy Joe Hall was HIV-positive.)

(But why had Carroll taken her to that terrible place? Didn't Carroll *like her*?)

(Of course, Carroll liked her! Of her girl-cousins, Carroll and Maggie had always liked her best, better than her sisters. They'd told her so, many times.)

She'd begun to shiver. She listened to Nick's message:

> *Hey Leanda, where are you? Did you forget to call when*
> *you got back from the Vineyard? Can I come over—*
> *tonight? Or—tomorrow?*

The second message:

> *Leanda? Where are you? Are you back from the wedding?*
> *D'you want me to vet your portfolio? Are you working on*
> *it now? When will it be finished? Maybe—supper tonight?*
> *Hey—I miss you. It's OK about the wedding.*

To her dismay, there were a half-dozen calls from Nick, plus text messages, which she hadn't somehow discovered until now. She couldn't bring herself to contact him.

The *male gaze:* she knew all about this, intellectually. In her Contemporary Culture seminar at Yale she'd written a paper on the subject. She'd quoted many impressive sources, included many terrific examples of the *male gaze* from Renaissance madonnas through odalisques by Manet, Renoir, Picasso and "exploited female figures" in Andy Warhol's lithographs. It wasn't just in pornography that the *male gaze* was evident but in serious classical art—virtually every-where. Yet, Leanda understood that she had no way of defining herself outside the *male gaze*. If it were not the *male gaze* of men of her own approximate age like Nick, or her male cousins, it was the (nurtur-ing, if judgmental) *male gaze* of older men: her professors at Yale, her instructors at the Parsons School, her male relatives, her father Jayson Johnston.

This gaze was like oxygen. Women who weren't aware of it were deceived into thinking that they could exist, they could *breathe*, on their own.

Girls were rarely so deceived. Girls understood, what women tried to forget.

Even in her fever-state, trying to work at her computer doggedly experimenting with Photoshop variants on her best photographs from the past year, Leanda couldn't escape the truth of this insight: that the *male gaze* so defined her, she could not imagine surviving, still less liv-ing, without it.

So, there was Nick. Before Nick there'd been other Nicks.

These hadn't been boys (like Mitchie) who'd teased and tormented her and laughed at her. These had been boys who'd been kind to her, drawn to her shy stammering manner, her beautiful but often down-cast eyes, the bruised-looking mouth that could be induced to smile. Of course, many of these boys, and now men, weren't tall—they were drawn to Leanda by her diminutive size. Here was a young woman who wasn't, well—*womanly*.

At least, at the start Nick had adored her. They'd met at the Par-sons School where Nick was teaching a workshop in Photoshop which Leanda had taken. Nick wasn't much older than Leanda but his pho-tography was so clearly superior to hers, she'd felt a kind of relieved gratitude, she wouldn't have to pretend otherwise as usually she did when she dated artists.

Two years they'd been together. But not living together. Nick complained that Leanda didn't answer her phone, didn't text back when he texted her. Gently he complained that she worried too much about her family, for a woman of her age.

"It isn't as if they worry about *you*."

She'd invited Nick to her sister's wedding, and to stay with her at the family "farm" on Menemsha Cross Road. She'd intended to introduce Nick to Jayson Johnston—at last. And if they slept together in the same room in the guesthouse, that would define Nick as Leanda's lover, unmistakably.

Her sisters thought Leanda was so sexless, so backward, she'd never had an actual boyfriend. Beautiful face and perfect straight-black glossy hair to her shoulders but disfigured by ineptitude as by acne. She'd never brought anyone home to introduce to the family, and certainly not to Daddy.

Two days before they were to leave for the Vineyard, after Nick had booked tickets for them on Jet Blue/Cape Air, Leanda had told him it wasn't possible, she had to go alone. Unforgivably she'd disinvited him by way of a text message—she hadn't had the courage to call him, or even to write an explanatory e-mail.

Of course, Nick had been disappointed. But not angry, as another man might have been.

He'd been, Leanda thought, *not so surprised.*

Now, she was feeling so sick—with guilt? regret? poison in her bloodstream?—she couldn't call him.

He'd believed that Leanda was a beautiful woman. He'd loved it that she was *mixed-race* and that she was vague about her probable background—all she really knew with certainty was that she'd been adopted as an infant by Jayson and Gabriele Johnston, who'd been forty-eight and twenty-nine at the time.

Now, she was looking so frankly sick—sallow-skin, lank hair, dry scabby lips—there was no disguising the fact that she was of *Filipina extraction.* She dreaded anyone seeing her in such a diminished state not as the delicate-boned Asian-American beauty the *male gaze* registered but as a totally ordinary-looking slant-eyed girl of the kind Nick had been seeing all his life in school, the kind who'd probably cleaned house for his mother, and registered in the *male gaze* as invisible.

So she hadn't called Nick whose father was a doctor associated with Columbia Presbyterian. She hadn't called any of her college friends who lived in the city and who might have come immediately to her. Instead she'd called Carroll and left a message she hoped didn't sound whiny:

> Hi Carroll? This is Leanda. I guess I don't feel so good—
> I think I'm sick—maybe the needle was infected?—the tattoo
> looks red—feels sore—I don't think it's healing right—could
> you come over if you're in the city? I—I'd really appreciate it.

This was 9:25 P.M., August 4. At 9:40 P.M. she called Carroll again.

> Carroll? It's Leanda. I'm feeling kind of—a little panicky,
> I'm kind of sick— I'm afraid to call 911. I'm afraid of the ER.
> I've been vomiting but I don't feel any better. I have a fever—
> 101.1 degrees. Could you come over, if you're in the city?
> I don't want to call my mother, you know what she's like she'd
> be hysterical . . . Please can you call me back, Carroll? Maybe
> you could come over . . .

In the space of several hours Leanda would call several other persons—her sisters Jody and Quinn, who had apartments in the city but who weren't in the city at this time; and her cousin Harriet. There were older female relatives (including her mother) she considered and dismissed.

No one answered her calls, and no one called back. By this time it was nearing midnight. She'd taken two capsules of Tylenol—that was good for a fever, wasn't it? She'd been vomiting—that meant she was in danger of dehydration. But when she tried to drink a glass of water, she choked, and vomited it up at once.

Her heart was beating strangely. Her skin itched, burnt. There were welts, terribly itchy welts, on her thighs, and inside her clothes on her belly and chest. She had sensitive skin: allergic to certain kinds of seafood, tomatoes, even onions. She wondered if she'd eaten something spoiled or contaminated.

In desperation finally she called her mother.

The phone number wasn't familiar to her, she'd forgotten it out of neglect. Had to look it up. Oh but she was so sick!—vomit leaking up into her mouth.

And the cool smug voice answered:

You have reached the residence of Gabriele Heideman-Johnston.
Ms. Heideman-Johnston is unavailable. If this is an emergency
you may want to contact Ms. Heideman-Johnston's secretary
whose phone is—.

It was her mother's revenge, Leanda thought. For her mother had been jealous of her and her father, the special bond between them.

As Gabriele, at a young age, had supplanted the middle-aged Mrs. Charlotte Johnston, whom Leanda had never met, who'd supplanted a woman named Marilynne Meyer, whom Leanda had also never met, who'd been the mother of her sisters and brother, so Leanda as a girl had supplanted her mother in her father's affections.

At the time, growing up, Leanda hadn't been conscious of this, or only barely conscious. It had become more evident, painfully so, when she'd graduated from college, and had been prevailed upon by her father to spend time on the Vineyard with him.

At Brearley, as at Yale, Leanda's father seemed to be "known"—

she hadn't had to speak of Jayson Johnston, and had rarely spoken of him, out of shyness.

In such schools there are *known* families. Amid most of those others, who are *not-known*.

Leanda Johnston's family situation had not been especially complicated, as such situations went. The majority of her Brearley classmates had been from families in which separation, divorce, remarriage, custody disputes, half-siblings/step-siblings, and adoptions were commonplace; not a few were, like Leanda, the children of an older father who'd married down a generation or two from his own generation, thus his youngest daughter had "older" siblings, practically of another generation. There were several Chinese girls who'd been adopted by Caucasian parents and these were among the very best Brearley students; there was a single dazzling-beautiful Ethiopian girl; but there was no other Filipina-American adoptee so far as Leanda knew.

Why did you adopt me, if you didn't want me. If you couldn't love me—this, Leanda had never asked Gabriele.

SHE'D BEEN TOUCHING the tattoo area, that throbbed and burnt her fingers. She was sure this had to be the infection. But to call 911—this would be an irrevocable decision.

She wondered if she was being ridiculous—Carroll would laugh at her.

She thought *If an ambulance comes for me, that will begin a process I can't stop.* She thought of her father in Chilmark, how upset and anxious he'd be to learn that Leanda had been admitted to a hospital in Manhattan, with an infected tattoo. Her father had become increasingly irrational in his dislike of Manhattan he called a *hellhole*, in the summer a *sauna*. He'd resent feeling that he should travel all the way to Manhattan to see his daughter in the hospital, if the ER didn't discharge her. She thought *He will hate this. He will know how weak I am.*

At some point that night Leanda lost her balance, slipped and fell heavily on the hardwood floor. Her stupid bad luck, she missed one of the rugs and struck her knee on the floor, stunned with pain. She began to weep, helplessly.

You deserve this! Whatever it is.

THE JOHNSTONS WERE *a distinguished old New England family.*

Invariably it was said of Jayson Johnston (b. 1938, Bangor, Maine) that he was *of a distinguished old New England family.*

In the 1870s, Jayson Johnston's great-great-grandfather moved to New York City. By the turn of the century, he'd built a small brownstone mansion at Park Avenue and Seventy-fifth Street and soon after the family acquired ninety acres of hilly land in the southwest corner of Martha's Vineyard, overlooking the Atlantic Ocean.

The brownstone had long ago been sold. Of the ninety acres at least twenty remained; the house was a shingle-board farmhouse with somewhere beyond a dozen sizable rooms. There was an old hay barn, and there was an old icehouse.

The irony was, Jayson Johnston (who was to live out most of the remainder of his life on Martha's Vineyard) frequently made the statement that he hated islands.

Jayson complained to interviewers, as to anyone who would listen, that as long as you were *on island*, you lived a myopic and miniature life.

He'd been coming to Chilmark for nearly eight decades. It wasn't a fact he was proud of, he said.

No matter that some of the most beautiful photographs of Jayson Johnston's "later years" had been taken *on island.*

There was a fragment of a bull's spinal column that had turned up in a field, Father used as a doorstop in his studio. Leanda had shrunk from seeing this, as a child. She shivered to think how a living creature had ended up in such a place. A bull was large, noble—handsome. All living things were recycled for the use of other living things, she knew. But it seemed so cruel.

He'd taken photographs of the vertebrae, in a patch of sunshine on a stone path. Dried autumn leaves, a crack in the stone path. Intricate shadows of the vertebrae, like lace.

AT THE WEDDING in the Old Whaling Church in Edgartown Leanda had sat with the family of course. She'd sat between her father (his foot in a cast! he'd fallen down a flight of steps and broken his ankle) and her aunt Elsie. It was a relief that she'd disinvited Nick—her father was in a sulky mood, you couldn't tell if he was feeling physically unwell or just brooding. He wasn't unhappy about the wedding—he hadn't so very much interest in his older children who'd long ago slipped free of his grasp and so seemed less real to him than the youngest girl who was still *his*.

Leanda understood this. Leanda knew it wasn't the time to challenge this assumption.

In the old Greek Revival church where the most elegant Vineyard weddings were frequently held, Leanda had felt something turn in her heart. It was beyond admiration for—envy of—her vivacious sister who was marrying Stanley Cummins III who was an investment banker in Boston. It was not even disappointment, that no effort of smiling could quite disguise, that Maggie hadn't asked her to be one of her bridesmaids. (In fact, Leanda hadn't expected to be asked. But pride wouldn't allow her to reveal this.) She'd been devastated to understand that never would she be married in this historic old church, never would she be married to any man of whom the Johnstons would approve, or even like. She *knew*.

For she'd had a birth mother of whom—(anyone could surmise)—she'd have been ashamed, if she'd known the woman. For the woman had *given up her baby*. What kind of person *gives up her baby?* People like the Johnstons and their friends and neighbors on Martha's Vineyard and in Manhattan didn't *give up their babies*. In their world, a baby is precious. A baby bearing their DNA is priceless. In the other world, which is most of the world, a baby is very often *unwanted*.

Leanda thought *It's a curse that can never be lifted. Yet they tried to love me, I think.*

Certainly, her (adoptive) father had tried to love her. Of all of the Johnstons it was Jayson who hadn't the capacity to be hypocritical. He said outright what he felt, and he felt exactly what showed in his face.

She'd tried to be "festive," however. She was the most reliable of people, not only willing to behave as others wished her to behave, but positively eager to do so.

She'd helped prepare for the party. Two hundred guests! She'd tried hard to prevail upon Gabriele to come, and had nearly succeeded. She'd helped organize the wedding rehearsal, the rehearsal dinner. She'd gone on errands into Vineyard Haven as she'd been bade.

She'd helped reason with Brook on matters of overwhelming if ephemeral significance. She spent time with her father who was irascible and depressed, shuffling about with his foot in a heavy cast. (He'd broken his foot in a mysterious fall, in the house. The close-mouthed way in which this fall was spoken of by the relatives, you had to suppose he'd been drinking.) If she'd burst into tears, it was safely in private.

At the party in the Chilmark house, she'd been urged to drink Champagne. A delicate "flute" of the most exquisite Champagne.

Fairly quickly people were drinking too much. Fairly quickly there was much laughter. Carroll and her half-sister Quinn were urging Leanda to dance with X, Y, Z. Names had flown past her, like inebriated hummingbirds. Leanda was wearing a pale blue silk sheath and a jade necklace her father had brought back to her from China; she'd begun to feel precarious in her high-heeled shoes, to which she wasn't accustomed.

A fizzing sensation in her nostrils, from the Champagne. In rapid succession she'd sneezed, squeaky little sounds of the kind a child might make.

Gesundheit! God bless you.

It was an idiotic custom. Leanda hated it. Some sort of holdover from a primitive superstitious past in which no one believed any longer and yet strangers intruded upon your privacy daring to wish you good health, succeeding only in embarrassing you.

The man who'd wished her good health leaned in upon her. Towering over her. He seemed to know her—a family friend? One of those admiring men her mother had gathered around her, in an earlier phase of her marriage when she'd still been young, and had been livened by the company of admiring men.

"Dance, dear? It's 'Leondra'—is it?"

She didn't bother to correct him—Mr. Hurst. Her smile was fixed to her face like plastic. She stumbled a little, in Hurst's awkward arms. The five-piece band was playing music with a hip-hop Latin beat to which the man was wholly unsuited.

She was feeling relief, Nick wasn't here. Very possibly, she would never see Nick again.

When they made love, at Nick's initiation, they were both very quiet. They were both very solemn. Nick's concern was with Leanda's comfort—he was concerned about hurting her, lying too heavily upon her, crushing her. Leanda's concern was with seeming not to feel the discomfort and pain she invariably felt.

You can tell me, Leanda—is there someone else? You're in love with someone else? Your mind is on someone else?

No! It is not.

Yet he'd seemed to know. Though he couldn't have known that the man on Leanda's mind was her father.

He professed not to understand why Leanda was so helpless when the Johnstons summoned her. It wasn't just Jayson, it was any of them.

If her mother called, Leanda hurried to her always expecting the worst—the woman lived alone except for a succession of houseguests in a sumptuous condominium on Central Park South. Relatives were always calling Leanda to plead with her, or berate her, about taking care of her father, and Leanda usually gave in. She told Nick that she was grateful to the Johnstons, they were her family. He said they were exploiting her good nature.

She had to think he meant *your servile nature.*

Nick said they'd probably bought her from her birth mother. He knew what private adoptions were: poor unmarried girls, well-to-do Caucasian couples. He told Leanda about a TV program he'd seen on the subject of American couples arranging to adopt Russian children, of whom a good number were "sent back" when they failed to "adjust."

Stubbornly, pointlessly Leanda said she wasn't Russian.

She'd said, the last time they'd been together, "I can't say no to my father! He's injured himself, he can barely walk. He's been depressed. He's capable of the most remarkable work, but he's been depressed."

"You have to assert yourself, Leanda. This has been going on for years. Your family will eat you up alive. Tell your father you've made other plans for this fall—you're going to Camden."

"I don't have a residency at Camden yet."

"You won't have one if you don't complete the application. I can help you."

"He doesn't want anyone else to assist him, now. He's feeling abandoned. He says he's convinced he will die, if he leaves the Vineyard."

"That's ridiculous! He's blackmailing you emotionally. It's what he's been doing since I met you. You should realize that you aren't a kid any longer, Leanda, who can throw away a year of her life."

He asked Leanda if she'd like him to accompany her when she explained to her father that she was going to Camden, Maine, for the fall and winter, to work on her own photography. "Tell him you've made other plans, that can't be changed. With me."

Leanda stammered yes—she would do that. Or—no. She could not do that.

Nick had taken hold of Leanda's hands. Now she eased her hands from his. She was laughing nervously. Nick said:

"You want to come with me, Leanda, don't you? To Camden? No one will bother you there, you can work twelve hours a day uninterrupted.

"Then—that's what I'll be doing."

He'd kissed her. She'd clutched at his neck, her thin arms around his neck, kissing him, desperate and elated.

COME HELP ME! I'm so afraid, Nick. I love you—if there is anyone I can love. Please help me, I don't want to die alone.

AT THE START of his drinking he was mellow, maudlin. Drawing his rough-calloused fingers across her cheek.

I hope you forgive me, Leanda. I know I've been a terrible father taking advantage of your sweet nature and your generosity.

You are my darling, you know that don't you?

Her older sisters, her brother Casey—he'd been disappointed in them. Even as children they'd eluded him. By traveling so much when they'd been young he had broken the bond between them—the bond between father and children. It had been painfully clear, he was capable of forgetting them for weeks, months. The gifts he brought to them were, in Casey's words, "airport gifts"—expensive "souvenirs" he'd picked up in airports, hastily, on his way home.

(Leanda didn't think that was always so. Her father had brought very nice things for her purchased on his travels, especially for her. She was sure of this.)

Tramping in the dunes. Miserable rainy weather on the Cape. The morning after a blizzard had left power out through most of the Vineyard. Yet as a girl of twelve she'd been Daddy's assistant-apprentice as he fondly called her. She was taking pictures, too. Daddy had bought her a good camera, and helped her with the settings.

Snow-draped dunes, foaming waves, rivulets on the wide sandy beach, driftwood, litter. Skeletons of once-living sea-creatures, washed ashore. Spines, vertebrae. Gliding across the coarse sand at their feet, shadows of gulls, hawks.

It was as Virginia Woolf had observed: there is so much more to be seen in a photograph than in the actual subject from which the photograph has been taken.

HERE WAS THE SURPRISE he'd wanted to tell her: the curator at the International Center of Photography had approached him to assemble a retrospective of his photographs. With his broken foot, his creased face, his eyes glistening in excitement—"Good news! But not possible without you."

She would help prepare the photographs. She would arrange for framing, which was expensive. She would label the photographs and she would write the catalogue copy which her father would then edit.

She'd studied the history of photography at Yale, to prepare for such tasks.

Shuffling with his broken foot in a cast, steely-gray hair in ridges above his forehead, tender-seeming, smiling like any proud father he'd escorted the bride into the Old Whaling Church and down the aisle to the altar where the bridegroom and the minister awaited her.

Leanda thought *That will never be me.*

A profound melancholy eased over her. She ceased to see what was before her.

Afterward at the Chilmark farm she'd been urged to drink Champagne. There were many toasts, and much laughter. Mr. Hurst had asked her to dance. Leanda had been too gracious, or too cowardly, to detach herself from him. He'd asked her about her college courses: the last time he'd spoken with her, Leanda had been an undergraduate at

Yale. Yet, he was confusing her with someone who'd gone to Welles-ley. His thinning white hair had been meticulously combed over his head. He wore black tie, and his starched white shirt was wine-stained. Soon, he would spill wine onto Leanda's dress. There is something so sad about a man who requires a woman, the desperation of such need. But he'd offended Leanda by asking, with a smile of admiration, how much she weighed.

Mr. Hurst was one of the Island's quasi-famous figures. There were many of these, who had achieved prominence in New York, or in Boston, in an indeterminate past.

"Jesus! I'm sorry . . . Let me see if I can wipe this with . . ."

Clumsily he'd dipped a napkin into a glass of ice water. But Leanda was departing, and would not return.

She'd gone into another part of the house with the excuse that she wanted to change her clothes. But she hadn't returned. Instead, she took two Ambien tablets and went to bed. And early next morning while the house was asleep—how many sleeping, in how many rooms, she had no idea—she slipped away without telling anyone.

Called a taxi, took Cape Air to Boston and Jet Blue to Kennedy, a taxi to West Tenth Street. She hadn't said good-bye to anyone even the bride. Even her father.

IT WAS A KIND of open secret, she was Uncle Jayson's daughter—actually. The mother was probably a cleaning woman, or—maybe—he'd been having physical therapy for some back problems—a physical therapist. Like I say it was a kind of open secret in the family but you never talked about it of course. He and Marilynne had been divorced, he'd married Gabriele, she'd had miscarriages and around that time the "adopted baby" came on the scene. They pretended it was adopted—or maybe Gabriele never knew. Anything Jayson Johnston wanted to do he more or less did.

He's a genius, they say. We see his photographs in museums and they look pretty good. It's hard when you know the man—the "genius." It's hard comprehending.

Sure it made sense, otherwise why'd Uncle Jayson adopt a baby when he already had so many kids, and didn't get along with any of them? A Filipina-American? Why'd his new, young wife want to adopt, except she couldn't get pregnant, and he maneuvered her into it, choosing the "adoption agency" which was really just a lawyer negotiating with them.

Did the girl ever know? Probably not.

Maybe when he'd gotten really old, he would've told her. Maybe he's revealed it all in his will. But that won't help her now, and it won't help him. He'll find someone else to be his "assistant," and he'll be distracted suing for malpractice. Maybe he'll even get married again but it won't be the same.

SHE WAS DESPERATE. She was begging. The *blondes* she'd adored, and feared. They'd called her *li'l dude, li'l dago.* They'd petted her like a little dog. She was begging Carroll.

> *Please will you answer Carroll? please will you please*
> *I'm afraid I am alone and I— I am afraid. . . .*
> *Please answer? Hello it's me. . . . Carroll are you listening?*

(She seemed to know that Carroll was listening. But no amount of begging could make one of the *blondes* do anything she wasn't in a fucking mood to do.)

SOME TIME LATER she called 911.

She'd thought (mistakenly) that this would be the end of it, in this way she could save herself though (also) she would humiliate herself. But calling 911 was not so routine.

The female voice at the other end sounded bored, cranky. *Yeh? What's your problem?*

She tried to speak. She stammered. She was sweating, and she was feeling nauseated. Her voice was so faint and thin, it might have been a child's voice. She'd taken Tylenol capsules, for pain, and for fever, but maybe—too many? And a single OxyContin she'd found in the medicine cabinet.

The cranky voice sharpened. *Hello? What is your age? What is the situation there?*

I—I—I—don't k-know . . .

Like water emptying through a drain. At first slow-seeming, you scarcely notice. Then, near the end, ever-faster.

Swirling down a drain counter-clockwise.

Sharply the voice said *Ma'am you got to speak up. What's your problem? What's your address?*

She was sweating, and she was shivering. She'd felt that thrill of sheer childish vengeance, that she'd left the wedding party, she'd left her father and all of the Johnstons without saying good-bye. As if they'd given a God-damn for her saying good-bye. But now, she was being punished for that blunder.

The 911 dispatcher was asking if there was anyone she could call, to come help her: mother, sister, friend. She seemed doubtful that Leanda needed an ambulance. She seemed to be warning Leanda that calling an ambulance was a serious matter. *How bad you feelin? Sound to me like you got some stomach upset. We don't send out ambulances for just like somebody sick to she stomach, see?*

She was whispering *Please! I'm afraid—afraid I am—dying* . . .

All right Ma'am tell me the address there, an ambulance will come for you.

SOMETHING BLACK AND hot in her brain. Black butterfly-wings fluttering open but the secret was—once the wings were *open*, they could not be *shut*.

MY CELL WAS TURNED OFF. I'd needed privacy. And when I was alone again, I went to bed without listening to my voice mail. Must've slept for ten hours. And there was my land phone ringing . . .

Or maybe, no. Maybe I'm remembering wrong.

Maybe it was my land phone she'd called, and I wasn't out—I was home. And there was someone with me, I didn't want to overhear anything private like in the family—that was it.

And I heard her voice, and I thought—Oh God! What's my cousin want, bellyaching about her God-damned tattoo not healing right. And I was feeling kind of anxious, I'd be blamed for this. My Uncle Jayson isn't exactly the forgiving kind. Hot shit, she'd gone to Yale and graduated summa like that was some major deal. I wasn't actually listening, only just heard her saying please would I pick up, if I was there please would I pick up, she was feeling sick, really sick, she didn't want to call her mother who'd be hysterical—"Please can you call me back Carroll? Maybe you could come over"—and—and I was feeling like I didn't have time for this right now—just let her leave the message and next morning didn't wake up until late and I guess I forgot about Leanda.

Yes I guess that was it. I forgot about Lee-lee.

How her message got deleted, I'm totally confused. Sometimes I just press DELETE and get rid of a lot of messages at once—it's easier that way.

HE WAS DEVASTATED. More than just his heart was broken.

The God-damned foot still in a cast. Unbearable pain sometimes despite painkillers washed down with Scotch.

Jayson Johnston hired his lawyer-friend who'd negotiated the agreement with the young Filipina physical therapist twenty-seven years before, when Leanda had been adopted. His lawyer-friend would work with a leading Manhattan malpractice attorney, filing a *wrongful death* suit on behalf of the grieving parents of Leanda Johnston who'd died in the Magdalen Hospital ER. Named in the $12 million suit along with the hospital were the resident physician who'd admitted

Leanda into the ER and had overseen her cursory examination, a nursing supervisor, and the nurse who'd failed to take Leanda's vital signs
as the young woman struggled to breathe over a period of forty-eight
hours, lapsed into a coma and died.

WHAT IS IT—something lacy-black on the girl's shoulder?

Sexy black butterfly, wings invitingly spread.

Evandela sees the tattoo and registers this is a junkie OD'ing. She
knows. Coke, or heroin—these are the "cool" downtown drugs, for
people like this, living in an apartment like this her daddy probably
pays the bills for, fancy computer and fancy art-works on the walls.

Evandela has seen plenty of junkies OD'ing. She's disapproving.
Disgusted. Folks taking up hospital beds needed by the legitimately
sick. Shoot up and kill themselves if that's what they want but not take
up hospital time needed for decent sick people.

At the trial, Evandela testifies for the defense, vehement, shining-
eyed. Evandela makes a strong impression on the jury which is a mixture of ages, skin colors, eight women and six men.

I WAS JUROR number five. I'm not ashamed of how we voted.

See, some of us have to work for a living. Some of us don't come
from a fancy "New England" family. I'm sorry for the girl, and her
family, but I'm not sympathetic with the artsy type. These kids you
hear about, they put their trust funds up their nose, they don't give a
damn for how their lives impact on others. The hospital lawyer said, it
was a tragedy she brought on herself. How was the hospital to blame
for a lifestyle. Even without the tattoo she was the type.

TATTOOS! DON'T GET ME WRONG, I think tattoos are cool. I'm not
against tattoos, there's people in my family, kids, with tattoos, piercings they call them, but that lifestyle, like the girl had, a downtown
kind of lifestyle, you take your chances OD'ing and wind up dead.

All the drugs she had in her, the hospital doctor listed. Some kind of Oxy-drug, which is basically heroin. Make your God-damn bed now lay in it. That's what my mother told us kids.

I WAS JUROR ELEVEN. My daughter works at Roosevelt, she's a nurse's aide got to put up with the most shit and she a good hardworking girl with two young kids, she don't complain. They work damn hard those aides and orderlies. They take the worst shit from the hospital you can imagine. They can't even park at the hospital, they got a car. Any nasty thing go wrong, they blame *them*. But this case, it clear who's at fault—that girl with the tattoo taking drugs, winds up in the ER and she's brain-dead and whose fault? Her fault! Her damn family thinking they so special on some island in the ocean.

We went through like ten ballots and we quarreled but in the end, the holdouts who wanted to make the hospital "negligent" gave in. There was a lot of sympathy for that nurse—the one singled out by name, and her reputation ruined. Like, a person makes one mistake in her life, which she did not see as a mistake. Like the hospital lawyer said, nobody can prove the girl would not have gone into a coma no matter what kind of medical care she'd received. If your time is up, it's up.

Jesus it got to be really late and we were really tired but some of us, we were not going to give in. So the others, they gave in. It was maybe twelve ballots. One thing we could agree it was a fact the prosecution didn't prove, she didn't die of an overdose. She was partying, she OD'ed on a mix of drugs and her heart gave out. They said her blood showed high amounts of—like, an infection. It's a tragic fact, she brought it on herself. Nobody makes anybody else take drugs or get slutty tattoos. My daughter tells me these things all the time, there's gangsters brought into the ER all shot up and dying and the hospital is supposed to save them?—no way. And no way we were going to give that rich family all those million dollars.

SHE'D BEEN HEARING her name—*Leanda? C'mon sit with us!*

The wedding dinner at Chilmark. Long tables beneath the trees.

They'd prayed it wouldn't rain and it had not rained. Moonlight glittering on the ponds linked, a visitor had once said, in Leanda's hearing, like the hemispheres of the brain.

Across the larger of the ponds was the old stone icehouse, you had to know was a stone building, to identify in the dark. Black rectangle amid the trees she'd had an uncanny feeling, like an optical illusion, but stronger, a hole gouged into the trees you could step into, and disappear.

Nearer the house were hydrangea, snowball bushes. Such beauty! Like a Chinese watercolor.

She told herself if I can think this, if I am seeing this, I am *on island*. I am not *in the city*. I am not tied down in a hospital bed, in a bright-lit screeching hospital. I can't be dying because someone would say Oh Lee-lee! How silly, you know you aren't dying. You are too young to die and besides, Daddy needs you.

You know, Daddy is waiting for you on island. Daddy can't walk without you. Daddy can't work without you. The new exhibit— retrospective at the I.C.P. It will be the opportunity of a lifetime. Daddy needs *you*.

DADDY WAS LIFTING HER, high over the beach grass so that she could see the Atlantic Ocean on the far side of the dunes. A fierce chill wind rushed onto land and through the spiky grasses making them shiver and shudder, like living vertebrae.

III

FORKED RIVER
ROADSIDE SHRINE,
SOUTH JERSEY

*K*EVIE WE MISS YOU WE LOVE YOU
Kevie may God be with you

SOMETIMES HEARING THIS makes me want to bawl. Sometimes it just pisses me, why they can't say five fucking words without dragging God into it.

Like God-damn fucking God gives a shit about what happened to me or'd give a shit about what happened to any of them, which they will discover for themselves. Jesus I have to laugh, or bawl, look at those girls' faces.

Kevie can you hear us? O Kevie we miss you we love you
Kevie?

FIRST THING YOU see from the road is the God-damn cross.

Three-foot-high homemade cross painted Day-Glo white.

And on this cross in red letters where the paint kind of drips down like smeared lipstick:

R
E
S
T

KEVIN ORR
Dec. 4, 1991–May 30, 2009

I
N

P
A
E
C
E

(Maybe *paece* is spelled wrong? It looks wrong. Shit!)

(Once you're a *decaesed person* all kinds of embarrassing shit can be said about you, you can't defend yourself.)

That shiny stuff wound around the cross is silver foil, looks like, the kind you put on a Christmas tree. And there's green-plastic vines and snowy-white-plastic flowers shaped like trumpets. At the foot of the cross are (laminated) photos, mostly iPhone pictures Chloe took of me, and pictures of Chloe and me, and me and the guys, and my mom and me, etc. There's pots of flowers—real flowers—that have got to be watered or they will wither and die, fast. And hanging from the crossbar is one of my sneakers—size twelve, Nike.

Must've come to the house and Mom told them to take whatever they wanted from my room. Whatever they needed for the shrine out Forked River Road. By this time she'd have been totally out of it on Xanax or OxyContin or whatever the hell it is, the God-damn shit-head doctor prescribes for her she's not supposed to take when she's drinking, or not supposed to be drinking when she takes it, but for sure Mom does. *Ohhh—what're you kids taking of Kevie's* and Chloe says *Just one of his sneakers, Mrs. Orr.*

I'm guessing: soon as the news came of *Kevie Orr, dead at Lenape Point* they got together, at my house. Hugging one another, crying and wailing, and some of them hysterical, and fainting like Chloe would do, hyperventilating, and my mom looking stunned like she'd been hit over the head with a mallet. No matter she'd been pissed as hell at me, and Chloe wasn't so fucking happy with me, nor any of the relatives in Mom's family—once it was known that I was *dead*, they'd want to remember me in a better way.

Jesus I am glad I was not there for *that.*

KEVIE—WE LOVE YOU.

Kev-ie? D'you hear us? Can you—see us?

It's Chloe, and Jill, and Alexa, and—

Oh shit they're bringing more crap for the shrine. Plastic lilies. Plastic roses, tulips. Plastic daffodils. Little stumpy candles what're they called—*votive candles.*

The little cross by the road is getting crowded so they've started putting things on a tree trunk a few feet away. This is the beech tree the SUV scraped rolling over downhill, tore off the left front fender like you'd tear a wishbone in two, and the tree trunk is scratched like a crazed tiger clawed it.

Josh is with them on crutches, Josh's face banged-up and part of his head shaved, but the motherfucker is *alive*, and there's Casey, and Fred, bringing Michelob beer, Red Bull, Cokes to position at the base of the tree. My kid brother Teddy looking like he hasn't slept since the accident, and what's he got to put by the tree—my hockey stick? And *VGHS*—the complete set, we'd watched together.

Each time they drive out here, they bring more pictures. There's me with my friends, and with my family—(minus my father). iPhone pictures of Chloe sitting on my lap, both of us laughing, Chloe's eyes look wet with tears, my eyes are shiny-red like a demon's squinting into the flash. Jesus, I wish I could remember when that was—wish I could slip back in time, to that moment.

It's like I am losing it—who I was. Whoever *Kevie Orr* was.

WHAT HAPPENED WAS, some kind of hot-white-blinding explosion— then *out*.

It was like getting tackled, that time in ninth grade—*concussed* they said it was. One minute I was OK and the next, I was being dragged on my knees, and my safety helmet was being yanked off, and there was dirt in my open mouth, and I was—*out*.

And this time when I woke it was quieter—a smell of something sweet and familiar—(lilac?).

The tow truck had taken the wreck away, in pieces. The body was gone, and buried. All that was finished. All that was just *material stuff*.

Just me left—*me*. And so lonely, my friends were gone . . . And I lifted my hand to see how bad it was, if my arm was broken or twisted which is how it felt, and I could see—*nothing there*.

Later, I looked and saw some kind of an arm, a grown guy's arm, a left arm, I think had to be Dad's.

This arm was attached to me, where my own arm was gone. And it was a muscular arm, and there was Dad's spider tattoo, with the red eyes, that was a consolation.

Dad? Hey Dad it's Kev—Kevie . . . Dad c'n you help me, please?

Dad I am so fucking scared. And cold, and—I guess kind of blind . . .

It wasn't Dad, but kids from school. Tramping in the grasses taking pictures on their cell phones. The big-toothed girl Barbara Frazier president of the senior class was tying ribbons around the beech tree, with knots and bows. And other girls, their faces known to me but not their names, shit! These kinds of girls that weren't anybody I'd gone out with, or had the slightest interest in, now Kevie Orr is *dead* anybody can drive out to the shrine and leave flowers and notes and all kinds of shit that's embarrassing to me, but can't be stopped.

Girls kneeling to hide their faces in prayer in the churned-up grass and rubble where the Jaws of Life tore open the SUV to pry me free too fucking late, the body pinned under the dashboard had *bled out.*

Blood mixed with oil, gasoline. The stink of gasoline.

Ohhh this tree, this is a beautiful tree. (What kind of tree is this?)

Let's put the balloons here.

I wanted to shout at them *Go away, Christ's sake! I don't want fucking kiddie-balloons, what the fuck are you thinking?*

(These are the hard-plastic balloons more like pillows than balloons. They don't deflate so easy as regular helium-balloons. And ugly bright colors so you can see them from the road, like fucking gonads or something, inner-body organs some asshole might think were Kevie Orr's insides strung up on a tree.)

Also there's a Christmas-tree star, a Christmas-tree angel, a plastic crucifix, pictures of *Jesus Christ*—(though I am not Catholic, none of the Orrs are Catholic).

A little American flag stuck in the ground, my grandfather Joe who'd been in the Korean War brought that out.

The poor kid. Threw it all away. Jesus!

Seventeen years old. Fuckin life should've been all ahead.

IF SOMEBODY ASKED THEM *Why make this shrine here, why when his body isn't here but buried in the cemetery in town* they'd have to think for a few seconds so you could (almost) see the thoughts rising in their heads like bubbles and then they'd say *Yes but Kevie's spirit is* here. *For here is where Kevie died.*

WHAT IS MEANT by *died,* I am not sure.

There was the body that *bled out.*

There was the body *pinned beneath the dashboard of the SUV.*

There was the body *broken, shattered, gutted, wasted.*

There was the body *like a sack of skin, leaking from a thousand wounds.*

There was the body *that had been Kevie Orr, trapped in the wreck.*

WE WERE RACING on Forked River Road. The guys in the Dodge Ram fell behind. Pressing the gas pedal to the floor, crazy sensation like wildfire rushing over me, such a terrific feeling I'm thinking it's about time—usually I'm kind of pissed, shitty-feeling, angry, resentful—the crystal meth we'd been smoking makes your heart pound really hard and that's a good feeling too—like gusts of wind lifting you, like you're a kite made of some crappy heavy material like wet canvas and it lifts you—Jesus!

We'd scored in the field behind the high school. We'd had a few hits and some beers and the idea was to see who could get out to Lenape Point fastest, and onto the beach.

The night sky was riddled with clouds. The moon was behind the clouds very bright. So you could see light through chinks in the clouds like torn cloth. It was a weird excited feeling that seemed to come down, from the sky. From the moon-like-an-eye, weird!

The Jersey shore at Lenape Point. The beach is pebbly and littered and the tide there leaves all kinds of crap behind some of it wriggling and smelly. The Jersey shore you don't think is on the Atlantic Ocean, seeing the ocean on a map you're—whoa!—that is *fucking large.*

Racing to Lenape Point in the SUV. Mom said, you can use it if you don't waste gas, OK Mom I told her, that's cool. I'm a good guy basically, I know this. I'm protective of my mom like Mom has any clue of any fucking thing. Seems like I'm always trying to argue this. People looking at me, at school, younger kids at Forked River High looking at Kevin Orr, Josh Feiler, Casey Murchison like they'd give anything to be *us.* And the girls. And this, our last God-damn year. Graduation in three weeks. And it wasn't clear what we'd be doing this summer let alone next year or the rest of our lives, at least not what I'd be doing—maybe a job at the stone quarry, if my uncle Luke could still get me in, maybe more likely we'd enlist in the U.S. Army where they train you for a job. The war in Afghanistan—where we'd be sent—is supposed to be ending. That's what people say. And we're saying *There'll be another war maybe—Iran? There'll always be a war.* We were high laughing how the "armed services" is a way of seeing the fucking world, there's no future in fucking Forked River, New Jersey, for God-damn sure.

Going into the turn at seventy-three miles per hour, the road sign posted for forty, sure I knew (I guess) that the (blacktop, much-cracked) Forked River Road turns sharply here, up onto the narrow ramp of the Lenape Point bridge which is one of those God-damn old single-lane plank-floored bridges of Lenape County and beyond it is an entrance to Lenape State Park and a half-mile inside the park, the Jersey shore at Lenape Point.

Should've known about the turn. The bridge. Jesus we'd been driving out to Lenape Point all our lives, far back as we could remember, young kids in such vehicles as the SUV driven by our fathers or older brothers or older guys but now three weeks from graduation from Forked River High we're the older guys and the weird thing is, this stretch of Forked River Road isn't so familiar by night, there's a mist rising out of the grasses at the edge of the road or out of the narrow strip of river you can't see from the road. Big sand-colored boulders, rocks and pebbles at the edge of the river where the water is just puddles or has dried up. The headlights behind us were blinding in the rearview mirror but are falling back now, the SUV is pulling away from the pickup Jimmy Eaton is driving, that belongs to his old man. Even at this time when the gas pedal is essentially pressed to the floor I'm kind of distracted by some fucking thing on the dashboard, can't keep my hand off the AC or the radio dial or the fan or whatever the fuck it is, lowering a window, raising a window, and so going into the curve I'm feeling the sick sliding sensation even before the SUV begins to veer out of control, the SUV that's registered in my mom's name, that's thousands of dollars from being paid off so at the back of my brain just before the moment of impact against the guardrail there's the shamed knowledge

It will never be paid off now.

SKIDDING TIRES. SUV hits the guardrail, smashes through the guardrail, overturns, rolls over, and again over down the (eight-foot) decline to the dry-bed edge of the Forked River, crashing against shrubs, trees, shearing bark from trees, overturned in the dry-bed and tires spinning, steam lifting from the radiator. The driver is pinned behind the wheel, and beneath the wheel, crushed beneath the dashboard. The driver wasn't wearing a seat belt. The three passengers were not wearing seat belts. Pretty badly injured Josh, Casey, Flynn manage to crawl out of the SUV, broken and bleeding like snakes that'd been stomped (you can stomp a snake so you'd think the thing was broke, all the vertebrae broke, so it's like a flattened piece of hose but a snake can fool you, a copperhead can fool you, even the little brain inside the bone-head you can stomp beneath your booted foot but the fucking thing is *not-dead* and if you're not alert it can leap at you and sink its poison-fangs in your leg)—and when the ambulance comes they are carried away and taken to the ER (at Atlantic City) fast enough to save them but not Kevie Orr who'd been driving *impaired and speeding, estimated thirty-five miles above the speed limit on the narrow winding road, not wearing a seat belt, pinned inside the vehicle and pried free by the Jaws of Life but too late.*

THE LENAPE LEGEND of the Death Song dreamt in the womb.

The Lenape Dream Festival. Ceremony of the Great Riddle.

Lenape Indians of all ages came forward to tell their dreams. The tradition was, women as well as men. Young as well as elders. A Jesuit recorded in 1689 that the Lenapes were pagans, they had no God but the Dream. *The Lenapes follow the Dream in all things blindly. Whatever the Dream bids them, they must do.*

In ninth grade New Jersey state history we learned. So much we forgot of what we'd learned. Like wind whistling through our empty heads like wind stirring the tall grasses of the cemetery behind the red-brick Forked River Church of Christ. But I remembered the Death Song. Don't know fucking why, when I forgot so much, I remembered the Lenape Death Song. How before the Indian baby was born the Death Song came to it in the womb and each song was different from the others. When the baby was born, the Death Song was forgotten. You open your eyes, you suck in your first deep breath of air—the Death Song is forgotten.

The young Lenapes would fast, hunt until they were exhausted, the young boys beaten with sticks by the older braves, their own male relatives. Dancing by firelight, torture by fire, starving so their bones showed through their skin, sweating—these are ways of bringing back the Dream. But these are incomplete ways. The Death Song is the song to be sung at death, your special revelation which is your Death Song. No one will know this Death Song except you.

O Jesus no one knows this except you. And you—you are obliterated now. You are gone.

AND MY MOM IS CRYING saying it's nasty and cruel for people to be blaming me, like it wasn't terrible enough how I died, bled to death trapped inside the upside-down SUV that she was nowhere near paying off and behind on insurance payments also. Jesus I wish she wouldn't drive out to the shrine, Mom and her sisters Stace and Claire, crying, and angry, and stumbling in the grass and Mom is saying *How dare they judge us what are they thinking* for her sisters have been telling her what people in town are saying, people who've pretended to be Mom's friends, shitheads she's known most of her life and never judged them—*How dare they judge my son, how dare they say anybody deserves such a thing to happen to them and Kevie such a sweet kid and only eighteen, his whole life before him.*

WET WIND OFF the Atlantic, pelting-down rain. Days of rain.

Parts of the shrine are sodden, ruined. Some of the photos are blown away in the grass. The Christmas-tree angel is gone. The geraniums survive, barely. The plastic vines and flowers have survived. The lone sneaker has survived, fallen onto the ground, soaked and leaden. The little American flag has toppled over in the grass.

But there's sunshine, suddenly—always, there is sun.

Sound of car doors slamming. Excited voices.

D'you think Kevie can hear us? Like, his spirit is here?

Walking in the sand wears you out quick. I remember that.

Trying to run along the beach, that's such a crappy "beach"—your feet sink in the sand, a kind of wet marshy smelly sand. Big trees had fallen over in some hurricane, years ago. Must've been ninth grade. We'd been drinking beers, smoking joints at the shore. And the day was hot-windy, the ocean waves were high, tall and white-frothed like some kind of video-game threat you'd have to waste with a submachine— quick before they got you.

Red-hot sun slip-sliding down behind the Lenape State Park pine forest.

Sometimes it's my mom, at the shrine. Mom with her sisters Stace and Claire, or Mom with my kid brother Teddy looking sick and scared and resentful at being here.

The shrine requires maintenance. The shrine is looking shabby after five or six weeks. Mom kneels in the grass, trying to repair it. Teddy stands back staring. Wide-eyed, anxious. Teddy's eyes drift over mine unseeing. *Hey Ted! Hey dude! It's me.*

He'd hated me, I guess. His asshole big-brother always teasing, poking him. *Why'd you do that, Kevin? That hurts.*

Because you're shit-for-brains, that's why. Got it?

Teddy has brought new, laminated copies of some of the photos posted at the shrine, that were damaged or lost. Teddy helps Mom tack them in place, on the tree trunk. And Teddy ties the single sneaker back up onto the cross.

Mom is saying in a bitter drunk voice *Kevie didn't deserve to die. They took their time getting out here—"Jaws of Life." The other boys, they were taken to the ER at Atlantic City and they were saved, they didn't deserve to be saved any more than my son. God-damn them leaving him to bleed to death in the wreck like a dog.*

It's a relief when Mom leaves. Jesus!—I wish I never had to see any of them again.

OK Mom I am sorrier than hell, what I did. Things I did, you don't even know about. OK Mom?—it was my fucking fault. I'm fucking sorry, OK? So let it go.

MAYBE IT WAS A MISTAKE, I was born. Maybe my mother didn't really want me, that was Mom's secret. They say a baby doesn't want to be born, a baby is "at home" in the mother's body and you remember all your life being "torn from the womb." On crystal meth these visions come so fast you can't deal with them, can't process them, it's like driving really really fast, all the windows lowered so your hair is whipping around your face, you're sweaty and oily-skinned and there's a burnt sensation like you've been out in the sun. Your brain is fucked and fried but it's OK. It's good!!! Too much!!! Flying at you like crazed comets like at the end of that movie—*2001.* Flying into Jupiter or something like that—wild.

DAYS PASS, no one comes to the shrine.

Then, there's a carload. Younger girls, not known to me. Not their names. At school, I'd see them—plain girls, you didn't look twice at. Girls with their cell phones to take pictures of themselves at Kevie Orr's shrine off the Forked River Road, Lenape Point.

One of them,

One of them, Janey Bishop it looks like. Feels these thoughts coming off me and looks up like she's been kicked.

Kevie? Kevie are you—here?

*Where the fuck do you think I am, here is where my brains splattered
in the SUV and drained out into the riverbed. All over the scrub trees, the
rocks is where the medics had to scrape me together and shovel me onto the
fucking stretcher, maybe you didn't know that.*

The girls are shivering saying *Kevie doesn't seem so nice now, does
he? It's like he has—changed. . . .*

*He has crossed over to some other place, maybe. He can see us and hear
us but we can't see or hear him.*

I can feel his thoughts! I think his thoughts are hostile.

Why'd Kevie be hostile to us?

It's just a feeling I have.

NOBODY KNOWS, Teddy bicycles out to Lenape Point.

My kid brother Teddy, alone.

It'd be God-damn embarrassing, if we had to see each other. If we
had to talk.

Teddy is taller and skinnier than I remember. Baseball cap pulled
down over his forehead. Like any kid you'd see on an ordinary bike,
hanging out at a 7-Eleven, or a school yard. You'd think *A loser. Glue-
sniffer.* It scares me to think that Teddy might turn out like that—like
it's my fault.

The fact is, I'd treated my brother kind of bad, I guess. Once, pushed
him into the fresh tar on our road. Made fun of him in front of the
guys. He'd said kind of plaintive *Why do you hate me, Kev?*—and it was
embarrassing as hell. *I don't hate you, fuck's sake! Just get out of my face.*

Long as I can remember Teddy was always hanging on to me,
following me around. Video games, TV. Whatever Kevin was doing,
Teddy wanted to do, too. When my father moved out and was living

across town he'd come to pick Teddy and me up, to take us out to eat like every Friday, it was a good time for me but not so great for Teddy who was always, like *When are you gonna come back home, Dad?*— kind of thing. Dad liked us to laugh, Dad likes people to be laughing not bellyaching, we'd laugh at our mother which was what Dad wanted, stupid woman, bitch, cunt, we'd sip Dad's beer and laugh, these were mostly great times except if Dad was in a shitty mood, and it didn't make any difference what you said to him, or how you acted. OK maybe—for a while—I was jealous of my brother, skinny Teddy snot-nosed Teddy whining and whimpering and because I didn't cry, no fucking way I was going to cry, or beg Dad to come back and live with us, Dad got it into his head that I didn't care about him so much—not like Teddy did. So, the quieter I got, the more Dad thought this. Some of the times, Dad got shitfaced drunk and I thought *Why don't you die. Right now.* But he never did.

It was just a few months ago, Teddy was sniffling and hanging out in my shithole room like he wanted to ask me something. I got pissed with him, I said the side of his face was going to get slammed inside the door, he just blinked at me like it was some kind of joke and didn't move fast enough and that's exactly what happened—his face got more or less slammed inside the door when I pushed it shut— Teddy screamed like he was being killed and I opened the door and, Christ, don't know why I pushed it shut again, harder—Teddy was screaming, blood running down his face, and Mom was downstairs, and called up to us—I grabbed him and said *You little cunt come off it, that doesn't hurt, you cocksucker little cunt I'll break your face into more pieces you don't shut up.* Why I was so angry, I don't know. I pushed them both out of my room—Teddy and Mom. I slammed the door and screamed at them I'd kill them if they didn't get out of my face. It's like a hot flame running through my veins. My hair on fire. Girls were scared of me, these moods. Chloe said it kind of turned her on but she was scared, too. *Jesus Kevie you should see yourself!*

I never did, though. I guess not.

The Indian dream chant, you smoke jimsonweed and dance. You wore special charms to stimulate special dreams. The smell in the night. Dream charms. There's a dream you sing when you are in battle facing death. Your special song, your Death Song.

On the radio in the SUV was (heavy metal) rap music, when the SUV went into the skid, hit the guardrail and overturned, and all of us guys screaming, like Teddy screaming, it was like God reached down and snatched up the SUV and threw it *You asshole kids see how you like this. My justice and My mercy see how you like this.*

It was a new morning. It was like debris from the dried riverbed. Forked River, that went shallow, dried out in the late summer. Stank of rotted fish, clams. Broken shells. Buzzing insects. Butterflies. A quarter-mile away, Lenape Point. The ocean, hard blue sky, tall waves.

Sand like a bad dream you are trying to run in, and can't make your legs move. I always loved running. I loved playing football, the guys grabbing at me, laughing and shouting, we were the same guy essentially, passing the ball among us. Roland Chermierz knocked me down, face-first, his knee in the small of my back, and there's dirt in my mouth. Roland is hooting and yelling like a crazy asshole, coach runs over and slaps him hard. The guys are running down the field. I'm trying to get up to run with them, there's sand pulling my legs down, I can't get balanced.

The shrine at Forked River they will call it. Through the fall months, through the winter and into the spring it's unbelievable how they loved me, and I never knew. Not just Mom and Chloe and my brothers and relatives but kids I don't know all that well. And the tall grasses growing up wild at the base of the tree. The holy shrine. There's votive candles they light—(though they don't burn long, the wind blows them out)—there are plastic flowers, geraniums, lilies, lilacs, the living flowers have died, a tangle of dried and desiccated things, flower pots, geraniums died over the winter. Beer bottles toppled over, bags of tacos blown in the wind, broken open by wild animals. Going to seed in the fall so beautiful. And beyond, the first wet snowflakes.

Shit I wanted Dad to come here, but Dad has not come here, ever. Not that I know, Dad has not come here. In Dad's eyes I am his shit-head son, he's washed his hands of me he'd said. Before the accident this was. He'd tried to get me a summer job at the quarry and it was a misunderstanding, I hadn't understood that I was supposed to drive out and meet the foreman, I guess I fucked up and Dad said he'd had it with me, fuck you Kevin he said and I thought Fuck you too, you God-damn old asshole. Like I give a shit if I work at the crappy quarry. Like I give a shit I'd wanted to tell him, but I didn't tell him. He'd cracked my face with the back of his hand once, I'd been five or six years old. You don't make that mistake twice.

Well it's a fact—I wanted Dad to like me better. Maybe love me, I don't know. It's what you can't have, you want. Want so bad you can taste it. My mom and my grandma—they love me, but I don't care so much about them. Your mom always loves you, big deal! It's like reaching in your pocket and there's a tissue you can blow your nose in—you do it, and you don't think about it. And you don't think *Hey I'm lucky for this tissue, else I'd have to blow my nose in my God-damn fingers.*

The thing is, my dad is ashamed of me. He's seen the photos in the newspaper about the shrine out at Forked River, it's a shrine in honor of Kevin Orr, seventeen when he died. Dad looks away, Dad doesn't want to see this. Dad didn't come to the funeral, Dad doesn't know where my body is buried. Dad would never drive out to the shrine for Dad does not want to speak with me. He sees his own death coming in me. I think that's it. I think that is it. He would never admit that, though. He gets drunk and says *That stupid kid. Didn't wear a seat belt either, he's seriously fucked now.* There's a wrong-ness in it, Dad per-ceives. Why Dad gets drunk four nights a week. The wrongness of a son going first. This is wrong. This is a violation of nature.

It's like he did it deliberately. Threw his life away.

It's like he did it to spite me. The asshole!

He was young, he was only seventeen. He was just seventeen—his birthday had been in the late summer.

Kevie was just a kid, an American kid. He was going to enlist in the army that'd shaken him up some, that'd mature him, unless it killed him. But he killed himself first.

GROPPEL DROVE OUT with three girls. He'd given them a ride out Forked River Road. Three girls, their hair blowing in the wind. Straight hair, dirty-blond, red-blond, and streaked brown. Janey Bishop, Melanie Trahern, Maggie Jones. Groppel wasn't a friend of mine he'd thought he was superior to me I guess. In tenth grade we got along OK then some of the guys came between us. Coach made us compete. I don't know what it was. Seeing Groppel out here in his nylon parka, his hands jammed in his pockets and the hood of his parka up, so he's trying not to show the tears in his eyes, I felt this sensation of—I guess— it's like love . . . I wanted to punch him in the arm, just for the hell of it, a good feeling, I wanted to pummel and kick, hey Groppel shithead, what're you doing here. He was bringing something for me, a plastic figure, superhero, Spider-Man, we'd traded Spider-Man comics when we were little kids. At school he was in another crowd. He'd taken college prep. He'd taken algebra. He'd sort of pretend not to see me on the stairs at school. Once, I sort of pretended not to see him and gave him a good hard shove, he'd have fallen on his face and broke his rabbit teeth if he hadn't been prepared, grabbed at the railing and stopped himself from falling. And he half-fell down the stairs, and people were watching us staring and excited and Groppel just kept going, walked quickly away with just this glance over his shoulder at me halfway up the stairs OK Kevie. *You go your way, and I will go my way.* It was like that a lot—a guy I'd been friends with sort of turned away from me, like he was scared of me—which makes me really pissed. Sometimes I saw, but I didn't let on.

One of my teachers drove out. Mr. Cranden, social studies. He took pictures of the shrine. Knelt, examined the laminated photos. The feathers, mirrors, girls' compact mirrors, hand mirrors edged with mother-of-pearl. Valentines, big cards from the drugstore, satin red hearts, faded from the wet and the sun, torn now, almost without color. Paper lace, ribbons, crosses, pictures of Jesus Christ, hiking boots (you were supposed to think were mine? They weren't, but resembled mine), gloves, pictures of U.S. Army soldiers marching. The wind blows some of the stuff away, that isn't secured to the tree. There's a lot of litter out here by the side of the road. Kids come here, and take down other pictures, and leave their own. Chloe comes out once a week at least, leaves letters for me. The girls are writing letters to me, in little coils tied with ribbons. Hanging from threads.

KEVIE? ARE YOU HERE? Hey Kevie. . .
   Hey we miss you, Kevie. We miss you a lot.

YOU CAN THINK OF your life as the mistakes you made that catch up with you finally. Ending in this. The shrine on Forked River Road. In the wind, there's the danger that most of the shrine will blow away. Hurricane-force gusts. The sky all twisted dark and clouds twisted. There was a sickening skid, a sound of tires on the pavement. Deafening crash, but already I was gone, I think. Shattered glass and twisted metal and the steering wheel column piercing my gut, my spine, crushing the vertebrae. A seat belt would've made no difference, seventy-three miles an hour going into the skid. Hitting the guardrail, and then the trees. And over and over, into the dried riverbed. It was like a video you can see over and over like on YouTube. A million hits. You can see it now. It's always now. The SUV collapses like something made of cheap tin. The doors fly open, my friends are thrown out. If we hadn't been hurt it would've been God-damn funny like the *Jackass* movies—*Don't try this at home.*

I WAS BLEEDING, a thousand wounds. I wasn't able to cry God I don't want this, this is not what I want, help me God. I wasn't able to speak, my mouth was filled with dirt and blood.

My brain was filled with blood. Seeping out my ears, my eyes. My mouth that would never speak again.

NOW IT'S A WINDY sunny-cold day. People feel good about coming here. Not so many are coming as came in the beginning but that's OK. It's a sign, Kevie was loved. The girls still come, and bring friends who didn't know me. My dad has not ever come here, my dad has moved to north Jersey. My mom and grandma still come out. In church they pray for me—it's something for them to pray for. But people feel good seeing the nice things on the tree, the plastic flowers, the ribbons and hearts. Tinfoil heart, with plastic lace. Kevie we love you. Rest in peace Kevie God be with you. Lifting their faces to the higher branches of the tree. Some of the girls will wipe away bird shit from the shrine. Rain keeps it pretty clean. Like they are seeing their best selves here. In the mirrors, people peek at their faces. Sometimes there's a weird little scare—it's like Kevie is peeking back at them.

FORGETTING I WAS THE KID who fucked up big-time. Every serious thing I tried to do, I fucked up. They don't remember that now. (Most of them don't remember.) It's over now. It don't matter now. They are forgetting me now, who I was exactly. They are remembering the boy-who-died. They are remembering the boy-people-have-a-shrine-for. It's been on TV and in newspapers. *Forked River Maintains Roadside Shrine for Teen Driver Killed in Crash. Forked River High Teens Maintain Shrine for Kevin Class of '09.*

IN ACTUAL LOVE like in sex there's always one who gets more of it than the other and you could say is using the other, because he doesn't care as much. I was always that kid, which was why the girls liked me I guess—each girl thought she'd be the one to make Kevie Orr grow up. I feel that I am growing up now I am "gone." I know that's weird as hell but I feel that my spirit is being refined. Like in the quarry, the marble is removed from the rock surrounding it. My bones are pulverized returning to dust in the church cemetery. My skull, that has holes for eyes, and a Hallowe'en mouth. Not where I am which is *here.*

Your body is not where you are, after you are gone. Your special place is where you died—"passed over." How long I will be here depends upon you, how long your love keeps this shrine.

MY CRAPPY-KID'S LIFE. It was mostly a shitty life wasn't it, OK but I miss it. I'd spend time with my dad at the pancake house, at Friday's, just laughing and relaxed, watching the games on TV. Why'd I have to want more than that from him, that was the mistake. And Teddy, why'd I have to be jealous of my kid brother. He'll walk kind of crooked all his life, the orthopedic doctor said, the way his knee got twisted and he fell with all his weight on it, and some of mine.

TEDDY FORGIVES ME, I guess. Teddy has never gotten over his big brother dying. He's taking drugs, smokes joints, hangs out with losers, serious losers.

DEER BROWSE HERE. In the early dusk they approach the tree. They've eaten the tacos, the potato chips. They nose around looking for food. Their eyes are large, beautiful. Calmly they seem to see me. Their white tails flick, nervously. Flick away flies. They are not frightened of me. They are aware of me because I am so still, I am transparent as vapor, I have no smell any longer, I am not their enemy. They approach me without fear. There is such happiness in this. I'd have wanted to shoot them, just a year ago. Now, I feel peace with them. I was never still for long, restless in my seat in school, always had to gun the motor of any vehicle, itchy, needing to move. My baby pictures are tacked on the tree, laminated. Affixed to the tree with tacks. Glow-in-the-dark Sacred Heart of Jesus.

I am happy now, I think.

I love and bless you all.

THE JESTERS

H E SAID, "DO YOU HEAR—?"

She listened. She'd just come to join him on the terrace at the rear of the house.

It was dusk: the calls of birds close about the house were subsiding. A flock of glossy-black-winged birds had taken over a hilly section of the lawn for much of that day, but had now departed. At the lake a quarter-mile away, not visible from their terrace, Canada geese and other waterfowl were emitting the random querulous cries associated with nighttime.

At first, she heard nothing except the waterfowl. Then, she began to hear what sounded like voices, at a distance.

"Our neighbors. Must be on West Crescent Drive."

The husband spoke matter-of-factly. It was not like him to take notice of neighbors unless in annoyance—which was rare, in Crescent Lake Farms. He seemed bemused and not annoyed.

They had never seen these neighbors. Whoever lived on the far side of the wooded area were strangers to them. There was no occasion for the husband and the wife to drive on West Crescent Drive which wasn't easily accessible from the cul-de-sac at the end of East Crescent Drive, where they lived: this would involve a circuitous twisting route to Juniper Road, which traversed the rural-suburban "gated community" called Crescent Lake Farms, an approximate half-mile north on that road, and then a turn into the interior of the development and, by way of smaller, curving roads, onto West Crescent Drive.

Like a labyrinth, it was! Crescent Lake Farms was not a residential area hospitable to strangers. Easily one could become lost in a maze of drives, lanes, "ways," and "circles," for the gated community had been designed to discourage aimless driving.

Their three-acre property did not include frontage on the man-made ovoid Crescent Lake. But a small stream meandered through it, to empty into the lake a short distance away.

"They sound *young*."

The wife heard what sounded like low thrilled throaty laughter. There was a strange unsettling intimacy to this laughter, as if their neighbors on West Crescent Drive were very near and not a quarter-mile away, at the very least.

You stared at the massed trees, expecting to see human figures there.

"Yes. And happy."

The wife had brought drinks for her husband and herself: whiskey and water for the husband, lemon-flavored sparkling water for the wife. And a little silver bowl of the husband's favorite nuts, pistachios.

Hungrily, noisily the husband chewed pistachios. Yet his attention was riveted to the dark cluster of trees which the sounds of voices and laughter teasingly penetrated.

It wasn't unlike hearing voices through a wall. Intimate, tantalizing. You heard the musical cadences but not distinct words.

Drinks outside on the terrace behind their house was their ritual before dinner, in warm weather. Though he wasn't any longer making his forty-minute commute to Investcorp International, Inc. in Forrestal Village, on Route 1, where the husband had directed the applied math and computational division of the company for the past seventeen years, the husband and the wife had not changed their before-dinner ritual.

They had lived in this sprawling five-bedroom shingle-board house in Crescent Lake Farms for nearly thirty years and in that time, very little had changed in the gated community which was one of the oldest and most prestigious in northern New Jersey.

There was a waiting list of would-be homeowners. Elsewhere, properties were difficult to sell; but not in Crescent Lake Farms.

The wife thought *We are protected here. We are very happy here.*

Thoughtfully, his head cocked in the direction of the massed trees, the husband finished his whiskey-and-water. The voices continued—softly, teasingly. A sudden squawking squabble among geese in the near distance, and the gentler sounds were drowned out.

In any case it was time to go inside for dinner which was more or less ready to be served—in a warm oven, and in a microwave. And on the kitchen counter a lavish green salad in a gleaming wooden bowl with feta cheese, arugula, avocado, cherry tomatoes—the husband's favorite salad.

"I think they must have gone inside. Over there."

Shyly the wife touched the husband's hand. He did not, as he'd used to do, turn his hand to grasp hers, instinctively; but he did not brush her hand away as he sometimes did, not rudely, not impolitely, but half-mindedly.

It appeared to be so: their neighbors' voices had faded. All you could hear was the quarrelsome sound of waterfowl and, startlingly near at their stream, the excited miniature cries of spring peepers.

She said, "Will you come inside, darling? It's late."

AIRY AND MELODIC the laughter, summer evenings.

Almost, the husband and the wife could hear through the woods a delicate tinkle of glassware from time to time—wineglasses? And cutlery.

The *neighbors-through-the-trees* frequently dined outside. Their voices were low and murmurous and no words were distinct but the sounds were happy sounds, unmistakably.

"Oh—is that a baby? D'you think?"

The wife heard something a little different, one evening in June. A sweet cooing sound—was it? Just barely discernible beyond the nocturnal cries of the waterfowl on Crescent Lake and low guttural bullfrog grunts in their grassy lawn.

The husband listened, paused in his pistachio-chewing.

"Maybe."

"Though we haven't heard a baby crying, ever."

The wife sounded wistful. Her own babies had grown and departed the house at 88 East Crescent Drive, years ago.

The wife was thinking *They are dining by candlelight probably. Their faces reflected in a glass-topped wrought-iron table on a flagstone terrace like ours.*

If the *husband-through-the-trees* brushed the hand of the *wife-through-the-trees*, the wife could not observe. If the *wife-through-the-trees* paused to take up the baby in her arms, to kiss him on his little snub nose, the wife could not observe.

"A baby *would cry*. So maybe it isn't a baby."

Yet, the soft cooing sound persisted. And adult voices, and throaty laughter. The husband and the wife listened acutely, sitting very still on their terrace.

It was their custom now to eat outside. In the past, the husband had not liked to eat outside which he'd thought too *picnicky*.

The wife did not mind the extra effort of carrying things from the kitchen and back again. The wife quite enjoyed the romance of mealtimes on the rear terrace, in the company, at a little distance, of their mysterious *neighbors-through-the-trees*.

For often, since his retirement, the husband was very quiet. The wife felt lonely even as she told herself *Don't be ridiculous! You are not lonely.*

It was strange that, in the past, they'd had no particular awareness of these neighbors. Possibly, a new family had moved into the house on West Crescent Drive?

Other, nearer neighbors, who lived on East Crescent Drive, were more visible of course and more annoying, at times; there were frequently large summer lawn parties, children's birthday parties with balloons tied to mailboxes, political fund-raisers involving vehicles parked on both sides of the narrow road. But overall, Crescent Lake Farms was a quiet place. In the Crescent Lake Farms Homeowners' manual *disturbing the peace and privacy of our neighbors* was expressly forbidden.

And the properties were large: a minimum of three acres. So your neighbors weren't inescapable, as in an urban setting.

Now the wife recalled: at Easter, on an unseasonably warm Sunday afternoon when their daughter Ellen had come to visit with her two small children, and they were walking on the back lawn, the wife had heard an unusual sound through the thicket of trees—a woman's voice, it might have been, so melodic as to seem like music, but indistinct, and soon fading. At the time she hadn't known what it was, assumed it was coming from their neighbors at 86 East Crescent Drive, and had paid no particular attention to it.

The husband hadn't noticed this female voice, at the time. Their daughter, distracted by her young children, hadn't noticed.

Ellen said, "This is a lovely house. I have such good memories of this house. It's a shame, you will probably be selling it . . ."

Selling it? The wife reacted with dismay, and did not glance at the husband; knowing that the husband would be upset by their daughter's careless remark.

". . . I mean, since it's so large. And it must be so expensive to maintain especially in the winter . . ."

The husband had walked stiffly on, headed for the edge of the property, where there was a gate, rarely used, that opened onto a no-man's-land—a densely wooded area that belonged not to any private landowner but to Hecate Township.

The wife was embarrassed by the husband's rudeness. But she, too, was offended by the question and did not want to think that their other children were speculating about their future.

The wife remained with their daughter and lively grandchildren, talking of other things.

Now, the wife recalled that awkward episode. And the way their daughter had lifted one of the children into her arms, with such confidence, and joy. Listening to the neighbors' cooing baby weeks later, she was feeling a pang of loss.

Inwardly protesting to her daughter *But we are so happy here! Why ever would we want to move?*

"WHAT IS *THAT?*"—the husband was baffled.

The wife listened: a soft blunted sound as of wood striking wood, she was sure she'd never heard before.

It was a morning in mid-June. The wife and the husband were outside on the deck reading the Sunday newspaper, that fluttered in the breeze. A part of the paper had gotten loose from the husband's grasp and had been blown into shrubbery close by, which the wife would retrieve.

"Is it coming from—*over there?*"

"I think so, yes."

"Some sort of—repair work? A kind of hammer striking wood?"

"Not a hammer. I don't think so."

They listened. Again the blunted sound came, a near-inaudible *crack.*

They were staring at the trees. Pine trees, deciduous trees whose names they didn't know—beech? Oak? Beyond their six-foot wire fence was a dense jungle of bushes, scrub trees, mature trees. However deep the woods was, whether a quarter-mile or less, it was as opaque to their eyes by day as by night.

The wife had to suppose that not one but two fences separated their property from that of the *neighbors-through-the-trees*. For the other property would be fenced-off as well.

In the land owned by Hecate Township there was a median strip kept mowed in the summer, probably no more than fifty feet across, where power lines had been installed.

The husband and the wife had never walked along the median. The wife had a vague recollection of stubbled weeds, marshy soil. Nothing like the fastidiously tended suburban lawns of Merion bluegrass, the preferred grass for Crescent Lake Farms.

Years ago when they'd walked more frequently, often hand in hand, they'd walked in parks, or along hiking trails; they had never explored the area behind their house which did not seem hospitable to strolling couples.

The wife assumed that there were signs posted in the woods behind their house, as elsewhere in Crescent Lake Farms, forbidding *trespassing, hunting with gun or bow.*

White-tailed Virginia deer dwelt in the woods of Crescent Lake Farms. Occasionally, no matter how vigilant homeowners were, no matter how high their fences, deer would manage to slip through, to ravage gardens in the night.

It had happened, the wife's roses had been decimated, years before. Her carefully tended little vegetable garden, even her potted geraniums. But the husband had had the fence repaired, and no deer had set foot on the property since.

Crack!—a light glancing sound.

It was utterly baffling, what this sound might be. At once sharp, yet muffled. A *playful* sort of sound, the wife thought.

The husband had ceased reading the newspaper. The politics of the day infuriated him: even when power lay with the politicians he supported, and the opposition appeared to be failing, so much in the political sphere seemed to him vile, vulgar, meretricious, inane—he threatened that he wouldn't be voting at all.

The husband, whose professional life had been involved with the most complex algorithms and equations, knew to distrust the sort of crude polls you saw reported in the media, and "statistical studies." The husband made the droll joke that *roughly 40 percent* of what was printed in the *New York Times* in such quasi-scientific or –economic terms was fabricated by researchers.

"Only naïve people take polls seriously. The publication of a poll is a stratagem of *persuasion*."

After degrees from Harvard the husband had begun his career at a mathematical research center in Cambridge, Massachusetts. Then, he'd been recruited by a medical science research center in White Plains, New York. Then, by a pharmaceutical manufacturer in Princeton, New Jersey, where he'd developed algorithms brilliantly forecasting consumer purchases. By the time he'd moved to Investcorp International, Inc. his work in mathematical computation was so complex, the wife had virtually no knowledge of what her husband did, or how it was related to the *actual world.*

"What is it that Dad *does?*"—so the children would ask one by one.

The wife recalled when her young husband had talked excitedly of his work to anyone who would listen. But in recent years, never.

She no longer made inquiries. Much of his life was separate from hers as if each was on an ice floe, drifting in the same direction and yet drifting inevitably apart.

"Something hitting against something else—that's what we're hearing. It sounds like wood."

"Croquet?"

The husband was impressed, the wife had solved the mystery.

"Yes of course! Such a civilized lawn game—*croquet*."

They did not mind the glancing *crack* of the mallet against the croquet ball, for the sound was diminished at a distance, like their neighbors' voices and laughter.

"I've never played croquet, have you?"

"Oh, long ago. At my grandparents' house on Nantucket."

The wife spoke wistfully. The husband spoke nostalgically.

"D'you think they have guests? They're playing croquet with guests?"

They listened. It was impossible to tell from the near-inaudible murmuring voices.

The wife half-closed her eyes. In twilight figures clothed elegantly in white were gracefully wielding mallets, striking painted wooden balls and driving them forward in the grass beneath little wire hoops.

The woman, or the women, wore long skirts. The men, white coats and trousers.

"I'd like to play croquet again. Would you?"

"Yes. I'd love to play croquet with you."

They smiled at each other. The wife felt an impulse to take up her husband's hand and kiss it.

On the backs of her husband's hands, bruises the hue of grapes. His blood was thin: he bled easily, beneath his skin. His medication was to correct for high blood pressure.

"We could order a set online, maybe. I doubt there are croquet sets for sale in town."

"Yes. Let's!"

They realized that the croquet game through-the-trees must have ended, when they'd been talking. It was past dark by now: fully night.

The trees beyond their property were a solid block of darkness like a gigantic mouth.

High overhead, a blurred moon that cast a blurred light.

"DARLING? COME HERE."

The wife called excitedly to the husband, who was working in his *home office* on the first floor facing the front of the house.

Though there was no longer an office at Investcorp International, Inc., yet the husband's office at home remained his *home office*.

"Hurry, darling! Please."

It was midday. Strains of music were penetrating the trees at the rear of their property, sweetly delicate, captivating. At first, the wife had assumed that the exquisite sound was the singing of an unusual species of bird but when she'd listened closely, and determined that the sound was coming *through the trees*, she realized that this was no bird.

"I think someone is playing the violin over there. I mean—it isn't a recording or a radio, it's an actual person."

The husband had come outside, frowning. He seemed irritable at having been interrupted at his desk yet he leaned over the railing, listening.

"Maybe a child? Practicing his lesson?"

The husband frowned, cocking his head.

"I'm not sure that I hear anything. I think you're imagining a *violin*."

They listened, intently. There came, from the roadway in front of the house, a sudden blaring of rock music: from one of the damned tradesmen's vans, or delivery vans, so prevalent in the neighborhood.

"I'm sure that I heard—something . . . It wasn't ordinary music but something special."

The wife knew: it was household protocol never to interrupt her husband when he was working in his *home office*. The children had never dared.

Apologetically the wife said she might have been mistaken. She was sorry to have called the husband and she knew that if she admitted her error at once, the husband would not be angry with her.

He was saying, petulantly, "I didn't hear a thing. Certainly not any *violin*."

The husband returned to the house. The wife continued to listen in a trance of expectation.

But she heard no more "violin" notes. Maybe the sound had been a bird's song after all.

Or blood pulsing in her ears. Beating in her heart.

That was what she'd been hearing—was it?

THEY HAD BEEN married for nearly forty years. Not an hour had they ceased to be married in forty years.

The husband had been "unfaithful" to the wife—probably. On those business trips. On company "retreats" to Palm Beach, Key West, Bermuda and Saint Bart's, Costa Rica and Mexico, to which wives had not been invited.

But these trips were of the past. The last one had been several years ago. The wife had ceased to think of these humiliations as one ceases to think of an illness, painful but not lethal, of long-ago.

The husband would be a domestic animal now, confined to the household and to the wife. And to his online life, in his *home office*.

The wife had not been unfaithful to the husband. Not with any man—any individual.

In her heart. In the mysterious and uncharitable way of the heart.

But I love him. That will never change.

"LISTEN! A DOG."

Not often but from time to time, when the *neighbors-through-the-trees* appeared to be in their backyard, or on their deck, adults and a child, or children, there came the sound of a dog barking—not protracted, not disturbing, just two or three short barks, then silence.

A dignified dog, the wife thought. A German shepherd, or a border collie. One of those elegant long-haired dogs she'd always fantasized owning—an Afghan.

"I think we should get a dog, darling. Everyone says . . ."

"Dogs are too needy, and demanding. Dogs have to be walked twice a day."

"Once a day, I think."

"Twice."

"It might depend upon the breed."

"*Twice*. And I don't have time."

You are retired. You have all the time in the world.

"A dog would be lovely company for us both. And a watchdog."

The husband laughed, the way the wife said *watchdog*.

"Oh, what's so funny?"

The wife wanted to laugh with him but the husband had turned his gaze to somewhere beyond the trees and had not seemed to hear her.

"LISTEN! Is it—Satie?"

This time there was no mistaking, they were hearing music through the trees: piano music.

Acutely they listened, on the terrace.

"Definitely, piano music. It seems remarkably near."

"An actual piano, being played. But not by a child—this would be an adult. Someone who has played for years."

The wife-through-the-trees, the wife thought. She herself had had ten years of piano lessons, as a girl, but had not seriously played for more than twenty years.

Delightful music! Just audible, at dusk.

Mixed with the sounds of waterfowl at the lake, frogs and nocturnal insects in the grass.

The poetic stately notes of Erik Satie. The wife was deeply moved—this was *her music*, she'd played with such eager pleasure for her piano teacher at college.

She'd had talent, her teacher had said. Beyond his words the subtle admonition she must not acknowledge, for fear of embarrassing them both—*Only not just enough talent.*

She knew, she'd understood and she'd accepted. *You have gone as far as you can go, very likely. You must not delude yourself, you will only be disappointed.*

Her life since that time had been a systematic avoidance of *delusion*. She had thought this was maturity, clear-mindedness. She had married her husband knowing that he could not love her as much as she loved him, for it was not in the man's nature to love generously and without qualification, as it was in hers. In matters of emotion, he had *gone as far as he could go.*

Yet, she would love him, and she would certainly marry him. For she was eager to be married. She did not want to be not-married. She did not want to be conspicuously *alone*. And whatever followed from that decision, she vowed she would not regret.

Three children, whom she loved (unevenly). For no mother can help loving one child above others, as no child can help loving one parent more than the other.

Before she'd married her husband, at the age of twenty-three, she'd had her single great emotional adventure, that would last her lifetime. This memory had crystallized inside her as a secret, insoluble as mineral. Her self had seemed to form around it, encasing it. And never would she reveal it.

The music of Satie reminded her. Tears shimmered in her eyes, the husband would not notice.

Gnossiennes. Gymnopédies.

The composer's annotations in the compositions were original, curious—*du bout de la pensée, sur la langue, postulez en vous-même, sans orgueil, ouvrez la tête, très perdu.*

How strange that had seemed to her, a girl: *très perdu.*

"'Quite lost!'"

She'd spoken aloud. The husband glanced at her, in mild curiosity.

When the husband was not critical of her, the husband was bemused by her. Their marriage had not been a marriage of equals.

Through the trees, the piano music ceased; then, after a moment, began again, what seemed to be a new composition by Satie, that differed from its predecessor only subtly.

Composed in the 1880s the piano music of Erik Satie sounded contemporary. It was eerily simple, beautiful. It was unhurried as time relentlessly passing second by second and it was seemingly without emotion even as it evoked, in the listener, the most intense sorts of emotion—melancholy, sorrow, loss.

A rebuff to Romantic music perhaps, with its many cascading notes and emotional excess, or to Baroque music, the fierce precision of clockwork.

"Isn't that something you used to play?"—the husband seemed only now to recall.

She said, laughing, "Yes. But not so well—I'd never played the music so well."

In fact she'd played Satie quite well. Her teacher and others had praised her, and they had not exaggerated.

The wife and the husband had not had an easy week, this week: there had been doctors' appointments, scheduling for "tests" and more appointments, stretching into the summer.

The husband's tenderness with the wife was just unusual enough to leave her shaken and uncertain. She knew it was his apprehension of the future—their future.

He is afraid. But I must not be.

The *neighbors-through-the-trees* lived in a house that mirrored their own, the wife presumed. Possibly, it was an identical house: artificially weathered shingle boards with dark red shutters, a steep roof, several stone chimneys. A three-car garage. Not a new house, for Crescent Lake Farms was not a new subdivision, but an attractive house, you might say a beautiful house. And expensive.

The wife had not driven by the house at 88 West Crescent Drive but she'd studied the Crescent Lake Farms Homeowners' map and saw how precisely the lots were positioned, three- and four-acre properties on each side of the man-made lake and each with its replica like halves of the human brain.

The property at 88 West Crescent Drive was three acres, like their own. It was equidistant from the man-made lake less than a mile to the east.

The wife had been fascinated, as an undergraduate, by human anatomy as well as by music. She'd thought—perhaps—she might apply to medical school—but requirements like organic chemistry and molecular biology had dampened her enthusiasm.

Yet, she remained (secretly) fascinated by illustrations of the human body, its labyrinthine yet symmetrical interior. The brain was the most complex of all organs.

Cortex, cerebellum, spinal cord.

Frontal lobe, parietal lobe, occipital lobe, temporal lobe.

She was fascinated with the possibility of "dissection"—the human body opened up, its secrets labeled. Yet she could not bear to look upon an actual human corpse. She certainly could not bear to see a human corpse dissected.

The mere sight of blood caused her to feel weak, faint. Even the thought of blood. It was an involuntary reflex like gagging.

"Hello? What are you thinking about?"

The husband was staring at her, smiling.

"I—wasn't thinking. I was listening to the music."

She'd forgotten where she was, for the moment. The pristine piano notes of Erik Satie had faded and in their place were the raucous cries of Canada geese, flapping their wings and squabbling on the lake.

"'*SEULE, PENDANT un instant*'—'alone, for a moment.'"

At the piano she'd neglected for most of her adult life she was playing—attempting to play—Satie. Inside the piano bench she'd found the yellowing photocopied pages she had annotated many years ago, precise instructions from her music teacher.

She did not want to think *Mr. Krauss must be dead. A long time now, dead.*

She'd loved him, at one time. How desperately, how helplessly—and yet, in secret. For he'd never known.

Her fingers had absorbed his interest. The sounds that leapt from her fingers. Of her, he'd had but a vague awareness, and very little interest.

He'd been at least thirty years her senior. And married.

He'd hummed with her piano playing, when she was playing well. Half-consciously he'd hummed, like Glenn Gould. But when she struck a wrong note, or faltered, the humming ceased abruptly.

She'd begun now with the simplest *Gnossienne.* Her fingering was awkward, she struck wrong notes. The very clarity of the music was a rebuke to her clumsiness but she continued, she returned to the beginning of the piece and continued through to the end; and, at the end, she returned again to the beginning and continued through to the end, with fewer mistakes. She did this several times before moving on to the second *Gnossienne.* She began to feel a small hesitant satisfaction—rising, almost, to elation—joy! *I haven't forgotten. The music is in my fingers.*

For ninety minutes she remained at the piano, playing the music of Erik Satie. Her shoulders ached. Her fingers ached. She was having difficulty reading the notes, that seemed to her smaller than she recalled. But she persevered. She was quite happy, with even her fumbling fingers. Someone came to stand in the doorway, to listen. Her heart reacted, she was startled. Though knowing it could only be the husband.

She waited for him to speak. He might say *Hey—that's pretty good.*

Or—*Hey, is that the music we were hearing through-the-trees?*

Or—*The piano needs tuning, eh?*

But when she turned, there was no one in the doorway.

She closed up the keyboard. She was strangely excited, and apprehensive. She foresaw returning to all her piano music, the many old and yellowed books and photocopied sheets, like an excavation of the past it would be, digging back into time.

The music is in my fingers. Anytime I want to retrieve it.

"LISTEN!"

It was just past 6:00 P.M. The midsummer sun was far from the tree line. The husband was on the deck at the rear of the house, for something had attracted him there.

He'd brought a drink with him. Earlier each evening he was leaving his *home office* until, this evening, he'd left to come out onto the porch before 6:00 P.M.

The wife came to join the husband, distracted. She'd heard him calling to her and hadn't realized at first where he was. There had been a telephone call from her oncologist—she'd had to call back, and to wait several long minutes.

It will be a simple procedure. A biopsy with a local anesthetic, a needle.

The husband had left the terrace and was standing in the fresh-mowed grass. He stood approximately fifty feet from the fence at the property line.

He was listening to—what?—the wife heard what seemed to her familiar voices, through the trees. A ripple of laughter.

But there were unfamiliar voices as well. The wife was sure she'd never heard these voices before.

These were dissonant sounds, somewhat jarring. The laughter loud and sharp and a dog's barking commingled with the laughter, distorted through the trees.

A party? A picnic?

There were children's voices as well, and shouts. And the dog barking excitedly as they'd never heard it bark before.

"They sound happy."

"They sound *drunk*."

The wife wanted to protest, this was unfair. She understood that the husband felt envious. It had been a long time since they'd hosted a party at their house.

An odor of barbecue, wafting through the woods. Fatty ground meat on a grill. Salsa, raw onion. Beer.

They had friends—of course. Numerous friends, and yet more friendly acquaintances. But their friends were *like themselves*—their political prejudices, children and grandchildren, homeowners' complaints, experiences in travel, physical ailments. Like mirror-reflections these friends were, and not flattering.

And their older friends were fading, irrevocably. Some of them had retired to the southwest, or to Florida. Some were mysteriously ill. A few had died—it was always a small shock, to realize *But she isn't alive any longer. There is no way I can reach her.*

The wife had accompanied the husband to his fortieth reunion at Harvard the previous year. The husband had arranged to meet old classmates, a former roommate, "friends" he'd maintained, to a degree, over the course of decades, though the men had rarely seen one another in the interim. The wife had liked these men—to a degree—and she'd liked their wives, who were making a special effort to be friendly with one another, under the strain of the college reunion which was tightly scheduled, boisterous, and exhausting. And on the drive home, when the wife said how good it was to see the husband with such old friends, one or two of the men "like brothers," clearly enjoying himself, the husband had listened in silence and not until they were home, preparing for bed, the husband brooding, slump-shouldered, and the flaccid flesh at his waist and belly pale as unbaked bread dough, did he say, in a flat cold voice, without meeting the wife's startled gaze, "Frankly, I don't care if I ever see any of them again."

Yet, hearing the festive sounds of the party *through-the-trees*, clearly the husband felt envy, as well as disapproval; he had to be thinking, the wife surmised, that since retiring from Investcorp, he saw relatively few people from day to day and from week to week. (Was it possible, the husband's Investcorp colleagues/friends were forgetting him? Those frequent e-mail invitations sent to a set group of individuals had ceased to show up in the husband's inbox, he'd only just begun to realize. And his e-mails to his former colleagues/friends were not being returned.)

The husband had only recently wielded *such power*—in his division at Investcorp. And now . . .

The husband said, "That sounds like—what?—furniture being dragged on the terrace?"

They listened. Through the trees came a sound very like furniture—heavy, wrought iron terrace furniture—being dragged along a terrace.

More voices, laughter. Raucous laughter, and braying laughter. The wife was shocked, their *neighbors-through-the-trees* had not seemed like such—well, gregarious people. Until now they had seemed like an ideal family, well-bred, private.

The husband said, "Maybe it's a political fund-raiser. It sounds *large*."

The husband detested noisy "fund-raisers" in the neighborhood. The husband had grown so contemptuous of politicians, even conservative politicians for whom he felt obliged to vote, in the effort of maintaining his accumulated investments and savings, the wife avoided bringing the subject up to him.

"I don't think it's that large. I think it's just—another family or two. An outdoor barbecue, in summer. I think they're just having *fun*."

Not just one dog was barking, but at least two. And now came amplified music, some sort of rock, or—was it "rap"?

The husband turned away in disgust, and stomped back into the house. The wife remained for a few minutes, indecisive, listening.

How loud they are. But how happy-sounding.

"THE JESTERS."

The husband must have been thinking aloud. For he hadn't addressed the wife, who was standing a few feet away, gardening implements in her gloved hands.

"What do you mean—'the Jesters'?"

"That's their name: 'Jester.'"

"I don't understand. Whose name?"

"Our neighbors through the trees."

The husband gestured in disgust, in the direction of the woods. Already, on this weekday morning, though it wasn't yet noon, there was a barrage of noise coming through the trees: lawn mower, leaf blower, chain saw.

The wife said, faltering, "But—everyone in Crescent Lake has lawn work done. We have our lawn mowed and serviced. How is this different?"

"It is different. It is God-damned *louder.*"

The wife recoiled, the husband was being irrational. Surely the decibel-level of the chain saw through the trees was no higher than that of the chain saws the husband had hired to trim away dead limbs from their own trees? (Of course, when the lawn crew was working on their large, sloping lawn, the husband and the wife made certain that they weren't at home.)

In any case it was too noisy, the wife had to concede, for she was trying to avoid a migraine headache, and nausea from medication, for her to work outside in the rose garden, which had suffered an onslaught of Japanese beetles and badly needed her care. She had wanted, too, to remove those tough little tendril-weeds from the terrace, that poked up between the flagstones, giving it a shabby look.

Too noisy for the sensitive husband to remain on the terrace where he'd brought some of his *home office* work—his laptop, investment accounts, sheets of yellow paper on which he penciled notes.

(When the wife asked the husband about their finances, the husband tended to reply curtly. She understood that they had "lost some money" in stocks, but then—who in Crescent Farms had not? The wife did not dare to ask more of the husband who would interpret such questions as a critique of his ability to handle their finances, thus of his manhood.)

The husband who'd been restless in his *home office* now returned to the house. The wife shut all the windows, and turned on the air-conditioning. And a ceiling fan in the husband's office, that made a gentle whirring sound.

"The lawn crew won't be there much longer, I'm sure. Then I'll help you move outside again."

The husband waved her away with a look of commingled disgust and dismay, that pierced the wife to the heart.

"THOSE DAMNED JESTERS! What did I tell you!"

This day, mid-morning, a lovely day in late June, there came what sounded like raw adolescent voices, boys' voices, through the trees. And barking. (Two dogs: one with a deep-throated growling bark, the other a petulant miniature, a high-pitched excruciating yipping.)

And there came too as the husband and the wife listened in fascinated horror, a harsh sound of slapping against pavement. Slap-slap-*slap.*

"A basketball? They have one of those damned portable baskets in their driveway so their sons can practice basketball."

"So soon!"

"What do you mean, 'so soon'?"

The wife wasn't sure what she had meant. The words had sprung from her lips. Faltering she said, "They'd just been young children, it seemed. So recently."

She was thinking *What has happened to the croquet set?*

She was thinking *We forgot entirely about it! Croquet.*

No longer could the husband linger on the terrace after breakfast where it was his habit to read the newspaper that so infuriated him but which he could not seem to resist—the *New York Times*.

(The wife knew that the husband sent angry e-mails to the *Times* editorial page, at least once a week. The subjects of the e-mails ranged from politics to global warming, from taxes, "earmarks," the President and the President's wife, to "sick cultures" in the Middle East and in the Far East.)

(The wife knew that the husband had sent angry complaints to the Crescent Lake Farms Homeowners Association. He had tried to call, but there was only voice mail, which was never answered. And the e-mail complaints were answered automatically, with a promise of "looking into the situation.")

Often then in the days following, intermittently and unpredictably through the day, there came the sound of teenagers practicing basketball, playing amplified rap music, exchanging shouts. It seemed clear that the Jester children had visitors—the shouts were various, at times the several young voices were quite distinct.

No words, only just sounds. Raw brash crude sounds.

And the dogs' nonstop barking, that continued after the young people left, often into the night.

(Were the dogs tied outside? Were no other neighbors disturbed? How could the *neighbors-through-the-trees* fail to hear and be disturbed, themselves?)

(Wasn't it cruelty to animals, to keep dogs tied outside? Ignoring their barking in the night?)

It was astonishing to the wife and the husband, how loud these noises were; how *close-seeming*.

"It's like they're just outside our house. They couldn't be any louder if they were inside our house."

"Maybe—we should go away. Sooner than August."

They'd planned two weeks on Nantucket Island, in August: in a rented house on the ocean, to which they'd been returning for decades.

But the husband was furious at the suggestion of being *driven out of his own house, by neighbors.*

"I wouldn't want to give them the satisfaction."

"But they don't know anything about us—they don't know *us.*"

"They know that they have neighbors. They know that their noise must carry through the trees. And what of their neighbors on West Crescent Drive? You'd think that they would have complained by now."

"Maybe they have. Maybe nothing came of it."

"Listen!"—the husband lifted his hand.

For now, there was the sound of a younger child, crying. Or screaming. Sobbing, screaming, crying.

Other childish voices, shouts. The teenagers' raw-voiced shouts. Must have been a game of some kind involving physical contact.

And the dogs' barking. Louder.

The husband and the wife left their house earlier than they'd planned for dinner in town. The husband could barely eat his food, the ignominy of being *driven away* from his own house was intolerable to him.

At least when they returned, the noise through the trees had abated.

Only nocturnal birds, bullfrogs and insects in the grass. And high overhead, a quarter-moon curved like a fingernail.

In gratitude and exhaustion, the husband and the wife slept that night, in their dreams twined in each other's arms.

"LISTEN!"—THE HUSBAND THREW down his newspaper, and heaved himself to his feet.

There came a child's cries, another time. Quite clearly, a girl's cries. Amid the coarser sound of boys' voices, laughter. And the barking dogs.

"But—where are you going?"

"Where do you think I'm going? Over there."

"But—there's no way to get through. Is there?"

"It sounds like a child is being harassed. Or worse. I'm not going to just sit here on my ass, for Christ's sake."

The wife followed close behind the husband. She had not seen him so agitated, so *activated*, in a long time.

They were descending the lawn, in the direction of the gate. The grass had been cut recently, not in horizontal rows but diagonally across the width of the lawn. The air smelled sweetly of mown grass, that had been taken away by the lawn crew.

Rarely opened, the gate was stuck in grass and dirt, and had to be shaken hard.

The husband was very excited. The wife felt light-headed with excitement, and dread.

For this was a violation of Crescent Farms protocol. No one ever approached a neighbor's house from the rear. It was rare that anyone "visited" a neighbor's house uninvited.

"There's a girl who's hurt. And that hysterical barking. Something is terribly wrong over there."

"We should call 911."

"We don't know their house number."

"The police would find it. We could tell them the situation—approximately where the Jesters live . . ."

" 'Jesters' is not their name."

"I *know that*. Of course, 'Jesters' is not their name. We don't know their name."

"And we don't know their address. We can't even describe their house."

"But we know—"

The husband had managed to get the gate open. It was a surprise to see that, like the fence, it was badly rusted.

They made their way then into the thicket of trees, onto township property. Here were scrubby little trees and bushes and coarse weeds, thigh-high. And there was the median, where the power lines were, that looked as if it hadn't been mowed for weeks.

Somewhat hesitantly the husband and the wife made their way into the woods on the other side of the median. Here, there were many trees that appeared to be just partially alive, or wholly dead; there had been much storm damage, broken limbs and other debris heaped everywhere.

There were no paths into the woods that they could discover. No one ever walked here. No children played here. It was not the habit of Crescent Farms children to wander in such places, as the generation of their grandparents had once done.

About fifty feet into the thicket, they encountered a fence. The six-foot fence belonging to their *neighbors-through-the-trees.*

They were panting, very warm. They peered through the fence but could see nothing except trees.

The noises from their neighbors had abated, mostly. The girl had ceased crying. The other voices had vanished. Only a dog continued to bark, less hysterically.

"Maybe we'd better go back? We don't want to get lost."

"*Lost!* We can't possibly get lost."

The husband laughed incredulously. A swarm of gnats circled his damp face, his eyes glared at the wife like the eyes of a man sinking in quicksand.

"The fence is like our own. Unless we've gone in a circle, and it is our own fence . . ."

"This isn't our fence, don't be ridiculous. Our property is behind us, on the other side of the median."

"Yes, but . . ."

The fence did resemble their own fence. It was (possibly) not so old as their fence but it was rusted in places and had become loose and probably, if they could locate the gate, they could force the gate open, and step inside.

Hello! We are your neighbors on East Crescent Drive.

We don't want to disturb you but . . . We are concerned . . .

The husband held back now. The husband was having second thoughts about his mission now that the alarming noises seemed to have ceased.

Again the wife said maybe they should turn back?

It seemed an extreme measure, to approach their neighbors' house from the rear, like trespassers. To come up to their neighbors' house from the rear, uninvited.

For this would be *trespassing* and Crescent Lake Farms expressly forbade *trespassing.*

THE CHILDREN CALLED. One by one, in sequence.

As if the calls were planned.

First, Carrie. Then Tim. Then Ellen.

The husband told them that things were fine, more or less. Except for the God-damned *neighbors-through-the-trees.*

The wife told them that things were fine, more or less. Except for the neighbors they'd never met, across the median on West Crescent Drive.

"For God's sake—Mom, Dad! Don't you have anything else to talk about except the neighbors?"

Their children were exasperated with them. Laughed at them. The husband was furious, and the wife was deeply wounded.

"But—you don't know what it's like, with these people. Your father is under such strain, I'm worried about his health."

"What about your health, Mom? We're worried about *you.*"

And: "If you're unhappy there, you can move. The house is much too large for two people. The maintenance must be out of sight, especially in the winter . . . Mom? Are you listening?"

No. She wasn't listening.

Yes. She was listening, politely.

Into one of those retirement villages? Your father would never survive.

They explained that they were not unhappy in their house, which they loved. In fact they were *very happy*.

Only just upset, at times. By their *neighbors-through-the-trees*.

"THE JESTERS! God-damn them."

Another party on the back terrace. From late afternoon until past midnight.

Amplified rock music. Throbbing notes penetrating the dense thicket of trees. The Jesters were thrumming with life: there was no avoiding the Jesters who penetrated the very air.

The wife returned from her chemo treatment ashen-faced, staggering. Fell onto a bed and tried to sleep for three hours during which time she tried not to be upset by the amplified music-through-the-trees and by her own nausea. The husband had shut himself in his *home office*.

Crack!—crack! Crack-crack-crack!

(Was it gunfire? From the Jesters' property?)

Hunting was forbidden in Crescent Lake Farms. As were firecrackers, fireworks—any kind of noisy activity that was a *disturbance of the peace and privacy of one's neighbors*.

Middle of the night, uplifted voices. Waking the husband and the wife from their troubled sleep.

The adult Jesters were arguing with one another, it seemed. A man's voice sharp as a claw hammer, a woman's voice sharp as flung nails. At 3:20 A.M.

(Were the children involved in the argument? This wasn't clear, initially.)

(Yes, at least one of the children was crying. A forlorn sound like that of a small creature grasped in the jaws of an owl, being carried to the uppermost branches of a tree to be devoured.)

"We have to speak with them. This can't continue."

"We should file a complaint. That might be more practical."

"With the Homeowners Association? Nobody there gives a damn."

"With the township police, then. 'Disturbing the peace'—'suspicion of child abuse.'"

"No! The Jesters could sue, if we made such allegations and couldn't prove them."

"Then we should speak with them. Maybe we can work something out." The wife paused, trying to control her voice. She was very shaken, and close to tears. "They're decent people, probably. They don't realize how disturbing they are to their neighbors. They will listen to reason . . ."

In their bedroom, in the night. The husband saw that the wife was ashen-faced, and trembling; the wife saw, with a pang of love for him, a despairing sort of love, that the husband was looking strained, older than his age; beneath his eyes, bruised-looking shadows. Yet he tried to smile at her. He took her hand, squeezed the fingers. He was like an actor who has forgotten his lines, yet will make his way through the scene, eyes clutching the eyes of his fellow-actor, the two of them stumbling together.

"I'm so sorry this is happening to us. Now you're retired, you should be spared any more stress. I wish I knew what to do."

"Don't be ridiculous. It isn't up to you. I should be more forceful. We can't let our lives be ruined by the Jesters."

It was quiet now. The terrible quarrel had flared up, like wildfire, and abruptly ceased. There had been a sharp noise like the shutting of a door.

Tentatively the husband and the wife lay back down in their bed, the wife huddling in the husband's arms. By slow degrees they drifted into sleep.

SLAP-SLAP-*SLAP.* The boys had returned to their basketball practice, early-morning. The dogs were barking. Someone shouted words that were nearly distinct—*Don't! God-damn you.*

"IF YOU'RE COMING with me, come on."

"But, are you sure . . ."

"We have no choice! We'll talk with them, and if they don't cooperate we'll file a formal complaint with the township police."

Bravely the husband spoke. The wife hurried to keep up with him, headed for their car. She saw that the husband had shaved hastily and that tiny blood-nicks shone in his jaws.

The husband always drove. The wife sat beside him, sometimes clutching at the dashboard when the husband drove quickly and erratically and spoke as he drove, distracted.

The husband was saying that there have been "primitive cultures" in which the populace cut down trees year after year—decade after decade—until at last there was but a single tree remaining on the island—(evidently, these were "island aboriginals")—and this tree, they cut down.

Then, there were no more trees. The people were amazed.

Amazed and mystified. *For there had always been trees.*

Where had the trees gone? Had demons cast a spell? The belief of centuries was, *there had always been trees.*

The husband said grimly, "You do not question inherited beliefs. That is blasphemy, and blasphemy will get you killed."

The husband laughed, "Yet: where are the trees?"

The wife had no idea what the husband was talking about. She had missed his initial remarks, as they'd climbed into their car, in haste and yet in determination.

She thought *Does he mean, we have no idea what will happen to us next? Or does he mean—we can alter our future, before it's too late?*

The husband drove along East Crescent Lake Drive, and at Juniper Road he turned right; a half-mile north on Juniper, and a right turn onto a smaller road, then another small road, then West Crescent Drive.

"These houses are beautiful. And the landscaping . . ."

The wife spoke admiringly. The wife was very nervous, both of the husband's driving which was too fast for the circumstances, and of their impending destination.

The husband said, "West Crescent isn't any different from East Crescent. The houses are no more beautiful here. The landscaping is similar. In fact, some of the houses are identical with houses on our road. Look—that Colonial? It's a replica of the Colonial a few doors down from us."

The wife wasn't so sure. This Colonial had dark green shutters, the Colonial on East Crescent Lake Drive had dark red shutters.

They came to 88 East Crescent Drive. The road curved as their road did, and the cul-de-sac resembled theirs. To their surprise, the mailbox at the Jesters' house was made of white brick and stainless steel, exactly like their own, but the Jesters' mailbox door was opened, and the interior of the mailbox crammed with what looked like an accumulation of rain-soaked junk mail.

Growing in a little patch at the base of the mailbox were ugly, coarse-flowering weeds. In a little patch at the base of their mailbox the wife had planted marigolds as she did every year.

"Oh my God! Look."

"What is . . ."

To their astonishment, the house they believed to belong to the Jesters resembled their own, though not precisely. It was a sprawling country house of weathered shingle board, large, with a horseshoe driveway like their own, but badly cracked and weedy. The elegant plantings in the Jesters' lawn had been allowed to grow wild. Rotted tree limbs lay scattered in the weedy grass.

The husband and the wife were stunned. The husband and the wife were nearly speechless. For it seemed that the Jesters' house had been damaged in some way, and was boarded-up.

"Do you think—no one lives here?"

"That isn't possible . . ."

The husband had parked their car at the curb. Cautiously now they were making their way up the driveway, staring.

Waiting for a dog to rush at them, barking . . . Two dogs.

It was so, the shingle-board house was shut up. Seemingly abandoned. No one lived here, or had lived here in a while. There was a dark stain across half the façade, like scorch.

It *was* scorch—smoke damage.

As the husband and the wife approached the house, they saw that there was a faded-yellow tape around it, at least so far as they could see. On the tape were repeated DO NOT ENTER BY ORDER OF HECATE TOWNSHIP FIRE DEPT.—DO NOT ENTER BY ORDER OF HECATE TOWNSHIP FIRE DEPT.— in black, badly faded.

The fire could not have been recent. But how was this possible?

Boldly the husband approached the house, stooping beneath the yellow tape. The wife protested, "Wait! Where are you going? It's a violation of the law . . ."

"No one is here. No one is watching."

"But—maybe it's dangerous."

(It might not have been correct, that no one was watching. Just outside the cul-de-sac, at 86 East Crescent Drive, there was a large putty-colored French Provincial house with numerous glittering windows. And a vehicle parked in the driveway.)

The husband approached the front door, stepping on debris on the stoop. As if to ring the doorbell, though obviously there was no one inside the wreck of a house.

They could see now that the fire damage was considerable. From the road, it had not been so evident. Much of the house had collapsed, at the rear; downstairs windows were boarded up, somewhat carelessly; part of the roof, burnt through, had collapsed. The wife was shivering in the midsummer heat. *Did anyone die in the fire? How many?* The wife did not want to think *Was it arson? And when?* Beside the heavy oak door there were inset windows, of stained glass, which were partly broken but not boarded up; through these, the husband and the wife stared into the house, into a foyer with a silly, forlorn-looking crystal chandelier, a badly stained tile floor, miscellaneous overturned furniture.

A chair lying on its side. A crooked mirror, reflecting what looked like mist, or gas. Smoke stains like widespread black wings on the once-white wall.

A smell of something terrible, like burnt flesh.

"Please! Let's leave."

"No one can see us."

"People have died here. You can tell. Please let's *leave*."

The husband laughed at the wife, irascibly. In the reflected light from the stained glass his skin was unnaturally mottled, rubefacient; his eyes narrowed with thought, a kind of frightened animal cunning. His nostrils widened and contracted as if, like an animal, he was sniffing the air for danger.

The wife pulled at his arm and he threw off her hand. But he relented, and followed her back to their car.

The wife saw that the husband had parked the car crookedly at the curb. It was a large gleaming new-model Acura, a beautiful silvery-green color, yet parked so carelessly it looked clownish. The husband saw this too and drew in his breath sharply.

"What the hell? I didn't park the car like this."

"You must have."

"I said, *I did not*."

"Then who did?"

"You drove."

"I did not drive! You drove."

"You drove, and you parked the car like a drunken woman or a—a senile woman. Lucky we aren't in town, you'd have a ticket."

"But I didn't here. I would never have driven here. I didn't even bring my handbag, with my driver's license."

"Driving without a license! That's *points* on your license."

The wife was deeply agitated. The smell of the burnt house and what had burnt inside it was still in her nostrils. Badly she wanted to flee home and lie down on the bed and hide her face and sleep but in the corner of her eye she saw a figure approaching her and the husband, from the house across the cul-de-sac. A white-haired woman, genteel, with kindly eyes, in gardening clothes, on her head a wide-brimmed straw hat. On her hands, gloves. The wife saw that the white-haired woman had been tending to roses bordering the driveway of her house, a striking red-brick Edwardian with a deep front lawn. Obviously, the white-haired woman had, like the wife, a gardener-helper who came at least once a week to till the soil for her and take out the worst of the weeds.

"Excuse me! Hello."

The white-haired woman removed her soiled gloves, smiling at the husband and the wife. Hers was a beautiful ruin of a face, soft as a leather glove; her nose was thin, aristocratic. Her small mouth was pale primrose-pink.

"Are you—by any chance—considering that house? I mean—to buy?"

"To *buy*? The house isn't in any condition to be inhabited."

"Yes. But it could be rebuilt and repaired."

"And it isn't for sale anyway, so far as we can see. Is it?"

"I wouldn't know. I mean—it might be listed with a Realtor. Realtors' signs aren't allowed in Crescent Lake Farms."

The white-haired woman smiled at them wistfully. She went on to say how hopeful they all were, on West Crescent Drive, that someone would buy the house soon, and restore it. "What a beautiful house it was! This is all such a shame and a—tragedy."

"Why? What happened?"

"The fire was—wasn't—an accident. So the investigators ruled."

"Who set the fire, if it wasn't an accident? One of the sons?"

Seeing that the husband was eager to know, the white-haired woman became cautious. She backed away, though with a polite smile.

"No one knows. Not definitely."

"*Was* there a son? A teenager?"

"There's an investigation—ongoing. It's been years now. I don't know anything more."

"You must know if they died in the fire? Someone did die—yes?"

"Who?"

"Who? The Jesters, of course. *How many of them died in the fire?*"

The husband was speaking harshly. The wife was embarrassed at his vehemence, with this gracious stranger. She tugged at his arm, to bring him back to himself.

" 'The Jesters'? I don't understand."

"What was the name of the family who lived here?"

"I—don't remember. I have to leave now."

The white-haired woman turned quickly away. That so gracious a person would turn her back on fellow residents of Crescent Lake Farms was astonishing to the wife though the husband grunted as if such rude behavior only confirmed his suspicions.

"Let's go. 'The Jesters' are taboo, it seems."

The husband drove. At the intersection of West Crescent Drive with a smaller road called Lilac Terrace he turned left, thinking to take a short cut to Juniper, and home; but Lilac Terrace turned out, as the wife might have told the husband, to be a dead end. NO OUTLET.

After some maneuvering, the husband and the wife returned home to 88 East Crescent Drive. In their absence, the house had remained unchanged.

THE HUSBAND SWUNG his legs out of bed in panic thinking that someone had entered the house to shoot them.

They went to the window which was a floor-to-ceiling window with a balcony, rarely used. Because of the Jesters' unpredictable noises, the husband and the wife no longer opened this window even on summer nights.

The husband's face was mottled with rage, and fear. The wife thought *I will comfort him all the days of our lives.*

It was the morning of July Fourth. The Jesters were celebrating early.

BETRAYAL

THE FIRST CLEAR SYMPTOMS WERE AT THANKSGIVING, last year.

Our son arrived hours late. It has long been our family custom to gather at our house at 4:00 P.M. and to sit down to eat at about 5:30 P.M. and yet it was nearly 6:00 P.M. when Rickie arrived—after having assured us he would arrive at about 1:00 P.M. We were so grateful to see him that no one, even Father, had a harsh word to say to him though we noted how defensive Rickie was saying he'd been driving six hours, stuck in traffic on the damned freeway and wasn't in a mood to be criticized now.

Outside it was deeply-dark, windswept and wintry. And wet. When Rickie entered the house a gust of wind accompanied him and struck at the crackling fire in the fireplace, that Father had been tending with a poker. And there came with him a smell of rain so sharp it seemed metallic, odors of earth and leaves and something rank as an animal's wetted hide that pinched at our nostrils.

We were already sitting at dinner. Rickie's place awaited him. He mumbled an excuse and disappeared upstairs for ten minutes presumably washing up, changing his rumpled clothes, but when he appeared again downstairs we saw that he'd done little more than run a comb through his matted hair, that hadn't been washed in a while, and he was wearing a long-sleeved T-shirt and jeans, not freshly laundered, and running shoes. He'd left off his Sigma Nu hoodie at least, upstairs.

Some of us were offended, frankly, that Rickie should sit down at Thanksgiving dinner looking so disheveled. His jaws were unshaven, his eyes were edgy and glittering. His laughter was high-pitched, a nervous sort of laughter, that faded abruptly like a switch shut off. Rickie's younger nephews and nieces and cousins were hurt that he paid virtually no attention to them, as he usually did.

Practically the first thing Rickie said when he took his place among us, as warm platters were being passed in his direction, was that he would "forgo" turkey this year, thanks!

Forgo turkey we protested, how can you *forgo turkey* when turkey is the point of Thanksgiving we pointed out to the unshaven boy in the soiled San Diego Zoo T-shirt but Rickie said with a smirk, Not for the poor turkey it ain't.

Ain't is not a word we use in our family. Not a word that Rickie with a *cum laude* B.A. degree from Stanford and whose SAT scores were in the highest fifth percentile would use. *Ain't* was a jab in the ribs meant to offend and annoy and so *ain't* did offend and annoy us, particularly Father who stared at Rickie speechless. Mother, who'd been preparing for Thanksgiving dinner for two days and who'd purchased an "organic" twenty-two-pound turkey for the occasion, blinked and stared at Rickie as if he'd slapped her.

We asked, are you a *vegetarian* and Rickie said yes that was right.

A *vegetarian*! Since when?

But Rickie just shrugged. He appeared to be starved spooning large portions of Mother's bread crumb stuffing, mashed sweet potatoes, candied carrots and broccoli-with-almonds onto his plate. We recalled his legendary appetite for any kind of meat including pizza-with-sausage and cheeseburgers, when he'd been a teenager in our household.

Mother said, trying to smile, "Well! At least I hope you are not one of those *vegans* . . ."

In Mother's mouth *vegan* was uncertainly enunciated. Rickie laughed and said, "No Mom: not yet."

Mother's bread crumb stuffing was particularly delicious this year, made with apples, prunes, chestnuts, thyme, tarragon, fine-cut onions and celery. In the lush salad of many gourmet greens were tiny sections of clementines, dried cranberries, chopped escarole, cherry tomatoes from Mexico. The mashed sweet potatoes were (secretly) laced with marshmallow—one of Mother's prized family recipes. All of these foods, plus chunks of thick raisin bread, Rickie ate as if he were famished. (It was curious to see how Rickie avoided even looking at the turkey carcass on the sideboard, that looked as if ravenous hyenas had attacked it. And even the harmless gravy boat, with its rich oily turkey gravy.) When we asked him about his closest friends from college he replied in distracted grunts. Mother dared to ask him about Holly Cryer, a prep school girlfriend whom Rickie often saw when they were both home from college, but Rickie only just frowned and shrugged. Instead he spoke excitedly of Mitzie, Claus, Herc (for Hercules), Kindle, Stalker, Big Joe and Juno. We said, "Oh but Rickie, those are *animals*. That is your *work*."

Rickie was currently an intern at the San Diego Zoo, at the bonobo exhibit. That day it seemed that, in our company, listening to our conversation, Rickie was frequently elsewhere, and listening intently to another conversation that drew him more powerfully. Almost dreamily now he paused in his rapid chewing to gaze at us one by one, around the table. As if he were counting us, or hoping to discover, in our familiar faces, something he recognized. We could see a fringe of dark-matted chest hair just visible at the stretched neckline of his zoo-issue T-shirt.

"Oh hey Mom, Dad—all you guys: I've been trying to tell you. My *work* is my *life*."

Certainly it was good news that Rickie was employed now, if only as an unpaid intern. (For an unpaid internship might lead to paid employment someday—that was the belief among the families of recent college graduates like ours.) And it was good news that Rickie seemed to be devoted to this work.

But since his employment was only temporary, at the San Diego Zoo, and not the employment for which he'd been preparing himself for four years at Stanford, this was possibly not so very good news.

It had been his parents' dream that Rickie would go to medical school. Or, failing that, Rickie might go into high-level medical research—at a pharmaceutical company, for instance. (Father, a quite successful corporate lawyer at Helix Pharmaceuticals in Vista Flats, California, whose long-ago dream for himself had been scientific research, had contacts in several prominent pharmaceutical companies.)

Yet, Rickie seemed happy. Rickie seemed *defiantly happy*.

Just after graduation, when he'd returned home to Saddle Creek, from his Stanford frat house, Rickie had seemed very unhappy. It would not be an exaggeration to say that Rickie had been seriously depressed. That spring he'd been interviewed for a number of promising entry-level positions with California employers but—(so far as we knew)—no offers had followed. Rickie had also, following Father's encouragement, applied to a miscellany of West Coast universities to enter a Ph.D. program in biology, but even where he'd been accepted as a graduate student, he hadn't been offered a fellowship. And so, he'd been inert with disappointment lying on his bed or sprawled on our family-room sofa stretched out like a rubber band that has lost its elasticity.

Son, don't do this, we pleaded with him. Don't *give in*.

Particularly, Father was repelled at the thought of *giving in*.

Rickie was unshaven then. Bristly whiskers marring his boyish face. And his eyes glazed with boredom, or something worse.

He wasn't *giving in*, he protested. He was *exploring, within*.

Anyway he couldn't help it. His generation was the Walking Wounded devastated by graduating from college and being expelled into the world that didn't give a shit for them, B.A. honors from Stanford or whatever.

Sure some of his college friends had definite *plans*. Not his closest frat-brother friends but others who'd gotten into med school, or law school, even if not first-rate schools, still the contrast with Rickie's own life narrow and circumscribed as his bed, or the family-room, sofa—no wonder he was feeling *down*.

Had to take solace from the fact that there were plenty of others in his generation who frankly had *no plans*, not even *prospects for plans*.

At Saddle Creek Academy which was in the highest percentile of California private schools Rickie had taken nearly every science course offered, most of them AP courses. And he'd had other AP courses. Usually high grades and the praise of his teachers. And the SATs—we hired tutors for him, reasoning that, as other parents hired tutors for their children, we would be disadvantaging our son by not hiring tutors; and the expenditure, which had been considerable, had paid off. With Father's encouragement Rickie had looked ahead to medical school at San Francisco, Yale, Harvard, as well as Stanford—the very best.

One of his closest Sigma Nu brothers had died only a few weeks after graduation, in his parents' basement TV room in La Jolla. A lethal combination of (prescription) Xanax and OxyContin the twenty-one-year-old had bought from a fourteen-year-old dealer in the parking lot of Saddle Creek High.

There were signs we might have noted, that Rickie might not get into his first-choice med school. For though he'd been an A-student in high school, in his first year at Stanford he'd run into a solid-concrete wall, as he described it, with organic chemistry, physics, and calculus, got messed up at mid-terms and never quite recovered his self-confidence; without informing his parents he had shifted to a less demanding major—some sort of science-culture studies, "environmental biology." Why'd he want to spend his life analyzing chemicals in a lab, examining the molecular underpinnings of animals without any notion of what the original animal looked like, or *was*; sure it was exciting that the genetic code was being broken, through such exacting experiments, but Rickie found abstractions *Bor-ing*!

He'd always liked animals—some animals. Like horses, giraffes. He'd loved our mixed-breed shepherd Strongheart who'd pined for Rickie when Rickie left home for Stanford, though, when he'd lived in our household, Rickie had had a decreasing amount of time to devote to the eager dog whose care and tending naturally fell to Mother. (Not that Mother complained!—Mother was never one to complain.)

Yet, Rickie's luck turned when he received a summer internship at the San Diego Zoo. We hadn't had any idea that Rickie had applied for such a position, at such a place, until, as Rickie proudly announced to us, it was a *fate accomplished*.

Father had said, speaking carefully as if fearing he might be misunderstood, "An internship is—unpaid?"

But Rickie's good spirits could not be dashed, now that they'd been fired up like gasoline sprinkled onto a dying fire. He told Father that working at the San Diego Zoo was known to be so cool for kids his age, everybody says they'd pay the zoo for the chance.

Mother said, "It sounds just wonderful! Rickie can try again applying to medical schools, or to graduate schools, and with this internship in his résumé, he'll be a—shoo-in."

Shoo-in was gaily uttered by Mother, in an outburst of optimism.

Shoo-in was not an expression ever heard on Mother's lips before this moment.

Two weeks after Rickie's first day as an intern at the zoo, we flew south to San Diego to visit with him. In his infrequent calls and e-mails home he'd told us how "great" his colleagues were and how "special" bonobos are—not just "great apes" but unique among these, genetically the closest of all primates to *Homo sapiens*.

Even before we saw Rickie in his zoo uniform assisting an older staff member at the bonobo enclosure, even before we saw Rickie grinning and "signing" to one of the friendly bonobos through the immense glass window protecting the bonobos from zoo visitors—we felt unease, that our son whom we knew so well was being seduced by this new milieu, which was so exotic and so strange to us.

We'd arranged with Rickie that we would meet him in front of the bonobo enclosure at about noon, and would take him to lunch; but when we arrived, breathless and just slightly intimidated—(for the San Diego Zoo is an enormous place!)—there was Rickie standing at the side of a tall broad-shouldered woman with ash-colored hair addressing a gathering of about a dozen visitors. Seeing us, Rickie only just smiled, nodded and waved, without speaking to us. You could see—(that is, we could see)—that our twenty-one-year-old son greatly admired this woman, as he'd admired a few of his Stanford professors; so intently did he listen to her words, observing the bonobos in the enclosure as she spoke of them, it was as if Rickie were memorizing the experience and didn't want to be distracted from it.

But how happy Rickie appeared! This was something of a surprise for we hadn't seen Rickie so boyishly enthusiastic since his small triumphs in high school athletics years before. And how very different he seemed, in his smart red San Diego Zoo cap, red sweatshirt and fresh-laundered denims, from the melancholy boy laid low by lethargy, depression, and irony in his boyhood room at Saddle Creek.

Mother whispered to Father, "Oh! is that *our son?* He looks so . . ."

"He does," Father said. "Thank God!"

Unobtrusively we drew near, to listen to the ashy-haired woman talk about the bonobos and answer visitors' questions. Truly, the woman, whose name tag identified her as HILARY KRYDY, was impressive. She was tall and fit and her face was both plain and powerfully attractive, with an energy and purposefulness that exuded from within. She might have been Mother's age but looked much more robust and youthful. We were directed to look closely at the bonobos, as Hilary spoke. An exhibit in a zoo at which we might have simply glanced—registering some kind of large antic "monkey"—now took on dramatic significance. In the enclosure, which looked like actual wilderness landscape with rocks and boulders, small exotic trees, a pond, the coarse-furred little apes were wonderfully lively and alert as if showing off for their human audience. They rose from all fours with a sort of gawky grace to their hind legs and "walked"—very like human beings. (Mother said, "Oh—are they imitating *us*?" Father chuckled saying, "Certainly not. Their species precedes *us*.") We could understand that Rickie would be drawn to the bonobos as crudely inferior types of himself.

Father observed in the gravely creased face of an older bonobo, who held himself apart from the cavortings of the younger bonobos, an expression of—recognition? *Identity?* For a moment it seemed almost that their eyes locked: each was an *elder*, and had reason to be exasperated with their young offspring. Then, to Father's surprise and disappointment, the seemingly dignified patriarch leapt onto a boulder, glared and grinned at Father with bared yellow teeth and, with rubber-like prehensile fingers, grabbed and shook his large fruit-like genitals in an unmistakable gesture of antagonism. Father winced—such vulgarity! Of course, the creature was just an animal. Father was grateful that Mother didn't seem to have seen this obscene display as other visitors pretended not to have seen it.

Younger bonobos, very lively, charmingly childlike, jumped about onto rocks, and off rocks; set up a high-pitched chatter of merriment that must have carried for some distance in the zoo; winked, grinned, spat and "signed" at observers who waved and called to them in return. Mother was most taken with the comely female bonobos nursing their hairy young, or hugging the young to their droopy enlarged teats, that did resemble the breasts of a nursing *Homo sapiens* female, to a degree; she saw, too, the uncanny flat-faced beauty of certain of the females, and the adorable gamin-faces of the very young. Rickie glowed with pride as if the bonobos were in some way *his*—a gift of his, for us.

It was thrilling to Rickie, we could see, when the ashy-haired Hilary turned to him, suggesting that he answer a visitor's question—which Rickie managed to do, quite intelligently. (We thought!)

Only when Hilary's mini-lecture ended and the visitors moved on to the next enclosure did Rickie hurry to greet us, with a hug for Mother and a handshake for Father; he was eager to introduce us to Hilary, a senior staff member. Impulsively Rickie invited Hilary to join us for lunch but she declined; she could see, as our heedless son could not, that we were not enthusiastic about the invitation, wanting to spend some time alone with our son.

At lunch in a restaurant inside the zoo Rickie chattered happily about his internship, his fellow interns and older colleagues; he'd become, within a remarkably short period of time, something of an expert on bonobos, it seemed, and spoke to us in an excited disjointed way about the exotic species of "ape" as if we'd made the trip to San Diego not to see him, but to see and hear about his newest-favorite animal.

Some of what Rickie recounted to us was an echo of the guide's talk. In his boyish voice, it did sound fascinating to us, initially.

"Bonobos, often called 'pygmy chimps,' should not be confused with the more common, more widely distributed and far more aggressive chimpanzees. That's an insult to us. I mean—to them." Rickie paused, as if to let this sink in. "Bonobos are much more attractive than chimpanzees, as you probably noticed—smaller, more slender, with heads that more resemble human heads, as well as other human-like features. " (In fact, we had not so much as glanced into any of the other ape-enclosures in our haste to get to the bonobo enclosure.) "Genetically, bonobos are our closest primate relatives. Bonobos 'laugh' as we laugh—virtually. Bonobos walk upright as we walk upright—almost. Wouldn't you know"—Rickie's voice lowered to a mournful growl—"of the great apes it's the bonobos who are the most endangered species. Go figure!"

"That is so sad!" Mother said.

"Shit, Mom, it's *tragic*."

Rickie seemed annoyed by Mother's innocent remark, as Father was annoyed by Rickie's profanity in Mother's presence.

"But not surprising," Rickie added quickly, seeing the disapproval in Father's face, "since bonobos are the most peace-loving and the least aggressive of apes. *Not* like *Homo sapiens*."

"Do chimps kill 'em and eat 'em?"—Father had to ask a facetious question.

Rickie winced. This was a topic he didn't like to consider.

"Well—maybe . . . Chimps are definitely 'opportunistic' carnivores and bonobos, at least bonobo babies, would be vulnerable to them. But I don't know for sure. I'll ask Hilary."

Father suggested to Rickie that they change the subject? We'd come to San Diego to talk about *him*.

"Sure Dad. Cool."

Slowly then the radiance began to fade from Rickie's face.

Rickie was clean-shaven and well-groomed. His wavy fawn-colored hair was neatly cut and his zoo uniform T-shirt and jeans were clean; his running shoes didn't look nearly so bad as Rickie's running shoes usually looked. Mother had to resist an almost overwhelming impulse to touch Rickie's smooth forehead with her fingertips as he and Father talked of more serious matters. The boy didn't look a day over seventeen!

Father was pointing out that the internship was just for the summer and Rickie had "no future" in the San Diego Zoo or in any other zoo without a Ph.D. in—zoology? environmental zoology? Seeing a sulky look in Rickie's face, Father said, with the air of a surgeon cutting into flesh just a little more emphatically than required, "It's a tragic time for *us*. I mean—*Americans*. We are reaching a saturation point of highly and expensively educated young men and women—like you—who have B.A. degrees from outstanding universities, even honors degrees. There are just too many of you—that's the fundamental, Malthusian problem. But you are not unified, you don't form a distinct cluster. You're likely to be scattered, living with your parents. Not at all the way the world was when your mother and I graduated from college, in the late 1960s and early 1970s—everyone couldn't wait to get away from home . . ."

But this struck a wrong note, a hostile note Father hadn't meant to strike. And at the moment, Rickie wasn't living at home but was renting an apartment near the zoo with another recent Stanford graduate whom we had yet to meet.

Father said, "Well—you're lucky to have part-time employment in this marketplace. Of course, you aren't exactly *employed*—you are *volunteering* your time. Some of your prep school friends who'd graduated last year or earlier seem to have given up seriously looking for jobs. There's a rush to graduate schools, too. In most fields, if you are second-best, forget it. Manual labor like lawn work and service jobs at Wendy's, Taco Bell, KFC is for illegal immigrants or the dumbest high school kids. No one wants an overqualified Stanford graduate. No one wants *adolescent irony*."

Rickie's boyish-tanned face darkened with the blood of adolescent humiliation.

Mother tried to soften Father's harsh words by speaking warmly of Hilary, whom she'd scarcely met, and the "pygmy chimps"—"So very *lively*."

There were exhibits at the zoo, Mother said, where the animals are just so boring, they don't move and don't look at you, because they don't have the brains to see you; and sometimes, like with the great snakes, or some kind of dwarf "tapir," you couldn't be sure that there was anything in an enclosure at all.

"Animal life *is* boredom," Father said. It was like Father, in times of crisis, to speak in such terse brittle remarks you were led to think that they were aphorisms of Montaigne you should have known, or clever cutting jokes of Oscar Wilde.

Rickie had been eating haphazardly, pushing food around on his plate. We'd scarcely noticed then—we would recall only in retrospect—that Rickie hadn't ordered a cheeseburger, chicken nuggets, or a pizza slice with pepperoni sausage but a large Waldorf salad containing no meat. With the sudden and surprising belligerence of the patriarch-bonobo who'd so offended Father he said, "Nooo Dad. Don't think so. The fact is, *animals* are not different from us: *we are them*."

"But," Mother said, flustered, seeing the anger in Father's face, "we are not *really*—are we? We can talk, and we—we wear clothing; we can add up numbers in our heads, and we can—well, make tools—cook food—*grow food*. Not many animals can do such things can they?"

Rickie shrugged as if Mother's question was so foolish he wasn't required to answer. Father said stiffly, "Well. We are *mammals*, I suppose—but not ordinary *animals*. I draw the line at that."

FROM THAT POINT onward, relations with Rickie became increasingly difficult.

We were expecting Rickie to return home in early September, when his summer internship ended, but, in late August, he called home excitedly to inform us that, though his applications for graduate programs had been rejected at sixteen California universities ranging from Stanford and Berkeley to San Jose State and U-C Eureka, his internship had been extended for another six months!

"Oh no," Father said.

In a stricken-voice voice Rickie said, "What d'you mean, Dad—*no?*"

Father said, "I can't continue to support you in a—hobby-kind of job. In a summer-vacation-kind of job."

Rickie protested, "Working with bonobos is *humanitarian work.* It isn't just some trivial pastime. Everyone I know at the zoo would inform you you are *so mistaken.*"

"Rickie, it's *unpaid labor.* The zoo pays its staff, you can be sure it pays its administrators generous salaries. Why should you, an intelligent young man, with a B.A. *cum laude* from Stanford, volunteer for *unpaid labor?*"

As Father spoke, Mother was listening to the conversation on a cordless phone. Quickly she said, hoping to deflect the conflict, "Rickie, what good news!"

"Mom, thanks. I'm glad that someone is on my side."

Later, when Rickie reluctantly came home for a weekend, Father tried to reason with him in private.

"You do understand, son, that you should be making a serious effort to support yourself at the age of—is it twenty-one?—twenty-two? You are welcome to stay with us while you're looking for employment or applying to graduate school, and we are willing to support you as an intern for a little while longer, but, you must know—the idea is to be *self-supporting.* If there is any lesson of evolution it is that each generation must become independent of the preceding generation—that is a law of nature! You will want to marry, Rickie, won't you?—you will want to have children?"

Rickie said, with a hoarse, deep-throated laugh, "I will? Who says?"

"But—it's *normal.* It's what is—*expected.*"

It was then that Rickie said, frowning severely as he scratched at his armpit, "Well—I look into the future, I guess, and it's like I'm look-ing into a mirror in which there's no reflection."

What a strange utterance! We had no idea what it meant at the time, nor would have we ever.

RICKIE HAD TO be cajoled into coming home for Christmas, which had always been his favorite holiday; another time he arrived late for dinner; another time he insisted upon "forgoing" meat—in this case, a delicious Virginia ham Mother had prepared with cloves, fresh pineapple, and brown sugar. Of course Rickie ate—in fact, stuffed himself—with everything else on the table including several desserts. We noted that his table manners had disintegrated—often, he ate with his fingers. His untouched napkin fell to the floor at his feet. Cagily Rickie didn't allow himself to be drawn out on the sensitive subject of the bonobos or what his future employment might be but simulated an intense interest in our conversation about—whatever it was our Christmas-table conversations were about. (It's impossible to remember even our most intense dinner-table conversations even a few hours later. Politics? Football? Illnesses, surgeries, therapies? Christmas presents, to be returned the next day for credit?) Near the end of the lengthy meal, when Rickie was finishing a second piece of chocolate-cream pie, Father leaned toward him and said, as if reluc-tantly, "Rickie, we should discuss—you know. What you might be doing when the internship runs out."

Rickie's expression froze. But he spoke politely enough saying, "Sure Dad. Cool."

"You have to understand, those—*bonobos*"— (Father pronounced the word with fastidious disdain)—"are not a serious future for you. You would have to return to school and get a Ph.D., at the very least. You'd have to be trained in—some kind of bonobo-zoology. There is no future at the San Diego Zoo, Rickie. Please understand. We are not being—controlling. We are only concerned for your future happiness."

"Good! The bonobo-work is my happiness."

"But—those are *animals*. They are not your *family*."

"We've been through this, Dad. They are my *family*."

Mother left the table, upset. Father tried not to raise his voice. The other guests—Father's brother and sister-in-law, Mother's sister and brother-in-law, Rickie's sister Amber and his younger brother Tod, cousins, Grand-daddy and Grand-mom, among others—sat hushed, embarrassed. Father said, "You are saying reckless things, son, which you can't possibly mean. Who is it who supports you, for instance? And who loves you?"

The words *supports you* had an immediate sobering effect. Rickie said OK he was sorry. Just that he felt strongly about his work, as other interns at the zoo did. It wasn't a job but a *vocation*. Mitzie, Stalker, Bei-Bei, Claus, Kindle, Herc, Big Joe, Juno, Juno's new baby Astrid— they were *so real* to him, there was nothing else like them in his life. The other day he'd been allowed to assist a vet who was examining Big Joe—Big Joe was the patriarch of the clan, whom the younger bonobos liked to tease. Big Joe had screwed up his face as if he'd been about to kiss Rickie but had spat at him instead. (Was this funny? No one except Rickie seemed to think so.) Big Joe was the alpha male, with a real sense of humor! Rickie smiled, recalling a private, precious memory.

Dryly Father said, "Good. I'm glad that someone sees humor in this pathos."

THERE FOLLOWED WEEKS of unanswered phone calls. Unanswered e-mails.

A steady stream of attempts from Rickie's family to contact him, ignored.

In late February Father left a phone message for Rickie, straining to keep his voice steady: "Son! I've calculated, we have spent more than two hundred thousand dollars on your education and what do we—or you—have to show for it?"

And: "Is this how you repay us, son? Going over to the *animals?*"

At last in March we returned to San Diego. We had little hope of confronting Rickie otherwise.

At the zoo, at the bonobo enclosure, we didn't see Rickie anywhere. A crowd of appreciative visitors watched the bonobos cavort and play—exactly as they'd done on our previous visit. In the animal world, time did not budge.

We inquired at an administration building but were told that Rickie was "no longer an intern" at the zoo. His internship had expired at the end of December.

No longer an intern! How was this possible? We'd been told that Rickie's internship had been extended for another six months . . .

We asked to speak with "Hilary Krydy" but were informed, somewhat rudely we thought, that the senior staffer was traveling in Africa right now and was not accessible by e-mail.

We had a street address for Rickie, in a haven of close-clustered stucco buildings a few miles from the zoo; the neighborhood was what Mother worriedly called "mixed-ethnic"—a predominance of Hispanics, Asians, and very black blacks. When we rang the doorbell at 1104 Buena Vida a bearded and shaggy-haired man with bloodshot eyes answered the door to tell us sourly that "Rickie Asshole" no longer lived there. We were stunned by this crude remark and when we tried to identify ourselves the bearded man said, smirking, "That asshole's your son? You can pay me then, he owes me fucking six hundred forty-six dollars in back rent."

Mother wanted to pay this "debt" at once—Father said he would "mail a chack." Mollified, to a degree, the bearded man had no idea where Rickie was and told us we'd be better off checking the zoo. He'd lost his internship but continued to hang out there, so far as anyone knew.

We returned to the zoo. Where is our son? we demanded. Our son seems to have disappeared off the face of the earth.

Again, the administrators spoke to us cautiously. We thought, evasively.

If only we'd recorded these conversations!

Desperate, we returned to the bonobo enclosure. Strangely, each bonobo in sight appeared to be female at that moment. The slender creatures were exceptionally affectionate, grooming, caressing, hugging and kissing one another amid much excited chatter. (They were sexually adventuresome with one another, and even with the youngsters, but we tried not to notice.)

Then, as if they'd just been released from another part of the enclosure, a swarm of males came in—the younger, playful bonobos and at the rear the patriarch who had to be Big Joe, who'd insulted Father previously. Big Joe moved with a stiff sort of arthritic dignity, the hair of his large head seemingly parted in the middle, like a gentleman banker of the 1950s. Rudely the younger bonobos rushed past him, jostling him and taking no notice of the furious glares he cast at their sleek backs. The younger bonobos were fueled by an infectious sort of energy—leaping, swinging, wrestling with the females and one another. (We tried not to stare.)

"Oh look!" Mother cried. "Behind that rock—do you see?"

There crouched a lanky male bonobo with narrow shoulders and a small head; his face was a childish gamin's face but his eyes were hooded and covert.

"Do you see? It's him—Rickie! Oh God."

Mother began frantically crying "Rickie! Rickie!" while Father tried to restrain her. Zoo visitors were astonished to see a well-dressed middle-aged woman making a gesture to climb over the railing, to press herself against the glass wall, arms outspread. "Rickie! Come back, Rickie! You know us—don't you? Rickie!"—so Mother pleaded. The female bonobos gazed at her with sympathy welling in their dark brown eyes. Big Joe was glaring, grinning, stomping his feet, scratching his belly and genitals in an effort to direct attention to himself. The lanky bonobo at whom Mother was calling had quickly retreated to the rear of the enclosure, hiding his eyes behind his hands.

Mother clutched at Father's arm to keep from fainting.

"You saw him, didn't you? Oh—you saw—didn't you?"

"Y-Yes. I think—yes. I saw our—son . . ."

We must have caused a commotion since security officers arrived, to escort us from the San Diego Zoo. Mother was so agitated she had to be driven in a motorized cart with Father seated despondently beside her.

"Oh what have they done to him, those terrible apes," Mother lamented. "How have we failed him, our son . . ."

Grimly Father said, "It's our son who has betrayed us. He has *gone over to the animals.*"

THE SAN DIEGO ZOO has refused to cooperate. No one in authority will take our allegations seriously nor even speak with us any longer. Through an attorney the zoo has issued a statement that our claims (of "abduction," "seduction," "coercion" of our son) are *totally unsubstantiated.*

The head of the great apes department has insisted to us, on the phone and through his attorney, that it is impossible that our son has in some way "disappeared" into the bonobo clan. There are just thirty-seven bonobos at the zoo, including newborns, and each is, of course, documented; approximately one-half of the bonobos were born in Africa and the rest had been born in the zoo. Certainly there was no possible "human male" who had hidden among the bonobos and dwelled with them—this was the height of absurdity.

Father agreed that what Rickie had done was absurd. That would be between Rickie and his family, someday soon. For the time being, we are convinced that Rickie is living in the San Diego Zoo bonobo enclosure in his new, bonobo form; he has, as Father charges, *gone over to the animals.*

This document is a preliminary draft of our prospective lawyer's brief. It is not intended as a legal paper and it is not (yet) in a state to be submitted to the San Diego County Courthouse.

Each Sunday we return to see Rickie. Clean-shaven now, our son has become lighter on his feet; his arms have grown longer, in proportion to his torso and legs. His toes are large and distinct and appear to be prehensile. His face is boyish yet wizened and quizzical, as with an ancient sort of wisdom; like his lively bonobo brothers he is shameless in his sexual proclivities with both young males as well as females of all ages. At our most recent visit last Sunday for the first time Mother said, with a sharp sigh of despair, "Oh maybe—it isn't our son. Maybe what we are looking at is—just an animal."

We gripped each other's hands staring into the enclosure. Mother was quietly weeping and Father stood tall, brave, and dry-eyed. We were gazing into what might have been a wilderness setting—somewhere in the depths of Africa—where amid a pack of bonobos, across a hilly distance of about thirty feet, the lanky-limbed bonobo with a curious ring of hair at the nape of his neck like the remnants of a collar observed us with an inscrutable expression—regret, exasperation, embarrassment, defiance? We saw as he turned away a just-perceptible wave of his furry hand as he trotted off with his brothers and sisters into a shadowy cave at the rear of the enclosure.

LOVELY, DARK, DEEP*

B READ LOAF WRITERS' CONFERENCE, BREAD LOAF, VERMONT. 18 August 1951.

HERE WAS THE FIRST SURPRISE: the great man was much heavier, much more *solid-bodied*, than I'd anticipated. You would not have called him *fat*—that would have been insulting, and inaccurate; but his torso sagged against his shirt like a great udder, and his thighs in summer trousers were a middle-aged woman's fleshy thighs. The sensitive-young-poet face of the photos—(at least, the photos I'd affixed to my bedroom wall)—had coarsened, and thickened; deep lines now bracketed the eyes, as if the poet had too often scowled, or squinted, or winked to suggest the (secret) wickedness of the words he was uttering. The snowy-white hair so often captured in photographs like ectoplasm lifting from the poet's head was thinner than any photograph had suggested, and not so snowy-white, disheveled as if the poet had only just arisen dazed from sleep. The entire face looked

---

* This is a work of fiction, though based upon (selected) historical research. See *Robert Frost: A Biography* by Jeffrey Meyers (1996).
  The Frost poetry quoted in this story is from *The Poetry of Robert Frost*, edited by Edward Connery Lathem (Henry Holt, 1969).

large—larger than you expect a poet's face to be—and the thick jaws were covered in glittering little hairs as if the poet hadn't shaved for a day or two. The eyelids were drooping, near-shut.

"Excuse me—Mr. Frost?"

My voice was tentative, apologetic. My heart had begun to beat erratically as some small, perishable creature—butterfly, moth—might beat against its confinement.

For here was the great man—so suddenly. In my nervous excitement I'd anticipated walking much farther along the path to the poet's cabin in the woods—the "Poet's Cabin" as it was called. I'd anticipated knocking at a door, and waiting for the door to be opened. (Surely not by the legendary Robert Frost himself but by an assistant or secretary? Widowed since 1938, as I'd made it a point to know, the poet would not have been protected by a wary wife, at least.) Instead, Mr. Frost was awaiting his interviewer outside the cabin on a small porch, slouched in a swing, seemingly dozing; slack-jawed, and a scribble of saliva on his mouth. In the bunched crotch of his baggy old-man trousers was an opened notebook and on the floor of the plank porch was the poet's pencil.

Mr. Frost seemed to have drifted into a trance-like sleep in the midst of writing a poem. I felt a stab of excitement at such unexpected intimacy—*Gazing upon Robert Frost asleep! And no one knows.*

On a table beside the porch swing was a pitcher of what appeared to be lemonade and two glasses, of which one was a quarter-filled; a strangely loud-ticking alarm clock; and a dingy red flyswatter.

Quickly I glanced about: no one appeared to be watching. The receptionist whom I'd met in the Bread Loaf Conference Center at the foot of the drive had sent me unaccompanied to Mr. Frost—"You're expected, Miss Fife. Just go on up to the Poet's Cabin. And remember, you must not stay more than an hour, even if Mr. Frost is generous with his time and invites you."

Primly this middle-aged woman smiled at me, and primly Evangeline Fife smiled back. *Of course! Certainly ma'am.*

The Bread Loaf Writers' Conference, as it was called, was a very busy place at this time of year; there were hundreds of visiting writers, poets, and students of all ages (with a preponderance of well-to-do middle-aged women). But this part of the grounds, behind the administrative offices and the white clapboard residences of the chief administrators, was cordoned off as PRIVATE.

Like an earnest schoolgirl I was carrying a large straw satchel weighted down with books, tape recorder, notebook, wallet. Out of this straw satchel came, now, quick into my hands, my newly purchased Kodak Hawkeye.

For it seemed that Mr. Frost hadn't heard my faltering voice—hadn't opened his eyes. In my shaky hands I positioned the camera—peered through the viewfinder at the shadowy figure within with its ghostly-white hair—dared to press the shutter. Very carefully then I wound the film to the next picture.

Like stopping to reload a shotgun, such photography was. You did not simply "take pictures" in rapid succession—each act of picture-taking was deliberate and premeditated.

How strangely vulnerable Mr. Frost looked to me, like an older relative, a father, a grandfather, whom you might glimpse lying about the house carelessly groomed and only partly dressed; it was said that the poet was vain of his appearance, and insisted upon exerting veto power over most photographs of himself, and so it was by chance I'd come upon him in this slovenly state between sleep and wakefulness, as in a hypnotic trance. On his bare feet, well-worn leather house slippers.

I smiled to think *Maybe he is dreaming of—an interview? An interviewer who has come to him, in stealth?*

In all, I took seven surreptitious pictures that afternoon of Mr. Frost slack-jawed and dozing on a porch swing. Sold to a private collector, resold to another collector, and one day to be placed in the Robert Frost Special Collections in the Middlebury College Library, discreetly catalogued *Bread Loaf August 1951 (photographer unknown)*.

Taking Mr. Frost's picture without permission was a brazen act, I know. I had never done anything remotely like this before in my life—at least, I didn't recall having done anything like this: appropriated something not mine, that I believed to be mine; that I believed I *deserved*. Yet all this while I was trembling in dread of Mr. Frost waking and discovering me. Exhilaration coursed through my body like a swift, sexual shock—*I will steal the poet's soul! It is what I deserve.*

IT WAS IN THE LATE SUMMER of 1951, when I was thirty-one years old and a candidate for a master's degree in English at Middlebury College, that I drove to the Bread Loaf Writers' Conference to interview Robert Frost for a special issue of *Poetry Parnassus*.

At this time, "Evangeline Fife" was a promising poet as well as an English instructor at the Privet Academy for Girls in Marblehood, Massachusetts, from which I'd graduated in 1938; since the fall of 1950, I'd been accepted into the rigorous master's program at Middlebury College. It was my hope to advance myself in some way, if only by improving my teaching credentials that I might apply for a position at a four-year college or university. (Of course, it was clear to me that few women were hired for such positions, except at women's colleges; and even there, men were favored. Still, I wished to think that I'd been encouraged by my professors in the Middlebury program; for I'd published poetry in several well-regarded literary magazines including *Poetry Parnassus*, whose editors I'd convinced to empower me to interview the seventy-seven-year-old Robert Frost.) My thesis advisor at Middlebury happened to be, not entirely coincidentally, the director of the summer Bread Loaf Writers' Conference, and he'd encouraged me in both my poetry and my academic studies; kindly Professor Diggs had intervened on my behalf with the famous poet who declined most requests for interviews—at least interviews with "unknown" parties and for little-known publications like *Poetry Parnassus*.

I was conscious of the great honor of being allowed to interview Robert Frost, the preeminent American poet of the era, and I prepared with more than my usual assiduousness. This meant reading, and rereading, virtually all of Frost's poems, many of which, without having intended to, I'd memorized as a schoolgirl. As early as middle school my grandmother had read to me such Frost poems as "The Road Not Taken"—"The Death of the Hired Man"—"Birches"—"Mending Wall"—"Stopping by Woods" (Grandmother's personal favorite). My English instructors at the Privet Academy had reinforced my admiration for Frost, and for poetry in general; at Berkshire College for Women, I majored in English, and published poetry in *Berkshire Blossoms*, which I edited in my senior year. As a junior instructor in English at Privet, I taught Robert Frost's poetry alongside the poetry of Shelley, Keats, Wordsworth, and Byron. Of course, I'd heard Mr. Frost read his poetry several times in Massachusetts and Vermont, always to large, rapturous and uncritical audiences. The atmosphere at these celebrated readings was reverential yet festive, for Robert Frost had become known as a Yankee sage who was also a Yankee wit—a "homespun" American who was also a seer.

Are you wondering what I looked like? No observer would have been surprised to learn that Evangeline Fife was a "poetess"—(as women poets were known at this time)—but it should certainly be noted that I was a pretty—*quite pretty*—young woman who'd always looked younger than her age which is, for women, the most satisfying sort of deception.

A man might enjoy being mistaken for being more sexually aggressive than he is, and richer. But for women, age is paramount.

It is true, I was not a strikingly beautiful woman, which would have involved an entirely different sort of strategy in confronting the (male) world—one far more cautious and circuitous—but my sort of wan delicate blond prettiness seemed preferable than beauty to many men. The *striking beauty* is the female a man can't control in the way he might imagine he could control the delicately blond *merely pretty* woman who at thirty-one can still pass for a girl of eighteen.

Also, I was *petite*. Men imagine that they can more readily intimidate a *petite* female.

"Evangeline Fife" was not married, nor even engaged. This you would note immediately by glancing at the third finger of her left hand—which was bare. Like most girls and young women of her sort, of the era, Miss Fife was certainly a *virgin*.

By *virgin* is meant not simply, or merely, a physiological state but a spiritual state as well. *Pure, innocent, unsullied, artless*—these were adjectives that might have described me, and would have been flattering to me, as to any young unmarried girl of the time.

Though at thirty-one, and still unmarried, Evangeline Fife wasn't exactly *young* any longer, I hoped that Mr. Frost, at seventy-seven, would see me differently.

"EXCUSE ME, MR. FROST? I am—Evangeline Fife? I have a—an appointment with you at one o'clock . . ."

Thrillingly my voice quavered. If you'd placed your forefinger against my throat, as the dozing poet might have been imagining he did, you would feel a sensuous vibratory hum.

The elderly poet's eyelids fluttered and blinked open. For a startled moment Mr. Frost didn't seem to know where he was—outside? On a porch swing? *Had he been sleeping? And what time was this?*

His first, fearful glance was at the alarm clock on the table beside the swing. From where I stood, I could not see the clock-face clearly but had an impression that the glass was glaring with reflected light. The clock was of slightly larger than ordinary size, trimmed in brass, with a look of a nautical instrument; its ticking was unusually loud, and seemed quickened.

The poet then saw me—blinking again, and even rubbing at his eyes. Ah, an attractive young stranger!—standing some ten feet in front of him in the grass, with fine-brushed pale-blond hair and widened "periwinkle-blue" worshipful eyes like a poetry-loving schoolgirl. As a portly peacock might do, quickly the poet took measure of himself, glancing down at his bulky body. His large hands lifted to pat down his disheveled hair, stroke his unshaven jaws, adjust his shirt where it swelled over his belt buckle. He frowned at me, and smiled, as a cunning look came into the faded-icy-blue eyes, and there emerged as through parted curtains on a brightly lit stage the New England sage "Robert Frost" of the famed poetry readings.

"Yes! Of course. I've been awaiting you, my dear. You are prompt— one o'clock. But I am *prompter*, you see, for I am already *here*."

Unfortunately the notebook precariously balanced in the poet's lap fell to the ground. Clumsy, flummoxed, and sensing himself not so nimble, Mr. Frost seemed disinclined to stoop over and pick up the notebook—so, with a little curtsey, I did.

(It was an ordinary spiral notebook, with a black marbleized cover. What I could see of the pages, they were covered in pencil scrawls.)

Mr. Frost seemed embarrassed, taking the notebook from my fingers. "Thank you, my dear."

Very like a schoolgirl I stood before the poet whose gaze moved up and down my body with the finesse of a practiced gem-appraiser. It is always an anxious moment before a woman understands the male judgment—*Yes! You will do.*

(After much deliberation that morning, before setting off on my pilgrimage, I'd selected a pink-floral-print cotton "shirtwaist" with a flared skirt that fell below the knee. On my slender feet were black patent-leather "ballerina flats." My pale-blond hair was brushed and gleaming and tied back with a pink velvet ribbon. Of course, the Kodak Hawkeye had vanished into my straw bag as if it had never been.)

Mr. Frost was murmuring what a lovely surprise this was, that the interviewer for *Poetry* was—*me*.

"So often the interviewer is beetle-browed and grim—if a young man; and thick-waisted and plain as suet—if female." The poet chuckled mischievously, rubbing his hands together.

There was the *Yankee sage*. Yet more beloved, the *mischievous Yankee sage*.

A blush rose into my face. Being so complimented, at the expense of other, less fortunate interviewers was an ambiguous gift: to accept would be vain, to seem to decline would be rude. A young female soon learns the *slitheringness* of accommodation to her (male) elders, by a faint frown of a smile.

Yet I had no choice but to murmur an apology: "Except, Mr. Frost, it isn't *Poetry*—but *Poetry Parnassus*."

Mr. Frost grunted, he wasn't sure he'd heard of *Poetry Parnassus*.

"You will be featured on the cover, Mr. Frost. As I'd explained in my letter."

Still, Mr. Frost frowned. A sort of thundery malevolence gathered in his brow.

Quickly I said, "I mean—the entire October issue will be devoted to 'Robert Frost.'"

This placated the poet, to a degree. He'd recovered something of his composure, placing the notebook on the table beside the swing, and taking up, in a playful manner, the red plastic flyswatter.

"And what did you say your name is, dear?"

"My name is—'Evangeline Fife.'"

Mr. Frost gazed at me with mirthful eyes. "'Evangeline Fife'—a truly inspired name. Is it authentic, or shrewdly invented on the spot, to prick the poet's curiosity?"

What a strange question! My thin-skinned face, already blushing, grew warmer still. My reply was a stammer: "I—I am—my name is 'authentic,' Mr. Frost."

"As authentic as 'Robert Frost,' eh?"

This was very clever! Or so it seemed to me. For *Robert Frost* was the ideal name for the individual who'd created the poetry of *Robert Frost.*

"Please have a seat, dear Miss Fife. Forgive an old man's rudeness, for not rising with alacrity at your approach . . ."

Mr. Frost made a courteous little gesture, simulating the action of rising to his feet, without actually moving; and extending a hand to me in a gentlemanly manner, though it was imperative for me to come to *him,* to allow my hand to be gripped in his plump-dimpled hand, and shaken briskly.

With a little grunt Mr. Frost tugged me up onto the porch to sit beside him on the swing—but discreetly I took another seat in a rattan chair.

"I think, my dear, the cushion on that chair is damp?"

Belatedly, I realized that this was so. But I only just laughed airily and insisted that the chair was fine, for I did not wish to sit close beside the elderly poet on the swing.

Mr. Frost was slapping the flyswatter lightly against his knee. "If it becomes too damp, my dear, please tell me—we'll find another place for your—for you."

With mock primness the poet smiled. Wanting me to understand how he'd refrained from saying *for your tender little bottom.*

Embarrassed, I was about to turn on my tape recorder and ask my first question, when, as if he'd only now thought of it, Mr. Frost said,

"And who are the 'Fifes,' my dear?"

My heart sank in dismay. I'd never thought of my family and relatives as *the Fifes*—it was rare that I gave them much thought at all.

The poet's faded-icy-blue gaze seemed to be pressing against my chest. I could not breathe easily. I managed to stammer a weak reply:

"My family and my father's relatives live in Maine, mostly in Bangor."

"Bangor! Not a hospitable place for the cultivation of poetry, I think." Mr. Frost smiled at me, tapping the flyswatter lightly on his knee. "And your mother's relatives, Miss Fife?"

"She—they—there were ancestors who'd lived in Salem, Massachusetts . . ."

Gleefully Mr. Frost said, "Ah, there's a history, my dear! Were your mother's Salem ancestors *witch-hunters*, or *witches*?"

"I—I don't think so, Mr. Frost . . ."

"If you don't know with certainty, it's likely that your ancestors were *witches*. The *witch-hunters* were the ruling class of the Puritan settlements, and no one is ashamed of being descended from any ruling class."

None of this made sense to me, entirely. Mr. Frost chuckled at my look of incomprehension. It would seem to have been an old, much-loved ploy of the poet's—confounding an interviewer with questions of his own.

He'd folded his large hands over his belly, that strained the white cotton shirt above his belt. I had a glimpse of the elderly poet's exposed navel, a spiraling little vortex of hairs around a miniature knob of flesh quaint as a mummified snail. Like a New England Buddha the poet reclined, a figure of complacent (male) wisdom.

Even as I asked Mr. Frost if we might begin our interview, he said, ignoring me, slapping the flyswatter against the palm of a hand, "'Thou shalt not suffer a witch to live'—the Americans understand this admonition, deep in their killer-souls. All that remains for our fellow citizens is to locate the 'witch' among us—for that, like the most vicious hunting dogs they require guidance." Mr. Frost smiled with a strange sort of satisfaction. "'I have a lover's quarrel with the world'—but I would not really like it, if the 'world' had any sort of quarrel with me."

In the way of a bull who is both rambling and aggressive, prone to whimsical turns the observer can't predict, Mr. Frost reminisced at length on the subject of witch-hunting and witches and the "witchery" of the poet, for poetry must always be "a kind of code"; by this time I'd switched the tape recorder on, and had begun to take shorthand in my notebook as well, for I did not want to lose a single, precious syllable of Mr. Frost's. I thought of Frost's bizarre poem "The Witch of Coös"— the bones of a long-ago murder victim hiking up the cellar steps of a remote old farmhouse in New Hampshire, nailed behind the head-board of a marital bed in an attic—like an ancient curse stirring to life. If the poet had written only this singular poem—along with one or two other poems spoken by deranged New England narrators—the reputation of Robert Frost would be that of a master of *gothic*.

"Do *you* believe in witches, Mr. Frost?"

It was the bold desperation of the timid, such an awkward query, made when Mr. Frost paused for breath; and met with a disdainful frown such as an impertinent child might receive from an elder. With a sneering smile Mr. Frost said, "Poetry isn't in the business of *believing*, Miss Fife. *Believing* is a crudeness that is the prerogative of other, lesser beings."

These words were a sort of rebuff to my naïveté but I was eager to transcribe the startling aphorism, which was entirely new to me. If Robert Frost had uttered it previously, or committed it to writing, I was unaware of it.

Poetry . . . not in the business of believing.

Believing . . . a crudeness the prerogative of other, lesser beings.

(Very different from the "homespun" Frost so beloved by people like my grandmother!)

As Mr. Frost spoke, his faded-icy-blue eyes darted shrewdly about, and with sudden alacrity he wielded the flyswatter—crushing a large fly that had come to rest on a porch post nearby. The black, broken body fell into the grass.

"If only the ignorant 'poetry-haters' among us could be dealt with so readily!"—Mr. Frost chuckled.

I was about to ask Mr. Frost if he felt that there were "poetry-haters" in the world, and who these individuals might be; I'd prepared to ask him about Shelley's bold remark that poets are the *unacknowledged legislators* of the world, but had not a chance to speak for Mr. Frost then reverted, with the air of an elder teasing a captive child, to the previous subject of *the Fifes*—as if he were suspicious of my identity, or pretending to be so. Asking me when *the Fifes* had emigrated to the United States, and from where, so that I told him that, so far as I knew, *the Fifes* had come to America in the 1880s, from somewhere in Scotland.

Mr. Frost seemed just slightly disappointed. "Ah well—so 'your Fifes' are not guilty of persecuting witches, at least not in the New World! And 'your Fifes' obviously were not slave-owners, nor did they profit from the robust slave trade of pre–Civil War United States—as so many did, whose descendants are canny enough to change the subject when it comes up."

"Yes, sir. I mean—no. They did not."

"And where in Scotland did they come from, Miss Fife?"

My tongue felt clumsy in my mouth. For my mouth was very dry.

The poet's perusal of me, the fixedness of his gaze, was making me feel very self-conscious; for it seemed to me that this was the way he'd been looking at the flies that buzzed obliviously about beyond his reach to swat. "I think—Perth, Inverness . . ."

Sharply Mr. Frost said, "Indeed! But not Leith?"

I had not dared claim this port of Edinburgh, for I knew that Frost's mother had been born there.

"No, sir."

"But have you visited Scotland, Miss Fife? Are you any sort of 'Scots lass'?" The poet's mouth twisted in a smiling sneer with the words *Scots lass*.

I told Mr. Frost that I was no sort of "Scots lass," I was afraid, and that there wasn't money for that sort of lavish travel in my family.

"Ah, a rebuke! Let me assure you, dear, there wasn't money for anything like that in *the Frost family*, either. We were all—very—as my poems indicate—*very poor*, and *very frugal*." But Mr. Frost was laughing kindly, seeing the abashed expression in my face. "D'you like the verse of Robbie Burns? 'O my Luve's like a red, red rose That's newly sprung in June; O my Luve's like the melodie That's sweetly play'd in tune.'" Mr. Frost recited the lines with exaggerated rhythm, sneering. "Gives doggerel a bad name, eh? All dogs might sue."

Feebly I laughed at this joke. If it was a joke.

A bully is one who forces you to laugh at his jokes, even if they are not jokes. That is how you know he is a bully.

A knitted-look came into the poet's forehead. The mocking eyes relented. "Though I will have to concede, Burns has written some decent verse, or rather—lines. 'Ev'n you on murd'ring errands toil'd, Lone from your savage homes exil'd . . .' The man *felt strongly*, which is the beginning of poetry."

(A ripple of panic came over me: at this rate we would never get to the poet's life, still less to the substance of the interview which was the poetry of Robert Frost. This, the man seemed to be hiding behind his back as one might tease a child with a treat the child knows is behind the back, and out of reach.)

Daringly I decided to counter with a question of my own:

"And where are your people from, Mr. Frost?"

But this was a blunder, for Mr. Frost did not like such contrary motions. Coldly he said: "That sort of elementary 'biographical information' you should already know, Miss Fife. In fact, you should have memorized it. I hope you've done some homework in your subject and don't expect the poor subject to provide information that is publicly available."

But for a moment I could not speak. I thought *He will send me away. He will laugh at me, and send me away.*

"Oh, Mr. Frost, I'm sorry—yes, I do know that you were born in San Francisco, and not in New England—as most people think. And your background isn't rural—you lived in San Francisco until you were eleven, your father was a newspaperman—"

Irritably Mr. Frost said, "That is but *literally true*. In fact I have a considerable 'rural background'—I was brought back east by my mother after my father's untimely death and soon—soon I was farming—my paternal grandfather's farm in Derry, New Hampshire. It was clear from the start that 'Rob Frost' was a natural man of the soil . . . a New Englander by nature if not actual birth."

Shutting his eyes, leaning back to make the swing creak, Mr. Frost began to recite poems from *A Boy's Will* and *North of Boston*, with perfect recall. These were: "Mending Wall," "The Wood-Pile," "After Apple-Picking" . . .

I am overtired of the great harvest I myself desired.

The poet spoke in a soft, wondering, lyric voice. There was great beauty in this voice. The New England drawl with its spiteful humor had quite vanished. Now, it was possible to discern the young Robert Frost in the flaccid and creased face—the young poet who'd resembled William Butler Yeats and Rupert Brooke in his dreamy male beauty.

The poet ceased abruptly as if he'd only just realized what this final line from "After Apple Picking" meant.

Quickly I asked, "What does that line mean, Mr. Frost? 'I am overtired . . .'"

"A poem's 'meaning' resides in what it says, Miss Fife."

The poet cast a look in my direction that, had it been a swat from the dingy red flyswatter, would have struck me flat in the face. As it was, I couldn't help recoiling.

Frost's second book, *North of Boston*, contained another of his early masterpieces, "Home Burial." This poem, the poet never read to audiences. I asked him if the "man" and the "woman" in the poem were himself and his wife Elinor at the time of their first son's death, in 1899, at the age of three; a death that might have been prevented except for the mother's Christian Science beliefs. I quoted the powerful line, of the woman: "I won't have grief so/If I can change it."

Mr. Frost stared at me for a long moment, with something like hatred. His eyes were narrowed, his face contorted in stubbornness. There was no mistaking the man for the kindly New England bard. But he did not answer my question. As if this were an issue that had to be set right he reverted to his previous subject: "Only a poet who knew rural life intimately could have written any of my 'country' poems. There is no other poetry quite like them, in American poetry. In England, perhaps the poetry of John Clare, and Wordsworth—but these are very different, obviously."

"Yes, sir. Very different."

"You see that, do you? Miss Fife?"

"Yes, sir. I think so . . ."

Mr. Frost tossed the flyswatter onto the table and was rubbing his large hands. I thought how curious, the backs of his hands were creased and elderly, but the palms smooth. A sly light came into the faded eyes. "I am wondering, Miss Fife—"

"Please call me 'Evangeline,' sir."

"But you must not call me 'Rob,' you know. That would not be right."

"Mr. Frost, yes. I would not presume."

"I have been wondering, *Evangeline*—are you comfortable in that chair?"

I was not so comfortable. But quickly I smiled *yes*.

"You've not become just slightly—damp?"

My bottom was in fact damp, for the cushion was damp and had eked through the skirt of my dress, my silk slip, and my cotton panties. But I did not care to betray my discomfort.

"Your bottom, dear? Your delightful little bottom? Your white cotton panties—are they damp?"

I hesitated, stunned. I had no idea how to respond to the poet's teasing query.

So shocked! My notebook nearly slipped from my fingers.

Seeing that he'd so discomfited his interviewer, Mr. Frost laughed heartily. He apologized, though not very sincerely: "I'm very sorry, my dear. My late wife chastised me for my 'coarse barnyard' humor. *She* was very sensitive—of course. But there are females drawn to such humor, I believe." Mr. Frost paused, gazing at me. The faded-blue eyes moved along my (bare) slender legs another time to my (bare) slender ankles, lifted again to my legs, my (imagined) thighs inside the flaring skirt, and the cloth-covered belt cinching my small waist so tight, a man might fantasize closing his large hands about it.

"You might want to change your panties, Evangeline. And take another seat here on the porch, one without a damp cushion." Again Mr. Frost patted the swing seat close beside him, and again I pretended not to notice.

I knew that Mr. Frost was teasing me. Yet, I had no other recourse than to say, with a blush, that I couldn't "change" my panties since I didn't have another, dry pair to put on.

"Really, my dear! You came to Bread Loaf to interview the revered Mr. Frost, with but a single pair of panties." Mr. Frost laughed heartily, seeing how embarrassed I was. "Risky, my dear. Reckless. For you must know that the notorious womanizer Untermeyer is on the premises—and the young, dashing John Ciardi." Mr. Frost peered at me, to see how I interpreted this ambiguous remark. (Of course, I had heard of Louis Untermeyer and John Ciardi, who were both poet-friends and supporters of Robert Frost; the poet was fiercely loyal to his friends, as he was said to be fiercely loyal as an enemy.) "And you are a poet—poetess?—yourself, I believe." Mr. Frost lay back against the porch swing at an awkward angle, as if inviting another to lie back with him; the old swing creaked faintly. His fingers were stretched over his belly as over a ribald little drum. "Or is it the lack of foresight of an innocent virgin?" The words *innocent virgin* were lightly stressed.

Seeing that his coarse jesting was meeting with a blank expression in his wanly blond young-woman interviewer, Mr. Frost sighed, in an exaggerated sort of disappointment, and may have rolled his eyes to an invisible audience, that reacted with near-audible laughter. With a wink he said, "Well! You must be the judge, dear girl, of the degree of dampness of your panties. No one else can make that decision, I quite agree."

Panties! What did the great man care about *panties*! I'd resolved to ignore these lewd remarks, as they were unworthy of a poet of such distinction; though of course, my tape recorder was recording everything Mr. Frost said.

My notebook was opened to the first page of questions, carefully transcribed in my neat schoolgirl hand, and numbered; but before I could begin, the mischievous old man peered at me again and said, "You are a 'good' girl, it seems, Evangeline! I should hope so. And what blue eyes! Of the hue of the New England 'heal-all'—has anyone ever told you?"

Did Mr. Frost expect me not to know to which of his famous poems he was alluding? Shyly I said, "Except if the heal-all is *white,* Mr. Frost."

"Eh! You are quite correct, my dear."

The oblique flirtatiousness of the *virgin poetess* had taken Mr. Frost somewhat by surprise.

An ideal opportunity! The poet was gazing at me as if hoping to be surprised further. And so in my low, thrilled, schoolgirl voice I recited that brilliant chilling poem that begins—"I saw a dimpled spider . . ."

Yet, if you had ears to so hear, you could detect, in the interstices of the schoolgirl breathlessness, something very far from school, or girlishness.

At the conclusion of my recitation Mr. Frost laughed and took up the flyswatter. He struck the porch railing in raucous applause. He couldn't have been more delighted if a small child had recited his poem without the slightest idea of its meaning.

"That is my most wicked sonnet, my dear. I'm frankly surprised you would have memorized it."

I responded that "Design" was a perfectly executed Petrarchan sonnet which I'd memorized as a schoolgirl years ago—"Before I understood it."

"And d'you feel that you understand it now, dear Evangeline?"

You little fool, trained in poetry by spinster schoolteachers, what do you know of me?

I was reluctant to take up this challenge. In my dampened undergarments I sat with meek-lowered eyes, turning over a page of my notebook, while on the table the alarm clock continued its relentless *tick, tick-tock, tick-tick-tock*—that would have been distracting except for the intensity of our conversation.

In a more serious tone Mr. Frost said: "In great poetry there is always something 'signatory'—a word, a phrase, a break in rhythm, a stanza break—that is unexpected. No ordinary versifier could come up with it. In Emily Dickinson's work, virtually every poem contains the 'signatory' element. In Robert Frost's work, it's to be hoped that many poems do. For you see, my dear, in reciting the poem, you blundered with one word—'wayside.' Instead, you recalled the more commonplace 'roadside.'"

Was this so? I tried to recall, confused. *Roadside, wayside?*

The poet said, more kindly than chiding, "If you can't sense the difference between the two words, you are not sensitive to the higher calculus of poetry."

"Mr. Frost, I'm sorry! It was a silly mistake."

"It was not a *silly mistake*, but a mistake of the sort most people would naturally make, trying to recall a 'perfect' poem. Of course, *you* could not recall, my dear Evangeline, because *you* could not have written the poem. As *you* could not emulate the conditions that give rise to the poem, originally: 'a lump in the throat, a sense of wrong, a homesickness, a lovesickness.'"

The poet seemed satisfied, now. Mr. Frost was the sort of bully, very familiar to girls and women, who is fond of his victim even as he is contemptuous of her; whose fondness for her may be an expression of his contempt, like his teasing. He lay back in the swing, fingers folded over the Buddha-belly.

The sun was shifting in the sky: now, the afternoon had begun to wane. Overhead, a *soughing* in the treetops.

Half-consciously I'd been smelling something both sweet and mildly astringent—a smell of fresh-cut grass. There came to me a blurred memory of childhood, like frost on a windowpane through which you can see only the outline of a figure, or a shadow. The poet is the emissary to childhood, and all things lost. I thought *He is not a wicked man, that he can lead us there. If only he would not misuse his power.*

The *ticking* of the windup clock merged with cries of crickets in the tall grasses at the edge of the clearing. Uncertain what I should do, I glanced through my notebook pages, as Mr. Frost sighed, and stirred. He opened a single eye, and regarded me quizzically: "In your printed piece, I suppose you will mention the alarm clock, dear Evangeline? It's because I hate watches, you see. Wearing a watch, as fools do, is like wearing a badge of your own mortality."

These mordant words, I recorded in my notebook.

"The poem is always about 'mortality,' you see. The poem is the poet's mainstay against death."

In the trees overhead, that *soughing* sound that is both pleasurable and discomfiting, like a memory to which emotion accrues. Except we have forgotten the emotion.

Belatedly Mr. Frost offered me a glass of lemonade, which I poured for myself, as I replenished the poet's glass as well; for Mr. Frost was one of those men who seem incapable of lifting a hand to serve themselves, still less others. This, I didn't at all mind doing, of course, for I'd been trained to serve, especially my influential elders.

I took a small sip of the lukewarm, oversweet lemonade. My mouth was very dry.

I resumed the interview with a friendly, familiar sort of question: "Mr. Frost, will you tell the readers of *Poetry Parnassus* what you hope to convey in your poetry?"

Mr. Frost laughed derisively. "If I 'hoped to convey' something, Miss Fife, I would send a telegram."

Very good! I laughed, and wrote this down.

In my schoolgirl fashion I went through a list of questions aimed to draw from the poet quotable quotes which would be valuable to the readers of *Poetry Parnassus*, virtually all of them poets themselves. Pleasurably, Mr. Frost leaned back, his hands locked behind his neck, stretched and yawned and answered my questions in his New England drawl which was both self-mocking and sincere. Countless times the great poet had been interviewed; countless times he'd answered these very questions, which he'd memorized, as he had memorized his carefully thought-out replies. Unlike other poets who would have become restless, irritable, and bored being asked familiar questions, Mr. Frost seemed to bask in the familiarity, indeed like a Buddha who never tires of being worshipped. How different this slack-faced old man was from the dreamy-eyed poet in his early twenties, on my bedroom wall! Long ago he'd composed his aphoristic replies, worn smooth now as much-handled stones. *Free verse*—"Playing tennis without a net." *Poetry*—"A momentary stay against confusion." *Lyric poetry*—"Ice melting on a hot stove." *Love*—"An irresistible desire to be irresistibly desired." *On invitations to poetry "festivals":* "If I'm not the show, I don't go." *Opinion of rival Amy Lowell*—"A fake." *Opinion of rival T. S. Eliot*—"A fake." *Opinion of rival Ezra Pound:* "A fake." *Opinion of rival Archibald*

MacLeish: "A fake." *Opinion of rival Wallace Stevens:* "Bric-a-brac fake!" *Opinion of rival Carl Sandburg:* "Hayseed fake! Always strumming his *geetar.* Everything about Sandburg is studied—except his poetry."

From time to time the vatic voice took on a sound of Olympian melancholy, as a god might meditate upon the folly of humankind from above. "Everything I've learned about life can be summed up in three words: 'It goes on.'"

(Yet even these somber reflections, the poet presented to the interviewer as one might hold out, in the palm of his hand, the most exquisite little gems.)

"And what *is* poetry, Mr. Frost?"

"Poetry is—what is lost in translation."

Mr. Frost paused, then continued, thoughtfully: "A poem is a stream of words that begins in delight and ends in wisdom. But, as it is poetry and not prose, it is a kind of music—a matter of sound in the ear. I hear everything I write. "

This I took up with a canny little query: "Do you mean you *hear*— literally, Mr. Frost? Words in your head?"

Mr. Frost frowned. Though he liked very much to be listened-to, he did not like being queried. "I—speak aloud—to myself. The poem is a matter of measured syllables, iambics, for instance, that produce a work of—poetry." Abruptly he ceased. What sense did this make? The young woman interviewer gazing at him so avidly with her widened heal-all-blue eyes had become just subtly disconcerting.

"A poem is 'sound over sense'?"

"No. A poem is not 'sound over sense'—not my poetry! The babbling of that pretentious prig Tom Eliot might qualify, or infantile lowercase e.e. cummings—but not the poetry of Robert Frost."

And again cannily I asked, "Do you ever 'hear voices,' Mr. Frost? As you are composing your poems?"

Mr. Frost frowned. The large jaws clenched. A look of something like fright came into the faded-icy-blue eyes. "No. I did not—ever—

'hear voices.' The poet is not, as Socrates seemed to believe, in the grip of a 'demon'—the poet is *in control* of the 'demon.'"

"But there is a 'demon'?"

"No! There is not a 'demon'—this is a way of speaking metaphorically. Poetry is the speech of metaphor." Mr. Frost was frowning at me, dangerously; yet I persisted, with my innocently naïve questions:

"But, Mr. Frost—what *is* metaphor? And why is metaphor the speech of poetry?"

The poet snorted with the sort of derision that would have roused gales of laughter in an admiring audience. "Dear Miss Fife! You might as well ask a mockingbird why he sings as he does, appropriating the songs of other birds, as ask a poet why he speaks as he does. If you have to ask, my dear girl, it may be that you are incapable of understanding."

This scathing rejoinder would have eviscerated another, more subtle interviewer, but did not deter me, for I felt the truth of the poet's observation, and did not resent it.

"But you have never 'heard voices' and you've never claimed to have 'second sight'?"—I pressed these issues, for I knew that Mr. Frost would not volunteer any truth about himself that might detract from his image of the homespun New England bard.

"Miss Fife, I've told you—*no*."

"And you've never had—'second sight'?"

Scornfully Mr. Frost asked, "What is 'second sight'?"

"The ability to see into the future, Mr. Frost. To feel premonitions—to prophesize."

Mr. Frost snorted in derision. In his eyes, a small flicker of alarm. "Old wives' tales, my dear. Maybe in your Scots family, but not in mine."

Adding then, in a smaller voice, "Why would anyone want to 'see into the future'! That would be a—a—curse . . ."

In the elderly poet's face an expression of such pain, such loss, such grief, such terror of what cannot be spoken, I looked aside for a moment in embarrassment. Thinking *But he is just an old, lonely man. It is mercy he deserves, not justice.*

And for that moment thinking perhaps I would take pity on him, beginning by destroying the humiliating snapshots in my Kodak Hawkeye. Then, Mr. Frost resumed his bemused, chiding, superior masculine voice: "Miss Fife! Tell your avid readers that poetry is very *mystery.* Quite above the heads of all. No matter what the poet tries to tell you."

But readily I countered: "Yet, the poet builds upon predecessors. Who have been your major influences, Mr. Frost?"

Mr. Frost looked at me startled, as if a child had reared up to confront him. "My—'influences'? Very few . . . *Life* has been my influence."

"But not Thomas Hardy?"

"No."

"Not Keats, not Shelley, not Wordsworth, not William Collins—"

"No! Not to the degree that *life* has been my influence."

The thundery look in Mr. Frost's face warned me not to pursue this line of questioning, for of all sensitive issues it is "influences" that most rankle and roil even the greatest geniuses, like the suggestion that others have helped them crucially in their careers. Yet I couldn't resist asking why Frost had so low an opinion of Ezra Pound, who'd been extremely generous to him when he'd been a struggling unpublished poet when they'd first met in England.

Mr. Frost shut his eyes, shook his head vigorously. No comment!

"Was Ezra Pound mistaken, or some sort of 'fake,' when he said that *A Boy's Will* contained 'the best poetry written in America in a long time'?"

Mr. Frost's eyes remained shut. But his large, lined face sagged in an expression of regret.

"Well—even a, a 'fake'—can be correct, now and then." Cautiously Mr. Frost opened one of the faded-blue eyes, his gaze fixed upon me in mock-appeal. "As a clock that can't keep time is yet correct twice each twenty-four hours."

Still, I wasn't to be placated. My next question was a sharp little blade, to be inserted into the fatty flesh of the poet, between the ribs: "But, Mr. Frost, weren't you once a friend of Ezra Pound's?"

"Miss Fife, why are you tormenting me with Pound? The man is a traitor to poetry, as he was a traitor to his country. A Fascist fool, an ingrate. No one can estimate when he became insane—he's insane *now*. Enough of Pound!"

"And what is your opinion of Franklin Delano Roosevelt?"

This was a sly question. For Mr. Frost's Yankee conservatism was well known. Even more than Ezra Pound, "FDR" enraged the poet who stammered in indignation: "That—cripple! That Socialist fraud! 'FDR's' brain was as deformed as his body! Tried to hide the fact that he wasn't a whole man—the idiot voters were taken in. And his wife—homely as the backside of a gorilla! Socialism is plain theft—taking from those of us who work, and work damned hard, and giving what we've earned to idlers and shirkers. My wife Elinor, a sensitive, educated woman, nonetheless raved about 'FDR' that if she could, she would've killed him!—which suggests the man's monstrousness, that he would provoke a genteel woman like Elinor Frost to such rage. You may call me selfish, Miss Fife—yes, I am a 'selfish artist' for I believe that art must be self-generated, and has nothing to do with the collective. 'Doing good' is a lot of hokum! I would not give a red cent to see the world 'improved'—for, if it were"—here Mr. Frost's voice quavered coyly, for he'd made this remark numerous times to numerous interviewers—"what in hell would we poets write about?"

My shocked response was expected, too. And my widened blue eyes.

"Why, Mr. Frost! You can't mean that . . ."

"Can't I! I certainly do, dear Evangeline. Have you not read my

poem 'Provide, Provide'—in a nutshell, there is Frost's economic theory. Provide for yourself even if it means selling yourself—'boughten'
friendship is better than none." The chuckle came, deep and deadly.
"Just don't expect *me* to provide for *you*."

"But—you are acquainted with poverty, Mr. Frost, aren't you?
Quite extreme poverty?"

"No."

"N-No? Not when you were a child, and later when you were married and trying to support a young family on your grandfather's farm
in Derry . . ."

"No! The Frosts were frugal, but we were not—ever—*poor*."

"When your father died in San Francisco, your mother was not
left—destitute?"

"Miss Fife, 'destitute' is an extreme word. I think that you are
insulting my family. This line of questioning has come to an end."

Mr. Frost's face was flushed with indignation, of the hue of an
overripe tomato. He'd been striking the swing seat beside him with
the flyswatter as if he'd have liked to be striking *me*.

"You don't think that we have a moral duty to take care of others?
Did Wordsworth feel that way?"

"Wordsworth! What did Wordsworth *know*! The old windbag
didn't have to contend with our infernal IRS tax, Miss Fife! He did
not have to contend with the slimy New Deal!"

Between us there was an agitation of the air. The very lemonade in
my glass quivered, as if the earth had shaken.

Seeing that the poet was about to banish me, having lost patience
with even my wanly blond good-girl looks, I plunged boldly head-on:

"Is it true, Mr. Frost, that as a young man not yet married you
were so depressed you tried to commit suicide in the Dismal Swamp
of North Carolina?"

Mr. Frost's cheeks belled in indignation. "'Dismal Swamp'! Who
has been telling you such—slander? It is not true . . ."

"Didn't you suspect that Elinor had been unfaithful to you, and so you wanted to punish her, and yourself, in a Romantic gesture?"

"Ridiculous! It's for effete poets like Hart Crane to commit suicide—or utter fakes or failures like Chatterton and Vachel Lindsay—not whole-minded poets. A man with a wife and a family to bind him to the earth doesn't go gallivanting off and *kill himself.*"

"But your poems are filled with images of darkness and destruction, Mr. Frost. The woods that are 'lovely, dark and deep'—except the speaker has 'promises to keep, and miles to go before I sleep.' The poem is obviously about a yearning to die, but a resistance to that yearning, and a regret over the resistance."

"Balderdash, Miss Fife! Though you are a pretty lass, you are also a hysterical female. Reading into poems nasty little messages that aren't there, like looking into a mirror and seeing a snake-headed female who *is there*, and who has your secret face."

Vehemently the poet spoke, and not very coherently. The red flushed face swelled and throbbed as with an incipient stroke. Yet, I persisted: "Why don't you ever read your 'dark' poems to audiences, Mr. Frost? Why only your perpetual favorites, which audiences have memorized in school? Are you afraid that they will be offended by the darker, more difficult poems, and wouldn't applaud you as usual? Wouldn't give you standing ovations, that so thrill your heart? Wouldn't buy your books in such great numbers?"

Flush-faced Mr. Frost told me that I had no idea what I was saying. And that I'd better turn off the damned tape recorder, or he would smash it. "Enough! This ridiculous interview is concluded. I suggest that you leave now—exactly the way you'd crept in."

Yet boldly I asked Mr. Frost about his patriotic poem of 1942, "The Gift Outright," with its remarkable line "The land was ours before we were the land's"—"Could you explain to the readers of *Poetry Parnassus* what this astonishing statement means?"

Mr. Frost had taken up the dingy red plastic flyswatter, tapping it restlessly against the swing railing. His voice was heavy with sarcasm: "Assuming the readers of *Poetry Parnassus* can comprehend English, I see no reason to 'explain' a single word."

"Mr. Frost, this is indeed a provocative statement!"

"Damn you, 'Fife,' what are you getting at? Frost is not 'provocative'— Frost is 'consoling.' Audiences have loved 'The Gift Outright' whether they understand it, or not. The poem tells us that our ancestors, who settled the New World, were 'of the land' in a way that later generations can't be, because we are American citizens; and that the 'land'—our country, America—is a 'gift outright.' It is *ours*."

Seeing the expression on my face, which was one of utter transparency, the poet said, irritably, "Is it each individual word that perplexes you, Miss Fife, or their collective meaning?"

"Mr. Frost, the collective meaning of your poem seems to endorse 'Manifest Destiny'—the right of American citizens to claim all of North America, virtually. It totally excludes native Americans—the numerous tribes of Indians—who lived in North America long before the European settlers arrived. British, Spanish invaders—'Caucasians.'"

Mr. Frost cast me a smile of glaring incredulity. "Miss Fife! For God's sake—are you seriously suggesting that Indians are *native Americans?*"

"Yes! They are human beings, aren't they?"

"*Human,* but primitive. *Beings,* but closer to the animal rung of the ladder than to our own." Mr. Frost tapped the flyswatter on his knee, with a dangerous squint of his eye. "You may put this in your interview, Miss Fife, that Robert Frost believes in *civilization*—which is to say the *Caucasian civilization*."

"But, Mr. Frost, the indigenous people you call 'Indians' were the original *native Americans.* Caucasians from the British Isles and from Europe came to this continent as settlers, explorers, and tradesmen— with no respect for the native Americans living here, they appropriated the land, exploited and attempted genocide against the natives, and are doing so even now, in less obvious ways, in many parts of the country. And your poem 'The Gift Outright,' which might have addressed this issue with a poet's sharp eye, instead—"

Smirking Mr. Frost interrupted, with a sharp slap of the flyswatter, "Miss Fife! 'Genocide' is a pretty hifalutin' term for what our brave settlers did—conquered the wilderness, established a decent civilization . . ."

"But there was not a 'wilderness' here—there were Indian civilizations, living on the land. Of course, the original inhabitants were not *city dwellers*—they lived in nature. But—surely they had their own civilizations, different from our own?"

How surprised Mr. Frost was by the passion with which I spoke!

You might have thought, as Mr. Frost was possibly thinking, that there was something *not quite right* about this interviewer from *Poetry Parnassus* with her tape recorder and notebook and straw satchel who was persisting, despite the poet's obvious agitation: "Mr. Frost—is it possible that your audiences have been deceived, and that you aren't a 'homespun New England bard' but something very different? An emissary from 'dark places'—an American poet who sees and defends the very worst in us, without apology—in fact, with a kind of pride?"

"And what is wrong with pride, Miss Fife!"

A fierce light shone in the poet's faded-blue eyes. His breath came audibly and harshly. You could sense the old, enlarged heart beating in his chest like a maddened fist as in the throes of a combative sexual encounter at which the poet in his inviolable *maleness* did not intend to fail.

But the interviewer was suffused with a sort of ferocity, too. Squaring her slender shoulders, leaning forward so that her pale-blond hair fell softly about her face, daring to inquire in her throaty, thrilled voice that hardly seemed the voice of a young virginal woman: "Did you not once say, Mr. Frost, imagining that your remark wouldn't be recorded, that you'd have liked never to see your children again—those who were living at the time, and causing you so much trouble; they were—are—'accursed'—"

"I—I did not say that . . . Who has been spreading such lies? I—did not . . ."

"You've written about this—in your sly, coded poems. Your inability to feel another's pain—your inability to touch another person. You've revealed everything in your poems that has been hidden in your heart. Which is why, in public, you deny your very poems—as one might deny paternity to a deformed or disfigured child."

"This is false—this is wrong! I have tried to explain"—Mr. Frost drew a deep breath, shut his eyes tight and began to recite through clenched jaws—"'To be too subjective with what an artist has managed to make objective is to come on him presumptuously and render ungraceful what he in the pain of his life had faith he'd made . . . graceful.'"*

Primly Frost uttered these words, as if the statement should be sufficient to convince the interviewer; but the statement did not have the desired effect.

"Mr. Frost, what do those words even mean? That those who see in your poetry something of the terribly flawed and dishonest man who wrote the poems are charged with being 'ungraceful'?—while the poet, who feeds like a vampire upon the lives of others, is imagined as being 'graceful'?"

"But—that's what poetry *is*."

"Not all poetry! Not all poets. The subject today is *you*."

"I—I—I have no reply to that, Miss"—the flyswatter had fallen from the poet's fingers onto the ground. His fingers appeared frozen, claw-like as if cramped—"whoever you are, and wherever you are from—Hell . . ."

---

* From *Robert Frost and Sydney Cox: Forty Years of Friendship* by William R. Evans (University Press of New England, 1981).

"But do you believe in 'Hell,' Mr. Frost?"

"I—I think that I do . . . I must . . . I believe—'This is Hell, nor am I out of it.' That grim and beautiful line of Marlowe's, I do believe."

This concession, rare for the poet, failed utterly to placate the interviewer, who pursued her panting quarry like a huntswoman and showed him no mercy.

"Mr. Frost. Do you remember when your daughter Lesley was six years old? When you were still a young man—a young father—living on that wretched farm in Derry, New Hampshire?—you wakened your daughter with a loaded pistol in your hand and you forced the terrified child to come downstairs in her nightgown, and barefoot, to the kitchen where the child saw her mother seated at the table, her hair in her face, weeping. Your wife had been an attractive woman once but, living with you in that desolate farmhouse, enduring your moods, your rages, your sloth, your fumbling incapacity as a farmer, your sexual bullying and clumsiness, already at the age of thirty-one she'd become a broken, defeated woman. You told the child Lesley that she must choose between her mother and her father—which of you was to live, and which to die. 'By morning, only one of us will be alive.'"

"No. That did not—happen. . . . It did not."

"Yet Lesley remembers it vividly, and will reproach you with the memory through your life, Mr. Frost. Is she mistaken?"

"My daughter is—yes, mistaken . . . My eldest daughter hates me without knowing me. She has never understood me . . ."

"And what of your daughter Irma, committed to a mental hospital? Why did you give up on Irma, when you might have helped her more? Were you exasperated and disgusted by her, as an extreme form of yourself? Your wild talk, your turbulent moods, your 'dark places'? You gave up on Irma as you'd given up on your sister Jean years before. Mental illness frightens you, like a contagion."

Mr. Frost protested, weakly: "I did all that I could for Irma, and for—my sister Jean. I could not be expected to give up my entire life for them, could I? All that I'd done, they felt no gratitude for, but were encouraged in their wildness and blame of *me* . . ."

"Why was poor Irma so obsessed with being kidnapped and raped? Forced into prostitution? You were scornful of Irma's terrors, you'd told her bluntly when she was just a girl that she was so unattractive, she needn't fear being raped; no man would be interested in her sexually; she wasn't worth 'twenty cents a throw.' Later, to Robert Lowell, you said laughingly that Irma Frost couldn't have 'made a whorehouse.'"

"That is not true. That is—a lie, slander . . . Lowell was a sick, distressed person. I spoke to him in a way to lift his spirits, to entertain him. He'd thought that he was *bad,* but old Frost was *badder.* But none of it was meant to be taken literally . . ."

"And your son. Your only surviving son. He'd said, 'My father is ashamed of me. My father has no more than glanced at my poetry, and push it aside.' He'd said, 'Sometimes I feel tight-strung—like a bow. I feel that I want to—that I must—be shot straight to the heart of . . .' And your son's voice would trail off, and he would hide his face in his hands."

The interviewer spoke in a soft condemning voice. The poet stared at her, uncomprehending. Small hairs stirred at the nape of his neck. It was very hard for him to draw breath. Barely he managed to stammer, "Who? Who is—'he'? Who are you speaking of . . ." A sensation of vertigo swept over him, the ground seemed to be opening at his feet. In desperation he'd snatched up the poetry notebook in both hands as if to shield himself with it.

"Mr. Frost, you know that he burnt his poetry. Fifteen years of poems. You'd thought so little of him, you'd never given him permission to live. He was always your 'son'—you never relinquished him, though you never loved him. He was thirty-eight when he died of a gunshot wound to the head. He'd seemed much younger, as if he'd never lived. All he wanted was approval from you, a father's blessing—but you withheld it."

"I've told you—I don't know what—who—you are talking about . . ."

"Your son, Mr. Frost. Your son Carol who killed himself."

"My son did not—kill—himself . . . He died of a regrettable accident."

"Your son you named with a ridiculous girl's name, for some whim of yours. He was so unhappy with 'Carol' he changed it to 'Carroll'—to your displeasure. It was too late, the damage had been done, as a young child he'd been marked. In his poetry he wrote of how you'd sucked the marrow out of his bones. You'd left him nothing, you'd taken his manhood from him. He knew your secret—you could never love any of your children, you could love only yourself."

Frost shook his massive head from side to side, frowning. Deep rents in his ashy skin.

"I—I loved Carol. He knew . . ."

"You never told him you loved him! He didn't *know.*"

"Carol was weak—immature. He *was not* a man. How then could he write genuine poetry? He was a versifier—his best poems were pale imitations of mine. He was a child who has traced drawings in Crayola. His rimes were stolen from mine—'though'—'snow'—'slow'—'near'—'seer.' Worse were his poems in which he'd attempted *vers libre.*" Mr. Frost laughed, a ghastly wheezing sound like choking. With the verve of a litigator arguing his case, the poet spoke with a righteous sort of confidence, though laced with regret: "My son thought that 'no one loved him.' Pitiful! His mind was one cloud of suspicion . . . his cloud became our cloud. Well, he took his cloud away with him. We never gave him up. He ended it for us—the protracted misery and *obstinacy* of a failed life." A brooding moment, and then: "It was an error to marry—initiating a sequence of worse errors, the Frost children. Soon it came to me, though I thought I'd kept it a secret, that I didn't care in the slightest if I ever saw any of them again—at least, after my dear daughter Marjorie died. *She,* I did love. I loved very much. Yet, what good was my love? I could not save the beautiful girl. She died as the child of anyone might have died—a disappearance. 'The only sound's the sweep of easy wind and downy flake'—nothing more in nature than that, of grief. A poet ought not to marry, and procreate. That was the fear of my wife Elinor—she would drag me down into her mortality, and we would make each other miserable, which we did. Poetry is more than enough of 'procreation.' Life is the raw material, like dough—but it is only 'raw,' and it is only 'dough.' No one cares to eat mere *dough.*"

The poet's large, slack-jowled face contorted into a look of sheer disdain, disgust. Astonishingly he reared up onto his legs, that barely held his bulk. The porch swing creaked in protest. The notebook fell from his lap, onto the grass. Like a wounded bull, suffused with an unexpected strength by pain and outrage, the poet swayed and glared at his tormentor. He was stricken to the heart, or to the gut—but he would not succumb. His enemies had assailed him cruelly and shamefully as they had through his beleaguered life but *he would not succumb.*

"You—whoever you purport to be—an 'interviewer' for a third-rate poetry journal—what do you know of *me*? You may know scattered facts about my 'life'—but you don't know *me.* You haven't the intelligence to comprehend my poems any more than a blind child could comprehend anything beyond the Braille she reads with her fingertips—only just the raised words and nothing of the profound and ineffable silence that surrounds the words."

Taken by surprise, the young blond interviewer stumbled to her feet also, a deep flush in her face; in dampened undergarments and schoolgirl floral-pink "shirtwaist" she gripped the straw bag, and backed away with a look of surprise and alarm.

Jabbing at this adversary with his forefinger the enraged poet charged: "You are *nothing.* People like you *don't exist.* You've never been called the 'greatest American poet of the twentieth century'—you've never won a single Pulitzer Prize, let alone several Pulitzer prizes—*and you never will.* You have never roused audiences to tears, to applause, to joy—you've never roused audiences to their feet in homage to your genius. Barely, you are qualified to *kiss the hem of genius.* Or—another part of the poet's anatomy. All you can do, people like you, contemptible little people, spiritual dwarves, is to scavenge in the detritus of the poet's life without grasping the fact that the poet's *life* is of no consequence to the poet—essentially. You snatch at the dried and outgrown skin of the snake—the husk of a skin the living snake will cast off as he moves with lightning speed out of your grasp. You fail to realize that only the *poetry* counts—the *poetry* that will prevail long after the poet has passed on, and you and your ilk are gone and forgotten utterly, as if you'd never existed."

The poet stumbled down the porch steps, not quite seeing where he was going. Something glaring was exploding softly—the sun? Blazing, blinding light? Overhead, an agitated *soughing* in the trees? He had banished her, the demon. His deep-creased face was contorted with rage. The faded-icy-blue eyes were sharpened like ice picks. In the grass, the poet's legs failed him, he began to fall, he could not break the propulsion of his fall, a fall that brought him heavily to the ground, the stunning hardness of the ground beneath the grass; all his life he'd been eluding the petty demons that picked at his ankles, his legs; the petty demons that whispered curses to him, that he was bad, he was wicked, he was cruel, he was *himself;* all his life they'd tried to elicit him to injure himself, as his only surviving son Carol had injured himself, and succumb to madness. In the vast reaches of the Dismal Swamp he'd first seen the demons clearly, and retained the vision through the decades; how, in daylight, it is a temptation to forget the terrible wisdom of the Swamp, and of the night; but at great peril. He had blundered this time, but he had escaped in time. *He was not going mad*—but madness swept through him like a powerful emetic.

Somehow, he was lying in the grass. Gnats flung themselves against his damp eyes. He'd fallen from a great height, like a toppled statue, too heavy to be righted. His fury was choking him. Like a towel stuffed down his throat. Somewhere close by a clock was ticking loudly, mockingly. He would grab hold of the damned clock and throw it—but the taunting girl-interviewer had vanished.

His notebook! Precious notebook! It had slipped from his fingers, he strained to reach it, to hold against his chest. Strangely it seemed that he was bare-chested—so suddenly. The shame of his soft, slack torso, the udder-like breasts, was exposed to all the world. He could not call for help, the shame was too deep. The poet was not ever a weakling to call for help. The obstinacy of his aging flesh had been a source of great frustration to him, and shame, but he had not succumbed to it, and he would not.

Just barely, the poet managed to seize hold of a corner of the notebook. The strain of so reaching caused him to tremble, to quaver—yet, he managed to draw the notebook to him, and to press it against his chest. His loud-thumping heart would be protected from harm, from the assault of his enemies. For here was his shield, as in antiquity—the warrior has fallen, but is shielded from the pain of mortality.

"Mr. Frost? Oh—Mr. Frost—"

Already they'd found him, he'd had scarcely time to rest. He was unconscious, yet breathing. The great poet fallen in wild grass in front of the Poet's Cabin at Bread Loaf, Vermont, in a languorous late-afternoon in August 1951.

Yet, the poet was breathing. No mistaking this, the poet was breathing.

IV

PATRICIDE

Before I saw, I heard: the cracking wood-plank steps leading down to the riverbank behind our house in Upper Nyack, New York.

Before I saw my father's desperate hand on the railing, that collapsed with the steps, in what seemed at first like cruel slow-motion, I heard: my father's terrified voice calling for—*me*.

And so on the stone terrace above I stood very still, and watched in silence.

If I were to be tried for the murder of my father, if I were to be judged, it is this silence that would find me guilty.

Yet, I could not draw breath to scream.

Even now, I can't draw breath to scream.

O god I knew: he would be angry.

He would be furious. He would not even look at me.

And it wasn't my fault! I would plead with him *Please understand it wasn't my fault. An accident on the George Washington Bridge . . .*

"Please, officer! How long will it be—?"

It was an evening in November 2011, five months before my father Roland Marks's death.

In desperation I'd lowered my window to speak with one of the police officers directing traffic, who barely acknowledged my pleas. For more than thirty minutes traffic had been slowed to virtually a stop in gusts of sleet on the upper level of the George Washington Bridge; ahead was a vortex of lights, red lights mingling with bright blinding lights, for there'd been an accident involving at least two vehicles, a skidding-accident on the slick wet pavement. In a tight space a tow truck was maneuvering with maddening slowness and a high-pitched beep-beep-beeping that made my heart race.

Police officers were signaling to drivers to stay where they were, and to remain inside our vehicles. As if we had any choice!

"God damn. Bad luck."

It was an old habit of mine, speaking to myself when I was alone. And I was often alone. And the tone of my speaking-voice was not likely to be friendly or indulgent.

I calculated that I was about two-thirds of the way across the bridge. In such weather the George Washington Bridge seemed longer than usual. Even when traffic began moving forward at a slightly faster pace it was still frustratingly slow, and sleet struck the windshield of my car like driven nails.

Once I crossed the bridge it was a twelve-minute drive to my father's house in Rockland County, Upper Nyack. If nothing else went wrong.

It was 7:50 P.M. I had awakened that morning at about 5:30 A.M. and had been feeling both excited and exhausted through the long day. And already I was late by at least twenty minutes and when I tried to call my father on my cell phone, the call didn't go through.

Telling myself *This is not a crisis. Don't be ridiculous! He won't stop loving you for this.*

To be the daughter of Roland Marks was to feel your nerves strung so very tight, the slightest pressure might snap them.

You will laugh to be told that I was forty-six years old and the dean of the faculty at a small, highly regarded liberal arts college in Riverdale, New York. I was not a child-daughter but a middle-aged daughter. I was well educated, with excellent professional credentials and an impressive résumé. Before the liberal arts college in Riverdale where (it was hinted) I would very likely be named the next president, I'd been a professor of classics and department chair at Wesleyan. A move to Riverdale College was a kind of demotion but I'd gladly taken the position when it was offered to me, since living in Skaatskill, New York, allowed me to visit my father in Upper Nyack more readily.

Don't take the job in Riverdale on my account, my father had said irritably. *I'm not going to be living in Nyack year-round and certainly not forever.*

I was willing to risk this, to be nearer my father.

I was willing to take a professional demotion, to be nearer my father.

In my professional life I had a reputation for being confident, strong-willed, decisive, yet fair-minded—I'd shaped myself into the quintessence of the *professional woman,* who is a quasi-male, yet the very best kind of male. In my public life I was not accustomed to being of the weaker party, dependent upon others.

Yet, in my private life, my private family-life, I was utterly weak and defenseless as one born without a protective outer skin. I was the daughter of Roland Marks and my fate was, Roland Marks had always loved me best of all his children.

This is the story of how a best-loved daughter repays her father.

❈

"YOU'RE LATE."

It wasn't a statement but an accusation. In another's voice the implication would be *Why are you late? Where were you?* The implication would be—*Darling, I was worried about you.*

"I can't depend upon you, Lou-Lou. I've had to make a decision without you."

"A decision? What do you mean?"

He is moving away. He is getting remarried. He is writing me out of his will.

"I've decided to hire an assistant. A professional, who's trained in literary theory."

This wasn't so remarkable, for my father had had numerous "assistants" and "interns" over the years. Each had disappointed him or failed him in some way, and had soon disappeared from our lives. Most had been young women, a particularly vulnerable category for *assistant, intern.*

Except now, since the breakup of my father's fifth marriage, and since my move to Riverdale, I'd been my father's assistant, to a degree— and we'd been planning a massive project, sorting and labeling the thousands of letters Roland Marks had received over the course of five decades, as well as carbons and copies of letters he'd sent. The letters were to be a part of Roland Marks's massive archive, which he and his agent were negotiating to sell to an appropriate institution: the New York Public Library, the Special Collections of the University of Texas at Austin, the Special Collections at Harvard, Yale, Columbia. (In fact the archive would be sold, Dad hoped for several million dollars, to the highest bidder—though Roland Marks wouldn't have wanted to describe the negotiations in so crass a way.)

It was unfair on Dad's part to suggest that he'd actually been waiting for me. Not in normal usage, as one individual might be "waiting" for another. With one part of his mind he'd probably been aware that someone was expected, after 7:00 P.M. and no later than 7:30 P.M., for this was our usual Thursday evening schedule. He would have been working in his study overlooking the slate-gray choppy Hudson River, from the second floor of the sprawling old Victorian house on Cliff Street; he might be writing, or going through a copyedited manuscript, or proofreading galleys—(for a writer who claimed to find writing difficult and who spent most of his time revising, Roland Marks managed to publish a good deal); he would have been listening to music—for instance, Mozart's *Don Giovanni*, which was so familiar to him, like notes encoded in his brain, he could no longer be distracted by it. Certainly my father wouldn't be waiting for *me* but his sensitive nerves were attuned to a waiting-for-someone, waiting-for-something, and until this unease was resolved he would feel incomplete, edgy, irritable and vaguely offended.

Yet if I'd arrived early, Dad wouldn't have liked that, either. "So soon, Lou-Lou? What time did you say you were coming? And what time is it now?"

My impossible father! Yet I loved Dad so much, I could not love anyone else including my clumsy well-intentioned self.

"And why exactly are you late?"

"An accident on the George Washington Bridge . . ."

"An accident! You should factor in slow-downs on that damned bridge, and leave early. I'd have thought you knew that by now."

"But this was a serious accident, Dad. The entire upper level was shut down for at least forty minutes . . ."

"You're always having accidents, Lou-Lou. Or, accidents are always occurring around you. Why is this?"

Dad was being playful, funny. But Dad was being cruel, too.

In fact it was rare that things went wrong in my life, and virtually never as a consequence of anything I'd done personally. A delayed plane, or a canceled flight—how was that my fault?—or an emergency at the college, which it would have been professionally irresponsible for me to ignore; or the plea of an old friend, calling at an inopportune time and badly needing me to speak to her, which had been the case several weeks before.

I'd tried to explain to my father that a friend from graduate school at Harvard had called me sounding distraught, suicidal. I'd had to spend time with Denise on the phone and had sent a barrage of e-mails to follow—"I couldn't just abandon her, Dad."

"How do you know that I'm not 'suicidal,' too? Waiting for you to arrive and wondering where the hell you are?"

This was so preposterous a claim, I decided that my father had to be joking. *Does an egomaniac kill himself?*

Dad persisted: "Do you think that, if you were in this person's place, she might not 'abandon' you?"

Though the subtext here was simply that Dad resented another person in my life, and felt threatened by the least disturbance of his schedule, it was like him to ask such questions, to make one squirm. His boldly serio-comic novels were laced with paradoxes of a moral nature, to make the reader squirm even as the reader was laughing.

I'd said that I liked Denise very much. I hadn't *wanted* to avoid her. (Though it was true, we'd grown apart in recent years; Denise had been the one to cease writing and calling.) "I've invited her to come visit me, if she wants to. If I can help her, somehow . . ."

"Lou-Lou, for Christ's sake! That's what I mean: you draw accidents to yourself. You're accident-prone." There was a pause, and Dad couldn't resist adding, "And losers."

This was particularly cruel. Since I knew that Dad considered me a "loser"—at any rate, not a success.

But now Dad was being funny, and not angry—at least, he'd been smiling. (For "losers" were the very material of Roland Marks's fiction, some of them loveable and others not so.)

His humor was the lightest stroke of a whip against my bare skin and not intended to hurt: if Roland Marks intended to inflict hurt, you would know it.

Only at my father's summons did I come, Thursday nights, to have dinner with him. This had been our schedule for some months since Dad had returned to the house in Upper Nyack—(he'd been writer-in-residence at the American Academy in Rome, and then a visiting fellow at the American Academy in Berlin)—but I couldn't take our evenings for granted, because my father disliked being "constrained."

That is, I had to leave Thursday evenings open for my father; but my father might make other, more interesting plans for Thursday without notifying me.

On weekends, Dad dined with other people in their homes or in restaurants. (I was rarely included.) Often, Dad was being "honored"—these events would often take place in New York City, forty minutes away by (hired) car. It wasn't unusual for my father to be invited to give talks, readings, onstage interviews every week in one or another city: in recent months Chicago, Los Angeles, Washington, D.C., Boston, Seattle, Toronto and Vancouver. If such events didn't conflict with my work-schedule, and if Dad wanted me, I would accompany him to these gigs, as he called them; his sponsors would pay for two business-class air tickets as well as two hotel rooms in luxury hotels. Since Dad's last divorce, he had not acquired a new female companion, and so I was grateful to be his companion when he wanted me.

Sometimes, I would be interviewed, too. *Tell us what it was like growing up with Roland Marks as your father!*

I'd rehearsed answers that were plausible but interesting—at least, I hoped they were interesting. What I said of Roland Marks was unfailingly upbeat and optimistic; my daughterly praise was warm and sincere; never would I hint at anything less "positive"— that remained for my sister Karin and my brothers Harry and Saul, who imagined that their opinions of Roland Marks really mattered to anyone.

Domestic routines, like our Thursday dinners, were sacrosanct with Roland Marks, as with most writers and artists. It's the "nervous" sensibility, as Dad said, that craves routine and stability. Of course, if Dad himself altered these routines, that was different.

Twelve years ago Roland Marks had been awarded a Nobel Prize for literature and in the wake of that cataclysmic award much in his domestic life had been overturned. His fifth marriage had ended in divorce, and a tremendous financial settlement to his embittered wife had depleted much of his award money. (Though even friends persisted in thinking that Roland Marks was wealthy.) Vulnerable to women, particularly young women, Dad was always "seeing" someone and always being "disappointed"—yet I dreaded the day when my octogenarian father might announce that he was "remarrying"—again!—and that our Thursday evening routine, the very core of my emotional life, was coming to an end.

Something was different about tonight. I realized—*Don Giovanni* wasn't playing. And a vehicle was parked at the curb in front of the house, which I was sure I'd never seen before.

My father had come to meet me in the front corridor of the sprawling old Victorian house, where a single wall-light feebly glowed. Roland Marks's habits of frugality contrasted sharply with his habits of overspending and overindulgence. Since my most recent stepmother's departure from his life, the Victorian house on Cliff Street was but partly furnished; the living room, with a beautiful dark-marble fireplace, was missing a leather sofa, a set of chairs, a Chinese carpet, and had the look of a minimalist art gallery in which the so-called art is a coiled rope, a bucket, a stepladder leaning against a bare wall. In my father's words the departing wife had "ransacked" the house while he was in Europe; I'd offered to help him refurnish but he'd dismissed my offer with an airy wave of his hand—"I'm a bachelor from now on. I don't use these damned rooms anyway."

At the rear of the house, not visible from the front hall, was a remodeled sunroom, where Dad spent much of his time when he wasn't working upstairs in his study. Beyond the sunroom, through a rear door, was a flagstone terrace in what one might describe as a comfortably worn state of repair, and descending from the terrace a flight of wooden steps that led to the riverbank thirty feet below, through a scrubby jungle of overgrown shrubs and trees. There had once been a small dock there, swept away by a ravaging river during the first winter of my father's occupancy.

Dad had joked that his marriage to Sylvia Sachs had been very like the dock—"Gone with the river!"

Gradually it had happened that, though I lived in a (modest) condominium of my own in the village of Skaatskill, just north of Riverdale, my father expected me to keep his house in reasonably good repair; it had fallen to me to pay my father's household bills with his checkbook, and help him prepare his financial records for his accountant's yearly visit; if my father had trouble opening a bottle or a jar, for instance, he would keep it for me to open—"Your fingers are strong and canny. Lou-Lou. You have peasant genes, you'll live a long time." It fell to me to hire cleaning women, handymen, a lawn crew, though my father invariably found fault with them.

Tonight my father was wearing not his usual at-home jeans and shapeless cardigan but neatly pressed trousers, one of his English "country-gentleman" shirts, and a green Argyll vest; his cheeks were smooth-shaven, and his silvery-brown hair, thinning at the crown but abundant elsewhere, falling to his shoulders, looked as if it had been recently brushed. Clearly, Roland Marks had not so groomed himself for *me*.

There was a sound upstairs. A murmurous voice, as on a cell phone.

"Is—someone here? Upstairs?"

My father's study was upstairs, as well as several bedrooms. My father's study was his particular place of refuge, his sanctuary, with a wall of windows overlooking the river, a large antique desk, built-in mahogany bookshelves. It was not often that anyone was invited into my father's study, even me.

Now a sly expression came into my father's face. I thought *A woman. He has brought a woman here.*

Despite his age Roland Marks was a handsome man; he'd been exceptionally handsome in his youth, with dark dreamy brooding eyes, a fine-sculpted foxy face and a quick and ingratiating smile. He'd dazzled many women in his time—and many men. Some of this I knew firsthand but much of this I knew from reading about him.

When you are related to a person of renown you can't shake off the conviction that others, strangers, know him in ways you will never know him. Your vision of the man is myopic and naïve—the long-distance vision is the more correct one.

"An academic. A 'scholar.' She's come to interview me. You know—the usual."

Roland Marks's genial contempt for *academics* and *scholars* did not preclude his being quite friendly with a number of them. Like most writers, he was flattered by attention; even the kind of attention that embarrassed him, annoyed or exasperated him. Each *academic* and *scholar* who'd met with Roland Marks, and had written about him, imagined that he or she was the exception. *What a surprise Roland Marks is! Nothing at all like people say but really, really nice . . . and so funny.*

"Is this your new—assistant?"

"We've been exploring the possibility."

This person, whoever she was, was unknown to me. I had the idea, since Dad hadn't mentioned her until now, that she was relatively unknown to him, too.

"Come upstairs, Lou-Lou, and meet 'Cameron.' We've been having a quite intense interview session."

It wasn't uncommon for people to come to my father's Nyack house to interview him. But it was somewhat uncommon for one of these interviewers to stay so late.

Though there was the *Paris Review* interviewer, a literary journalist, who'd interviewed Roland Marks in 1978, in his apartment at the time on the Upper West Side, who'd virtually moved in with him and had had to be forcibly evicted after several weeks.

Dad led me upstairs with unusual vigor.

In his study, a tall skinny blond woman—a quite young, quite striking blond woman—was slipping papers into a tote-bag. On the table before her was a laptop, a small tape recorder, a cell phone, and a can of Diet Coke.

"Cameron? I'd like you to meet my daughter Lou-Lou Marks. And Lou-Lou, this is Cameron—from . . ."

"Cameron Slatsky. From Columbia University."

With a naïve stiffness the young woman spoke, as if one had to identify Columbia as a *university*.

Awkwardly we shook hands. Cameron Slatsky from Columbia University smiled so glowingly at me, I felt my face shrink like a prune in too much sunshine.

Of course, Dad had to tease a bit calling me his "Dean Daughter"—

"Dean Marks, Daughter"—which drew a breathy laugh from Cameron Slatsky and a look of wary admiration as if she'd never seen a dean before, close up.

In fact, Dad was proud of my academic credentials. Unlike my sister and my brothers, who'd tried to "compete" with Roland Marks by writing—(fiction, poetry, plays, journalism)—I was the daughter who'd impressed him with her diligence, intelligence, and modesty; if I published essays, they were of esoteric literary subjects—Sappho's poetry, the tragedies of Aeschylus and Sophocles, for instance— which Dad read with the avidity of the intellectual whose knowledge of a subject is limited. The point was, Lou-Lou Marks knew her *place*.

I gathered that Cameron had just been speaking on her cell phone and that she was, as a consequence perhaps, somewhat agitated; though she continued to smile at my father.

"Mr. Marks? I wonder if we could confirm our date for—"

"Please, I've asked you: call me Roland."

"'R-Roland' . . ."

"Thank you, my dear! 'Roland' it is."

My dear. I felt a stab of embarrassment for my father.

Roland Marks, who often didn't try at all to be charming, was trying now. Hard.

"—our date for Monday? As we'd planned?"

"Sure. Just don't come before four P.M., please."

It seemed that Cameron was writing a dissertation on the "post-Modernist-polemic" fiction of Roland Marks for a Ph.D. in English. Exactly the kind of *theoretical bullshit* my father usually scorned.

Cameron wore metal-rimmed eyeglasses of the kind that, removed, reveal myopic but beautiful thick-lashed eyes, as in a romantic comedy. (And so it was in Cameron's case, in fact.) She was thin, willowy. She shivered with the intensity of an Italian greyhound. Her shoulders were just perceptibly hunched. For she was a tall girl, taller than my father; and she would have sensed that Roland Marks was vain enough to resent any woman taller than himself.

Cameron's strangest and most annoying feature was her hair: a kind of ponytail shot out of the side of her head, above her left ear. The hair was straw-colored and stiff-looking like a paintbrush. Long straight uneven bangs fell to her eyebrows, nearly in her eyes. If she'd been a dog she would've been a cross between a greyhound and a Shih Tzu, face partly obscured by hair.

Her sexy red mouth just kept smiling! I could imagine this arrogant young woman gloating to herself as soon as she was alone—*Pretty good, I think! Not bad! The old man likes me for sure.*

The way Dad was looking at Cameron, frowning and bemused, blinking, smiling to himself—it was obvious, the old man liked her.

As offensive as the grade-school ponytail was the young woman's attire, which had to be totally inappropriate for an interview with a Nobel laureate: she was wearing jeans foolishly frayed at the knee and so tight they fitted her anorexic body like a sausage casing. I swear you could see the crack of her buttocks. You could see—(though I didn't want to look)—the cleft of her pelvis. And her small perfect breasts strained against a tight black turtleneck sweater adorned with a white satin star like a bib.

Her ears glittered with gold studs and there was a tiny, near-invisible gold comma through her left eyebrow. Her skin was pale, pearly. Beneath the silly bangs, probably her forehead was pimply.

And the insipid mouth just kept *smiling*.

I could barely bring myself to look at this Cameron, I disliked her so intensely. I felt an impulse to grab hold of the ridiculous ponytail and give her head a good hard shake.

In dismay I thought *She will be the next! She is the enemy.*

In one of my father's bestselling novels of erotic obsession—(well, to be frank, virtually all of my father's novels were about erotic obsession however cloaked in intellectual and paradoxical political terms)—not a tragic novel but a comically convoluted melodrama titled *Intimacy: A Tragedy,* he describes the male response to the most obvious sorts of sex-stimuli, in terms of newly fledged ducks who react to the first thing they see when they leave the egg: a cardboard duck-silhouette, a paper hanger in the shape of a cartoon duck, a wooden block. All that's essential is that the thing, the stimulus, is in motion; the ducklings will follow it blindly as if it were the mother duck. So too, Roland Marks said, the male reacts blindly to a purely sexual mechanism, stimulated by certain sights and smells. *Instead of a brain, there's the male genitalia.*

Such knowledge hadn't spared Roland Marks from several disastrous marriages and, I didn't doubt, numberless liaisons.

Cameron was saying, apologetically, in a voice that scratched at your ears, "Mr. Marks, I mean—Roland—this is disappointing, I'm really sorry, but I can't stay for dinner—I have to leave now. . . ."

"But I've ordered dinner. I've ordered for three."

"Oh I know—I'm so sorry! It's just something that came up, I've been on the phone . . ."

"When? Just now?"

"Yes. A—someone—just called, I had to t-take the call . . ."

Dad was aggrieved, angry. It disturbed me how quickly he was flaring up at this stranger, as if she'd betrayed an intimacy between them.

He'd never seen her before today. His reaction was totally irrational.

"I really can't stay, it's a personal matter . . ."

My father's face was livid with emotion—surprise, hurt, jealousy. For the past fifty years or more, Roland Marks had become accustomed to being at the center of most scenes involving women. He'd had the whip hand.

"Well, Cameron. Whatever you like."

Dryly Dad spoke. I wondered—had he asked this young woman to be his new assistant? How impulsive he was becoming!

"May I return, Mr. Marks? On Monday afternoon as we'd planned?"

"Better call me first, to see if I'm here. Good night!"

It was like a grating yanked down over a store window—Dad's conviviality toward the striking young blond girl had ceased.

It fell to me to see the abashed Cameron downstairs and out the door as she clumsily repeated that she was sorry, she hoped my father would understand, maybe another time they could have dinner . . .

No. You will not. Not ever.

I shut the door behind her. I did not watch her drive away from the curb. I told myself *But I must not be jealous of her, if he lets her return. I must be happy for my father. If that is what he wishes.*

Brave Lou-Lou Marks staring at her blurred reflection in a mirror in the front hall while a floor above, in his study, door pointedly shut, my father Roland Marks was already talking and laughing too loudly, in a phone conversation with someone I could not imagine.

THE FACT IS, my name isn't *Lou-Lou* but *Lou*. Yet *Lou* is so bluntly unlovely, inevitably the name became vapid *Lou-Lou*.

My father had wanted to name me after Lou Andreas-Salomé, a hot-blooded female intellectual of the nineteenth century whose most heralded achievement in the popular imagination is to have lived in a ménage à trois with her lover Paul Rée and Friedrich Nietzsche and to be photographed with the two men in a *dominatrix* pose.

You've seen the famous photograph—Lou Andreas-Salomé in a little cart pulled by Rée and Nietzsche in the role of donkeys. Andreas-Salomé looks oddly twisted, in a dress with a long skirt; she's wielding a little whip. The men, who should look doting, or as if they're enjoying a joke for posterity, look like zombies. Andreas-Salomé was said to be a beautiful woman but, as is often the case with alleged beauties of the past, photographs of her don't bear out this claim but show a snoutish-faced woman with intense eyes and a heavy chin. (Yes, I do somewhat resemble Andreas-Salomé except that no one would have described me as beautiful.)

My namesake, admirably "liberated" for a woman of her time, also had affairs and intimate friendships with Maria Rilke, Viktor Tausk, and Sigmund Freud. She'd become a psychoanalyst and published psychoanalytic studies admired by Freud; she'd written novels, and a study of Nietzsche. I'd tried to read some of her writing years ago but had soon given up, it had seemed so dated, so sad and so—*female.*

Once I'd asked my mother why she'd agreed with my father to name me after Lou Andreas-Salomé and not rather someone within the family—(which is a Jewish custom)—and my mother had said she had no idea—"He talked me into it, I suppose. Why else?"

He was uttered in a way so subtle, you'd have to listen closely to hear reproach, accusation, woundedness, resignation in that single syllable.

At last count I have four stepmothers, in addition to my own mother. They are Monique, Avril, Phyllis, Sylvia. There are step-brothers and –sisters in my life but they are younger than I am, of another generation, and resentful of me as their father's favorite.

I think of my stepmothers as fairy-tale figures, sisters united by their marital ties to Roland Marks, but of course these ex-wives of Roland Marks detest one another.

Sylvia Sachs was the New York actress, and the youngest. Just fifty-six, and looking, with the aid of cosmetic surgery and the very best hair salons in Manhattan, twenty years younger.

Monique Glickman was old by now—that is, Dad's age. For a woman, *old*.

She was living in Tampa, Florida. She'd disappeared from our lives—good riddance!

Avril Gatti was the litigious one—a former journalist, Italian-born, now residing in New York City with an (allegedly) female lover.

Of Phyllis Brady what's to say? The daughter of a distinguished Upper East Side architect might have expected to be better treated by her Jewish-novelist-husband whose father had owned a (small, not-prosperous) bakery in Queens, but she'd been mistaken.

My mother, Sarah, had been Roland's second wife. He'd been still young at the time of their marriage—just thirty-two. Mom must have thought that, impassioned as the handsome young Roland Marks had been, eager to leave his "difficult" wife Monique for her, that his love for her would be stable, constant, reliable—of course, it was not. And after four children, certainly it was not.

"You must have wanted to kill him, when he left you for—whoever it was at the time"—so I'd said to my mother impulsively, one day when we were reminiscing about those years when we'd been a family in Park Slope, and the name "Lou-Lou" wasn't so inappropriate for me;

and my mother said, with a wounded little cry, "Oh, no, Lou-Lou—not *him*."

A neutral observer would have interpreted this remark as—*She'd wanted to kill the woman he left her for.*

But I knew my mother better than that.

AFTER CAMERON LEFT, the very air in the house was a-quiver.

"Not an auspicious beginning. If she wants to be my *assistant*."

Dad was muttering in Dad's way: an indignant thinking-aloud you were (possibly) meant to hear, and to respond to; though sometimes, not.

Casually I said, as often I did in such circumstances: "She may have wanted to exploit you, Dad."

"Oh well—'exploit.' That's what everyone pins onto *me*."

"You can't trust interviewers. They can edit the tape as they wish, and make you out to seem—"

"She certainly knew my work. My *oeuvre* as she called it."

With a wounded air Dad spoke. He might have been lamenting *My penis.*

Of course, Dad was disgruntled. Not just the beautiful blond girl had left, trailing a sweet-smelling sort of mist in her wake, but he had to content himself for the evening with *me.*

His favorite daughter. Poor plain hulking Lou-Lou.

Not that Dad didn't like me. Even love me. (So far as he was capable of love.) But it was clear that he didn't regard me as attractive, or particularly feminine; he didn't *admire* me. This had always been evident, even as a young girl I'd seen it in his eyes, as I'd seen his pleasure in female beauty, female grace, *femaleness,* in the presence of one or another of his wives, or my older sisters who were both quite attractive as girls. "Beauty is skin deep: we perceive it immediately. What's beneath, if it's ugly, will require more time"—so Roland Marks had observed more than once, with an air of vengeful melancholy.

All that day, Dad said, until the interviewer had come at 3:00 P.M. to "interrupt and distract him," he'd been working in his study. It is expected of Nobel Prize winners that they begin to slacken their pace after receiving the award but this wasn't the way of Roland Marks who was as committed to, or as obsessed with, his work as he'd been as an aggressive young man out of the Midwest fifty years before. It had been his aim to combine the "many voices of our time"—the elevated, the intellectual and the poetic, and the debased, vernacular, and the crudely prosaic. It was an ambitious aim—it was a Whitmanesque aim—which struck a nerve in the literary community as well as in the vast unchartable American community that responds to some—a very few—works of "art" with genuine enthusiasm and pleasure. Yet, Roland Marks had detractors. After reviewers celebrate a "brilliantly promising" young writer, they are not so easily placated with his more mature work. The many awards bestowed upon my father didn't soften the hurt of the barbs and stabs he'd received as well, some from old friends whose admiration had turned to resentment as Roland Marks's reputation grew.

The cruelest blow had been a lengthy, quasi-sympathetic but finally condescending review of a novel by an old writer-friend of his, a literary rival, who ought never to have written such a veiled attack on another writer of Roland Marks's stature and age—in the *New Yorker*.

Roland Marks never wrote reviews. But if he had, he would not have retaliated—such "low-down, down-dirty" behavior was beneath him, he said.

Never again would he speak to that writer, whom he felt had betrayed him. If the man's name came up, Dad was likely to walk away, wounded.

Through all this, Dad's work had continued. It was a joke to suggest that the man was a womanizer when the deeper truth was, he was wed to *work*.

Dad had recently finished a project—a lengthy novel set in New

York City in the 1940s and 1950s, the era of World War II, post-War
and Cold War America. Gleefully he'd been telling interviewers that
he'd "named names and burnt bridges"—even as he insisted that *Patricide* was purely fiction. There was anticipation in publishing circles,
for a novel by Roland Marks invariably managed to excite controversy.
Feminists loved to hate him; haters of feminism loved to praise him;
every Jewish literary figure had a strong, even vehement opinion about
him; and there were the ex-wives, one of them the moderately famous
Broadway actress of a certain age who'd said some very damning—and
funny—things about Roland Marks in uncensored TV interviews. In
any case he'd put the manuscript in a drawer, and would not look at it
for another six months. He was anxious about his work, and superstitious. If he waited too long to revise, he might die before he finished!
The novel would be published *posthumously*. He would be criticized
posthumously, for not having polished it to Roland Marks's characteristic high sheen.

"Daddy, don't fret! You always say the same things."

"Do I? The same things?"

"You've been worrying about 'dying too soon' since you were in
your fifties. That's twenty years at least."

"Those were premature worries. But now . . ."

I'd hoped that Dad would ask me to help him with the novel in
some way—fact-checking, retyping. But he wasn't quite ready to share
Patricide with anyone else, just yet.

Patricide. A strange title.

It was not an attractive title, I thought. But I dared not ask Roland
Marks what it meant.

That day Dad had been going through a copyedited galley of an
essay he'd written for the *New York Review of Books* with the intriguing
title "Cervantes, Walter Benjamin, and the Fate of Linear Art in a Digital Age." Roland Marks was as impassioned, and often as unreasonable,
about his non-fiction work as he was about his fiction: he'd ended up

revising most of the essay, and yet he was still dissatisfied. And his head ached, and his eyes hurt. (No one knew, but me, that Roland Marks had a still-mild case of macular degeneration for which he was being treated by injections to the eye, at an enormous expense only partly covered by his medical insurance.) He couldn't bear any more reading today, he said—"Or thinking. I'm God-damned tired of *thinking*."

It was Thai food my father had ordered, from a Nyack restaurant. For our Thursday dinners we alternated among several restaurants— Chinese, Italian, Thai—which my father found not too terrible, though nothing like his favorite New York restaurants, to which he was usually taken as a guest.

On our domestic Thursdays we often watched television in the remodeled sunporch while we ate take-out dinners from the Thai Kitchen, reheated in a microwave.

"What would you like to watch, Dad?"

"Anything. Nothing."

I knew that he was still thinking of Cameron whose last name he'd forgotten. I knew that he was anxious, embittered, and yet hopeful— that was Roland Marks.

He'd been unjustly angry with me earlier, but he'd forgotten why. Now he was unjustly angry with the gawky ponytailed blond without remembering why. He said, taking the TV wand from me, "Anything distracting. Entertaining. But *something*."

This wasn't so. My father couldn't tolerate TV advertisements. I would have to find a movie for us, on one of the few cable channels without interruptions.

"What about *A Stolen Life*—Bette Davis and Glenn Ford. *The Bridge on the River Kwai*—William Holden. *The Entertainer*—Laurence Olivier."

"*The Entertainer*."

"You've seen this, I think?"

"Yes, I've seen *The Entertainer*—'I think.' When you're seventy-four you've seen everything. But not recently. And Olivier is brilliant."

I brought in our heated-up Thai food from the kitchen, on trays. I used attractive earthenware plates and paper napkins of a high quality that almost resembled cloth napkins. I would have opened a bottle of wine for us but Dad avoided alcohol in the evenings because it made him sleepy. I tried not to notice the anger in his face, and the sorrow beneath. I fussed over him as I always did, tried to chide and joke with him, for he expected it of Lou-Lou, no matter what mood he was in.

The love-affair of a daughter with her father encompasses her entire life. There has never been a time when she has not been her father's daughter.

I thought *None of them can take my place. None of them can know him as I do.*

It was so, Laurence Olivier was brilliant in a role in which he, one of the great actors of the twentieth century, plays a second-rate vaudeville entertainer in a dreary English resort town—Brighton?—who, from time to time, onstage, in the spotlight, amid burlesque routines of stultifying banality and vulgarity, reveals flashes of genius.

Olivier was so compelling in the role of Archie Rice, so utterly convincing, both my father and I sat in silence, enthralled. Roland Marks could not think of any clever remark to underscore what we were seeing—the saga of an aging, hypocritical, hollow-hearted vaudeville comedian who connives to make a comeback by exploiting his elderly father, and finally killing him. Yet Olivier's character is so very human, my eyes filled with tears of sympathy. He's a fraud, but "charming"— women continue to adore him! He's a heel, and a cad, and a drinker, yet it was love I felt for the man, impersonal as sunshine.

There is a particularly poignant scene midway in the film in which the young Joan Plowright, in the role of Archie Rice's daughter, tells the "entertainer" that he can't possibly be serious about marrying a naïve young woman who has been seduced by his charisma—"She's my age! The age of your daughter!"

Archie Rice is chastened, embarrassed. But his daughter's scandal-ized plea makes no difference: he's determined to marry the second-place beauty-contest winner just the same, in order to borrow money from her father.

Dad began to laugh. Dad had been picking at his Thai food, that was too spicy for him though he'd insisted on ordering *hot*. And now something pleased him mightily.

"Here's a fact, Lou-Lou: Olivier married that very actress, Joan Plowright, within a year. He divorced Vivien Leigh and married Plow-right who was young enough to be his daughter." It was a curiosity, how Roland Marks seemed to know so much of popular culture, which in his books and lectures he disdained as *drek*. Now Dad laughed his loud Rabelaisian laugh, that made me shudder.

Though he hadn't had any wine, Dad was very sleepy by the time the movie ended. (The final scene of *The Entertainer*, when Archie Rice is disintegrating onstage before a sadly diminished audience, had made him laugh, initially; then cast him into a bleak mood I thought it most prudent not to notice.) I helped him up the stairs, said good night to him and cleaned up downstairs; it gave me pleasure to darken the rooms of the house, preparatory to leaving, and returning to my condominium in Skaatskill.

Except: before I left, in Dad's study I looked for a note-sized piece of paper. I knew it was there somewhere, and finally I found it in plain sight beside Dad's shut-up computer: *Cameron S., 212 448 1439,* cslatsky@columbia.edu.

Crumpled it and took it away in my pocket.

Thinking *This will do no good, probably. But I will have tried.*

IT WAS MY VOCATION: TO SPARE MY FATHER FROM RAPACIOUS females.

I hadn't done a very good job of it, you might say. And you'd be correct.

I tried to protect Dad from harm. At least when he wasn't traveling abroad and far off my radar. I was the *constant* in his life, I wished to think.

Swarms of women, of all ages, tried to attach themselves to Roland Marks in one guise or another. Some were wealthy socialites eager for celebrity-writers to perform—"For zero bucks," as Dad said dryly—for their charity fund-raisers; some were young like Cameron Slatsky, relatively poor, unattached and, who knows?—desperate, if not deranged. No one is so alert to the dangers that beset a famous man than a daughter.

It's true, Dad might have been seeing quite reasonable women, divorcées or widows just slightly younger than himself, yet not embarrassingly *young*—except that Dad wouldn't have been seen in public with any woman within two decades of his age.

In Washington, D.C., a few years ago, where Dad had been honored by the president at the National Medals ceremony in the White House, he'd been accompanied by a chic skinny girl who might've been a model, very gorgeous, and so young that the president's wife had said, utterly without irony: "It's so nice of you to bring your granddaughter to our ceremony, Mr. Marks!"

It's well into the twenty-first century. The era of Women's Liberation was the 1970s, or should have been. Yet, women are still bound to men. The majority of women, regardless of age. And a famous man attracts women as a flame attracts moths—irresistibly, fatally. Some of the most beautiful moths want nothing more than to fling themselves into the flame which destroys them.

"Go away. Steer clear of him. Don't you know who he is?"—often I wanted to cry at the foolish women.

My own mother, in fact. Poor Mom had been clinically depressed, frankly suicidal, for years after their divorce, though she'd seen a succession of therapists and "healers" and had been prescribed a virtual buffet of tranquillizers, anti-depressants, organic and "whole" foods. (She'd been a rising young editor at Random House when Roland Marks had met her but she'd quit her job, at Dad's insistence, shortly after they were married.) As a mother she'd often been distracted and hadn't been able to focus, as she'd said, on her children, as she'd have liked; for Roland Marks was her most demanding child.

Belatedly, Sarah has tried to be a "devoted" mother—too late for my sister and brothers, I think.

In a divorce, a child invariably chooses one or the other parent to side with. It was never any secret, though he'd moved out of our house and out of our lives, I'd sided with my father.

Though my mother was the one who'd loved *me*, and cared for *me*.

My father never knew that I'd spared him the embarrassment of an *ex-wife-suicide*.

I'd been twelve at the time. Mom had been still fairly young— not yet forty-five. Dad had been living elsewhere for several months as details of the "separation" were being worked out. (In fact, there was to be no "separation" everyone but my mother and I seemed to know.) She'd told me in a matter-of-fact voice, as if she were discussing the weather: "I don't think that I can go on, Lou-Lou. I feel so tired. Life doesn't seem worth the effort . . ."

"Please don't talk that way, Mom. You know you don't mean it."

I was frightened because in fact I didn't know that my mother didn't mean it. In the slow, then rapid decline of her sixteen-year marriage with Roland Marks, she'd lapsed into a chronic melancholy. When I'd been a little girl it was said that she'd suffered from postpartum depression but in fact, as people close to our family knew, it was my father's infidelities that wore her down.

She might've divorced *him*—so one might think.

My sister Karin, my brothers Harry and Saul were impatient with my mother. Her weakness was a terror to us all. She frightened them as she frightened me but, cannily self-absorbed adolescents as they were at this time, they reacted by ignoring, rebuffing, or fleeing her, as I did not.

One afternoon when I returned home from school I couldn't find Mom, though I knew she was home. And then I did find her, locked into an upstairs bathroom.

I could hear her inside, beneath the noise of the fan. She was talking to herself, or sobbing; when I knocked on the door, she told me please go away.

But I didn't go away. I continued knocking on the door until at last she opened it.

I don't think that I will describe what I saw.

I will spare my mother this indignation, out of numerous others.

I called 911. I may have screamed, and I may have wept, but I only remember calling 911. For already at the age of twelve I was *Lou-Lou the brave, the stout, and the reliable.*

It was for the best, Mom was saying. Her eyes were dilated, her voice was faint and cracked. He'd all but told her—told her what to do . . . He'd shown her how, in his new novel. How to clear the way for an impatient husband who has fallen in love (guiltily, ecstatically) with a younger woman . . .

Mom was referring to Roland Marks's newest novel *Jealousy* in which an unloved wife kills herself in these circumstances and is much mourned, much regretted, even admired by survivors for her *sensitivity, generosity.*

I held my mother, waiting for the emergency medical workers.

I thought *If I weren't here she would die now. He would have killed her.*

Dad came to see my mother in the hospital, repentant, remorseful, very quiet. He brought her flowers. He brought her new books in bright paper covers, conspicuously women's fiction of the kind Roland Marks scorned. He took certain of her relatives, visiting the hospital, out to dinner at a good restaurant. He spent time with my sister, my brothers and me. And after Mom was discharged from the hospital, he filed for divorce.

Except at court dates and incidental meetings at family events, Roland Marks would never speak to my mother again.

AND YET, I loved him best. Can't help it.

"MY GOD, WHAT'S THAT? A TOOTH?"

He was astonished. He was aghast. Yet you could see that already he was formulating the terms in which he would relate the story to his friends: how his teenaged athlete-daughter Lou-Lou was struck in the mouth with an opponent's hockey stick, tripped and fell on the field entangled in opponents' feet, yet nonetheless managed to scramble erect and grip her stick hoping to continue in the frantic game until—at last—though it could not have been more than a few seconds—the referee pulled her out of the game.

"Hell, Dad. I'm OK."

The athlete-daughter was me. Panting, dribbling blood down her chin, staining her lime-green hockey-team uniform. Cursing but laughing. The referee hadn't seen how badly I'd been hit.

"Jesus, Lou-Lou! Is that a *tooth?*"

It was. A front, lower tooth, with a bloody root, in the palm of my shaky hand.

"I've got plenty more, Dad. It doesn't hurt one bit."

This was true. In the adrenaline-charge of the moment, my bloodied mouth didn't hurt. Spitting blood to keep from choking didn't hurt.

Worth it, to see the aghast-admiring look in my father's eyes.

Before the sheer *physicality* of life, Roland Marks seemed at times mesmerized, paralyzed. His large intelligent eyes blinked and shimmered like an infant's eyes yearning to understand, yet overwhelmed by understanding.

"Dad, hey—don't look at me like that. It's not like, you know—I'm some kind of fashion model, and now my career is ruined." And I laughed again, and spat out blood.

I was scared, but high. No sensation like being high on adrenaline!

I was Roland Marks's exemplary daughter, his favorite daughter, but I was no beauty. Gamely my father liked to compare me to certain classic paintings—female portraits—by Ingres, Renoir, even Whistler—but my broad Eskimo-face, my small eyes given to irony, my fleshy sardonic mouth resisted mythologizing. Hulking and needy, but disguising my need in robust good spirits and a laugh that, as Dad noted, sounded like fingernails scraped upward on a blackboard, I resisted idealization.

I'd weighed nine pounds, twelve ounces at birth. So I'd been told many times.

I wanted to scare my fastidious father, a little. He'd almost missed this game. He'd *wanted* to miss this game, but I'd begged him on the phone the night before—my mother had arranged not to come to Rye so that my father could come—and so he'd given in. But I knew he'd resented it. He'd had other plans, in Manhattan. I wanted to suggest now in my swaggering manner that, even as I assured him I felt fine, really I'd been stunned, shaken. Violence had been done to me by a meanly-wielded hockey stick which despite my big-girl body I hadn't been able to absorb. And I wanted to punish Roland Marks for staring so avidly at certain of my teammates—my friend Ardis and the sloe-eyed Estella with thick dark hair like an explosion of tiny wires. He'd even gaped after some of the St. Ann's girls.

"Maybe the tooth could be put back *in*? Some kind of fancy orthodontic surgery . . ."

Roland Marks was looking faint. Nearly wringing his hands. The sight of blood was confounding to him. Infamously he'd written about *female blood*—a notorious passage in an early novel, frequently quoted by hostile feminist critics as an example of Marks's *unconscionable misogyny.*

But Dad was no misogynist. Dad loved *me.*

I laughed. I was feeling excited, exalted. This was a key moment in my young life—I was fifteen years old. I had not always been so very happy and I had not always been so very proud of myself despite my exemplary status in my father's eyes. I believed now that my team-mates were concerned about me—and that they knew who my father was—who Roland Marks was. I'd seen the curiosity and admiration in their eyes, a hint of envy. The Rye Academy was an academically prestigious school (it was ranked with Lawrenceville, Exeter, Ando-ver) but it was not Miss Porter's, St. Mark's, or Groton—there were not nearly enough celebrity-daughters enrolled. So Roland Marks—a much-awarded, much-acclaimed and frequently bestselling literary author whose picture had once been on a *Time* cover—a name partic-ularly known to English instructors and headmasters—carried some weight. As Dad complained to his friends *It's a come-down to discover you're the celebrity yourself. You know what Groucho Marx said.*

(Did I know what Groucho Marx had said? I wasn't sure. As a young child, I'd assumed the name my father meant was Groucho *Marks.*)

Dad had given me one of his handkerchiefs to press against my bleeding mouth. Not a tissue—a handkerchief. White, fine-spun cot-ton, neatly ironed and folded. My mother would have grabbed me tight not minding if I got blood on her clothing.

"Lou-Lou darling, we'll—sue! Someone is liable here! This is worse than Roman gladiatorial combat, you don't even get a decent crowd."

Dad's lame attempt at humor. The more nervous he was, the more he tried to be "funny."

As soon as he'd arrived at school, as soon as he'd seen the number of spectators in the bleachers before our game with St. Ann's, he'd been vehement, disapproving. Where was "school spirit"? Why weren't the field hockey team's friends and classmates supporting them in greater numbers? And where were their teachers, for Christ's sake? (This was unfair: there were teachers amid the spectators. No choice for them, our fancy private school decreed that instructors attend as many sports events as they could, as well as concerts, plays, poetry slams. Our teachers were substitute-parents, of a kind. You could see the strain in their faces, before their cheery-instructor smiles broke out.) Dad's quick alert eye had moved about my teammates' faces—and figures—seeking out those images of female beauty, utterly irresistible female beauty, that made life worth living—or so you'd think, from Roland Marks's novels; and during the game, even as I ran my heart out to impress him, stomping up and down the field like a deranged buffalo and wielding my hockey stick with bruised hands, even then I saw how he was distracted by certain of my teammates, and one or two of the St. Ann's girls, whose field-hockey ferocity didn't detract from their young sexy bodies.

My father didn't know what to make of me, beyond marveling at my "pluck"—"physical courage"—"recklessness." He should have held me, hugged me—but of course, he'd have risked soiling his J. Press sport coat and tattersall shirt if he had. Easy intimacy wasn't one of Dad's notable traits.

At five foot ten I loomed over Dad who habitually described himself as "just-under six-feet"—I didn't want to think that I intimidated him, as sometimes I intimidated my smaller classmates. Roland Marks was an elegant figure—slender, narrow in the torso, straight-backed and always impeccably dressed. In literary circles he could be depended upon to wear what is called, with jaw-dropping pretension, *bespoken suits*. The tattersall was his "country gentleman" shirt—he had others, dressier and more expensive. His neckties were always Italian silk, very expensive. Though this afternoon at the girls' school in Rye, Connecticut, he was wearing a beige-checked shirt with no tie beneath a camel's hair coat; neatly pressed brown trousers and dark brown "country" shoes with a high luster. If you hadn't known that my father was a famous man, something of his prominence, his *specialness*, exuded from his manner: he expected attention, and he expected a certain degree of excitement, even melodrama, to stave off the essential boredom of his life. (This, too, is taken from Roland Marks's memoirist fiction.) In his youth he'd been strikingly handsome—as handsome as a film star of the era—(Robert Taylor, Glenn Ford, Joseph Cotten?)—and now in late middle age he exuded an air still of such entitlement, women turned their heads in his wake, yes and young women as well, even adolescent girls—(I'd seen certain of my classmates stare openly at my father before dismissing him as *old*).

In my mother's absence, Dad had driven to Rye, Connecticut. Mom was now his ex-ex-wife and his feelings for her, once a toxic commingling of pity, impatience, and repugnance, were now mellowing, as his feelings for his more recent ex-wife, the notorious litigant Avril Gatti, were sharp as porcupine quills. In the accumulation of former wives, my mother Sarah Detticott was not the most vivid; her predecessor, and her glamorous successors, had figured in my father's fiction more prominently, pitiless portraits of harshly stereotyped *bitch-goddesses* that were nonetheless entertaining, rendered in Roland Marks's beguiling prose. Even feminists conceded *In spite of yourself you have to laugh—Marks is so over-the-top sexist.*

The fact was, Dad had missed several visits with me that fall. He'd had to cancel—"unavoidably, if unforgivably." He'd insisted that I attend the Rye Academy since it wouldn't be "too arduous" a drive for him from New York City—(compared to the smaller Camden School in Maine which I'd preferred)—and so it was a particular disappointment when he called, sometimes just the night before a scheduled visit, to cancel. Especially if we'd arranged it so that Mom wouldn't be coming that weekend.

Like the Swiss weather cuckoo-clock, in which the appearance of one quaintly carved little figure meant the absence of the other, my two so very different parents could not be in my company at the same time.

He was looking at me now with dazed wounded eyes. I thought *He really does love me. But he doesn't know what that means.*

By this time Tina Rodriguez, our phys. ed. teacher and our hockey coach, who'd been refereeing the game, was headed in my direction. "Lou-Lou! What's this about a tooth?"—she would have pried open my hand if I hadn't opened it for her.

"It doesn't really hurt, T.R. It's just bleeding a lot, but—it isn't any kind of actual *injury*."

"A knocked-out tooth is an *injury*, Lou-Lou. Don't be ridiculous."

In his anxiety Dad began to berate the referee for allowing "all hell to break loose" on the hockey field, and his daughter's tooth knocked out in a "brutal scuffle."

T.R. was startled by my father's vehemence. Possibly, she knew who he was. (I'd intended to introduce them after the game.) Yet she didn't apologize profusely, she didn't defer to an angry parent so much as try to placate him, and assure him that his daughter would get the very best medical treatment available in Rye.

So, despite my protests, an ambulance was called. An emergency medical crew took me to a local ER for a dozen stitches in my gums and lower lip, a tetanus shot, painkillers. I was furious and crying— the last thing I'd wanted was to be expelled from the hockey game. I'd hoped only to be praised by my father, and a few others; my teammates, for sure; and our coach T.R. Naïvely I'd seemed to think that I might have been allowed to continue, for what was a silly lost tooth compared to the exhilaration of the game? (Win or lose didn't matter to me, it was the game, the *girl-team*, that mattered.)

In my ER bed surrounded by tacky curtains I shut my eyes to suppress tears seeing my teammates rushing down the field oblivious of Lou-Lou Marks's absence, having forgotten their valiant teammate already, wielding hockey sticks with fierce pleasure and rushing away into the gathering dusk.

Wait, wait for me! Come back! I am one of you.

But they ignore me. They are gone.

Long I would recall—more than thirty years later I am still recalling—how quickly my fortunes had changed on that November afternoon in Rye, Connecticut. A single misstep! Not ducking to avoid a wildly swung hockey stick! And a knocked-out tooth! Dad would pay for fancy orthodontic surgery as he'd promised, and the new, synthetic tooth was—is—indistinguishable from my other lower front teeth: that isn't the point. What I was struck by was the swift and unanticipated change of fortune: one minute you're in the game rushing down the field wielding your hockey stick—(a light rain beginning to fall, threaded with snowflakes that melted on my fevered cheeks)—exhilarated, thrilled—yes, frankly *showing off* to Roland Marks in a way that was desperate and reckless if not adroit and skilled like the better field-hockey players that afternoon whom I so badly wanted to emulate, but could not: for they were agile on their feet even if their feet were large as mine—one minute *in the game* and the next, *out*.

It was a revelation worthy of Roland Marks's fiction. *One minute in the game and the next, out.*

For intense periods of time—years, months, weeks—he loved his women. Then, by degrees or with stunning swiftness, he did *not*.

In the hospital my father paced about my bedside excited and distracted.

"Oh, Lou-Lou. Poor Lou-Lou! This is so, so . . ."

So unexpected, probably Dad meant. When you considered that he'd done his daughter a favor by driving to Rye, Connecticut, from New York City—when (as the daughter had to know, even in her adolescent myopia) there were so many more far more interesting people craving Roland Marks's attention in New York City than she. But this generous gesture had turned out badly, and who was to blame?

Also, being stuck in the ER with me, groggy with codeine and awaiting the results of X-ray tests, and the game continuing without us, or, by this time, having ended—*so boring.*

Partly I'd dreaded being taken to the ER for this reason. I worried that my father would become impatient and annoyed with me—his instinct was to blame the victim. He wasn't one to "coddle" weakness in others, though weakness in himself was an occasion for lyric self-pity of a Rilkean quality.

". . . we could sue, possibly. You girls should be wearing mouth-guards—masks—like ice-hockey goalees . . . Jesus, the puck could have gone in your *eye.*"

"It wasn't the puck, Dad. It was a stick."

"Puck, stick—fucking monosyllable. Comes to the same thing, in a 'negligence' suit."

"Please tell me you're not serious about suing my school, Dad." Everyone would hate me, then. Now, they mostly just pitied me, or felt sorry for me, or half-admired me, or tolerated me. I had more than a year and a half to endure at the Rye Academy, before I graduated, if I graduated. *Just let me get through, Dad. Then—I'm on my own.*

So I wanted to think. My sister and two brothers had fled Roland Marks's gravitational pull. He liked to say, dryly—*The older kids are on their own. If that's how they want it—fine.*

"We'll get the tooth replaced, Lou-Lou—I promise. We'll fix you up fine. Better than new."

For years I'd had to suffer orthodontic braces. Now that my teeth were reasonably straight, I'd lost a crucial front tooth. Dad didn't appreciate the irony. Or, Dad had other, more pressing things to think about.

I couldn't know, or wouldn't have wished to know, how what was preoccupying my father was nowhere near: not even in Manhattan.

An individual whose name I didn't (yet) know, who would become Roland Marks's next wife; at the present time living in Berkeley; the object of his current concern, or obsession. Yet it had seemed slightly odd to me, a quizzical matter, how Dad chattered about West Coast residents: "They seem younger somehow, more naïve and innocent, on the West Coast. Here it's six P.M.—they're still at three P.M. We're the future they're headed for."

In my codeine daze I tried to object: "Dad, if the world ended, it would end for them *at exactly the same time it ends for us.* Don't be silly."

" 'Silly'! I guess I am, sweetie."

And Dad gazed at me, or rather toward me, not-seeing me, with a fond, faint smile of such heartbreak, I knew that I would love him, and forgive him, forever.

WEEKS LATER—(you will not believe this!)—over Christmas break in Manhattan, at Dad's apartment on West Seventy-eighth Street, I would overhear a call between my father and—could it be Tina Rodriguez?

For it seemed, they'd already met at least once in the "city"—that is, New York City. Evidently they'd had drinks together. They'd talked over an "issue"—exactly what, wasn't clear.

T.R.! And Roland Marks!

I don't think that anything much came of it. I'm sure that nothing came of it. Roland Marks was always "having drinks" with women—friends, editors, agents, journalists, admirers. To his credit, not all were glamorous young women; some were his age at least. You might hear that he was seeing X, but you might not ever hear of X again. Instead you'd be hearing of Y, and of Z.

I was shocked, and felt betrayed. Not by my father but by Tina Rodriguez.

Why would she want to see my much-older father in the city? What had she thought that a meeting with Roland Marks might lead to?

I hoped T.R. wasn't disappointed. As I was disappointed in her.

We'd wanted to think that our wiry-limbed phys. ed. instructor with the snapping-dark eyes was a lesbian, at least. Not susceptible to men.

I would never tell my teammates. I would never play field hockey again.

⚛

"HELLO, MISS MARKS! SO GOOD TO SEE YOU AGAIN."

"Hello . . ."

In my discomfort I couldn't recall her name—the skinny blond ponytail girl of the previous week with the insipid ingratiating smile.

Except today she wasn't wearing her hair in a ponytail jutting out of the side of her head but brushed straight, to her shoulders. Shimmering and lustrous as a model's hair, not at all straw-colored or paintbrush-like but dazzling-pale-blond like Catherine Deneuve.

And she was wearing a trim little designer-looking mauve wool jacket, with a matching pleated skirt. And stockings, and high-heeled shoes.

The eyebrow piercing had vanished. Quite proper gold studs in her creamy ears.

" 'Cameron'—remember me? Your father is out in the sunroom, Miss Marks. We're almost finished for the day, come right in."

I'd been unlocking the front door of my father's house on Cliff Street, the following Thursday, when the door was flung open for me by the smiling blond stranger—the Ph.D. student/interviewer from Columbia. Vaguely I'd assumed that, since my father hadn't mentioned her, she'd been expelled from his life.

And what an insult, an arrogant blond stranger daring to *invite me inside my father's house that was practically my own house as well.*

Like a pasha Dad was sprawled on a bamboo settee in the sunroom sipping a muddy-looking cup of coffee which I had to suppose smiling Cameron had prepared for him. To be Roland Marks's assistant was to be his personal servant, as well.

Just barely, my father managed a smile for me.

"Lou-Lou. You're a little early, are you? No 'accident' on the bridge today?"

I'd wanted to lean over my father and brush his cheek with my lips in a tender-daughter greeting, to impress Cameron Slatsky; but I knew that my father would recoil, maybe laughingly—we rarely indulged in such sentimental *female gestures.*

"I'm not early. I'm exactly 'on time.' But I can go away again if you'd like, and come back later."

I spoke in a voice heavy with adolescent sarcasm. A few seconds in a parent's presence can provoke such regression.

I didn't like the bemused and condescending tone of my father to me, his favorite child, as it might be interpreted by the shining blond stranger.

On a glass-topped table in front of my father were many sheets of paper, some of them photocopies of pages from Roland Marks's books, as well as a laptop and a small tape recorder. And a can of Diet Coke which the intrepid interviewer must have brought for herself since it represented the sort of "toxic chemical cocktail" my father had always banned from his households.

I could see that the interviewer was systematically questioning my father about his career, making her way through his book titles chronologically. Her questions, numbered for each title, appeared to be elaborate.

For the first time, I wondered, is the girl serious? about Roland Marks's *oeuvre?* Her interest had to be a calculated campaign—didn't it?

I had never read a page of my father's allegedly brilliant fiction for its aesthetic properties. I'd read only to pursue an ever-elusive glimpse of my own self through Roland Marks's eyes though I'd read—and reread—obsessively.

Smiling Cameron Slatsky said, "Miss Marks, may I bring you something to drink? There's more coffee, and wine. And I brought Diet Coke . . ."

Dad said, "For God's sake call her 'Lou-Lou,' Cameron. 'Miss Marks' sounds like one of those cryptically unfunny *New Yorker* cartoons."

Stiffly I told Cameron Slatsky no thank you, I didn't want any of her Diet Coke. Or coffee or wine either, for that matter.

In fact I'd have loved a Diet Coke. But not in my father's presence.

"We're not quite finished for today, Lou-Lou. Cameron has been asking some very provocative, tough-minded questions about the 'internal logic' of my novels—I'm being made to feel flayed. But it's a good feeling, for once."

A good feeling—flayed? This had to be ridiculous.

Shining-blond Cameron cast her eyes downward in a semblance of modesty. Indeed they were beautiful gray-green eyes, once she'd removed her glasses.

She was looming above my father dazzling and willowy in the mauve wool suit, that had to be of very high quality, though possibly purchased at a consignment shop; the brass buttons were just slightly tarnished. She was slouch-shouldered as a too-tall teenaged girl might be, which made her appear touching, vulnerable. In the instant in which my father turned to Cameron I sensed how *the exemplary daughter* disappeared from his consciousness, as if a portion of his brain had been severed.

Of course, I was upset. I hadn't expected this—again. In the intervening week I'd tried to erase the arrogant young woman from my memory.

However, in my role as a college administrator I'd long ago learned to disguise upset. Emotions were not permitted in one in authority. In an unperturbed voice I asked my father—smilingly—what sort of food he wanted for dinner; and my father gallantly asked Cameron what sort of food did she want?—"There's Chinese, Italian, Thai—but we had Thai last week . . ."

The way—gently crumpling, a catch in his throat—in which my father enunciated "Cameron" was not reassuring.

Bright-vivacious Cameron said, like any high school girl aiming to be liked, "Please choose anything you want, Mr. Marks—I mean, Roland. I'm not a fussy eater. I like all kinds of things." It was the sweetly subservient manner of one who understands that to manipulate others in serious matters you should always acquiesce in small matters; you should give an impression of *pliancy*.

"Except sushi—the thought of raw fish makes me feel queasy."

Cameron shuddered, and laughed. Roland Marks shuddered and laughed, too.

Cynically I had to wonder if Cameron knew that, many years ago, Roland Marks had gotten deathly sick after eating sushi at a publisher's banquet in Tokyo; since then, the mere thought of raw fish made him feel queasy, too.

I said, "I'll order Chinese. I'll specify—nothing raw."

I left them and went into the kitchen. I must have been upset, I collided with doorways, chairs, countertops. In the other room I could hear their laughter, that was chilling to me.

I'd interrupted a domestic scene—was that it? Unbelievable.

It must have been my father's age. Everything had to be accelerated, even as it was being repeated. And ever-younger women, to be confused with not *daughters* but *granddaughters*.

I bit my lower lip. This was unfair! Unjust.

The deluded old man can't fall in love so quickly—so soon again.

It was a measure of my upset, I'd thought of my father as an *old man*. In a normal state of mind I would never have thought of Roland Marks in such a way.

Several times during the past week I'd called my father, spoken with him or left phone messages. I had not mentioned the young Ph.D. candidate who'd been interviewing him nor had my father mentioned her to me and so I'd felt justified in thinking that she might already be out of our lives.

As always I'd been a dutiful and devoted daughter. Dad had very little idea of how hard I worked at Riverdale College and of how much the college expected of me. For him, I'd made several telephone calls which he hadn't had time to make himself and I'd arranged for a furnace repairman to drop by the house, since Dad was having trouble with the furnace. (Roland Marks was helpless as a child living in an adult's house: he had no idea how to keep up with repairs, whom to call, how much to expect to pay; he just suspected all the locals to be taking advantage of him.) The wooden steps at the rear of the house, leading down to the beach, badly needed repair; at the end of the summer I'd tied yellow tape across the top of the steps, to discourage people, primarily my father, from using them; but Dad had ripped the tape off, of course— "Lou-Lou is always exaggerating 'safety measures.'" (Walking along the riverbank with his Nikon camera was one of Dad's few relaxing hobbies.) I was trying to find a reliable carpenter to repair the steps but, like plumbers and building contractors in Rockland County, reliable carpenters were in short supply.

When Dad had tried to deal with local handymen and tradesmen, and they'd failed to call him back, he'd given up in disgust. Nothing was so insulting in Roland Marks's elevated world than someone failing to call you back—Roland Marks was the one who failed to call others back. But an administrator knows that such disgust is but the first rung of the ladder you must climb routinely, if not daily.

In the kitchen I called Szechuan Village. I ordered several dishes which we might share. Cameron seemed the type who'd want brown rice, so I ordered brown rice as well as white. I was very much in control but my hand shook gripping the phone and the Chinese woman at the other end of the line seemed to have trouble understanding me.

"Speak English?" she said uncertainly, and I said, vehemently, "I am speaking English!"

In the next room I could hear them. The girl's uplifted soprano voice, and the man's deeper voice. It was a duet in which I was not welcome—I had no musical voice.

Also, I was feeling intense jealousy. For the one thing that Roland Marks had never been able to abide from anyone in his family, adult children as well as wives, was talk of his "career": his "writing." All that was Roland Marks's professional life was out of bounds to his family, as it would have been out of bounds for his children to have asked him how much money he made a year, or which of his women he'd loved best.

She has a way into his soul that you just don't. You can't.

This past week I'd been particularly diligent about asking my father how he was feeling, and if he needed me to drive him to any medical appointments; for some time, he'd been having water therapy at a local clinic to ease arthritic pain in his neck, lower back and hips, and as often as I could I drove him to the clinic; but my workdays at the college were long, and frequently my father had to drive himself, or take a taxi. Now I would feel anxious that the vigilant interviewer would take my place without my even knowing.

There was a (new) crisis imminent in Roland Marks's life at this time. Very soon, a Manhattan judge would be ruling in a civil suit brought against my father by his fifth wife Sylvia, the flamboyantly "wounded" and "sexually abased" actress who was charging, with the panache of the obsessively litigious Avril Gatti, the third wife, that she'd been virtually a *collaborator* with my father on at least two of his bestselling books, and deserved more money than he'd paid to her at the time of their divorce settlement.

This was ridiculous of course. This was outrageous. And—wasn't it illegal? Sylvia and her attorney had accepted the generous settlement at the time, which preceded her post-marital campaign of revealing comically vile slanderous "facts" about my father to a repelled but fascinated public—(interviews on *E!*, profile in *New York*. "The woman has made me her hobby," Dad said ruefully). Yet, in a courtroom anything can happen. Even judges who'd read and enjoyed Roland Marks's fiction were perversely likely to side against him. We had noted this phenomenon over the years—the decades. The more outrageous a former wife's demands, the more somberly the demands were considered in court.

My mother Sarah had been an exception. She'd been so emotionally fragile during the last several years of her marriage to my father, and at the time of their divorce, she'd hardly cared to contest him; despite her (female, feminist) lawyer's urging she hadn't asked for much money, and for a minimum amount of child support. (To my father's credit, like his friend Norman Mailer he'd never stinted in child support and had often contributed more than legally required.) Poor Mom! She'd been a pushover, in Dad's slangy term. He'd insisted that he had loved her, he said—"But it burnt out. Like a flame that just gets smaller and smaller and finally it's gone."

He'd assured us kids at the time of the divorce that his love for us would never change—which turned out not to be true, so far as my sister and brothers were concerned.

To deal with Sylvia's *collaboration* charges my father had hired a very good—and very expensive—lawyer to defend him, in New York City where the lawsuit had been initiated. As usual he seemed to think that the self-evident outrage of the litigant's demands, not to mention the injustice, on which expert (literary) witnesses would testify in court, would influence the judge to side with the beleaguered author, and not with the vindictive ex-wife. But I wasn't so convinced, and hoped to shield my father from the shock of another massive judgment going against him.

After a judge had awarded Avril Gatti two and a half million dollars as well as ordering Roland Marks to pay her crushing legal fees, my father had managed to pick himself up and limp along, as he described it, like a horse with three broken legs; with gleeful commiseration his (male) writer-friends who'd gone through more or less the same experiences called him, to welcome him to the club. It had been considered that Roland Marks might be "finished"—"close to finished." But out of an equal mixture of stubbornness and desperation he'd immersed himself in work, in "exile"—(that is, here in Nyack)—in a novel unique among Roland Marks's oeuvre in that it is mostly dialogue, though dealing with his usual subject of erotic obsession, in a mordantly comic style that made the book a number one bestseller.

Out of its own ashes, the Phoenix rises triumphant. Poor Phoenix!—(my father joked, in interviews)—*has he any choice but to survive?*

Living with a genius you come to realize: the "genius" is hidden from you, somewhere inside the deeply flawed if loveable and mortal person.

Waiting for the Chinese food to be delivered, I joined my father and his young blond companion in the sunroom, as they were stepping out onto the terrace, to look at the river.

Often my father stood on the terrace, taking photographs. In the relative tranquility of Nyack he'd learned to take quite beautiful photographs of shifting lights and weather on the Hudson River but disparaged them as "amateur"—he who had so pointed a respect for "professionals" in any field.

Of course, Dad couldn't resist inviting Cameron to climb down the wooden steps with him to the riverbank. Though the light was rapidly fading, and the steps were unsafe.

Quickly I said: "Dad? Remember, those steps are getting wobbly? I tied some tape there, that you ripped off . . ."

But my father scarcely listened to me. Nor did Cameron, laughing as the gallant elder gentleman slipped an arm through hers, seem to hear.

You would think that an intelligent and sharply observant young woman would be cautious about stepping onto rotted wood, even on the arm of a Nobel Prize winner. But in the gaiety of the moment nothing could have seemed more pleasurable than accompanying Roland Marks down the thirty-odd steps to the riverbank below— "All my property, Cameron. It's two point five acres."

I was relieved to see that the steps held beneath them. I must have exaggerated the danger. If there were individual steps that sagged, and one or two that had broken, at least the overall structure held firm.

I heard their laughter from below. Dad might have called me to come join them—but he didn't.

He's forgotten me. Wishes I weren't here.

They were down there for quite a while, walking on the riverbank with some difficulty since the bank was overgrown. I could hear my father chuckling about the swept-away dock—"Gone with the river!"

I wondered if my father continued to hold Cameron's arm, through his. Or whether he might be holding her hand, to prevent her stumbling.

Then, returning to the terrace, naturally my father had a little more difficulty ascending the steps, since the angle was steep, almost like a ladder. Cleverly Dad husbanded his strength pausing several times to point out to Cameron something of interest in the distance; he didn't want the girl to hear him breathing heavily. Nor did he want her to notice how he slightly favored his (arthritic) right knee.

Safely back up on the terrace he said to me, with an indulgent smile, "You worry too much, Dean Marks. 'Live dangerously'—as your old friend Nietzsche said."

Your old friend Nietzsche was an allusion to Lou Andreas-Salomé, I supposed. It was an allusion probably lost to Cameron Slatsky.

When the Chinese food was delivered, I prepared it as attractively as possible, and brought it to my father and Cameron in the sunroom, that now overlooked a murky river; when Cameron saw me carrying the tray, she made a pretense of leaping up to help me.

At dinner most of the talk was between my father and Cameron. At a certain point she even switched on the tape recorder—"I hope you don't mind, Mr.—Roland. The things you so casually say deserve to be kept for posterity."

Well, this was true. But Dad wouldn't have liked me to say so, and would have been furious and incredulous if I'd suggested "recording" his off-the-cuff conversation.

Wide-eyed and somber Cameron said to me, "Miss Marks, your father has been like this all day. Since I arrived. They say that Swinburne was a brilliant conversationalist. And Oscar Wilde, of course. And—Delmore Schwartz."

My father had known Delmore Schwartz. This was a (fairly crude) ploy to stir him into speaking of Schwartz, I supposed—but Dad, involved with chopsticks, merely grunted an assent.

"Miss Marks—I mean, 'Lou-Lou'" (this girly-frothy name Cameron spoke with the expression with which you might pick up a clumsy insect with a tweezers)—"as you must know, your father is—remarkable."

Benignly I smiled. It was pleasing to me, that I could handle chopsticks much better than Cameron Slatsky.

"Of course. Otherwise people wouldn't be begging to interview him and cluttering up his calendar."

"The most remarkable man I've ever met."

"But not the most remarkable *person* you've ever met?"

Cameron blinked at me naïvely. Dad intervened with a grunt of a laugh.

"Lou-Lou, you might not want to stay too long tonight. We won't be watching a DVD, obviously. Cameron and I have more serious things with which to occupy ourselves, OK?"

What could I say? That my Thursday evenings were reserved exclusively for my father; that this was what remained of "family night" in my life? That the prospect of returning home to the chilly, sparely furnished condominium in Skaatskill, and to my computer and administrative work until midnight, was heart-numbing?

"Of course."

They continued to talk of my father's books almost exclusively. It was astonishing to me that Cameron Slatsky had certainly read these books with care and with (evident) enjoyment. The early, "promising" novels; the massive "breakthrough" novel that had won major literary awards for its twenty-nine-year-old author; subsequent titles, some of them "controversial"—"provoking." My father's face was flushed with pleasure. Particularly my father enjoyed Cameron leafing through her photocopied pages to read aloud passages of his "mordant humor"—he laughed heartily, with her.

This conversation he would never have allowed within the family clearly gave him enormous happiness. There was no comparable happiness I could offer.

I had little appetite for dinner, though no one noticed. Dad and his avid young visitor drank wine. They were festive. They were *fun together* as if linked by an old, easy intimacy.

Plainly I saw: my father was mesmerized by Cameron Slatsky: that is, by the mirror she held up to him, of a "brilliant" man, a "remarkable" talent, one of the "major American writers of the twentieth century." It would have required a will of steel to resist such flattery, and my father had rather a will of gossamer; cotton candy. I thought *And yet, she's probably right. The words she utters. He is a great writer, if only he could believe it.*

For that was the paradox: like other writers of his generation, Roland Marks was both ego-centered and insecure; he believed that he was a literary genius—(otherwise, how could he have had the energy to write so many books?)—while at the same time he believed the worst things said of him by his critics and detractors. Even the Nobel Prize hadn't shored him up for long.

(When Norman Mailer died in 2007, at the age of eighty-four, Roland Marks had publicly lamented—"Now Norman will never win the damned Nobel! That's their loss.")

There was no hope, I thought. He would fall in love with this Cameron Slatsky—("Slutsky"?—I dared not joke about her name to him)—he had already fallen in love with her. *Brain, (male) genitals. Irresistible.*

I said, a little sharply, "But what about you, Cameron? We haven't heard a thing about you."

Sitting so close to the girl, it was difficult not to succumb to her warmly glowing personality; if I had not resolved to hate her, I would probably have liked her very much. She was beautiful—but awkward, unsure of herself. She was certainly very smart. As a professor I was inclined to like my students unless they gave me reason to feel otherwise, and Cameron Slatsky wasn't much older than our Riverdale undergraduates.

With a stricken look Cameron said, "Oh—*me?* There's n-nothing to say about *me* . . ."

"Well, where are you from?"

"Where am I *from* . . ."

Cameron shook her head mutely. Her face crinkled in an infantile way. At first I thought that she was laughing, fatuously; then I saw that she was fighting back tears.

"Oh well—my life is *too sad.* I don't want to talk about my life—*please.*"

This ploy had an immediate effect upon my father: he moved to sit beside Cameron, taking both her hands in his and asking her what she meant. I hadn't seen such an expression of tenderness in the man's face since—well, the incident on the hockey field. Presumably Roland Marks had been deeply moved by other events in his life—(the births of his youngest children, for instance)—but I hadn't witnessed them.

What a blunder I'd made, asking the girl about her personal life!

I'd taken for granted that it would be a conventional, proper, dull sub-urban life which would provoke my father's scorn; but quite the opposite had developed.

And it seemed to have been already arranged, to my surprise, yes and dismay, that Cameron would be staying the night in Nyack—"Since we have work tomorrow morning, it makes sense for Cameron not to commute all the way back to New York City."

All the way back! It was no farther than my "commute" to Skaatskill.

Calmly my father regarded me with bemused eyes. Asking if I would please check to see if the guest room was "in decent shape" for a guest?

I would, of course. I did. Like a house servant—or a slightly super-annuated wife—I brought in a supply of fresh towels for the adjoin-ing bathroom. The guest room was drafty from ill-fitting windows but that wasn't my concern.

Cameron had the graciousness to express embarrassment. She saw me to the door, since Dad wasn't inclined to rise to his feet after the intense two-hour dinner.

I would have slipped away with a muttered farewell, but Cam-eron insisted upon shaking my hand, and thanking me—for what, I couldn't imagine.

"I'm so happy to have met you, Lou-Lou!—as well as your amazing father. *So happy,* you can't imagine."

Yes. I could imagine.

I left them, trembling with indignation. Driving to the George Washington Bridge where once again wet rain was whipping into sleet, and the pavement was slick and dangerous.

"Accident. 'Accident-prone.' Who?"

NEXT DAY WHEN I telephoned my father, it was Cameron's bright voice that greeted me.

"Oh Lou-Lou—guess what! Your father has asked me to be his

assistant, and I've said 'yes.' I think that I can add my experience in some way to the dissertation material—like, a journal as an appendix?"

A memoir, most likely. Which you will write after the man's death.

DREAMS OF MY father's death.

"It was an accident. He didn't l-listen . . ."

Quickly before the will is changed. Before the *executrix* is changed.

Distracted by resentment and anxiety I made an effort to be all the more friendly, helpful, and alert in my dean's position. I was sympathetic with everyone who complained to me, I even shook hands with particular warmth. I stayed up until 2:00 A.M. answering e-mails including even e-mails from "concerned" parents. It was reasonable—(well, it was wholly unreasonable)—to think that, if I was a *good person*, I would be rewarded and not punished by Fate.

ONCE, I'D SAVED ROLAND MARKS'S LIFE.

I'd been twenty years old. I was to be a junior at Harvard, within a month.

My father was staying with wealthy friends on Martha's Vineyard in late August. With his third wife, gorgeous/unstable Avril Gatti. I was in a smaller guest house, that overlooked the water, when a girl in a bikini drove into the driveway in a little red Ferrari convertible.

She was sharp-beaked, like a hungry bird. Crimped dyed-red hair as if she'd stuck her finger in an electric socket.

"Is Roland Marks here? I have to see him."

"He isn't here. Is he expecting you?"

"Where is he? He's here."

"I'm sorry. This is not Roland Marks's house, and *he is not here.*"

"I know whose house this is. And I know *he is here.*"

Since the publication of *Jealousy*, and Roland Marks's figure, in tennis whites, on the cover of the *New York Times Magazine*, many people had tried to contact him. The usual sorts of people, but now others as well. A more *American-suburban* spread, not primarily Jewish-background as before. Dad laughed at the commotion but was beginning to become concerned.

"Philip is absolutely correct"—(Dad was referring to his friend Philip Roth)—"people naïvely think they want to become 'famous'—but it's nothing like what you expect. Instead of having the luxury of failure, which is being left alone, you're fair game for every idiot."

Rudely the bikini-girl was staring at me, in my shapeless Save-the-Whales T-shirt and drawstring sweatpants. Even my bare feet looked pudgy and graceless.

"Are you one of his daughters? Karin?"

"No."

"The other, then—'Lou-Lou.'"

"Louise."

"'Lou-Lou.'"

"Well, my father isn't here. He's in London."

In fact, Dad was sailing with our hosts. He'd be back within a few hours.

"No. He's on the island. I asked in town. There are no secrets here."

The bikini-girl was edging toward me in a way that made me nervous. Her body was fleshy and full yet her face looked drawn and there were distinct shadows beneath her eyes. She was glancing about, suspiciously. "He's—where? Down by the water? Upstairs in the house? And his wife—'Avril.' Where's she?"

I thought *She has something in that bag.*

It was a large Bloomingdale's sort of bag made of elegantly woven straw. The handles were tortoiseshell. The way the girl was gripping it, I understood that she had a weapon inside.

Calmly I said, with a forced smile, "I can leave a message with my father. He can call you."

She laughed. "Call me! Are you joking? He will never *call me*, he has said so."

"Then . . ."

"There was a time when that hypocritical son of a bitch called me, but now, I can't even call him; he never calls back. Your father is a terrible man. You know this, I'm sure. You don't look stupid—only just moon-faced and fat. I don't think that your father should be allowed to live."

Barefoot, with garishly painted toenails, the bikini-girl was edging toward the veranda of the main house, which was shingle board purposely stained to appear weatherworn, with a steep-pitched roof. Inside the house there were voices—I didn't know whose. I'd begun to sweat. My fatty upper arms stuck to my armpits. I was calculating that I would have to wrench the bag away from the bikini-girl with no hesitation, within seconds; if she stepped back from me, she could take out her weapon . . .

With my strained mouth I continued to smile. I saw that the girl had tiny rosebud or pursed-lips tattoos on her back. I saw that her bikini was striped iridescent-purple and that her flushed-looking hips and breasts were tightly constrained; she was breathing audibly.

"Wait, please."

"I'm just going to knock at the screen door."

"No, please—wait."

"I'll just call 'hello' inside. I won't go fucking *in*."

As the girl edged past me I stumbled to my feet and threw myself at her, and wrenched away the bag—it was heavy, as I'd suspected.

She began screaming. Cursing me. She clawed at me but I didn't surrender the bag. Our hosts' adult daughter came out of the house, astonished. A Portuguese water spaniel, that had been sleeping on the veranda nearby, began barking hysterically. The girl ran stumbling to the little Ferrari, where she'd left the key in the ignition;

haphazardly she backed out of the driveway, all the while cursing us.

In the elegantly woven bag was a snub-nosed revolver. In fact it was a Smith & Wesson .25-caliber "snubbie"—a semi-automatic with a mother-of-pearl handle that carried six rounds. It would turn out to be a stolen gun, sold to the bikini-girl in New York City; a *female* sort of gun, though close up it could be fatal.

Our hosts' daughter called the Vineyard police and the girl was arrested within a half hour as she tried to buy a ticket for the ferry.

It would be said that she was *one of Roland Marks's girls. One who hadn't worked out.*

My father refused to discuss her. My father professed not to know her—never to have heard of her. His wife Avril did not believe him. The bikini girl was older than she'd seemed: thirty-two. She'd been arrested for carrying an unlicensed and concealed gun. She lived in TriBeCa and described herself as an actress associated with La MaMa. Later, we would learn that, the previous summer, she'd stalked Philip Roth in Cornwall Bridge, Connecticut, though, like my father, Philip had declined to press charges against her.

Dad had not wanted to talk about the bikini-girl. No one could make Dad talk about the bikini-girl. Not even Avril Gatti. To me he said, with his utterly charming abashed-Dad smile: "Thanks, kid. You did good."

ANOTHER TIME WHEN I CALLED MY FATHER, IT WAS CAMERON who answered the telephone.

"Hi! Lou-Lou? We have news here—we're flying to Miami tomorrow."

And so there was no Thursday evening dinner that week. Nor the next week. Rudely, I wasn't notified until I made a call, and Cameron called back to explain apologetically that she and my father were flying to Key West from Miami—"You know, the Key West Literary Seminar? Roland is giving the keynote speech."

I had known that the revered Key West seminar was imminent. But I'd been led to believe that I was to accompany my father.

At last I managed to speak with him. My voice must have been quavering with hurt for Dad chided me kindly.

"Lou-Lou, things have changed. Cameron's coming with me—of course."

"You told me—'mark on my calendar. Key West.' You told me 'don't make other plans.'"

In red ink several days in early January had been marked on my calendar. There was no mistaking this.

In fact, I'd been invited to a party, or—to something . . . I hadn't accepted of course since I'd planned to be in Key West with Roland Marks.

I came close to blurting out *Take me with you, please! I will pay for my own way.*

I didn't, though. A dean is dignity.

Shamelessly and unapologetically they went together, and without me. And my father had the temerity to ask me to "check in" on the house in his absence.

THE FURNACE WAS REPAIRED, finally. Faulty smoke detectors were repaired. I called a carpenter to inspect the shaky wooden steps leading to the riverbank that needed to be strengthened and the man promised to call me back with an estimate. He couldn't begin work, he said, until at least late March when the weather was warmer and ice had melted from the steps.

Daringly—cautiously—I climbed down a half-dozen of the steps, to see how rickety they actually were. The January air was cold, and windy, rising from the steel-colored river. Obviously each winter had weakened the steps; the structure had to be at least twenty years old. (The house itself was 106 years old—an Upper Nyack landmark. I wanted to think that one day there would be a brass plaque on the front: *Residence of Roland R. Marks, Nobel Prize in Literature.*)

Tightly I clutched the railings imagining the rickety structure suddenly buckling beneath my weight, collapsing, and my body falling heavily to the rocky ground below . . . My father would find me when he returned, a broken body, frozen . . .

Why didn't I invite Lou-Lou to come with us! How could I have been so selfish!

And Cameron would say *Don't blame yourself, Roland! You could not have foreseen.*

In my melancholy mood, almost I wouldn't have minded falling—or so the thought came to me.

I didn't fall. The steps held. Though some of the steps were shaky, the structure held.

YET IT COULD *happen to him. An accident. Accidental death.*

AN ACCIDENTAL DEATH is always a surprise. At least, to the one who dies by accident.

In the days, twelve in all, that my father and Cameron were in Florida, I spent more time than I could really afford in the house in Upper Nyack.

I was thinking how Roland Marks disliked *surprise*. The element of *surprise* was vulgar to him, like the antics of circus clowns.

Except if he were the one doling out the *surprise*, then it was fine. Then, it might be classified as "humor."

I knew this, for I knew him—thoroughly. Others have imagined they've known my father, unauthorized biographers have sniffed and snooped in his wake and much garbage has been written of him—but no one has plumbed Roland Marks's *essence*.

I wondered what Cameron Slatsky would write about him, some-time in the future. When my father wasn't alive to read it, and to recoil in horror and disgust.

I had to protect him against her, I thought. Or better—(since another "Cameron" would appear, probably within a few months)—I had to protect Roland Marks against himself.

DAD HAD ALWAYS been admiring, in his way.

Grudging, yet admiring.

For he'd had a habit of saying, even when I was much too old for such personal remarks, "You're my big husky gal. You don't need any man to protect you. Nothing weak or puling about *you*."

The emphasis—*you*. Meaning that I was to be distinguished from the weak, puling, manipulative females who surrounded my father and other luckless men.

"In the female, sex is a weapon. Initially a lure, then—a weapon. But there are those who, like my exemplary daughter, refuse to play the dirty little game. They *transcend*, and they *excel*."

He'd actually said such things in company, in my presence. As if I were an overgrown child and not a fully mature young woman.

Sometimes, he'd been drinking. He'd become sentimental and maudlin lamenting the "estrangement" of his other children, and the "bizarre, self-destructive" behavior of their mothers.

It was painful to me, yet I suppose flattering—how my father boasted of his "exemplary" daughter. Often, I felt that he didn't know me at all; he was creating a caricature, or a cartoon, adorned with my name. Even when he was looking straight at me his eyes seemed unfo-cused.

"Lou-Lou's my most astonishing child. There's nothing mysteri-ous or subtle about Lou-Lou—she is *all heart*. She isn't obscure, and she isn't devious. She's an athlete." (Though I hadn't been an athlete for years. Most girls give up team sports forever after high school.)

"Did I ever tell you about how Lou-Lou played field hockey—really down-dirty, competitive field hockey—at the Rye Academy? Up there in Connecticut? I'd drive up to watch her play—stay overnight in the little town—at one of the championship games she was hit in the mouth with a puck—no, a hockey stick—and just kept charging on—running down the field bleeding from the mouth—and made a score for her team. And afterward she came limping over to me where I was standing in front of the bleachers anxious to see what had happened to her and Lou-Lou says, 'Hi Dad'—or 'Hey Dad, look'—and in the palm of her hand, a little broken white thing. And I said, 'What's that, Lou-Lou?' and she said, 'What's it look like, Dad?' and I looked more closely and saw it was a tooth, and I said, 'Oh, sweetie—it looks like about five thousand bucks. But you're worth it.'"

This was a wonderful story. One of Roland Marks's wonderful family stories. In his fiction most of his family stories were comical catastrophes but when he was talking to friends, or to a friendly audience, his family stories were wonderful.

Even his detractors warmed to Roland Marks at such times. Even those who knew he was confabulating, in his zeal to tell the ideal, the perfect, the *family story*.

In my father's absence, I cherished such memories.

In my father's absence that was a betrayal, and a warning of betrayals to come, I visited my father's house on Cliff Street, Upper Nyack, with a pretense of "checking" the house; wandering through the drafty rooms, standing outside on the terrace and gazing at the broad misty river below, shivering in the cold I told myself *There have been precious memories even if they are laced with lies.*

"LOU-LOU? WHAT'S THIS I HEAR? ANOTHER—? AGAIN—?"

People began to call me. In the wake of the Key West Literary

Seminar at which the celebrated Roland Marks and a "very young, very blond" Ph.D. student from Columbia were clearly a *couple.*

Dad's longtime agent called. Max Keller had known Roland Marks for more than forty years, why was he so surprised? I wasn't in a mood to share his incredulous indignation commingled with pity and, yes, envy: "At least, tell me her age. People are saying—twenty-four? And Roland is *seventy-four?*"

Through clenched teeth I told Max that I didn't know the young woman's age.

"Her name?"

"I don't know her name. I've forgotten."

"And is she good-looking?"

"I have no idea. I've barely glimpsed her."

"And is she *smart?* People are saying so . . ."

"Max, I have no idea. I'm going to hang up now."

"And Roland is in love? This is serious? Maybe?"

"Look. He's elderly. He needs an assistant—his papers, manuscripts, letters are a mess. And he needs a full-time attendant to take care of him—he has let his house go, he's like a baby when it comes to *living.* It can't be me to take care of him—I have my own life. She came to interview him, and essentially, she stayed. She is young, and she is blond. What else? In the past, Dad just took up with 'women'— good-looking, glamorous women—the assistants and interns were a separate category. But now, this might be the first time he combines the two so maybe that will be an improvement."

I'd spoken breezily, to hide my anger. I'd meant to be amusing but Max didn't seem to think that I was very funny.

"She'll get Roland to sign a pre-nup. She'll insist on money up front, if she's smart. (She sounds smart.) And she'll wind up the executrix of his estate, Lou-Lou—not you. So don't be so amused, my dear." And he hung up.

Executrix of his estate. But I was Roland Marks's executrix!

After the last divorce, he'd made me his executrix. Before this, he hadn't had a will: he'd assumed, as he said, that he would be around for a "long, long time—like one of those giant tortoises that live forever." But in his late sixties, after batterings in court, he'd begun to feel mortal. He'd told me frankly that he would be leaving money to all of his children, even those who'd disappointed him pretty badly, and from whom he was estranged—"I don't want to single you out, Lou-Lou. They would just hate you." But what Dad would do for me, beyond leaving me money—(which, in fact, I really didn't need, as a professional woman with a good job)—was to name me executrix of his estate, which would include his literary estate, for which service I would be paid a minimum of fifty thousand dollars a year.

I'd been deeply moved. I may even have cried.

I'd said, "Dad, I can't think of this now. I can't think of you—not here. But I will be the very best 'literary executrix' who ever was—you deserve nothing less. I promise."

"I know, Lou-Lou. You're my good girl."

AFTER KEY WEST, they returned to Nyack briefly. No time to see Lou-Lou—though at least Dad spoke to me on the phone.

They were on their way to Paris, where Roland Marks was to be feted on the occasion of the publication of a newly translated novel; and from Paris, to Rome, where another newly translated novel was being launched; and from Rome to Barcelona and Madrid . . .

By now, they were lovers. Of course.

I wondered *how*.

(At seventy-four, my father was still a virile man—it would seem.)

(Yet, at twenty-four, his new lover might be repelled by him—wasn't that reasonable to suppose?)

(No. This is not a reasonable situation.)

(Yes. It is utterly reasonable—it is *pragmatic*. She will marry him for his money and his reputation and not his "virility.")

Lying in my bed in Skaatskill, I was helpless in the grinding maw of such obsessive thoughts.

"He won't betray me. Even if he marries her . . ."

(Ridiculous! He'd betrayed virtually everyone in his life, every *female*. Why not reliable old Lou-Lou with her pearly false tooth?)

Dad had asked me to continue to "check" the house, so of course I did. Bitterly resenting being treated as a servant and yet—grateful. More than I needed, I visited the house; I brought in Dad's mail, which was considerable; sorted it, left it in carefully designated stacks on his desk—the work of an assistant; but the assistant wasn't on the premises, *I was*.

At Riverdale, I now left my office promptly at 5:00 P.M. most days, where once I'd remained until much later. And now on Friday afternoons, I sometimes left as early as 3:00 P.M. ("Family matters"—"my father, medical appointment.") Or took the entire afternoon off.

There were academic events I had to attend, national conventions— these I cut short, to return to Nyack and drive past the house on Cliff Street which was looking shut-up, unattended. With my key I let myself in and prowled the rooms like a clumsy ghost. I knew the house so well, yet stumbled. I collided with things. Seeing my reflection in mirrors—"Oh, Lou-Lou? What has happened? You were just a girl . . ."

I was doing my father's bidding and yet: I was an intruder.

Easily, I might become a vandal.

For there was some secret in this place, that might be revealed to me if I prevailed. Though Dad would have been furious, I looked through his desk drawers, and his filing cabinets; there were literally thousands of papers, documents, manuscripts in his keeping, in his study and in an adjoining room; his older manuscripts, galleys, page proofs and drafts were stored temporarily at the New York Public Library, which was negotiating to purchase the entire Marks archive. It was not true that my father's papers were a mess as I'd told Max

Keller—but they did require a more systematic organization, which only I could provide, I believed.

Only I! The exemplary beloved daughter.

I lay on the bamboo settee in the sunroom staring out at the sky and the river below. Soon, my father and Cameron would return—she was now his "fiancée."

The Hudson Valley: such beauty! But it was not always an evident, obvious beauty—the beauty of a river depends upon weather, gradations of light. The ceaseless shifting of sunshine, shadow. Cloud formations, patches of clear sky. An eye-piercing blue. Dull gunmetal-gray. The river reflecting the sky, and the sky seeming to reflect the river.

I was thinking of the English explorer Henry Hudson who'd sailed up the river for the Dutch, in the early seventeenth century, until, about 150 miles north, the river became too shallow for him to navigate. How bizarre it seems to us, Hudson had been looking for a route to the Pacific Ocean, as his predecessor Christopher Columbus had been looking for a route to the East Indies . . . I thought *The routes we think we are taking are not the routes we will take. The routes that take us.*

I must have fallen asleep for I was rudely awakened by a loud rapping at the front door.

It was the carpenter I'd tried to engage to repair the steps. I had not heard from the man in weeks and now, as if on a whim, or more likely he'd happened to be driving by the house, he'd stopped to speak with me.

We went out onto the terrace, to look at the steps. He'd given me his estimate for the repair but I had no way of knowing how reasonable it was, for I hadn't called anyone else. He said, "I could begin next week, Mrs. Marks. I've got the lumber, and I've cleared away the time."

"Next week—really?"

Then for a long moment I stood silent. Almost, I'd forgotten the man, the stranger, standing close beside me, the two of us looking down at the steps; then I said, "I'm truly sorry, but my father has changed his mind. He says he wants something more ambitious. He's been talking to an architect."

"An architect? For just some steps?"

I laughed, awkwardly. "Well, he wants something more ambitious for the terrace, and the steps, and down below on the riverbank, something like a gazebo. You might know my father Roland Marks—he never does anything simply."

Of course, the carpenter didn't know Roland Marks. He had no idea who Roland Marks might be, and judging by the disgruntled noises he was making, he didn't care.

THEY RETURNED. The *fiancée* was now living at 47 Cliff Street, Upper Nyack.

Not often, not every week, but occasionally they invited me to have dinner with them. And when they were away, to check on the house and bring in my father's mail.

On the third finger of her left hand, Cameron wore an engagement ring. A large diamond—ridiculous! Roland Marks had often commented disparagingly on the absurdity of engagement rings, wedding rings; he'd never worn a wedding ring, himself.

When are you planning to be married?—I did not ask.

Cameron was kind to me, at least. Kinder than my father who often seemed irritable at the sight of me as if it might be guilt he truly felt, but couldn't acknowledge.

Though Dad surprised me one day by asking if I kept in contact with my mother and when I said yes, asking me how she was.

The truth was, my mother had survived. She'd long ago remarried and was living in Fort Lauderdale with her (aging, ailing) second husband, and was on reasonably good terms with her adult children, whose children she adored. And she never asked after Roland Marks as one might never speak of a virulent illness she'd narrowly survived.

I said, "Mom is doing great, Dad. Thank you for asking."

"Why 'thank you'?—that's a strange thing to say." Dad lowered his voice, so that Cameron in the other room wouldn't hear. "I was married to your mother once, for almost twenty years! Of course I would want to know how she is."

Years ago, as a girl, I'd have felt a clutch of hope in my heart, hearing these words from my father. *Maybe he will return. Maybe he will love us again.* But now I knew better. I knew the words were only words.

ONCE, I FOLLOWED Cameron Slatsky in Nyack. By accident I'd seen her on the street, a tall leggy blond girl in jeans and a pullover sweater looking, from a distance, like a teenager.

Heads turned as she passed. She seemed not to notice.

Why, she was *preoccupied*. Somber-seeming. Her hair tied back in an ordinary ponytail. And her shoulders slouched. By the time she was forty, she'd be round-shouldered.

But Roland Marks wouldn't be alive to see her then.

At a discreet distance I followed her. It wasn't so very unlikely that I might have been in Nyack that day—if Cameron saw me, I could explain convincingly.

She stopped by the Cheese Board. Buying my father's special cheeses, and his special (pumpernickel) bread. She stopped by the Nyack Pharmacy. Picking up my father's prescription medications. She stopped by the Riverview Gallery where there was an exhibit of new paintings by a local artist.

The gallery had a side entrance. Through the doorway I observed the young blond woman moving slowly from canvas to canvas, with the sobriety of a schoolgirl. No one else appeared to be in the gallery except a female clerk.

The painter whose work was being exhibited was Hilma Matthews, a woman in her late seventies with a respectful reputation as an abstract artist; she'd once had a Madison Avenue gallery but had been exiled to Nyack, where she lived about a mile from my father. They were old friends: not lovers, I don't think. Once Hilma had said bitterly to my father, "Some of us don't make the cut. It isn't evident why." And my father had blushed, guessing that this remark was meant to be an insult to him, who'd clearly made the cut; at the same time, it was enough of an oblique insult that he didn't have to acknowledge it. Gallantly he said, with a squeeze of the woman's hand, "Posterity judges, not us. Be happy in your work, Hilma. It's beautiful work—enough of us know. That's the main thing."

As Cameron moved about the gallery, very seriously considering Hilma Matthews's art, I continued to observe her. I wondered at her motive—was she planning to talk about the exhibit, to impress my father? Had she been invited with my father to a local event, where she might meet the artist? I couldn't believe that she was acting without motive, out of a genuine interest in these large abstract canvases by Hilma Matthews, in the style of a more hard-edged Helen Frankenthaler.

Cameron and the woman at the front desk fell into a conversation. It seemed that they were talking about the exhibit, though I couldn't hear most of their words.

I did manage to hear the woman ask Cameron if she lived here and Cameron said yes—"For the present time."

I waited to overhear her boast of *Roland Marks*. But Cameron said nothing further.

I had an impulse to come forward and say hello to Cameron. She couldn't have known that I'd followed her here—my greeting could have been spontaneous, innocent.

I thought, if I hadn't known her, I might have introduced myself to her in the gallery. I might have thought *A sensitive, intelligent person. And beautiful.* I might have asked *Are you new to Nyack?*

THAT SPRING.

That final spring of my father's life.

It was my work at Riverdale College from which I was becoming increasingly distracted. Initially I'd thrown myself into it with renewed energy as a way of quite consciously *not thinking about my father's fiancée*; then, I discovered myself daydreaming in my office, rehearsing scenes with my father and Cameron Slatsky. Sometimes it seemed urgent to me that I *act quickly*, before they were married; at other times, I was gripped with lethargy as if in the coils of a great boa constrictor.

I should have spoken with Cameron in the gallery, I thought. Or met up with her on the street.

Just the two of us: the women in Roland Marks's present life.

I'd tried to make discreet inquiries about Cameron Slatsky at Columbia, but had been reluctant to provide my name; if it were revealed that I'd been prying, I would have been humiliated; my father would have been furious at me, and might not have wanted to see me again. He was famous for *breaking off* with people he'd known well, and had loved, if he believed he'd been disrespected.

What I'd been able to learn about Cameron Slatsky online was not exceptional, nor did it conflict with what she'd told us. She had graduated from Barnard with a B.A. in English and linguistics; she'd been a summer intern for a New York publishing house, and for the *New Yorker*; she'd traveled briefly in Europe, with friends; she'd enrolled in the Ph.D. English program at Columbia. She'd grown up in Katonah, Westchester County. Her parents must have had money, for someone was paying her tuition at Columbia.

Since moving into my father's house, with an upstairs room designated as her study, Cameron continued to work on her dissertation, as she said, *on site*. Living with the subject of a doctoral dissertation! Quite a *coup* for one so young.

Obsessively I rehearsed my conversation with Cameron.

Pointing out to her that any relationship with my father was doomed to be impermanent; that, even if he claimed to adore her he didn't adore *her*; he adored the person who adored *him*.

And then I thought, she knows this. Of course.

She knows, and doesn't care.

If he adores her as his muse, or just wants to have sex with someone so young—why would she care? She'd spent enough time perusing the more sensational literary biographies and collected letters to come to a realization that, in a sequence of wives, it's only the final wife—the widow—who inherits the estate.

In this matter of the serial womanizer, it's the elderly serial womanizer you want to marry.

At Dad's age, and at her age, Cameron Slatsky would prevail: she would survive. The other wives had been sloughed off like old skins.

How many American (male) writers, including writer-friends of my father, had entered into marriages exactly like this! Elderly distinguished men with international reputations who'd long ago worn out their first wives; who'd married women young as their daughters, or younger; in some cases they'd even sired children, of the age of their grandchildren. The dominant male married the subservient female: there could be no question of equality in these relationships.

My father's friend the poet Mordecai Kaplan had been committed to a psychiatric nursing home by his wife who was forty years younger than he; at the time, Kaplan was eighty-nine. The fiery young woman, herself a poet, had managed to acquire his power of attorney—"When a man gives up his power of attorney, he's finished. Like castration, it's final," my father said. Kaplan's middle-aged children tried to protest; tried to get a court injunction, to take him from the home; younger poets who'd been his students came to his rescue, or tried to; Roland Marks had pleaded with the wife but they'd had an ugly scene and she'd ordered my father never to try to see her husband again, or she'd have him arrested. She might have been mentally unbalanced, this young wife. (Not so young: at least forty.) She'd made a project of pursuing and capturing Mordecai Kaplan and plucking him from his wife of more than thirty years. The Kaplans' marriage had been a reasonably happy one and yet, as Dad liked to say—*Instead of the brain, there's the male genitalia.*

Eventually, the situation spilled over into the press. There was an article sympathetic to Kaplan and his supporters, and by implication critical of the wife, in the *New York Times*. Still, Mrs. Kaplan refused to allow anyone to arrange for her husband to be moved from the nursing home; though he wasn't senile, only just physically frail and needing a wheelchair. She succeeded in restricting his visitors, which was the deepest blow. She succeeded in curtailing his letters to family and friends, from the nursing home, by threatening the staff with lawsuits. She'd been named Kaplan's executrix in his will and so she was to have total power over his estate, when he died; she would inherit his many copyrighted titles, his royalties, his letters, his treasures—everything.

I thought that I would bring up the example of my father's tragic friend to him but I knew that Dad would respond angrily: "Look. Mordecai was ninety-two when he died. I'm twenty years younger, or nearly. His wife was a vicious psychopath. My wife will be my closest friend."

I could not bear to hear Dad say those words—*My wife.*

"Dean Marks? Is something wrong?"

My assistant Olivia stood in the doorway of my office, looking very concerned. She was a gracious woman of approximately my age, whom I'd inherited with the dean's office. Quickly I told her that my father had a medical condition—"Not an emergency. Minor. But upsetting."

Olivia asked if there was anything she could do?

"Thank you, Olivia, but no."

Then, a few minutes later, ringing her in her office: "I think that

I'm going to be leaving a little earlier today . . . Could you cancel my appointments, please?"

"NOT GOOD, LOU-LOU. Terrible news."

But it was news my father could only share with *me*.

The lawsuit initiated by the aging Broadway actress Sylvia Sachs had gone badly for Roland Marks. In addition to the large sum of money he'd had to pay Sylvia at the time of their divorce six years before, he now had to pay $750,500. The judge had somehow been convinced by Sylvia's lawyer that her claim to have helped written—"supplied primary material for"—my father's most recent novel wasn't preposterous, as everyone knew it was; he'd been convinced that Roland Marks was a "sexual predator" and "exploiter of women." All of Roland Marks's fiction written since he and Sylvia had begun living together was the result of "intimate, protracted conversations" between them; at least two of his female characters were based upon Sylvia, she claimed. (It was true, my father had published a devastating portrait of a vindictive, small-minded "quasi-Broadway" actress in a recent novel, but the character was a fictional construct, not in some way a "real person.") Years before, my father had been found liable for "defamation" of Avril Gatti in the novel *Travesty*, couched in the tones of his hero Rabelais. *Travesty* could not be confused with "realistic" writing—of course. This genre of fiction was a kind of tall tale told with a ribald gusto, male speech addressed to male readers, as distorted a reflection of "real people" as Japanese anime figures are distorted. Anyone with more than a high school knowledge of literature would have understood that Roland Marks's portraits of people out of his personal life bore the relationship that Francis Bacon's or Picasso's portraits bore to their subjects. Where there is art, there is *no literal representation*.

Yet, the words Avril Gatti had contested were damaging, and damning, read aloud in the silent courtroom by the litigant's lawyer in a voice of fastidious disgust. No one dared laugh: no one wished to laugh. I'd wanted to protest: "But my father is a *great writer*, like Rabelais! You can't put an artist on trial."

Of course, this could only have made things worse. Such special pleading for the uniqueness of the artist doesn't go over well in a democracy.

Even now, Avril Gatti wasn't finished with litigation, my father had been warned. And just yesterday, this devastating award to Sylvia Sachs!

My father's lawyer had suggested an appeal. And so my father was going to appeal.

"They can't touch future work of mine, at least," Dad said bravely. "Now—I have to live."

It was a solace to me, that my father discussed the lawsuits with me rather than with Cameron. Or at least, in addition to Cameron.

My opinions were more valuable to him, than hers. For I'd known the litigants involved—my fierce stepmothers.

I DID NOT LIKE THESE CONVERSATIONS ABOUT THE FUTURE, that left me faint and anxious. For I could not truly envision a world in which Roland Marks did not live, even if Roland Marks's living caused pain for some persons including me.

I did not want my wonderful father to die. I did want the besotted old fool of a father, who'd become infatuated with a girl who might've been his granddaughter, to—well, *pass away*.

That Dad was both wonderful and a besotted old fool at the same time was difficult to comprehend. Like juggling two large and unwieldy clubs above my head, risking the prospect of being struck by one or both.

In his life, Dad believed in a tragic destiny for humankind: there were shelves in his library crammed with books about the Holocaust, many of them memoirs. He'd known Holocaust survivors, of course; a few had been his relatives, from Eastern Europe. But in his art, Dad believed in the sunnier realms of comedy: the idiosyncratic twist that the human imagination could give to any story, no matter how steeped in sorrow. To Roland Marks, comedy meant *freedom*; tragedy meant *imprisonment*.

He'd developed elaborate arguments on the subject. He'd published essays on the subject. He'd resented the predilection of certain reviewers for the "tragic vision" over the "comic vision"—to Dad, shaping comedy out of contemporary American life was much more challenging than shaping tragedy. He was furious that his *oeuvre* might be confined to the second tier, beneath works of tragedy. It didn't help to consider that Shakespeare's most profound works were his tragedies and not his comedies.

In recent novels, in the interstices of antic and convoluted plots, Dad had taken up speculating about mysticism. Not Jewish mysticism, not the Kabbalah, which would have made a kind of sense, but his own mix of idiosyncratic interpretations of Zen Buddhism, Hindu pantheism, and 1960s sexual liberation. (Dad did not ever "do" drugs—he considered drugs dangerous as a "leveler" of intellect and imagination.)

But ordinary life with its sane perimeters and marital and parental responsibilities did not much appeal to my father, for its very ordinariness. You could not win awards—you could not win a Nobel Prize—by writing about ordinary Americans leading ordinary lives.

Cameron once said to me: "Lou-Lou? Does Roland really—you know—*believe* in this 'spirit stuff'? Or is it kind of wishful thinking?"

"You'd have to ask him."

Though I might have said *My father is a secular Jew, a rationalist. He is not a half-baked mystic.*

"Oh, no—I couldn't ask *him*. Roland would be offended. The novels he writes he says are 'fiction'—not him. What's in the novels is a kind of bread baking, he says, with all sorts of ingredients, and spices—and yeast: it's there to make the bread rise, and bake. That's the purpose. Not if you 'believe' in yeast, you just use it."

Cameron spoke so ardently, with such wide-set unblinking eyes, I found myself staring at her, at a loss for words.

IT HAD BEEN hinted to me from the start of my deanship at Riverdale College that one day, before too long, I might be invited to take over the presidency. And so when the president asked me to have lunch with her privately, in the dining room of the president's residence, I prepared myself for this possibility. *Thank you so much. But with a current crisis in my life—my family life . . . I think the responsibility would be too much.*

It was flattering to be asked, however! Flattering to be considered.

Though, as Dad would point out, Riverdale College is "pretty small potatoes." He'd have preferred me to stay at classy Wesleyan, or "move up" to one of the Ivies.

The president of our college knew very well who Roland Marks was, of course. She asked about him at our luncheon and I said, with an airy laugh, for I'd been feeling light-headed after a very bad sleepless night, "He is entering upon his final folly."

The president chose to interpret this as a witty, though not a very funny, remark.

Quickly I said, more seriously: "Oh, he's fine. He has just completed a major new novel—*Patricide*. You'll probably be hearing about it in about a year. Over spring break I hope to read it, and confer with him about it, as I usually do with his novels . . ."

So we spoke of Roland Marks for a while. The president of our little college had been trying to inveigle—that is, to invite—my father to visit the college, and to accept an honorary degree at commencement, for years; even before my arrival, the college had issued invitations to the distinguished writer who lived "just over the George Washington Bridge" from the college. But Roland Marks, who hated the pomp and circumstance of commencements, accepted such invitations only from the top Ivy League universities, or smaller institutions that *paid*. (Dad could command somewhere in the vicinity of ten thousand dollars for a commencement speech which he'd adroitly tailor to fit the situation. A single commencement address had served him for decades like one-size-fits-all sweatpants and had yielded somewhere in the vicinity of two hundred thousand dollars.) The problem was, Riverdale College had a small, eroding endowment and so hoped to acquire my celebrity-writer father for no fee, and I'd been the awkward go-between for several seasons. Dad said, chuckling, "What a sap I'd be, Lou-Lou, to sit through your commencement ceremony, give an 'inspiring talk,' have lunch with the trustees, for *zero bucks*. Bad enough to get *zero bucks* at Harvard, but hell—that's Harvard."

Each time, I was embarrassed to return to the college to make excuses for my father who was to be traveling in Europe at commencement time, or committed to another commencement. Each time, the zealous president promised to invite my father for the following year.

"... have seemed distracted, Lou-Lou. For the past several months. And so I've been thinking, maybe it's time for you to consider stepping down—that is, returning to teaching ..."

These words out of the president's mouth I did not entirely fathom.

Was the woman asking me, in this roundabout way, to take her place as *president*? Was she asking me to *step down* from the deanship, that I might *step up* as president?

"I—I'm sorry—I don't quite understand?"

" ... your performance as dean has been, I'm afraid, increasingly erratic. Your staff has become demoralized, and faculty have complained ..."

In a haze of incomprehension I sat at the president's cherrywood dining room table, as the woman spoke on, on and on; for there was no way to stop her, and no end to all that she had to say in her kindly-yet-unhesitating manner.

" . . . finish up the term of course, we hope . . . I've asked Esther Conrad to assist you . . . move her office into the room adjacent to yours. A complete physical exam might not be a bad idea . . . our insurance will pay . . . And at faculty meetings, if . . ."

The haze like cotton batting had invaded my ears. Pushing into my brain that had gone numb. Blindly I reached for my water glass—and knocked it over. Water and ice cubes went spilling. The president veered back but couldn't escape an ice cube or two in her lap. Nervously laughing I recalled, as a girl, overturning my water glass during meals at home, and my father, for whom domestic occasions were something of a strain, an interruption from his far more urgent writerly life upstairs in his study, saying wittily, if sarcastically—*Well if there's a fire on the table now it's out. Thank you, Lou-Lou!*

How young he'd been then. Wickedly handsome with a bristling dark goatee.

I rose to my feet. I was shaky but undefeated. I would report to my father this outrage. Yet calmly I said, "I will think over your proposal, President Lacey. I will think it over and get back to you, soon."

A dignified exit. No looking back.

DRIVING HOME THAT EVENING confounded *Did she really mean to demote me, or—promote me? Was it code for—would I want to become president?*

" 'Thank you, but no. My life with my father has to take precedence right now.' "

APRIL 14, 2012. NOT A DAY I'D PLANNED TO SPEND IN UPPER Nyack.

It was a sun-warmed fragrant Saturday, and—who knew?—possibly my father and Cameron were away for the weekend, or in

New York City; frequently they spent evenings in the city, or stayed overnight as guests in one or another of my father's (usually wealthy, Upper West Side) admirers' apartments. It was Cameron who told me about such evenings, casually—"They said to say hello to you, Lou-Lou. The Steinglasses."

"Who?"

"Edythe and Steve? Steinglass?"

No idea who this was but I smiled as if in gratitude at being remembered, by someone.

"Well—thanks! Is their place still so great?"

"Yes. It is *fantastic*."

"Overlooking the park?"

"At Seventy-third Street. Yes."

Each weekend they were away, or mysteriously unaccounted-for, I dreaded to hear, belatedly—*Lou-Lou guess what! Your dad and I are married.*

Or, more somberly, though with a helpless baby-smile, from Dad—*Lou-Lou, sorry! We wanted a private ceremony, no fuss.*

What relief then, that day, to so casually drop by the house on Cliff Street, and there was Cameron in jeans and short-sleeved T-shirt raking the neglected front lawn in which, in jagged clusters, daffodils and jonquils were brightly blooming; ponytailed Cameron who waved at me, and smiled—"Hi, Lou-Lou! We've been missing you."

This had to be a lie. But it was a gracious sort of lie.

Very different from Dad's grumbling greeting, as I knocked very lightly on the (opened) door of his study—"Lou-Lou! Good! I need to talk to you about these God-damned *bills*."

Dad frequently confused those bills he asked me to pay for him, out of his checking account, with bills he'd paid, or intended to pay, himself; inevitably, there were mistakes. Sometimes we both paid the same bill, sometimes no one paid. When I told Dad that it would be easier for us both if I paid his bills via computer, he refused to listen—

"And what if the damned computer 'crashes'? What then? Paper checks are at least something you can *feel*."

This had been going on for years. This was a disgruntlement that felt easy and comfortable, like worn bedroom slippers.

I laughed thinking *This is what a family is. This.*

And later that afternoon, when, it seemed to have developed, I would be staying for dinner, and Cameron and I were to prepare together one of Dad's favorite meals, chicken tagine with prunes, dried apricots, almonds, and couscous, another incident occurred that gave me, if not hope exactly, a sense that things might not be so hopeless as I'd been thinking: by chance, I overheard my father speaking in a low, sarcastic voice to Cameron, in an adjacent room.

Poor Cameron! I felt a thrill of sympathy.

Recalling how many times I'd heard Roland Marks speak in this way, within my hearing or not-quite, to one or another of his wives—my mother, Phyllis, Avril, Sylvia. Inevitably, Roland Marks would *find fault* with a woman, or rather, the woman's imperfection would be revealed. In this case, so far as I could gather—(for truly I didn't want to eavesdrop, and especially I didn't want to be caught eavesdropping)—the zealous and well-intentioned assistant had filed away some of my father's papers on her own accord, without his having instructed her; or possibly, something was "lost" in my father's office, that had been the assistant's responsibility. And so Dad spoke harshly to Cameron, who didn't seem to be defending herself; only perhaps murmuring *Yes yes I'm sorry* in the way that, if a whipped dog could speak, a whipped dog would speak in such a circumstance.

Not all of Roland Marks's women had been so meekly apologetic, so subservient. Even my mother had tried to defend herself, sometimes. And others had quarreled with him, quite fiercely, even hatefully, at a time in their relationship when it was clear that Roland no longer much loved or respected them. But Cameron Slatsky—so young, inexperienced—so in awe of *the great man*—seemed to have been struck dumb.

The scolding went on and on, and on. I felt sorry for the blundering assistant and at the same time gratified for it was the first time I'd heard my father address Cameron in such a way; and I understood it would not be the last.

Later, Cameron was upstairs in "her" room. She'd hidden herself away in tears, or shame. She'd been embarrassed to have been scolded when I was in the house, perhaps; but I wouldn't let on, when we prepared dinner, that I'd heard anything at all. I would talk of other things, perhaps as if casually I would bring up the exhibit at the gallery in town, Hilma Matthews's paintings; or, I would ask how her dissertation was developing *on site*.

At dinner, I would entertain Dad and Cameron with a humorous recounting of the luncheon with the president of my college—"I told her, as graciously as I could, 'Of course I'm honored but I couldn't possibly take your place. I have more than enough to do taking care of my famous father.' " And we would laugh together.

Dad was wonderfully *tease-able*, if the teasing was in reference to his reputation, his popularity, his "women."

So happy: the happiest I could remember myself being, in many years.

Maybe when Dad had looked at me with eyes of unabashed and helpless father-love, as I'd stood with the silly little tooth in the palm of my hand. That long ago?

Except, stiff and sulky, Dad came downstairs from his study, and seeing me said, "You're still here?" and I said, "Dad, you and Cameron invited me to stay for dinner, don't you remember?" and Dad said, with a shrug, "Fine. You can go check on her, see how she is, you know how emotions upset me," and I said, "You mean, other people's emotions, Dad—your own are sacrosanct." And he said, on his way outside, "Wise guy."

The last words my father said to me, which he hadn't said to me in probably thirty years—*Wise guy.*

He'd had his camera. He must have intended to take photographs. I watched him outside on the terrace and at the same time I was thinking about Cameron upstairs and how he'd told me to check on her, and what this meant to me, how much it meant to me; and so, when Dad headed for the steps, I wasn't observing very clearly, or lucidly—just stood there in the sunroom smiling to myself, a big husky not-young overgrown girl in her father's house.

It did not strike me—*He is in danger. Those damned steps!*

It did not strike me—*If I'd wanted someone to fall, I might have sabotaged the steps. I might have loosened nails, supports.*

Though I was drawn to run upstairs to Cameron, yet I found myself following my father outside. A chilly wind from the river, and sun splotches in the heaving water.

The Hudson River is a living thing, so close by. The massive breadth of water wind-rippled and agitated, never at rest, mesmerizing to watch as liquid flames, and this afternoon a curious slate-blue-gray color, the hue of molten rock.

"Dad? Be careful . . ."

He didn't hear. He wouldn't have heard. Too many times I'd warned him, he had no awareness of any real danger. And there was a swagger to his walk, a stiff sort of bravado, as if he believed that someone—it would have to be Cameron, she was the only "woman" in residence—was watching him, and admiring him; he took care not to lessen the weight of his right leg, his arthritic knee.

High overhead several hawks flew. I felt a premonition—but then, I often felt such premonitions here on the terrace above the river. My father laughed at "premonitions"—though he took his own seriously, for he was a superstitious man. I was smiling still, foolishly. I tasted something metallic, cold. I did not want my father to fall and injure himself on the rocks below, all that was the most ridiculous fantasy. I squinted upward at the sky—*They are vultures. They sense an imminent death.*

Then, as in a dream, or a nightmare, I heard the cracking wood-plank steps, an abrupt and angry-sounding noise, like a rebuttal. It was a sound somehow familiar to me as if I'd heard it—rehearsed it—many times already.

Before I saw, I heard: a portion of the steps was collapsing, beneath my father's weight.

Dad had gained weight this past winter: though he would not have acknowledged it, in his masculine vanity, he must have gained at least twelve pounds. He'd blamed the bathroom scales for giving erratic and unreliable readings of his weight. But no longer was Roland Marks what one would call *slender, very fit-looking.*

Before I saw my father's desperate hand on the railing, that collapsed with the steps in what seemed at first like cruel slow-motion, I heard: my father's terrified voice calling for—*me.*

I think this is so. I think he was calling for me.

Or maybe—he'd only been screaming for help.

Or maybe—only just screaming.

What happened was in slow-motion yet also quickly.

More quickly than I could comprehend in my haze of foolish-daughter happiness.

And so on the terrace above the collapsing steps I stood very still, and watched in silence.

If I were to be tried for the death of my father Roland Marks, if I were to be judged, it is this silence that would find me guilty.

Yet, I could not draw breath to scream.

Even now, I can't draw breath to scream.

NO NO NO no no!

Cameron was crying hysterically. Cameron was shocking to me—her young face contorted, shining with tears. Her young body broken-seeming, defeated and without strength, so that I had to hold her.

In the crisis and confusion, my dean-self prevailed: I made the call to 911, an ambulance came, but too late: my father had died.

His skull had been badly fractured, it would be discovered. He had hemorrhaged into his brain.

It would be a long time before I could grasp the irremediable fact—Roland Marks was *dead*.

Which is to say, *my father was dead*.

Is dead.

(For death is a state that is perpetual: all who'd ever lived and who had died *are dead*.)

My memory of the collapsing steps, the scream, the fall—my memory of rushing to the edge of the terrace, to stare at my father fallen and twisted in the broken lumber below—is very vague.

Like the windshield of my car, grimy and scummy. Sunspots further obscure vision.

She'd been upstairs, in hiding. She'd heard the sound of the collapsing steps, and my father's scream.

No no no no no.

It was foolish of us, it was risky, dangerous, yet we never thought of not doing it—climbing down, slip-sliding and falling, whimpering in fear, making our way down the near-vertical slope to where my father lay fallen amid rocks. And once there, seeing that he was unconscious—(but still breathing?)—we understood that we must call an ambulance; one of us would have to climb up to the terrace, or to the side of the house.

Precious time was lost. Minutes . . .

It would have made no difference, we were told. My father's skull had been so severely fractured.

The camera, fallen a few feet away, broken on rocks.

And the river, only a few yards away, rushing past, noisy, jubilant, with a smell of early-spring, elevated muddy water—indifferent.

It was Dean Marks who climbed up, who made the sobbing/panting call.

It was the young blond assistant who was too stunned, too stricken, to move from my father's body.

His body had never looked so *slight*. So *inconsequential*. His head, turned at a painful angle.

His handsome face streaked with blood.

"MY FATHER DIED, two years ago. And my mother—she'd died five years ago. My father hadn't ever recovered from losing her, I think. I tried and *tried* with him. To make him think of something else—to make him happy. To keep him company. All the family did. But it made no difference, I guess—he just stopped wanting to live, and he *died*."

Cameron wept in my arms. A tall gawky young girl trembling in my arms.

It was stunning to me, that my father was *gone*.

Yet also stunning to me, that this stranger seemed to have loved him so much.

For Cameron Slatsky was devastated, clearly. We were sisters in grief, despite the disparity in our ages. Certainly I could not resent her. I could not wish, as in my lurid fantasies I might have wished, that my father's assistant had fallen in those crashing steps and died with him.

FOR SOME WEEKS then I was sick.

Sick with grief, and also remorse. And shame.

Cameron too was sick, with the shock of loss. But Cameron was younger and stronger than I was, and would be more resilient. She came to me where I was lying on the settee as the strength had drained from my body. I was thinking *But now I am his executrix. That is what I wanted.*

"Lou-Lou! My God. *Where is he?*"

It did not seem possible that my father was gone. That, if we searched the house, he wouldn't have been here—somewhere.

Laughing at us, maybe. But touched by our grief too.

He'd have known that we loved him. He would not have felt that our love was smothering, or a burden; boring-dull, like so much *female love*.

Roland Marks's obituary was prominent on the front page of the *New York Times*, on the left side of the page below the fold.

The photograph showed Roland Marks lean-cheeked, dreamy-hooded-eyed, handsome and smiling. He would have liked it, I think.

Cameron Slatsky and I commiserated together. There was a luxury of pain, a rush of pain neither of us could have borne alone.

I took the remainder of the semester off from Riverdale College. In any case, I was finished there.

In his will, he'd left her nothing. He hadn't had time to update his will and so in Roland Marks's will, Cameron Slatsky did not exist.

This was proper, he'd left the house to *me*. I felt sick with guilt, yet gratitude, to have been treated with justice for once.

Very few of the mourners who came to Roland Marks's memorial service had heard of Cameron Slatsky, let alone knew her. I introduced the silent ravaged-looking girl as my father's *fiancée*, and added that she'd been, initially, my father's *assistant*. No one quite knew how to speak to her, especially Dad's older friends, for whom she would have appeared to be the age of their grandchildren. Tall, slump-shouldered, very pale and very blond Cameron wore black clothing, a black jersey dress that fell to her ankles. The diamond ring she'd unobtrusively turned inward, toward her palm, so that the sparkling stone wasn't visible. Apart from my introducing her to a few people, at the memorial service she stood just slightly apart, ignored as if invisible.

I felt the injustice, and the irony, of her situation. Her elderly fiancé had died too soon, before she was firmly—legally—attached to his name.

Dad had loved her so much! How good that the last months of his life had been happy, entering upon his *final folly*.

I tried to explain to Cameron, as to others, whoever would listen among the many mourners who came to the memorial ceremony in New York City and to our house in Nyack, that my father's death was my responsibility—"My father had depended upon me to keep the house in good repair. You know what he was like—he never *saw* things for himself. The way he'd drive a car with the gas gauge at empty, or a tire losing air—somehow, it worked out. Even Avril shielded him. And Sylvia! When they'd loved their genius-husband, they'd insisted upon taking care of him. We'd all provided a buffer for him, to protect him. He'd had faith in me, his daughter. Those steps should have been repaired. I'd told him, he knew, but—he'd never done anything about it. Like the flagstone terrace, that needs repair. The house is beautiful but a century old. I see him in every room, I hear his voice. I hear him calling—*Lou-Lou! Where the hell are you?* I let him down. I am to blame for his death."

They held me, those who'd loved Roland Marks. Even the litigious ex-wives came to grieve with me, to hold me and absolve me of patricide.

Or, if they'd halfway believed that I might be halfway responsible, they couldn't agree that my father's actual *death* was my fault. Roland Marks had cheated death a number of times, like a wily cat. He'd run out of lives, that was all.

"Roland almost died in that car crash on Long Island—Montauk. That was before his career had even begun. Imagine, he'd only published his first novel. And that crazy girl who tried to shoot him on the Vineyard. And the spoiled sushi in Tokyo . . ."

They would spin legends of Roland Marks. They would mythologize him. His enemies and detractors as well as his friends.

They would agree: Roland Marks would have wanted to depart this earth in the way he had, suddenly, and without time for reflection; without a debilitating or humiliating illness, or a crushing decline like poor Mordecai Kaplan. In some versions of the story of Roland Marks's death in April 2011, when he'd been seventy-four years old, it was said that he'd been hiking in the Catskills with his young fiancée, or wife; he'd insisted upon climbing in a dangerous area, and had fallen to his death. He'd defied the young woman who'd been with him who had begged him to come back to even, safer ground . . .

We drove back to the house in Upper Nyack together. It was my house now, or would be when my father's will was fully probated. Cameron wept softly. Cameron wept almost without pause. I felt a thrill of deep imperturbable grief that was the most exquisite sensation I'd ever known. As we entered the darkened house Cameron groped for my hand: "We have each other now."

IT IS TRUE, TO A DEGREE: THE *FIANCÉE* AND THE *DAUGHTER* HAVE each other.

As executrix of my father's estate, I have hired Cameron as my assistant. Quite simply, Cameron Slatsky is the most qualified person for the job. Jointly we work on my father's massive archive which will soon be sold to a prominent American institution; at the last minute, the Beinecke Rare Book and Manuscript Library at Yale is making an unexpected bid. Dad would be pleased!

There is much more to Roland Marks's literary estate than anyone might have imagined. I had no idea of the numerous uncompleted, unpublished manuscripts and drafts he'd kept in cardboard boxes, in storage, dating back to his high school days at Stuyvesant High School in the 1940s; in all, thousands of priceless pages.

In the evening we sit in the sunroom, or on the terrace. Few people visit us here, for we've invited virtually no one; not my sister and brothers, who'd avoided my father when he was living, and have no right to mourn him now, at least in my company; not the "younger children" whom I scarcely know, and who I believe have not even read their father's books. And none of the ex-wives except my mother, Sarah, who isn't likely to make the trip, with her ailing husband in Fort Lauderdale, in any case.

Now the weather has changed to a cool summer, the air is mild and daylight prevails until nearly 9:00 P.M. Cameron has suffered more visibly from grief than I have, I think—(though I have lost eighteen pounds, and am not quite such a husky fleshy healthy-looking gal as my father had seemed to cherish); her skin is sallow, her eyes are ringed with fatigue, and her beauty has corroded, somewhat. Like Lou Andreas-Salomé and like me, she has a slightly overlong nose, a too-intense look about the eyes, a clenched mouth.

She commutes to Columbia University two or three times a week and returns home exhausted. The dissertation *on site* has stalled, though as my assistant she's an able and diligent worker, far more patient than I. Sometimes I hear her crying in "her" room. I enter, and approach her quietly. I slip my arms around her and she turns to me and presses her face against my thigh. She says, "Without you, Lou-Lou, I couldn't make it."

She'd told me more about her father who'd died of a stroke two years ago. And about her mother who had died of a quick-acting pancreatic cancer three years before that, in the last semester of her senior year at Barnard. She said, "Mom told me—'Don't give up! I'm counting on you.' She'd tried to hide the fact that she was *dying*. I think I was furious at her. All I could do was put on my armor. It felt like actual armor—my makeup, my clothes. Deflecting people's questions by looking funny, girly. There's a character in *Jealousy* who behaves just that way—it's prescient. Roland got her down perfectly! I needed something to protect me, like a steel vest. So bullets or rocks might be thrown at me and I would feel the shock but not be killed."

She said, "I know that people, like you, Lou-Lou, thought that Roland and I scarcely knew each other. But I knew *him*. Long before

I'd met Roland Marks I'd fallen in love with him, reading his books. I'd memorized passages. He really knew women well—you could say, the masochistic inner selves of women. All that was Roland Marks is contained in his books, really. His 'voice . . .'"

Tenderly she said, "I will take care of you, Lou-Lou. Anything you want from me, I will provide."

Since my father's death, I am often short of breath. I find it difficult to sleep on my back. Of course I'm frightened to see a doctor and have an EKG—(I'm a physical coward like Dad)—but Cameron insists that she will drive me to Columbia Presbyterian Hospital, which would have been Dad's choice, if I made an appointment.

I never had a daughter. I'd never had the experience of being pregnant.

Though Dad would have laughed at me in scornful pity, I'd never had the experience of sex with a man, or a woman. Never the experience about which Roland Marks wrote with such corrosive humor and such unabashed delight.

If Roland had married Cameron, she would be my step-mother.

How strange it would have been, perhaps how wonderful, to have a step-mother young enough to be a sister.

Strange, and wonderful. Though I would not have thought so at the time of our first meeting.

OUR NEWS IS, we will be attending the Los Angeles Book Fair together, to represent Roland Marks whose first several novels are being republished in classy trade paperbacks. Then, we are going to Book Expo America, in New York City; then, later in the summer, London and Stockholm for similar publications. We will be interviewed at literary festivals, and on TV.

Onstage, we wear black, side by side: we are not likely to be mistaken for sisters, but we may be mistaken as kin.

By slow degrees Cameron is becoming beautiful again, something of the luster in her eyes returning. Though she's still pale, and wears her shimmering blond hair pulled back and tied at the nape of her neck, in a way I think too prim and *widow-like*. I am not so pale, rather more putty-colored, which Cameron tries to correct by "making up" my face—with startling results, I have to concede. (How Dad would laugh at me—"I can see through your fancy makeup, kid.") For these occasions Cameron wears tasteful black dresses that fall to her ankles, often with a shawl or a scarf around her shoulders; I have urged her to stand up straighter, to resist the impulse to make herself shorter, now that there is no reason for her to make herself shorter. I wear dark trouser-suits, that fit my less hulking body flatteringly; my graying hair is trimmed short as a man's, in fact shorter than my father's hair had been. Audiences gaze at us with fascination. They know something of Cameron's story, and something of mine. As if spontaneously we clasp hands onstage. We do not rehearse such scenes. Tears spring from our eyes like shining jewels. The audience draws in its collective breath.

Women who love each other. Women who will stand by each other. How unexpected, this is Roland Marks's legacy.

WHO WOULD HAVE THOUGHT, this posthumous life of Roland Marks is so—celebratory! For his admirers, his survivors, are many; and his literary reputation, buoyed by rumors that *Patricide*, scheduled for fall publication, will be the author's strongest novel, a masterpiece to set beside the major works of Hemingway, Faulkner, Fitzgerald, Mailer, and Bellow, has never been higher. Requests for reprints of all kinds, republications of titles long out of print and seemingly forgotten, come to us continually. The Library of America will be issuing a large volume titled *Roland Marks*, and Cameron and I will be co-editors. Dad's longtime publisher has commissioned a biography and Cameron and I will be interviewing prospective biographers including the distinguished Nelson A. Gregorson whose biography of Melville Dad had so admired.

Of course, we will be editing the *Selected Letters*. A volume of at least seven hundred pages, a treasure trove of brilliant prose, flippant prose, gossip, scandal, candid snapshots of the writer's secret life, "visionary" insight.

There is even movie interest, from Miramax Films, in *Intimacy: A Tragedy*.

Though Roland Marks had haughtily refused to sign over any of his titles to be "mongrelized" by Hollywood, Cameron and I are willing to negotiate with the filmmakers. We joke about our "cameo" roles . . .

When we miss him terribly, we seek each other out. We clasp hands. Cameron says, swiping at her eyes, "Oh God, he was so *funny*. I loved his humor, his laughter." I said, "I can hear him laughing, sometimes." And we listened.

Trying not to hear instead the final desperate scream that might have been my name.

The other night after Cameron returned late, exhausted, from New York City, I was awakened hearing her walking in the house, as the floorboards creaked; I went to her, where she was lying on the settee in the sunroom, that was flooded with moonlight. I brought her an afghan, because the night was cold; and Cameron is very thin, and becomes chilled easily. And I held her hands, to warm them. And I thought *We both loved him. And now we have each other.*

This is not the ending that I had envisioned, just months ago. It is no kind of an ending anyone might have envisioned, especially my father, and yet—here it is.

This night, when I can't sleep, I curve beside Cameron on the settee, and pull part of the afghan over myself. If Cameron is covered, including her bare feet, and I'm part-uncovered, that's fine with me: of the two of us, I'm the stoic. I've brought a bottle of red wine, and we drink from the same cloudy glass, by moonlight. A rich red sensation begins in my throat and spreads through my chest, my belly and my loins. I feel the stirring of sexual desire, but it is not a desire for paroxysmal pleasure; I think it is a desire like the opening of a flower, petals spreading to the sun. It is the purity of desire, that requires another person to coax it into blooming.

"I love you, Cameron. I am so grateful that you've come into my life."

"I love you, Lou-Lou. If Roland could see us, he'd be—well, he'd laugh, wouldn't he? He'd be jealous, maybe."

High overhead the moon is moving through the night sky. Venus, the brightest star. And Jupiter. We are planning an exhibit of Roland Marks's photography, taken in the last three years of his remarkable life; some of the photographs are of the night sky shot with moonlight above the Hudson River. Dad would have been embarrassed, and abashed: he'd been an "amateur"—he hadn't been competing with "professionals." Already we've shown a portfolio of the Hudson River photographs to the gallery here in Nyack, and the proprietor is eager to mount the exhibit; yet we're thinking perhaps this is premature, and we should show the portfolio to some galleries in Chelsea or TriBeCa as well. Tell me a story about your father, Cameron says in a voice husky with sleep, and so I tell her about the incident at the Rye Academy. "I was playing field hockey and Dad was in the bleachers—he came to a surprising number of my games that year—and a girl struck me in the mouth with her stick, and one of my teeth—this one, here—was knocked out. And Dad said, 'What's that in your hand, Lou-Lou?' and I said, 'What's it look like, Dad?' and he said, not missing a beat, 'It looks like about five thousand dollars, Lou-Lou. But you're worth it.'"